WINSLOW BROTHERS BOOK TWO

max monroe

New York Times & USA Today Bestselling Author

The Pact (Winslow #2)
Published by Max Monroe LLC © 2021, Max Monroe

All rights reserved.

Without limiting the rights under copyright reserved above, no part of this publication may be reproduced, stored in or introduced into a retrieval system, or transmitted, in any form, or by any means (electronic, mechanical, photocopying, recording, or otherwise) without the prior written permission of both the copyright owner and the above publisher of this book.

This is a work of fiction. Names, characters, places, brands, media, and incidents are either the product of the author's imagination or are used fictitiously. The author acknowledges the trademarked status and trademark owners of various products referenced in this work of fiction, which have been used without permission. The publication/use of these trademarks is not authorized, associated with, or sponsored by the trademark owners.

Editing by Silently Correcting Your Grammar
Formatting by Champagne Book Design
Cover Design by Peter Alderweireld
Cover Photo by Wander Aguiar Photography
Cover Model: Gil Soares

AUTHOR'S NOTE

The Pact is a full-length romantic comedy stand-alone novel in the ***Winslow Brothers Collection***. This book is outright hilarious, as you might expect, but also, Flynn is the kind of hero who brings a little something extra to the table—hot, mysterious, dirty-talking, this man will make your ovaries explode.

Honestly, we're highly tempted to add a disclaimer about using protection while reading, but apparently, Trojan doesn't offer condoms for electronic devices. So, just consider this a warning. A *big* warning. *The Pact* is going to make you laugh your ass off, but its HOT LEVEL is so OFF THE CHARTS, there's a chance this book could get you pregnant via osmosis.

Also, due to the hilarious and addictive nature of this book's content, the following things are *not* recommended: *reading while waiting in the carpool lane at your child's school, reading in bed next to a light-sleeping spouse and/or pet and/or child, reading on a first date, reading this book at your mother-in-law's Thanksgiving dinner instead of lavishing her with compliments about her broccoli casserole, reading during your child's sports game/recital/school event, gifting this book to your mother-in-law for Christmas (unless your mother-in-law is a horny mofo who loves romantic comedies), reading while eating and/or drinking, reading at work, reading this book to your boss, and/or reading while operating heavy machinery. Also, if suffering from bladder incontinence due to age/pregnancy/childbirth/etc., we recommend wearing sanitary products and/or reading while sitting directly on a toilet.*

Happy Reading!

All our love,

Max & Monroe

DEDICATION

To dirty-talkin', mysterious men: *Dayuuum*, we like your style.
To the word that starts with an **F** and ends with **U-C-K**: Keep up the good fucking work.

INTRO

Saturday, April 6th, Las Vegas

Flynn

The four Winslow brothers in Vegas. What could go wrong?

Ha. Pretty much *every-fucking-thing* can go wrong when all three of my brothers decided a boozy brunch to start the day was a grand idea.

Although, so far, their only drunken sins revolve around stumbling steps and being a little too loud for the early afternoon casino crowd, but my track record of knowing them for my entire life predicts this day to be one hell of a chaotic ride.

Says the bastard who always chooses to be the responsible, sober brother of the group.

"What time is it?" Ty asks, but he quickly answers his own question when he glances at the time on his phone. "Holy shiz, it's only noon?"

Jude snorts from behind a blindfold that's tied around his face. "My dudes. I feel pretty fuggin' drunk for noon. How'd that happen?"

I almost laugh out loud. *How'd that happen?* Most likely, the bottomless margaritas the three fools drank at brunch is the root of the cause. Not to mention the round of tequila shots Ty ordered…three fucking times.

"Took the words right outta my mouth, bro," Ty agrees and locks arms with Jude in a sloppy attempt to lead Mr. Blindfold through the casino.

These clowns' need for a chaperone is so real it's nearly violent.

Unfortunately, I am that man, and there's only one person to blame—my brother Jude. The very bastard who decided to fall in fucking love, and late next month, he'll say those two infamous words—*ones that will sure as shit never leave my lips*—and marry his fiancée, Sophie.

"Alls I gotta know," Jude slurs, "is where we goin' and when can I take this blindfold off?"

Is he getting drunker by the second? *Fuck.*

My eldest brother—*and currently least drunk brother*—Remy lets out a deep, heavy sigh that perfectly showcases how I feel. "Jude, *you* put the blindfold on."

"What?" Jude questions, glancing from side to side, even though he can't see shit. "No, I didn't."

"Actually, yeah, man, you did," Remy states, annoyance more than apparent in his voice.

"I blindfolded me?" Jude scoffs. "That doesn't make any-fucking-sense, bro."

No shit, Sherlock.

Frankly, I don't have a clue why Jude insists on wearing that blindfold. What was meant as a one-time use when we surprised him with a trip to Vegas to celebrate his upcoming nuptials has turned into him putting the damn thing on in the name of "staying true" to his fiancée, Sophie like it's some kind of chastity belt for his face. It's beyond me how walking through the Wynn's casino could pose any risk, but I've never pretended to understand my youngest brother's mind.

In quite the turn of events, he went from a steady stream of women to what some would call "whipped," otherwise known as completely and undeniably in love with his bride-to-be. I might not be the type of guy who buys into relationships and marriage and shit, but I can't deny my baby brother is one-hundred-percent committed to Sophie.

So much so that he proposed four times before she said yes.

Four fucking proposals. If that doesn't prove commitment, then punch me in the dick and call me the craziest Winslow brother.

Jude just laughs off Rem's words, still leaving that stupid blindfold on, and mumbles something that apparently only Ty can hear.

"*Puh-lease,*" Ty comments through a sarcastic chuckle from behind me and stumbles arm in arm with Jude. "Remy probably spends most of his time picturing himself makin' women look like toaster strudels."

Jude cackles, and Remy turns around and punches Ty in the shoulder.

"Ow," Ty howls obnoxiously. "What was that for?"

"For saying shit about me I don't understand and probably don't want to know either."

My eyebrows lift, and a tiny smirk curves the corner of my lips. I know exactly what Ty's talking about—though I wish I fucking didn't—and he better write a personal letter to God, thanking him for Remy's unexpected innocence, along with a request to forgive him for all his past and future sins. I guarantee if Remy knew what Ty was really talking about, I'd be making an unscheduled trip to the hospital. I don't know what it is about Ty and alcohol, but mix the two together, and you get one of the most inappropriate men on the planet. It's almost like a disease.

Currently, we are on day three of my youngest brother's bachelor party extravaganza, and leading up to this day, I've endured over forty-eight hours of drunken debauchery, chaotic-as-hell nightclubs, and overly friendly strippers.

Don't get me wrong, I'm more than happy to celebrate Jude; I just wish I didn't have to be surrounded by the obnoxious Vegas party scene in order to do it.

Personally, I prefer quiet surroundings. Relaxed vibes. *Sober* people. And while I'm probably in the minority when it comes to most men, going to strip clubs has never been my thing. Of course, I can appreciate the beauty that is the female form. I just prefer to enjoy it when it's a consensual situation devoid of money and tips and fucking lap dances to songs that helped make *Magic Mike* a box office hit.

This is exactly why Ty shouldn't have been in charge of planning this weekend.

Hindsight is a real bitch, isn't it?

You'd think, since all four of us Winslow brothers are over the age of thirty-fucking-five, a trip to Vegas wouldn't be a shitshow, but yeah, it's been the very definition of that.

After two days of subjecting myself to my brothers' shenanigans, I honestly can't believe I showed up to the third. If I'd been smart, I would have taken off on my motorcycle and left them to their own messes without looking back.

Hell, I might be based in New York like the rest of my brothers and baby sister, Winnie, but I have a house that's about twenty minutes outside of the Strip. I could've easily sequestered myself away from their antics for a few hours to get some sanity.

But no, here I am, subjecting myself to the circus. Sometimes my love for these jokers comes at the price of my own mental detriment.

Drunken, sloppy, cackling brothers in tow, I head to the casino table that looks the most promising, the buzz of excitement and flashing lights ringing out all around us. I slide more than I probably should in cash across the felt to the dealer and sit down. It takes Ty a couple tries to land his ass on the chair, and the motion of its teeter throws Jude off-balance on his feet. Overwhelmed by dizziness, he finally removes his blindfold and tucks it into the back pocket of his jeans.

I snort and shake my head as they sit next to me and start digging in their pockets for money to make bets of their own. Unfortunately for them, I emptied their pockets right after I watched them take tequila shot number three at eleven in the damn morning, knowing just how far down the gutter their ability to make sound decisions would go as this day progressed.

"Damn," Ty huffs, turning his pockets inside out and picking at the thin white material. "I could'a sworn I had some more chops—haaa—chiiips in here."

I flash the dealer a look that conveys "Please ignore them," and his eyebrows rise only slightly as he takes my money and stacks up chips on my behalf. Jude immediately reaches over for some of my stack, and I slap his hand like a mom who's just taken the turkey from the oven on Thanksgiving.

Remy laughs. "Ohhh! De-nied!"

I clear my throat, and the three of them straighten in their seats mockingly. "I think Flynn wants us to behave, fellas," Jude says in his normal, jovial voice. Despite their teasing, I can't help but kick up one corner of my mouth as I watch them all comply.

Carefully, I flick a five-hundred-dollar chip at each of them. Jude and Remy practically fall on the table to claim theirs, tapping the felt to get the dealer to count them in, but Ty takes his and carefully, almost methodically, tucks it back into his pocket.

"Not playing, Ty?" I ask slowly, almost like a parent would to a toddler. It's really the only way to handle people when they're this drunk.

"Nope. I'm saving it for somethin' special."

I nod. Fine by me. With the group finally settled, the dealer starts flinging cards.

I'm not much for gambling, not much for taking unnecessary risks that aren't in my favor, but given a weekend of choosing between hanging out in clubs or playing cards, I'll pick blackjack every time. I know the game, know the strategy, *and* I have a ninety-nine-percent lower chance of being grazed by an unknown, dirty cooch. It also means my brothers are at least trying to be on their best behavior to keep from getting kicked out of the casino.

If I'm being honest, I'd admit that I'm also capable of counting cards to the point of having a pretty good idea what's left in the dealer's decks and making a goddamn killing, but I'm in Vegas, and as most people know, counting cards is highly illegal.

Acknowledge that you can count cards out loud? You might as well prepare yourself to be dragged into a windowless room and play Fight Club with a couple of muscle-headed, steroid-taking casino security.

The dealer shows an eight of hearts, and I show two tens, one of spades and one of diamonds.

Blackjack odds place me in a position to hold at a strong twenty.

Now, some people might think it's a good idea to split the tens, but I'm here to tell you that splitting tens will bring you nothing but bad blackjack juju and will almost always fuck you out of money. *A lot* of money if you double down.

The rest of my table—including my two participating brothers—play their hands. Remy and Jude hold at eighteen and nineteen, some guy wearing a gold ring busts by getting a seven on a soft sixteen, and the last one, an older gentleman with a Yankees baseball cap who looks like he's been playing for three days straight, manages to pull a blackjack out of his back pocket by getting a seven of spades added to his jack of hearts and four of clubs.

The dealer flips over his cards and showcases a ten, which means I'm in the money on my hard twenty and Remy and Jude break even. All in all, good for the table, not good for the house.

And the game pretty much rolls in a similar fashion. The same guy who busted on the first hand continues to bust three out of the next five hands. The guy in the baseball cap makes risky choices against the typical odds that end up paying off. And I base all my decisions on actual statistics to keep my chips steadily multiplying.

When another guest joins our game, the dealer pauses to cash in the new player's chips, and I relax back into my seat while the people at my table make chitchat about random things, like where they're from, what their plans are for the night, and which casino has the best buffet. Basically, a whole bunch of useless chatter that I have no desire to partake in.

I'm anything but a small-talk kind of guy.

Out of the corner of my eye, I catch sight of a wild mane of light-brown curls walking down one of the long, carpeted casino paths and grow intrigued. The owner of the curls is a petite female dressed in jeans, white sneakers, and a white T-shirt that showcases just a hint of a trim stomach. She looks to be late twenties, and everything about her outfit, even down to the white luggage on wheels in each of her hands, matches perfectly.

My first instinct is to write her off. All that perfect coordination screams of anal-retentive tendencies and impossible standards for every man she meets. She probably expects expensive gifts and flowery words and no food on the couch, even snacks.

"Ah, dammit," Jude shouts, tossing his cards down on the felt and startling me out of my surveillance. "This hand's about as good as a pair of saggy old nuts."

Ty snorts and tips his chair back, accidentally teetering on two legs until

Remy smacks him forward with a straight arm, making him bump into the table. The dealer's nostrils flare accordingly.

"I'm sorry," I apologize, though I doubt drunken idiots are anything new for someone who works in a casino on the Las Vegas Strip. "They missed obedience training when they were puppies."

Placated enough to not call security, the dealer lets out a long sigh and goes back to his job, and my eyes bounce back over to the woman with the wild curls. They're blithely out of place from the rest of her.

As she pulls her two small suitcases behind her, her eyes grow big with delight when her gaze locks on to a slot machine.

Instantly, there's a pep in her step as she hurries over to the empty seat and plops down, and it doesn't take long before she's sliding money into a machine with gold lights and pictures of buffalo all over the front of it. When the big screen lights up, she giddily taps her finger on one of the buttons to bet money on her first spin.

My brow furrows as I watch her, and I almost startle when she claps her hands and outwardly shouts, "Let's go!" as the slot machine starts to do its thing. She's completely on her own, completely by herself, but she acts as though she's at the center of a crowd. It's entirely at odds with what I expected—it's not at all refined or uptight or worried about keeping up appearances.

She doesn't seem to have a care in the world—a lone wolf in a sea of sheep that are worried about what other people think.

Frankly, she's a breath of fresh air.

She taps the button again and raises both hands in the air for a brief second to cheer, "C'mon, buffalo! Let's do this! Move your big hairy asses, and show me the money!"

I fucking loathe slot machines. They're the biggest waste of money that anyone who steps inside a casino can engage in, and if I were a man who wore his emotions on his sleeve, I'd probably be shaking my head at her blind enthusiasm for the stupid game.

Yet it's that same enthusiasm that has your mouth curving up into a distinct smile…

"Yes! Yes! *Yesssss!*" Her long, wild curls bounce against her back as she dances in her chair. The big screen lights up, and the speakers begin to sing out the word *"Buffalo!"* while the sounds of a running stampede add to the ambiance.

When I hear the man sitting a few seats away from me say, "Hit me," I quickly switch my focus to the felt. I calculate the dealer's card, my cards, and the rest of my table's cards, but my attention is quickly pulled back to that damn slot machine when the woman shouts something, jumps out of her seat, and fist-pumps the air.

The big screen in front of her flashes with some kind of bonus round, and early risers in the casino begin to stop near her slot machine just to watch the show.

A show that has you completely riveted.

She's over the top, but I can't deny her continued excited reactions don't disappoint. Hell, I'm pretty sure I'm laughing—on the inside, at the very least.

The woman's mane of curls bounces against her back as she twirls and cheers and even gives high fives to random passersby and casino staff.

"Sir?" The blackjack dealer grabs my attention, and I look back to my table to see he's waiting on my next move. I assess my cards quickly—a king of hearts and another ten—and then see that a nine shows for the house.

"Stay," I decide, and the play moves to Remy.

But my eyes veer back to that stupid-ass slot machine where the happiest woman in Vegas is still bouncing around in joy. In the foreground, Ty flits his eyes over to mine and they catch, and then he turns to look where I am.

I barely register the rest of my blackjack hand, let alone my brothers hooting and hollering, only noting that I beat the house when the dealer slides more chips my way.

Knowing full well that, unless you want to lose money, distraction and blackjack don't mix, I know I need to start the process of exiting the table.

"*Dayuuum*, she's pretty," Ty mutters loudly. I presume he meant to keep that comment to himself, but the amount of booze he's had is not at all conducive to volume control. Remy's head turns slowly to match his gaze, and Jude covers his eyes dramatically, crooning, "Oh no, no, no… Me no *lookie* at the *cookie*."

Without warning, Ty jumps up, bumping the table awkwardly, and practically wags his tail as he scoots across the casino floor toward the woman at the buffalo slot machine.

Oh, here we go…

Remy glances at me with a goofy grin, and I nod with a sigh, scooping Jude off his chair as I move from mine and follow Chipper Chuck toward a wild head of curls.

God help me because I can only imagine how this is going to go.

Daisy

I think I'm in love with Vegas.

Sure, I've only just arrived in Sin City, haven't even checked in to my room, but Lady Luck is smiling down on me. Flashing her pearly whites and shaking her tits and telling me I'm the best little slot girl in the whole wide world.

"Buffalo! Bonus round!" my slot machine chants, and I watch the screen flash with excitement as the big wheel spins around and more money is added to my bankroll.

Technically, I'm here for work not pleasure, but *holy shit, this is fantastic!*

I don't even like gambling, and I sure as shit don't know what made me stop at this slot machine before heading up to my room, but damn, I'm glad I did.

The sounds of a running stampede fill my ears when I manage some kind of triple bonus with a screen full of buffalo. Truthfully, I don't have a clue about this game. I don't know what any of it means or why I'm winning, but when I look down at my bankroll, I see the numbers keep going up, up, *up*.

"Woo-hoo!" I cheer and do a little two-step dance beside my chair. When I glance over my shoulder, I force one of the casino staff who's emptying out the trash cans to give me a high five.

Considering I'm the crazy woman jumping around like a banshee, he mostly looks confused, but eventually, a little grin spreads across his lips.

"Good luck, ma'am," he says and moves across the casino floor, in the opposite direction from me and my lucky slot machine.

"Holy hell, I can't believe this," I whisper to myself and force my ass back into my chair as my bonus spins finish up and my winnings are calculated.

$135.13 Fantastic Win! sits front and center on the screen.

Somehow, after only putting a twenty-dollar bill into this machine, I'm up over a hundred bucks.

Viva Las Vegas, baby!

The rush of adrenaline pumping through my veins makes me understand why people love Vegas so much. I mean, I've just barely gotten off my plane from LAX, and I'm an official winner.

But now, the big question remains. *Do I stay or do I go?*

Do I keep playing? Or do I cash out my winnings and head up to my room to take a shower and a nap before I have to get ready for my work party?

I mean, you did just get off an early morning flight from LAX and probably smell like sweat and stale pretzels…

"Don't get too cocky," a man says from over my shoulder, making me whip my head around. He's cute in a seriously obvious way with his playful light brown-blond hair and big smile, but the glaze in his eyes makes it equally apparent how drunk he is. "Trusts me, Lady Luck loves to hit cocky shits in the balls. I know because I'm one of 'em."

Raucous laughter follows him in the form of two more almost heinously attractive men, one of whom is curiously holding a hand over his eyes.

"Ty," the dark-haired one says, "stop bothering people."

"Who's he bothering?" the one covering his eyes asks, earning a smack to the back of the head from his dark-haired counterpart.

"Just uncover your eyes, Jude. I'm pretty sure Sophie knew you were going to have vision when you came here. You're not cheating, for fuck's sake."

"Sophie is a goddess," the man recites then, making me smile big for the first time during this interaction. They're all drunk, which can be intimidating for a woman on her own, but they're funny too, and I take that as a good sign.

Maybe my relaxed state is why I'm so caught off guard when a fourth man approaches, but perhaps it's because he immediately strikes me as different.

Given his strong jaw, swirling ocean-blue eyes, perfectly messy dark hair, and a body that looks fit and trim beneath his jeans and white shirt, there isn't a single cell inside me that's upset by his presence.

I quirk an amused eyebrow in his direction as I address the first man, the playful one I now know is named Ty. "So…you're saying I should cash out before this slot machine can eat up all my winnings?"

Mr. Reserved doesn't say anything, but I swear his mouth almost hitches up at the corners.

"Yep," Ty answers, a little too loudly for our close proximity. "But no matter what you decide," he continues and places one single black casino chip in my hand. "It's my patriotic duty to make you leave here a winner."

"Patriotic duty?" I question, and he just winks. The other two drunk companions burst into laughter, but my eyes, they jump to the fourth man—the one who's yet to say anything.

I glance down at the chip in my palm. *Holy shit. Five hundred dollars?* It sure seems like Lady Luck likes my balls just as they are.

"Wow. Thank you. This is beyond generous, and I'm not sure I can acc—"

"Yeah, you can," the man interrupts me with a sway and a smile. "I'm not paying you for sex or nothin'. Just doin' my patriotic duty." He punctuates that statement by saluting me as if I'm a soldier in uniform, and it spurs a giggle to jump from my lips.

"Jesus," the dark-haired one chastises, grabbing Ty by the shoulder and pulling him farther away from me. An apologetic smile crests his lips when he meets my eyes. "I wish I could say he's never like this, but I'd be lying."

"Remy's right," Ty agrees with a lazy grin. "I am, in fact, always this charming and resistible."

"Resistible?" Jude, the man who is still covering his eyes, bursts into laughter. "I might be blitzed, but I think that's the wrong word, my man."

"Nah, I think it's the perfect word," Remy, the tallest and not-quite-as-drunk one, comments with a big grin.

So far, through this crazy conversation that I'm only half involved in, I've gathered three out of the four men's names—Ty, Jude, and Remy.

Which only makes me more curious about the most reserved one of their group. He has yet to say a word, but somehow, his presence is the most undeniable. He's confident without uttering a word or showing any sort of obvious expression. And for some reason, that only makes me more intrigued.

I almost open my mouth to ask him his name, but the raucous ringleader and the gifter of my chip performs a deep bow, saying, "My lady, I bid you adieu."

The other two start to laugh, but after a silent command from the fourth stalwart companion, they turn away and leave, stumbling slightly as they walk.

Without another word or explanation, Mr. Mysterious and the gang are just…gone.

I don't know what in the hell just happened. But seeing as it ended in me being five hundred dollars richer, maybe I need to come to Vegas more often.

ONE

Daisy

"Daisy girl!" my boss Damien greets me with a huge smile on his handsome face and walks straight over to place two European-style air kisses to my cheeks. "How was the flight in?"

"It was fine," I remark, smoothing the satin of my blouse with a delicate hand. I swear, I just put it on five minutes ago, but the damn thing is already threatening to wrinkle.

"Fine?" he repeats with derision in his tone. "Girl, you flew commercial out of LAX. Unless you consider the pits of hell fine, I know it wasn't anywhere close to that."

Damien Ellis is rich, sophisticated, and one-hundred-percent spoiled to the point of not understanding what life is like for most folks. I honestly think when people reach a certain level of success and income, they lose sight of what the day-to-day is like for those without eight-figure bank accounts and investment portfolios.

"You act like flying commercial is some kind of atrocity." I roll my eyes. "We're not all living the luxury lifestyle, you know. Plus, *you* sign my paychecks and pay for my flights and accommodations…"

I mean, I can't deny that flying commercial isn't what it used to be. Every airline gives you the minimum amount of space and makes you pay a fortune for bags, even though they overbook their flights to the point of having to stuff carry-ons in the cargo.

Not to mention, the snacks and drinks are a thing of the past. You want a Coca-Cola on your flight? Prepare to cough up ten bucks.

But still, that flight saved me several hours of driving, so I'm not going to complain.

"Whatever, sis." He just smirks and sassily shrugs his shoulder. "How did the setup go in Malibu?"

"You mean the ten-million-dollar beachfront home with a master walk-in closet bigger than my apartment?" I tease. "Oh, it went just fine and dandy. Didn't make me want to move in or anything."

He chuckles. "I can't wait to see what you did with it."

"Frederick was already there getting pictures before I left for the airport, so I'm sure come Monday morning, he'll have them ready for you to look at."

"Fantastic," he comments. "Forcing you to emigrate from Canada and join my team was the best decision I've ever made. I'm never letting you go."

Forcing me? Ha. Working on Damien Ellis's team was the epitome of career goals. I would've sold both my kidneys on the black market and offered up my firstborn just to be a part of one of the most successful real estate firms in the US.

"Well, that's good news because you're stuck with me."

Los Angeles, New York, Las Vegas, Miami, EllisGrey is the top name in the real estate game. If you're not a part of Damien Ellis and Thomas Grey's team, you want to be on their team. And if you have a small obsession with Patrick Dempsey like I do, you fantasize about having the company's name on your business card a little more. Seriously, though, for someone like me, who specializes in interior design and staging homes for the market, unless I manage to start my own firm and skyrocket to success, there isn't any higher achievement.

It's the whole reason I moved from Vancouver to LA and the whole purpose I was seeking when I started Daisy Designs's social media presence.

Though never in a million years did I think my Instagram following and popularity would get me on a guy like Damien's radar. To this day, I still feel like there's been some sort of mistake.

"What time did you end up getting in?"

"A little before noon."

"Doll, you've practically been here all day. What in the hell have you been doing? You should've called me."

"Oh, don't worry, I know how to keep myself busy." I waggle my brows. "Shower, nap, slot machines, and a delicious room service lunch, to be specific. Though not in that order."

"Slot machines? For real?" he questions on a laugh. "And how did that treat you?"

"I'm up five hundred."

He jolts his head back. "You're up five hundred on fucking slot machines?"

"Well, technically, I broke even on this addictive buffalo game, but apparently, I was so entertaining while playing, a random stranger gave me a five-hundred-dollar chip."

"A random stranger?" he questions. "Girl, tell me he's tall, dark, and handsome with a big cock and you got his number."

"Technically, he was tall, medium-brown, and handsome. His hair was a little on the lighter side."

"And the cock?"

"Shoot." I snap my fingers. "I knew I forgot something. It totally slipped my mind to have him drop his pants so I could take a look."

Damien grins. "Did you at least get his number? Any man who's willing to cough up money because he thinks you're entertaining shows some serious sugar-daddy potential."

"Oh my God!" I exclaim on a giggle. "I don't want a sugar daddy."

"I do."

"Damien, I hate to break it to you, but you *are* the sugar daddy."

"You think Mateo is just using me for my money?"

"Don't get me wrong, Dame, you're handsome. But your boyfriend is a twenty-five-year-old Brazilian model with the prettiest face and tightest ass I've ever seen."

He winks. "He has a big cock too."

"TMI!" I cough on my own saliva. "TMI!"

"Don't be such a prude, Dais." Damien just laughs and presses a soft kiss to my cheek. "Now go get yourself a drink and enjoy the party."

And then he's off, doing his usual Damien-thing of schmoozing and impressing everyone in the room. I swear, I've never met anyone like him. Successful, hilarious, insanely fashionable, and sophisticated, yet he's unapologetically himself.

It's the kind of confidence and contentment that only come with age and wisdom and experience. I wish I could bottle it up and add it to my daily vitamin regimen.

The bar in my sights, I head on over and snag a glass of the complimentary champagne that sits out for everyone in attendance. Glass to my lips, I take a sip and enjoy the odd sensation of bubbles tickling my throat as it slides down into my belly.

"Daisy Diaz." A familiar male voice fills my ears, and I turn to find Duncan Jones striding toward me with his signature smile etched across his lips. "I was wondering when you'd get here."

I lift my glass in the air and offer a neutral smile. "Well, I'm here."

"And I'm glad." He pulls me into a friendly hug, and it lingers about five seconds longer than I would deem appropriate. "I'm hoping you'll finally let me take you to dinner this weekend."

"Considering it's already Saturday night, and Damien and Thomas have plenty planned for this evening and all day tomorrow, I'm thinking you're going to have to take a rain check."

Ever since Damien hired me, one of his most successful agents, Duncan Jones, has been heavy on the flirtation and charm in an attempt to get me to go out with him.

He's not bad-looking or anything. Blond hair, blue eyes, and an attractive face, Duncan is incredibly eligible in his bachelordom, but dating isn't something I'm focused on at the moment.

I'm open to the idea, but I'm not looking for just any guy to fill the time. I'm waiting for the guy who *makes* me make the time.

Some might say I'm too picky, but personally, I think it's more about timing. And now isn't the right time. I'm only twenty-nine, and my career goals are far more important to me than finding someone to settle down with.

Not to mention, several of my female coworkers let me know from day one that Duncan Jones is like this with *all* the women in the firm. Which, to me, only gives off red flags and stay-away vibes.

"Really? A rain check?" His lips crest into a confident smirk. "And when do I get to cash in my *rain check*?"

I shrug cheekily. "I don't know."

He grins and reaches out to slide a rogue piece of my hair behind my ear. "One day soon, you're going to let me take you to dinner. And I promise, you won't be dis—" He pauses midsentence when the sound of his cell ringing urges him to pull it out of his jacket pocket. One finger in the air toward me, he says, "Hold that thought. I need to take this real quick."

I kind of want to roll my eyes at the obnoxiously oblivious contradiction between his rabid pursuit and his inability to finish even a sentence without prioritizing me behind his call, but I just offer a small smile and nod as Duncan steps away to a quieter spot in the crowd. Frankly, it's a relief to be rid of him for a little while.

I make a point to wander away inconspicuously while he's busy talking LA real estate with whoever is on the other end of the line, but I only get a few steps toward the table filled with appetizers when my phone vibrates in my purse and grabs my attention.

Gwen: *How is Vegas, darling?*

I've known Gwendolyn Ross since I was a fifteen-year-old lifer in the foster care system and she took me in. She's pretty much the only family I have, but she's more of a best friend than a mother figure. Still, I'm not entirely sure where I'd be without her.

Me: *It's fabulous. How's your Saturday going?*

Gwen: *Also fabulous. And Sunday is looking to be the same. I have an art class in the morning with the girls and a brunch date with David around noon.*

Me: *David? I take it you've found a new flavor of the month?*

I grin over her always-busy social calendar. It's honestly one of my favorite things about her.

She doesn't let life lead her; *she* leads her life.

Gwen: He's a pepper-gray stallion who always picks up the check. Who knows? I might even let him entertain me for two months instead of one. ;)

I shake my head on a laugh.

Gwen has never been married, and besides taking me in when I was fifteen, she's never had any kids. But her dating life is always thriving, and it's certainly far more entertaining than mine.

She may be in her sixties now, but the woman never has any issues finding new men to date. She just never keeps them around for long.

Me: Okay, Miss Thang. I better get back to my work party. Phone chat soon?

Gwen: Of course. Call me when you make it safely back to LA. Kisses, darling.

Before I slide my phone back into my purse, I pull up my email inbox to see if Frederick sent any of the photos he took at the Malibu beach house my way. To say I'm proud of what I created for the interior of that unspeakably gorgeous home would be the understatement of the century. Looking avidly through my inbox for the picture proof in the middle of the party so that I can avoid chitchatting with random strangers for the time being is merely a bonus.

For the last month, I've put my heart and soul into that space. Every single detail was meticulously chosen to create an airy, relaxed, sophisticated atmosphere that will make wealthy home buyers drool over the idea of living there.

I slide my finger down the screen to refresh my emails, but unfortunately, when five new emails populate the screen, not a single one of them is from Frederick.

Sheesh. It's like he's taking the weekend off or something.

Most of them are the usual spam everyone gets for giving stores their information for those stupid rewards cards that do jack shit. But one email in particular stands out like a boner in a pair of skinny jeans.

From: U.S. Citizenship and Immigration Services (USCIS)

Subject: Urgent Update Regarding Work Visa Lapse

My heart starts to pound furiously in my chest as I tap the screen to open the email, and a sick, cloying feeling immediately takes up residence in my throat. *No, no. Surely I'm misreading the subject.*

I click furiously and swallow hard as I wait for the interior of the email to load on the Wynn's sluggish public internet. My spine curls over on itself, and I lick my lips roughly. When the message finally loads, I'm not the least bit comforted by the words inside.

Daisy Diaz,

We are writing to inform you that, as of forty-five days ago, your work visa has expired, and the USCIS Los Angeles field office has not received Form I-765 for an extension.

Holy fucking shit! My work visa is expired?! It's… No. It can't be. There's no way I've been in LA for over a year…

What month is it? I know it's past Valentine's because I did that whole singleton Chinese food thing while watching Jennifer Garner lose her shit on Jessica Biel's piñata. And my neighbor Batshit Bob puked all over our hallway on St. Paddy's Day, so it has to be at least late March.

Shit. No. I'm in Vegas for the Vegas thing, and that's an April thing…meaning… Oh my God, is it April?!

Oh God, oh God, no.

You are no longer permitted to work and live in the United States. If you would like to extend your work visa, you will have to submit Form I-765. Average processing times are twelve to fourteen months.

Oh my God. Oh, holy hell.

I can't even finish reading the rest of the email because my heart is pounding so hard in my chest it's making my vision blurry, and simple tasks like breathing feel impossible.

You have seriously fucked up big-time, Daisy.

The room feels as if it's closing in on me, and my breaths are harsh, pathetic little pants of distress.

My fucking work visa has expired, and I'm pretty sure I'm the only one to blame.

Considering you're supposed to send in a yearly extension application to keep it active and you've been in LA since February *of last year, it's safe to say you are* to blame.

How in the hell could I be so stupid? Surely they sent me a notice that I ignored.

Did I mark it as a spam email? *No, that's dumb.* There's no way they sent the only notice of my visa expiring as email, right? It had to come with the rest of the snail mail. Which, *of course*, I have no respect for, whatsoever.

Gah. Why am I so cavalier about dumping junk mail in the garbage? I should save every goddamn piece of paper that deigns to bestow its presence in my mailbox. I should file it by date, chronologically, in a, like, supersized filing cabinet with reminder alerts on my phone to check every folder each month. I should pay attention to my freaking life's documents and, I don't know, get a safe-deposit box like a real adult.

Well, it doesn't matter now, Dais. It's too late. You just single-handedly fucked your career.

"Now, Daisy, where were we?" Duncan is back, and he's all up in my personal space, smiling and grinning and showcasing all the emotions that I am not feeling right now.

He reaches out to slide my hair behind my ear again, and the urge to run is so fucking strong that that's exactly what I do.

I fucking run.

Away from Duncan.

Away from the big party that Damien and Thomas are throwing for their staff, at which my presence is *absolutely* expected.

"Daisy!" Duncan's voice is behind me, but I don't stop.

Out into the casino area, I run as fast as my feet will take me. And I'm not stopping until I run out of oxygen or break through the time-space continuum and land a couple of months in the past—whichever comes first.

TWO

Flynn

At a little after eight, I take a right into the Wynn's entrance and head toward the main valet.

Of course, I have no plans to let some twentysomething dude hop onto one of my favorite possessions and park it for me. Just give me the valet ticket, and I'll park my own bike, thank you very fucking much.

The valets are a little busy, and I ease the throttle to a stop as I step my right foot onto the pavement and wait patiently behind the line of cars.

Phone out of my back pocket, I check the screen to find a few missed text notifications from my brothers, finally awake from their afternoon drunk-naps, most likely asking me my ETA so we can start with the late-night portion of the slop-fest. Seeing as I'm here and I'll be inside soon enough, I don't bother with a response.

Once we finished with brunch and blackjack and headed back up to the penthouse suite we rented for the weekend, those bastards passed the fuck out in the middle of trying to make plans to go to the pool.

And, like the mom who gets out of the house the instant her husband gets home just to get some peace and quiet from the kids, I took that as my cue to get a little fresh air and open road on my bike for a couple hours.

Comparing my adult brothers to children might seem harsh, but anyone who witnessed Ty's big lap-dance debut in the middle of a Las Vegas strip club for a half-naked stripper named Sapphire while Jude and Remy threw dollar bills at him would strongly agree with the sentiment. Though, it should be noted, Jude had blindfolded himself by that point in the night, and his dollar bills were landing on a table of college guys who gladly pocketed the cash.

The line of cars edges forward, and I ease my bike up after I slide my cell back into the pocket of my jeans.

"Oh my gosh! I'm sorry!" A female voice grabs my attention, and I glance toward the entrance doors of the Wynn to find a blur of wild curls running like a banshee. She bumps into several people trying to get outside, and more apologies blurt from her lips as she almost takes out an older gentleman wearing a cowboy hat.

The man is none too pleased, but his annoyance doesn't stop her. Out onto the pavement of the driveway, she stumbles a bit on her sky-high heels as she continues her fast-track path to who knows where.

And it's then I recognize who she is—the beautiful woman from the slot machine this morning. The one Ty saluted and gave a five-hundred-dollar chip to.

She comes to a halting stop in the center of the entrance driveway, in the middle of cars and only a few feet from my bike, and looks around manically with her big green eyes.

What is she doing?

Aesthetically, she's still downright fucking beautiful and dressed in the kind of clothes that ooze sexuality and a good time.

But mentally? She now appears to be a quick step away from out of her fucking mind. Her breaths come out in harsh pants, and she chaotically brushes pieces of her wild mane of curls out of her face.

"You okay?" I find myself asking, and she snaps her eyes toward mine.

She stares at me like I just asked her to solve an advanced calculus problem, and I lift the visor up on my helmet to repeat my question. "You okay?"

She shakes her head and digs her teeth into the meat of her full, red-painted lips. But just as she opens her mouth to respond, a man in a well-fitted suit comes bursting out of the entrance doors, yelling, "Daisy!"

The beautiful but possibly insane woman shuts her eyes on a heavy sigh, and by the sag in her shoulders and frown on her lips, I have a feeling she's the *Daisy* he's calling for.

"Daisy! Honey! Wait up!"

"Fuck," she mutters, and it doesn't take a genius to figure out Crazy Daisy wants nothing to do with this guy.

Maybe he's the reason for her abrupt departure and reckless sprint out of the casino?

This guy could be her boyfriend. Fiancé. *Husband.* I don't fucking know what. But whoever he is, she wants distance. That much is apparent.

And even though I'm supposed to meet my brothers at one of the Wynn's bars in about ten minutes, the urge to help her is too strong to ignore.

It's a rare thing for a guy like me, to be honest. I don't meddle in other people's shit, but the panicked look on her face makes me want to give her the escape she needs.

But before I know it, before I can even offer the help, she takes it for herself.

One leg over the seat of my bike and her arms around my waist, she leans into my back harshly and declares her intentions without pause. "I need a ride."

THREE

Daisy

I wait there, shaking and quivering as I cling to this stranger's back like an uninvited monkey. He seems paused in time, a boot to the ground to hold the bike steady, and his stormy blue eyes fixate on me over his shoulder.

Gah. I need this more than I need the air in my lungs, and the thought that he might deny me makes a knife cut at the sensitive lining of my stomach. Frankly, I need a lot more than a ride to fix this monumental fuckup, but I can't think in sweeping measures of time—I can only consider right now, this moment, and how glorious the feel of a cool wind blowing on my flushed face will feel. In fact, I'm truly surprised at how much I like the idea of hopping on the back of a complete stranger's bike altogether.

"Please," I say then, the shake in my voice apparent to even my own ears.

I can only see his intense—*and eerily familiar*—blue eyes through the flipped-up dark screen of his black helmet, but the combination of *those mesmerizing eyes* and his visibly fit body that's currently clad in dark jeans, black boots, and a James-Dean-*Rebel-Without-a-Cause*-style black leather jacket, he's...pretty damn enticing. If all the women in the world combined their fantasies of the quintessential bad boy to experience hot and wild fun with, this guy would be the poster child.

"Daisy, what are you doing? Come back inside!" I glance over my shoulder to see Duncan standing at the entrance doors of the Wynn, and a sigh escapes my throat.

I have nothing against Duncan Jones, but also, I don't want anything to do with him. Especially right now. I have no actual concrete reason for this internal response, but it's undeniable. He's the very last person I want to deal with.

I look back toward Mystery Guy, and he slides his helmet off his head, and I don't miss the stark reality that the rest of his face is the same caliber as his eyes. Strong jaw, sexy, full lips, this guy could actually have given James Dean a run for his money back in the day. And when you add in the perfectly messy dark hair that sits on top of his head, it's almost too much to comprehend.

Goodness, where did he come from? A fucking fantasy?

And then it hits me. He's *the* guy. The silent, mysterious man who commanded his drunken, five-hundred-dollar-chip-bestowing companions without even a word.

"I know you," I announce. "Your friends chatted me up this afternoon at my slot machine. One even gave me a five-hundred-dollar chip."

"My brothers, actually," he corrects.

His brothers? No wonder all four of them were insanely attractive. Only strong genetics could make something like that happen.

"Put this on." He turns his body enough to hand me his helmet, and then he kicks his heel down to throw the motorcycle into gear. "And hold on tight," he adds quietly, and I don't hesitate to obey, sliding the helmet over my head and wrapping my arms around his firm waist once again. The material of his black leather jacket is rough against my forearms, but for some reason, I don't hate the sensation.

Just as the engine revs, I look toward the entrance again and spot Duncan standing there with wide, shocked eyes. And before he can even open his mouth to say something, Mystery Guy releases the brake, cranks the throttle, and we're off on a slight jolt.

I grip my arms tighter around his abdomen as he weaves us in and out of the Wynn's valet traffic, and it doesn't take long before we're taking a right onto the main road of the Las Vegas Strip and heading toward the unknown.

Holy hell. What have I just signed up for?

FOUR

Flynn

Unsure of where my unexpected passenger wants to go or what has her so worked up that she hopped on the back of my bike, I pull into a gas station about a mile off the Strip. Once I pull my Harley to a stop, she eases herself off the saddle.

My helmet is off her head a few moments later, and I don't even try to be inconspicuous as I watch her wild mane of curls fall past her shoulders and the green of her eyes shimmer beneath the obtrusive neon lights of the gas station.

Daisy. I silently test her name in my mind. Oddly enough, the name matches her to a T. Beautiful, but also a bit wild. I sense she's the type of woman who is full of surprises.

Frankly, I'm just happy it was me sitting at the entrance and not some deranged psychopath looking for a vulnerable victim.

Her energy is manic as she paces the pavement next to my bike, her teeth sinking into the flesh of her soft red lips repeatedly. I avert my eyes briefly and focus on cutting the engine and popping out the kickstand of my bike, and it's only then, after being divested of the weight of my scrutiny, that she finds the will to speak.

"I'm…uh…Daisy." Her words grab my attention, and I look up to find her holding out a petite hand toward me. "Daisy Diaz."

I consider her closely before taking her small hand in my own. Mine envelops hers easily, and I think the feeling must make her nervous because she starts babbling again before I give her my name.

"So…I'd like to make it clear that I'm not the type of woman who just hops on random guys' motorcycles. Not usually, anyway. I guess you could say I'm currently in the middle of a bit of a mess and was overwhelmed, and you sitting there was an escape option I couldn't resist." She looks up toward the night sky and sighs. "God, what is wrong with me?"

Obviously, I, personally, have not a fucking clue what's going on with her.

"I probably seem nuts, don't I?" Her green eyes meet mine. "Like a total lunatic. I mean, who does that? Who just sprints out of a work party and hops on some complete stranger's bike? Holy moly, I'm totally losing it!"

She turns on her heel and begins to pace in front of me. After a few groans and even more sighs, she eventually stops and turns to face me again.

"You don't say much, do you?"

The assertion is obvious, but her comfort in voicing it is much less so. Most people are afraid of me—something about the silence makes them think I'm based in sin. I raise my eyebrows, and she sighs briefly before mixing it with a laugh.

"That's…that's good. You don't ramble in circles like me, which I have to tell you is not always convenient." Her words are open and honest, and by the giant smile on her face, it's obvious she is mostly just amused with herself than anything else. "It can get you into some real pickles, actually, and I've got the stories to prove it. Some real foot-in-the-mouth scenarios, you know?"

I smile. I can't fucking help it. There's something so purely honest about her. It's endearing.

"I bet."

She nods enthusiastically as if I've just delivered a moving address to the nation. "Exactly! You get it. So, you don't have an obsession with hearing yourself speak," she states, and I nod. "That's freaking admirable. All the men I've ever known in my life are blabbermouths."

"The guy back at the casino?"

Her brow furrows in confusion. "What guy?"

"The guy you were running from."

"I wasn't running from—" She pauses midsentence, and her eyes go wide for the briefest of moments before a shocked laugh jumps from her lips. "Oh my God, *no*. I wasn't running from Duncan. I might've abruptly sprinted away from him while he was doing his usual flirting routine, but I definitely wasn't running *from* him. He's just a coworker. Nothing more than that."

My eyes narrow, and she starts to pace again, her earlier agitation coming back with a vengeance.

"I was running from something much more life-altering than the office flirt. Something that I can't actually run from… So, I guess, in a way, I was attempting to run from my own stupidity, but as you can see, I can't really run away from myself. I just…just thought maybe I could run from tonight, you know?"

I don't have a fucking clue. This woman is intriguing, but also confusing as hell, and I don't have a scrap of the time and energy it would take to figure her out.

But I don't have to crack the code of her innermost workings to be a little bit of what she needs tonight. To be an escape from reality. Surely my brothers can handle keeping themselves alive for one night without me. They're all grown.

Mind already made up, I pull my cell phone out of my pocket and shoot off a message.

Me: Something came up. Go ahead and start tonight's festivities without me. Catch up with you later.

Instantly, Remy responds with a, **What are you talking about, bro?**, but I promptly lock the screen and move my attention back to a still-pacing Daisy.

I hold out my helmet again and jerk my chin to the space behind me.

"Get on."

"Get on?" She repeats my words, surprise evident in her voice. "Why? Where are we going?"

"Away from the Strip, and away from tonight. You in?"

She considers me for a long moment, her eyes positively churning with the angst of endless possibilities. Whatever's driving her inside, though, it wins.

Taking the helmet from my hands, she nods and swings a leg over the bike again, leaning into my back. I pause before firing it up, three words making my chest rumble under her hands.

"My name's Flynn."

FIVE

Daisy

Bright lights dance through the dark window, and a car's headlights flash by on the street. I follow the stimuli like a gnat searching for a place to land, even with an entire rectangle-shaped bar and several tables beyond that between me and the outside.

The truth is, I haven't known what to say since my new friend Flynn pulled up outside this little bar on a quiet street removed from the busy Vegas Strip. The glitz, the glamour—we left it all behind for life just outside the bubble, and with the way he is, that means neither one of us has uttered a syllable in over twenty minutes.

It's awkward—as I would expect it to be with a complete stranger—but somehow comfortable at the same time. There's no overt pressure, no prying. In fact, he seems content to sit here and let me stew on myself for as long as I want.

The bartender sets a fresh glass of ice water in front of me—a pointed choice I made given that I'm on the verge of a huge breakdown *and* in the presence of someone I know virtually nothing about—and I heave a sigh as Flynn stares blandly at the TV above us. There's a game of some sort on, but I can't tell for the life of me what's actually going on. I think it's something European.

Rubbing my lips together roughly, I swallow once before finally clearing my throat, turning a little bit on my stool to face my companion, and I find my voice.

"I guess you're probably wondering what would possess a person to go screaming from a hotel in the middle of the night and hop on some random stranger's motorcycle, huh?"

He lifts his eyebrows, turning away from the TV to look at me directly, and I can only imagine the things he's thinking. Probably that I'm reckless with my own well-being and maybe that I'm needlessly wild with my life at all times. Maybe he thinks I sleep around or prostitute myself or something. I mean, who knows at this point? I wouldn't blame him.

His blue eyes are calm, kind even, but as far as what's running through his mind, they give nothing away.

I nod to myself, answering for him. "Well, of course you are. I know I would be." I scoff. "I'd be half tempted to call the police on my crazy ass, to be honest."

He smirks, and a nervous niggle makes my chest ache. *Oh God, I hope he doesn't call the police.* They'll report me to Immigration, and if I'm convicted of a crime, they'll never give me another visa!

I calm down briefly by reminding myself that he's a big, tough guy and probably doesn't have nearly the hair trigger about calling the police that a petite woman like myself would. On that thought, I lay out my thinking for him to digest. Plus, it's always good for a man to get a little reality check about life as a woman.

"Not that you've got as much to worry about as the average woman does. Statistically, nearly one in every five women is raped in their lifetime, and that fact doesn't even take non-sexual assault into consideration. I mean, mugging and murder and all that included, it has to be like one in three, right?"

"I'm not gonna call the police," he says easily, and I'm almost surprised his voice isn't scratchy from disuse.

"Oh. Well, that's good. For sure. I don't want to be at the Wynn right now, but I don't necessarily want to be in jail either, ya know?"

He almost smiles, sitting back in his seat and rotating his body slightly to face me. It's a small change physically, but mentally, I feel as though he's placed a big, warm hand on my thigh and squeezed. I shift and fidget a little under the extra attention. It's so intense, it almost feels like scrutiny.

"Jail would be really bad, actually," I state with a shake of my head. "Pretty sure it would make everything worse."

"It usually does."

"Ha!" I laugh. "Yeah, you're right. It does. But in this case, I'm pretty sure it would mean I was completely and totally screwed, like, no take backs ever. And right now, I'm just in the utterly fucked department."

His forehead wrinkles slightly, but if it weren't for that, I'd swear he didn't even care to know what was going on with me at all. I don't get it. If some stranger shanghaied me like I did him, I'd be doing the million-question march right now.

I rub at the condensation on my water glass and sigh. Maybe he really wants to know, but he's not asking out of politeness. Maybe I just have to be the one to break the ice—to offer up an explanation so he doesn't have to come digging for one. Resolute in my conclusion, I nod, pushing my glass away slightly and turning to face him so our knees just barely rub each other's. "Okay, I'll tell you. It's not like telling you is going to change the situation, but maybe it'll feel good to get it off my chest."

He shrugs, jerking up his chin as though to tell me to proceed.

So, I do. I proceed like a goddamn spinning top that can't slow down once its momentum gets started.

"I, well…I'm Canadian…from Canada. I mean, I don't live there right now.

I live in LA. But I was born in Canada and came here because I got offered my dream job a year ago. Well, one year and two months, to be exact."

"Canada, eh?"

"Wow," I remark. "I guess that joke really transcends all Americans. Even the ones who otherwise barely speak."

He laughs but doesn't say anything else, instead taking a sip of his own water. For a couple of people at a bar, we make quite the boring pair.

"Well, as it turns out, I'm kind of challenged when it comes to keeping up with my mail and important documents and such, and I just got notice tonight that I let my visa lapse. You know, just the very essential visa that was making sure I was in this country legally."

His eyebrows lift, more than they have before, a sign that he realizes how serious my situation is, and I nod vigorously. "Yeah, it's bad. It's, like, end my career at my dream company, go back to my sad life in Canada with no clear direction for my future bad. I don't know what I'm going to do or how I'm going to fix it. I don't have connections with the overlords at the immigration office, and processing times to get a new visa are over a year. I have zero options. Hell, I never even date, so there's no American man in the picture who would be willing to make some kind of marry-me-to-save-my-ass-from-deportation pact. Basically, I'm just waiting for ICE to come take me away in handcuffs and put me on a plane back to Vancouver."

I take a huge swig of my water and slam it back down on the bar before turning to face him again, my whole face collapsing. "So, yeah. You're kind of stuck dealing with me on one of my worst nights, and if I had any kind of inner peace whatsoever, I would apologize to you. As it is, though, all I can do is sit here and whine. And hydrate, though I'm considering switching to vodka. And quite possibly, go on the lam."

He leans forward into the bar, puts his elbows onto the surface, and lets out a quiet breath that I'm surprised I can hear over my own breakdown.

It's easy—not at all troubled like my own—and I think that might have something to do with just how caught off guard I am when he speaks.

"Fuck it. I'll make that pact."

"Huh?"

"I'll marry you."

I whip my head toward him violently, so much so that a pop in a tendon of my neck makes stars flash on the surface of my eyes. Still, the beginning stages of an aneurysm or stroke or whatever can wait.

"I'm sorry, *what?*"

He looks at me closely, his eyes reading mine with careful intent. His posture is calm, his stature poised, and he doesn't repeat himself. I know he doesn't waste words, ever, and so I can only assume he doesn't reiterate the same ones when he doesn't need to.

"You just said you'd marry me."

He just stares. Relaxed, cool as a cucumber, and not all freaked out by what he just offered.

"You just said you'd marry me, and you don't even know me. How does that make any sense?"

He shrugs. "Because you don't need a husband. You need a green card. And I don't have any plans to have a real wife."

"You don't even really speak."

He shrugs. "You talk enough for the both of us."

That's…well, that's true. Especially right now, in the midst of my freak-out. But should I really make the completely insane, rash, life-altering decision to get married while I'm this mentally unstable? I don't even know anything about this man! Nothing. Zilch. Zero.

"I don't even know your last name."

"And?" He smirks. "You worried it's not going to go with Daisy or something?"

"You want to make a marriage pact with me, a woman you don't know anything about? I'm starting to think I'm having a stroke or I've suffered some serious accident and I'm actually in a coma." I laugh. Almost hysterically, really. I am one of the hyenas from *The Lion King*, and I can't seem to stop it. "We just…we can't…"

He raises his eyebrows and takes a drink of water before standing up from his stool and holding out a hand.

"Flynn. This is crazy."

But just crazy enough to get you a green card…

I stare into his magnificent eyes and try to find a shred of doubt or worry in them that matches the absolute scrambled-egg feeling going on in my insides, but try as I might, I can't see anything in there but steadiness.

My hand, shocking me to my core, doesn't even shake as I slide it into the hollow of his. As his fingers close around mine, so does the reality of the impending domino effect my lapsed work visa will create.

Awesome job? Done for.

All my goals and hopes and dreams? Poof. *Gone.*

I take a deep breath. "And what are the terms of this marriage…well, *fake* marriage pact? You marry me so I can get a green card? And that's it, no strings attached?"

He nods. "Pretty much."

"This really is crazy." I giggle through a shaky smile. But also, I can't bring myself to do anything but accept the life vest he's just tossed into my ocean of chaos. "Okay, yeah, count me in."

"Winslow," he says, and I quirk a brow. "My last name."

Winslow. Flynn Winslow, I silently recite his name. *Welp, at least it actually goes with Daisy and doesn't put you in a Julia Gulia situation…*

"Right. Next stop…Mr. and Mrs. Winslow."

SIX

Flynn

Neon lights that read *Happy Chapel* flash obnoxiously in front of us, and I pull my bike to a stop in a small parking lot just off the main drag of the Strip. Just as I push my foot against the kickstand, I cut the engine and plunge us into pseudosilence. It's not quiet—not with the buzz of the Vegas nightlife so close by—but without the sound of the engine rumbling in my chest, it's damn near tranquil.

Daisy's arms don't loosen like I expect them to, so I prompt her with a couple generous words I'd usually not bother with.

"We're here."

I feel the edge of her chin in my back as she nods against it, but still, the hold of her grip doesn't loosen.

Rather than rush her, I put the weight of my bike onto the kickstand and wait. Red neon lights outline the chapel's big sign, and a pair of kissing doves are painted on the side of the white brick.

Given our proximity to the desert, the spring night is more balmy than cool, but I swear I feel a shiver run up my clinging companion's spine.

It's only afterward that her iron grip softens, and one of her toned legs makes a move to step down onto her sky-high heels.

I stay still, acting as a steady brace as she finds her feet off a leaning bike, and climb off only when she backs away several steps and wraps her arms around herself.

Her curls poke out from the bottom of my helmet, and I have to bite my lip to keep from grinning as I take a couple steps toward her and help her remove it.

"Oh," she says through a laugh as the padding scrapes over her ears on the helmet's way off her head. "Right. I'm supposed to take that off, I guess."

She's nervous, obviously, but after living with my sister Winnie for as many years as I did, I'm not sure there'd ever be a woman who wasn't when in this scenario.

And most men would be, too.

I set my helmet on the bike and lock the ignition, and then I head for the door, placing a hand on the small of her back and gently guiding her along with me as I go.

She moves freely and with ease, but her eyes are the size of very pretty saucers.

A happy, laughing, clearly drunk couple stumbles out through the doors ahead of us, and I sidestep, taking Daisy with me to keep them from barreling into us.

Daisy watches them with avid interest, and I have to squeeze the side of her hip to get her to precede me when I hold the door open.

Steps careful, she eases her way into the entry of the chapel, where red carpet, disco lights, busts of naked women, and dozens of bouquets of flowers await. *This place certainly lives up to the Vegas wedding scene that most people picture.* The front desk isn't occupied by any other couples, so we're able to step right up to it, and to the waiting man behind it.

"Welcome to the Happy Chapel!" he greets cheerfully, leaning into the plexiglass top with his elbows. "What can we help you with tonight?"

Daisy's body locks, her muscles turning to stone and her eyes rivaling those of a cartoon. She looks like the lead character in a Disney movie, her wild curls dancing in the breeze of the air conditioning and tickling at her face.

"Ha!" The man at the desk laughs then, completely ignoring my companion's audition for the movie *Frozen*. "Just kidding, obviously! It's safe to say you're here to get hitched, which means you're in the right place. Step right up and take a look at our different packages! We've got the quicky, the slicky, the all I want's the dicky." His cackles take over, and Daisy's frantic eyes come to me briefly.

I know she's looking for some kind words and comfort, but the only thing I can manage is a soft, reassuring smile. Interestingly enough, the entire expression of her face changes at the sight of it, and all of the tension leaves—at least as far as I can feel—her body.

Nodding swiftly, she steps up to the counter and looks down below the glass as the front desk comedian runs through the options in more detail. "The quicky's just the ceremony without the thrills. No flowers, no décor, just the quick and dirty contract. It does include a witness if you don't have one of your own, though. The slicky has a lot more pomp and circumstance, two gold wedding bands, and you get to choose a bouquet and a slice of cake. It's twice the price, but honey, can you really put a dollar limit on love?"

Daisy glances over her shoulder at me, and I offer an amused raise of my eyebrows. This guy is really something. When she turns back toward the desk, I don't miss the longing way she looks up at the display of cakes and bouquets above the man's head. Eventually, though, she replies, "I guess just the quicky will be fine."

That look of hers is the same one I saw cross her face after we left the Clark County Marriage License Bureau and she spotted a small shop with tuxedos and dresses.

It's also the reason my attire tonight transformed from jeans and a T-shirt to full-on black tuxedo.

"You don't want to hear about the dicky?" The man behind the desk questions with a quirk of his brow.

"Um, no," Daisy says through a giggle, glancing back at me.

"Are you sure?" he asks again, looking me up and down. "It's very sexual, and the tension between Mr. Tall, Dark, and Silent back there and you is pretty thick."

I also want to laugh at his absurdity, but I step into the fray and place a soft hand on Daisy's back that nearly makes her jerk several joints out of their sockets trying to contort to see it.

"Actually, we'll take the one with the flowers and the cake."

Daisy's big green eyes meet mine. "What?"

"A wedding, any wedding," I tell her, "has flowers and some cake." When she doesn't respond, I pointedly touch the lapels of my black tuxedo and then smile at the formfitting cream silk dress she's been wearing since she tried it on at the rental shop.

We've dressed the part, Daisy. It wouldn't feel right not to include the cake and flowers, too.

She nods then, studying me closely, and a tiny, breathtaking smile lights her up from her smiling mouth to her now sparkling eyes.

"Okay, then," front desk man chirps, spinning in a circle and grabbing some forms from a tray. "Just fill these puppies in with the important information, and I'll get it all typed up and ready to go." He leans forward and points to the papers. "See here? This is the section where you pick the flowers and cake flavor, okay? They're all labeled up there."

"Great," Daisy replies, taking the forms from his hands, placing them on one of the waiting clipboards from the counter, and grabbing a pen to fill everything out. I follow her to the other side of the room as she takes a seat in a chair and starts writing. I shamelessly watch over her shoulder.

Daisy Marie Diaz. Twenty-nine years old. Birthday December 25.

"Christmas baby, huh?"

She laughs a little. "So the city of Vancouver tells me."

The city of Vancouver tells her? Not her parents? Interesting.

Done with her information, she offers the clipboard to me, where I quickly scribble down my information. It's nothing too thorough—just very basic information and a home address.

When I'm done, I get up and walk the clipboard back over to the counter, carefully checking the sheet to see which bouquet she's selected.

Number 2A.

Big, bright Gerbera daisies all packed together in an overcrowded cluster. *Very interesting.* I really thought she'd go for one of the more refined sets of delicate whites and pinks, but then again, I'm finding that this woman never hesitates to surprise me.

Settling the clipboard onto the desk, I turn and head back in her direction, where she's no longer sitting in the chairs in which I left her. Instead, she's up and moving.

She waves frantic hands at her face, the crimson red wave of her anxiety cascading off her cheeks and down the line of her neck, and I step back as her red-tipped fingers swing out and almost hit me in the face.

"Okay. Okay," she repeats to herself, spinning in the world's tiniest circle. "Everything is fine. This is no big deal. People do crazy things like this all the time for far less rational reasons, and I'm just…taking care of business. Handling my shit. Making life my bitch. I can do this."

I step back and out of the way as she does some sort of power-skip, half-jump thing and lands on her toes. My eyebrows lift slightly, but I don't say anything else. I'm not even sure there's anything that can be said to calm her down at this point.

That's not entirely true. You could tell her she doesn't have to do this. That life happens for reasons, and maybe it'll turn out to be a good thing that her visa expired. My stomach flips in protest, and I shake my head slightly to clear it. No, we're doing the right thing. Saving her career. Her future. It's not a big deal.

I'm a practical guy, rationality and logic always the foundation for my decisions. A guy like me doesn't do impulsive shit unless it serves an actual purpose. And this, obviously, serves a very important purpose.

Actually, you don't do impulsive shit, period.

I can't deny this is, hands down, the most impulsive thing I've ever done in my life. My brothers would certainly lose their fucking minds if they were here to witness it.

But they're not here, and according to Ty's last update, they're at some bar with beer pong tables and cocktail waitresses that make Hooters' tight outfits look prim and proper. I know this because he sent me a photo of an oblivious and blindfolded Jude, smiling toward the camera, while two of the scantily clad cocktail waitresses stood beside him.

Jude would be at risk for a fucking stroke if he found out you were getting married before him...

I almost start to marinate in that thought and allow the reality to sink in, but the doors to the chapel swing open so dramatically they hit the wall with a shocking bang. Instantly, a very broad-shouldered man wearing a white halter top dress and a face full of show makeup steps into the space.

"Oh my God," Daisy whispers, her voice rising at the very end to an almost silent shriek. "Is that…uh…Marilyn Monroe?"

I almost snort, but in deference to her obvious freak-out, I don't. One thing is for sure, though, that is most certainly *not* Marilyn Monroe. But it's a pretty damn good showing by a man trying to look like her, I have to admit.

"Daisy Diaz and Flynn Winslow?" Fake Marilyn calls out with a movie-star smile and flutter of eyelashes, and Daisy's hand shoots out and grabs me by the forearm, her fingernails digging into my skin, even through the material of my tux jacket.

"Us? Already?" Her eyebrows practically shoot up past her hairline. "But you just handed in the clipboard, like, a second ago. What kind of operation are they running here?"

I can't help but chuckle. "Seems like a quick one."

Daisy's glare is pointed and strong and oh-so amusing.

"Ready?" I ask with a simplicity the two of us know isn't all that simple.

She takes a moment of consideration, but it's not more than a few seconds before she's nodding and taking me by the arm to lead us toward Marilyn. "That's us."

"Great," Marilyn coos, shooting us a wink before waving a hand and escorting us through the doors to the chapel. "Let's do it."

The door bobs and bounces against itself as I reach out to catch it without pushing through. Instead, I turn to Daisy with a raise of my eyebrows. *You sure about this?*

Her words are a declaration—and the first step in a whole new part of our lives. "Let's do it."

For better or for worse and until Daisy gets a green card, Mr. and Mrs. Winslow, here we come.

SEVEN

Daisy

Flynn tosses the keys to his motorcycle into the bowl beside the door and walks down the hall, leaving me to follow. I watch silently as he puts down the duffel bag from his bike that houses our normal clothes and then works off the tie at his neck. His strong shoulders work to take off his tuxedo jacket, and I bite my lip to stop my mouth's nervous quiver when he reaches back to ruffle the hair at the back of his head with long, tanned fingers.

And I thought he looked good in leather. This sophisticated tux look takes Flynn Winslow's hotness to a whole new level. It's almost a shame it's a rental that will have to be returned.

You do realize that this marriage is fake, right? You're not going to, like, move in with him and pop out 2.5 kids…

His house is dark, but lights set to motion sensors illuminate each space as we move through it. First, down a long, large, high-ceilinged hallway, and then through a living room with modern, dark-green velvet sofas, and finally into a huge kitchen, set against a wall of floor-to-ceiling windows and a terracescape in the backyard. Even outside, lights begin to dot the hillside as Flynn walks in front of the windows.

Wow. This place is… Well, it's not my dinky apartment in LA, that's for sure. It's a place for someone with money.

The silence, for the first time all night, is heavy. It's laden with things unsaid—things I'm afraid to say—and even as I chip away at the block with my mental ice pick, I'm having the damnedest time trying to find some words to say.

I mean…what do you say in this situation? When you find yourself at the remote house of your new husband, about whom you know next to nothing?

"Do you…do you have a shirt I could sleep in, maybe?"

Oh God. I'm pretty sure that's not it.

Under normal circumstances, with the men of my past, I might actually have the opportunity to be embarrassed. To wonder what he's thinking as he stares at me in sheer disbelief. But not with Flynn. No. He turns without a word and walks down the hall. And, yeah, it's things like that that let me know how wrong I am every time I try to convince myself that anything about what I've just done is normal.

That's my *husband*. And I don't have a freaking clue what he's going to do from one moment to the next. *For the love of God, I kissed that man, not even an hour ago, after promising ourselves to each other until one of us reaches our ultimate demise.*

Drag Marilyn fanned herself and asked someone for a glass of water, and all I could do was stare into the deep ocean of his eyes and wait for a tidal wave to knock me out of my misery.

The kiss…it was *powerful*. Gravity shifting. So fucking exceptional that my lips have yet to stop tingling.

You just need to go to bed. Get your head right. Calm down, for Pete's sake.

For now, though, while I wait on him to return with either a shirt or a weapon of some sort, I stand there swaying on my feet and survey the modern interior of his desert home. It's filled with cool concrete on the floors and counters, and the black cabinets look perfectly in place. It's not my personal taste, but as a designer, I can appreciate the intention of it and how good it looks juxtaposed against the heated backdrop of sand and shrub.

His footsteps are quiet, so I don't hear him coming back until he's there, exiting the mouth of the hallway and holding out a neatly folded T-shirt for me to take, his own now noticeably missing. I accept it gratefully, letting the folds fall open in front of me as I pull it toward myself and swallow hard at the ripple of his well-defined muscles.

The borrowed shirt is huge in comparison to my small frame, and for the first time since I wrapped my arms around him on the motorcycle leaving the Wynn, I'm reminded just how large he actually is.

"Thank you," I murmur.

"You're welcome." The sound of his deep voice on those two simple words slides over my skin like a warm wind. I never realized how much I'm used to hearing people babble like me. Nevertheless, the simple exchange feels as if it unlocks the vise around my throat, and finally, I explode all over the room with hundreds of words.

"I'm sorry if I'm getting in the way of your plans. Surely you had things you intended to do before I asked you to take me on a wild ride. If you need to get back to them, I completely understand, you know? I'm…well, I'll be fine, and now that we're married—ha!—I guess I need to figure out what that means for what I need to do with Immigration."

"It's fine."

"Okay, good. I mean, not good. None of this is good. It's…well, it's crazy, is what it is! I married you—a complete stranger—with Marilyn Monroe as the officiant. If that's not worthy of a little bit of a freak-out, I don't know what is. Liberace, sure, I could see that. But Marilyn Monroe as a member of the clergy? Seems like a stretch, you know?"

He raises his eyebrows but, by and large, doesn't do anything else other than grab a glass from the cabinet beside the sink and turn on the tap to fill it halfway with water.

I swallow thickly as he turns his shirtless back to the counter to take a swig. When he tips his head forward again, he holds out the glass in offering.

I almost wheeze. "Oh, no. Thank you, but no. I don't want to take your water."

He smirks then, turning around and pulling another glass from the cabinet. *Oh, right.* He was offering to get me my own, not to meet in the middle of the noodle like we're fucking Lady and the Tramp.

Placing the glass under the faucet, he fills it until it's about an inch from the top and then holds it out to me. I tuck his T-shirt to my chest and reach out to take it.

"Thanks. Really. For all of this. You've been incredibly patient with me tonight, and I know that's not the easiest task under the circumstances." I laugh almost manically again. "I, um, think I'll just take this to bed with me. Try to get some sleep if that's all right."

He jerks up his chin, and I nod. "Um. Sorry, but, uh, which bedroom?"

"Second door on the left, bathroom is in the hall."

"Great. That's…great. Okay, well, thanks again. And goodnight."

"Goodnight," he replies softly, so softly I almost don't even hear him.

I take a hugely deep breath as I spin around and only let it out when I'm safely tucked into the hallway bathroom with the door shut and locked behind me. I set my glass on the counter and look at myself in the mirror, and for the briefest of moments, I don't even recognize any of my features. My eyes are wide and bright, and my hair is wild in a way I never let it get. I suppose, however, that messy hair is to be expected after going on an unexpected joyride on a motorcycle.

I look down at the gold wedding band on my left ring finger and spin it around a few times with my thumb.

I'm *married*. Freaking legally bound to a man whose middle name could be Herbert for all I know. *Oh God, what if it's Muriel like Chandler on* Friends?

Jesus, Daisy, like that's what matters at this stage in the game. You got married. Pretty sure his middle name and whether it's mockable aren't what's important here.

"Okay, relax. This is…good. We're well on our way to solving this whole visa debacle, and tomorrow morning, I'll go back to reality and work and figure out all the details. This will just be a fun night that I look back on and tell my grandkids—only after their grandfather has passed. Just in case he's got a hair trigger about divorcing a crazy lady. Right? Right. So just…wash your face, Daisy," I tell myself in the mirror like a freak. "Wash your face and go to bed. Sleep it off."

I lean back off the counter and shake out my arms for good measure. Surely the vibration will help with letting all the anxious juju make its way out through the ends of my fingers.

Quick and efficient, like a trained soldier, I set out to follow my own orders. A quick rinse of my face, a brush of my teeth with my own finger, a little potty break, a quick change into—*swallow*—Flynn's large, loose T-shirt, and a run of my fingers through my hair, and I'm ready for bed.

I click off the lights first before opening the door a crack and peeking out into the hallway, my own discarded rental dress clutched to my chest. It's dark and quiet, and after a brief surveillance to make sure that's not going to change, I open the door the rest of the way and prance toward the bedroom on ninja-like feet. To be honest, I imagine I look a little bit more like the Grinch as he prepares to steal Christmas than anything else, but hell, it makes me feel better, so I go with it.

Safely in the bedroom, I shut the door behind myself with a soft click and step back to look at it, tossing my dress on a high-backed chair to the side. I never take my eyes off the door. It's completely inanimate, and yet, it seems to say so many things.

I jump forward quickly and engage the lock brusquely before breaking into a jog for the bed. The sooner I'm in and tucked under those covers, the sooner I can fall asleep, which, ultimately, means I'll be able to let all of this go for a short period of time and just…rest.

Recharge. Reset. Recalibrate.

I shuffle and wiggle and scoot until nothing but my chin sticks out from the thick white comforter, my two eyes blinking rapidly in the silent darkness.

There is no city out the window, no hustle and bustle of the freeway just beyond the fence behind my apartment building—only the great, expansive nothingness of the desert and beyond.

I roll to the side and tuck my head in the pillow, hoping to smother some of my unrelenting thoughts.

Married, Daisy. You're married.

I shake my head to, I don't know, hopefully cause some minor brain trauma so the little cerebral workers shut things down for the night, but every time I try to close my eyes, they just pop back open like they're spring-loaded.

I do an alligator death roll, spinning and spinning until the sheets are so tangled around me, I don't know that I'll ever get free.

"Well, this is good," I murmur softly to myself, wrestling my limbs until I finally get my arms free and flop them on top of the covers.

God. Now I'm hot. Like, fucking swampy, to be honest. Why, why, *why* didn't I bring my glass of water to bed with me? Whyyy did I leave it in the bathroom?

"Ugh," I huff, pulling the covers down and off me completely while my internal oven cranks up the temperature to 500. *For the love of everything, my organs will never survive this roasting.*

I sigh. Sit up. Stare at the door.

Surely Flynn's gone to bed now, right? I could just sneak back into the bathroom, grab my glass, fill it up one or five times, and that'll be that. A gulp of some H2O and back to bed.

The fact that you're trying to avoid your husband on your wedding night is quite the turn of events…

On a sigh, I shove the covers down to the end of the bed and turn my body so that my feet dangle off the edge. I crane my neck and strain my ears to hear anything outside of the bedroom—any signs of life—but as hard as I try, I can't hear anything at all.

Just go, you lunatic. The night can't get any weirder than it already is.

Moving boldly, I jump down from the bed and take off on another Jim Carrey in a green suit style run for the door. I unlock it, open it, peek outside, and then creep my way to the bathroom swiftly. I shut the door, lock it behind me, and then flick on the lights only to find my glass of water is…gone.

Nooo. Jesus, where did it go? Don't tell me this place is like the Beast's castle, and candlesticks are doing some light housekeeping in the dark of night.

Shit. I'm going to have to go back to the kitchen. Whipping out my virtual UNO reverse card, I exit the bathroom with the same stealth and speed with which I entered and head down the hallway toward the land of concrete and black cupboards.

The lights are all out, and the motion sensors must have a timer or something, because I'm left to the safety of the darkness as I make it into the kitchen, grab a glass from the cabinet I watched him get it out of before, and fill up my glass at the sink.

I put it to my lips, take a hard swig, and then settle my frantic hips against the counter with a deep sigh.

"Can't sleep?" a rough, thick voice says from the darkened breakfast nook at the side of the kitchen. The jump it produces from me rivals that of Earvin Johnson, the Magic man himself.

"Holy shit," I snap, a hand to my chest as I gasp for breath. Frankly, it's nothing short of a miracle that there's not shattered drinking glass fucking everywhere. "You're still up."

Flynn doesn't respond, only shifting slightly in his seat and changing the shape of his shadow on the wall.

"I'm sorry. I didn't mean to disturb your…quiet time or whatever. I just had to have another drink. P-a-r-c-h-e-d, that's me."

This has to be the weirdest, most awkward wedding night that has ever occurred.

My eyes close of their own accord, embarrassed for all sorts of reasons. Though, mostly due to the fact that I'm stuck inside the body of a lunatic.

"My mind…it keeps running and running like it's Usain Bolt or something," I ramble, because, well, why not? It's not like Flynn hasn't caught on to the reality of my manic mental state. I mean, I was like this *before* he married me. You know, when I hopped onto his bike without even knowing his first name. "Big night, huh?" I question, even though I know the odds of him answering are slim to none. "Lots of shifting life parts or whatever." I stick a fist in the air and do some kind of weird cheer thing, and that's when he moves. Up and out of his chair, he comes toward me, stalking almost, his walk is such a prowl.

My back hits the counter as I try to work my way through the concrete, but it's no use. Between one breath and the next, his front is six inches from mine, and I can't seem to keep any air in my lungs.

"You're worked up," he says, his big hands tenderly running a path up my arms and knocking my equilibrium right off planet Earth and catapulting it straight to flipping Mars.

All I can do is nod.

"Too worked up."

I nod again.

"You know what I think you need?"

"A tranquilizer dart to the neck?"

He smirks, shakes his head, and his hands go to my hips. My mouth gapes, and before I know it, I'm two feet to the left and my bare ass is on the cold stone of his counter and a rush of pent-up frustration floods between my legs.

Hell's bells, why am I so turned on right now?

"You can't seem to calm down, and in order to sleep—which I haven't been able to do in two fucking nights thanks to babysitting my drunken brigade of brothers—I need you to." His voice rumbles and rasps in the most delicious way, like it's my own personal ASMR soundtrack, only suited to what triggers my desires. "So, I'm thinking the only way to make that happen is to fuck the anxiety right out of you."

Time halts and my ears bleed—and my soul? Well, I'm pretty sure it just up and leaves my body.

Holy shiiit. Is this happening right now?

Please, please, please say this is happening right now.

EIGHT

Flynn

"Do you think I'm right, Daisy?" I ask her. "Do you think you need me to fuck the anxiety right out of you?"

She nods, and the way her green eyes blaze makes my cock grow hard beneath my zipper.

Fuck me.

Daisy gasps as I cover the flesh of her bare ass with my hands and pull her closer to the edge of the counter. With pressure on the insides of her knees, I spread her legs apart to the point at which I know she's on the brink of pain and grab a handful of those sexy goddamn curls to pull her head back and expose her throat.

"Do you want this? Yes or no."

"Yes."

A long, purring moan rolls out of her mouth, and her eyes flash with both surprise and arousal.

I seal my lips to the skin of her neck and suck, the sweet perfume of her body making the tip of my nose tingle. It's been several months since I've had sex, but it's not been from lack of opportunity.

Truthfully, I've been bored—unexcited—and if there's one thing about me that's absolute, it's that I don't ever do anything with the intention of going through the motions. Sex without pleasure, words without meaning, friendship without life enrichment—it's all frivolous. I don't need pointless fucking, and I don't need pointless people. Period.

That said, I don't have to be in love either—quite the contrary. All I need is the thrill of a partner who's willing to push the limits with me. Someone who's interested in doing more than lying back and spreading their legs. Someone who's open to being pleased and eager to please me in return.

And if there's anything I've surmised about Daisy Diaz in the last four hours, it's that she's extremely eager to please.

Her knees rise up, skimming my sides and tucking into the flesh just above the bones of my hips. Her core gyrates toward me, and her tension increases. Her body bows with each breath, suggesting she's all too eager to get my cock inside her dainty little cunt.

I push her knees wide again and sink down to the floor, and the direct view I get of her bare pussy is enough to make my cock jump inside my jeans. She smells sweet, and I can tell without even touching her that she's making my counter wet.

"I'm going to tongue you so deep, I'll remember the taste of you every time I eat in this kitchen."

Her fingernails dig into the muscles of my shoulders through the thin material of my T-shirt, and my cock swells some more. *If she got off on that, this is going to be good.*

"Lie back," I instruct, reaching up with a flat hand to press on the center of her chest. She acquiesces immediately, and the new position makes it that much easier to get her legs as wide as they'll go and anchor her heels into the cool concrete counter.

Her breathing is heavy, her whole body shaking, but for the first time since I met her this afternoon, she's quiet. And it's not because she's scared—I can tell by the glisten on my finger as I run it around the rim of her pussy—she's excited.

I skim my finger over her clit, eliciting a moan and a jerk of her hips, and then suck the juice off the surface of her pussy. She tastes like a cherry popsicle on a hot summer day. *Fuck.*

Easing her open, I push one finger inside, and the squeeze of her around me is enough to make me sink my teeth into the flesh of my bottom lip. It's a stretch, so I go gently, but adding a second finger to the first is as sweet as I imagine.

"You have no idea what you've gotten yourself and your tight little cunt into, Daisy. But I'm sure as hell about to show you."

"Oh my God," she breathes, her legs shaking so hard you'd think Vegas was experiencing an earthquake. I run my hands up the length of her thighs firmly, settling them in their place again.

My dick throbs in my pants, and I know I can't wait any longer to taste her again without breaking in half from the anticipation. With steady hands, I hold open the spread of her legs and put my mouth to her pussy. It spasms against my lips, inciting a pointed flick of my tongue at the entrance before dipping it inside to really drink her in. She's soft and supple and every bit of the woman I imagined she'd be when I first wrote her off.

She's immaculate—tidy—and used to a certain amount of restraint. Her back bows, and she scratches her hands at the top of my head, desperate to find purchase in the dark locks of my hair, though. And I know it's because the way I'm eating her—the messy, voracious strokes of my tongue—is better than anything she's ever felt before.

I suck and stroke and lap at her patiently until I've drunk every drop of come her pretty little pussy has to offer and make it give me more. It spasms and quakes with her orgasm, and the sound of her howl echoes off the walls of my kitchen like a boomerang. She's as slick as silk, and my cock is going to love the feel of her around me.

Standing softly, I unbuckle my belt and undo the button of my pants. She's motionless, the only indication that she's still with me, the heave of her returning breath.

I realize that then I don't have a condom. Ironically, I should've had the foresight to have one in my pocket to keep a drunken Ty out of trouble this weekend, but apparently I dropped the fucking ball.

My cock is pulsing, damn near purple from arousal, and Daisy is right here, with her thighs spread and her pussy wet with need.

Fuck.

"I don't have a condom."

"It's fine," she breathes out in a raspy, needy voice, but her eyes are still half closed. "I'm on the shot. I'm clean. And I haven't had sex in, like, eleventy-billion years."

Her commentary almost makes me laugh, but again, I'm so fucking hard right now, I could hammer nails.

A rational guy like me doesn't have unprotected sex, but tonight, I don't fucking know. I can't stop looking at her, staring at how gorgeous and downright tempting she looks with her legs spread wide for me.

And you sure as shit can't find the will to stop whatever is happening here.

"I'm clean too," I tell her, and like a fucking masochistic psycho, I slide a finger inside her to remind myself of how damn good she feels.

"Then we're all set." A tiny moan escapes her lips, and she wiggles her hips closer to my hand. "It's *allllll* good. All set to consummate," she rambles, and it's only then that she gathers enough strength to lift her head from the counter, her glazed-over eyes landing squarely on my girth. "Uh…wow…" She licks her lips. "Uh…you're…"

"Big," I finish for her. It's not a brag or a flex or some stupid ego type of bullshit. It's just a fact. To be honest, I've found it scares more women than it excites.

"How… Is that… Is it going to fit?"

"Oh yeah. I made sure your sweet little cunt would be ready for me."

And just imagine how she's going to feel wrapped around your cock…

Fuck.

I don't miss the way she swallows hard, the bob of her throat visible even in the moonlit kitchen.

"Are you sure you're okay with this?"

Her head stutters, but she ultimately nods. By the fifth or sixth bout up and down, it's much more resolute. "Yes. I-I want you, Flynn. I need to know what you feel like."

Fuck it. I can't hold back. I have to be inside her, too.

Her words hit like a buzz, sending my mind into a tailspin of naughty—really fucking dirty thoughts. If she wants to know what I feel like, I'm going to make sure her pussy walls remember every goddamn stroke like I've written them in braille.

NINE

Sunday, April 7th

Daisy

I pull open the bedroom door—*Flynn's* bedroom door—to the hallway, my clothes back in place thanks to a stealth mission at the crack of dawn and Flynn's folded T-shirt in my arms, and head for the kitchen. I don't know how long I've been staring at the door, working up the nerve to come outside and face everything I did last night in the light of day, but it's bordering on way too long.

His bed. The walls. The black chair in the corner in front of the closet. They all *know* things. Things I'm not even sure I knew about myself before Flynn opened up an erotic portal to a place I've *never* been before.

Sweet land of the living, the man is…well-informed about the female body. He knew all the spots, all the buttons to push. I swear, if I weren't sure it would make me sound entirely crazy, I'd consider asking him if he went 50/50 with God on all the details of the clitoris.

Deep breaths in and out, over and over again, I straighten my spine and force myself to walk toward the kitchen with my head held high. I'm a strong, independent woman. So what if I had insanely hot—*condomless*—sex last night with my husband who isn't really my husband but a conduit in helping me get a green card. It's no big deal.

No big deal? Ha. That's cute.

Surprisingly, the room is completely quiet as I step inside, and Flynn is nowhere to be seen. The counter pulls my attention immediately, and a tiny crimson tidal wave starts its ascent up the skin of my throat.

That counter…knows the details of my labia.

Shocked by my own thoughts, I squeak, cover my mouth, and power walk across the kitchen, grabbing a glass from the cabinet and taking a peek in the fridge. I'm happy to find some orange juice—the vitamin C is definitely needed today—that's within its expiration timeline and pour it into the waiting vessel.

"Finding everything okay?" Flynn asks, making my heart shoot through a self-inflicted hole in the ceiling. *Cripes. Maybe I'm more on edge than I thought.*

But, gah, what am I supposed to be like? I got *married* last night. Not in practice, of course, but in *documentation*, and hell, the mind-bending sex probably added at least a little fine print at the bottom.

At least, for me, it did. As per usual, I don't have a flipping clue what he's thinking.

Casual and calm as ever, he walks past me to what's becoming known as *the cabinet* and gets himself a glass, filling it once again from the tap.

Does he ever drink anything other than water?

He's showered, damp hair curling softly around the backs of his ears, and he's dressed in a slightly different version of the same outfit from earlier last night. Black jeans this time, with a light blue T-shirt that makes his eyes seem otherworldly.

God, he looks good.

And I can't seem to stop myself from taking in the view. The *insanely hot* view, mind you, and before I know it, I'm taking a mental inventory. I don't want to forget even a sliver of what's in front of me when I'm back home in LA, with only my hands and a vibrator to satisfy myself.

Wide, muscular shoulders? Check.

Prominent biceps? Check.

Slim but firm stomach showing through the material of his shirt? Check.

And a delectable hint of a perfectly equipped bulge whispers secret promises of what I know lies beneath those jeans of his? Check. Check. Check.

The beauty that is his body is just standing there, proffered to me like the most delectable meal on a silver platter. If I had to compare his physique to anything, I'd say his body is reminiscent of those hot Olympic swimmers who make it very apparent they spend hours upon hours in the pool.

Before I know it, I'm blurting out a question. "Have you ever…swam competitively?"

"No…" Flynn glances up from his phone, which I didn't realize he was holding in front of himself, and cocks his head to the side. "Why?"

Because your body looks like someone sculpted it out of fucking stone, and I'm wondering if what I did last night was the best thing for me.

I realize that Flynn's and my marriage arrangement isn't fueled by love at first sight and butterflies. If anything, we've entered into a business contract without any hint of emotion. Besides, well, him feeling bad enough for my situation to take pity on me and offer up his pseudocommitment.

But he's my husband. Temporarily, sure, but still my husband. And you should definitely fuck your husband before you get a divorce.

Right? *Yes.*

I did the right thing last night.

A memory of Flynn's hips between my thighs, his hands to the counter behind me as he thrust inside me so powerfully my teeth chattered, plays like a film behind my eyes, and I have no choice but to close them and gather myself. *Oh, yeah, you SO did the right thing.*

"Uh…no-no reason," I manage to mumble, gathering myself enough to place his T-shirt on the counter next to him with a small smile before walking around to the other side to sit down on one of his stools.

It's only seconds before my mind runs away again, back to last night and the bad and sexy things that happened to make this a slightly less sterile environment.

I picture my head falling back and my heart rate skyrocketing and Flynn's warm breath as he grunts softly into the skin of my throat. Good gracious, *he's hot.* Like, *forgive me, Father, for I have really, really sinned* kind of hot.

Dirty, crude, uninhibited…I will never forget the sound of him whispering in my ear and telling me to *fuck him like I wanted to be fucked.*

His hips slowed, his chest slick with the effort he'd put into leaving an impression inside me, and I'd wrapped my arms around his shoulders and ordered him to carry me to bed.

And carry me to bed, he did. *His* bed, in fact, with careful, measured steps while his cock was still pressed to the hilt inside me.

I swallow, my hand drifting down to just above my pubic bone, where there's been the most delicious ache rolling through me since I woke up alone in his bed this morning.

Geez, Daisy, get yourself together here. There'll be plenty of time to remember all the details of your night together when you get back to LA—alone and horny and desperate to make yourself come.

Flynn is quiet and focused, his eyes back on his phone as he scrolls through something, and my eyes flick from the strong, chiseled lines of his face to the clock on the microwave display behind him.

Shit. "It's already nine?"

Flynn's eyes flit up to mine, considering me for a moment, and then he nods. "Yes."

I jump up from the stool and hustle toward the front door where I know I dropped my purse upon arrival last night.

Flynn's footsteps are soft, but not so much so that I don't hear the pattern of them following me down the hall at a slightly slower pace. With the length of his legs, however, I'm sure he's keeping up with me.

I grab my phone from my purse, saying a small prayer that it still has some battery juice, and scroll over to the Uber app to call myself a car.

"Have somewhere to be?" Flynn asks then, making my head whip up from my phone and my lips roll into my mouth.

"Oh yeah. I'm sorry, but I was supposed to be at another work function about half an hour ago."

He raises his shoulders nonchalantly. "Of course. Do you want me to take you back to the Wynn? I have to go anyway."

It's a nice offer, one I'm not sure I'd be able to resist if I didn't have a reason, to be honest. "Thanks, but no. It's a brunch at an old client's house—not at the hotel. I don't know much about Vegas geography, but I'm pretty sure it's in completely the opposite direction."

I search his eyes for disappointment and could almost swear that I see a flash of it, but the amount of trust I have in myself right now, in my current state of emotional turmoil, is minuscule at best. Frankly, I'm probably just projecting.

I lick my lips, tightening my grip on my phone to get up the courage I need before suggesting, "I-I would like to get your phone number, if that's okay. And give you mine? I'm pretty sure I'm going to need to send you some immigration paperwork at some point, and this is probably the easiest way to get in touch with me." I laugh at myself, self-deprecation all too ripe with the evidence of my current situation. "Clearly, I can't be trusted with the mail."

Flynn actually smiles at that, and immediately, it's melted butter where cartilage should be in my knees.

He reaches out and steadies me with one hand while easing my phone out of my hand and into his with the other. With a lot of pushing of buttons, he enters his number into my contact list and then pushes the call button to bestow his phone with the same information from me.

And just like that, I have a lifeline to the most interesting man—*who just so happens to be my husband*—I've ever met in my life.

I stare down at his programmed number. *Damn.* I really didn't dream it. I got married last night.

In a rented wedding dress with Marilyn Monroe officiating, no less…

"Oh shoot!" I look up at Flynn. "My dress…the rental shop. It's still on the chair in the bedroom and—"

"I'll handle it," he says with a soft smile, promptly stopping me from diving into a needless ramble about return policies.

"Thank you, Flynn," I blurt as my eyes stay locked on his face and refuse to let go. "I'm really not sure if I said it in all the chaos of the night, what with my freak-out and basically making you convince me that it was the right thing to do to marry you…to *pact* with you." I laugh, and he grins. "But *thank you*. You've quite possibly saved my life, and you've done it without even asking for anything in return. Please, if you ever figure out a way for me to repay you, I'm telling you now, don't hold back. Okay?"

"Okay, Daisy."

I nod then. Okay. That's…done. My frazzled brain nearly mocks me. *Oh yeah, Dais, you've really got everything completely buttoned up.*

Light lasers through the window, a perfect beam of illumination reflecting off the paint of my Uber as it pulls into Flynn's driveway and comes to a stop.

I glance back at my contracted husband and plaster the biggest smile on to my face that I can manage. "Well, I guess it's time to go."

He nods and then surprises me by moving forward, putting his strong, firm hands to my jaw, tipping my head back, and pressing his lips to my own.

It's a delicate, strangely innocent kiss, given the intimate knowledge we have of each other from last night, but the jolt it rockets through my pounding chest is nearly enough to send me to the hospital.

"Goodbye, Daisy Winslow."

My stomach turns over on itself as he reaches around me and opens the door, holding it for me gallantly.

I look from him, back to the house, and then out to the car.

I guess that…is really that.

"Goodbye, Flynn."

TEN

Flynn

In an expensive Las Vegas penthouse stood a man with a crappy cup of hotel coffee made from a temperamental Keurig, the logistical, legal side of his life having changed dramatically overnight.

I, Flynn Winslow, am that man, and what a night it was.

I'm officially the first Winslow brother to be married, and no one's ever even going to know about it. *Fucking hell.* That's funny enough to almost make me laugh.

I take another sip of my coffee and stare out the massive windows of the penthouse suite that Remy, Ty, and I reserved for Jude's bachelor party weekend. For once, the Strip looks calm and quiet, and very few tourists mill about on the sidewalks. Hell, even the neon lights of the desert city look almost reserved beneath the Nevada sun.

Now this is the kind of Vegas I can get behind.

"Damn, Flynn, you're up early."

I glance over my shoulder to find my eldest brother Remy shuffling toward the kitchen, most likely in search of coffee, and jerk my head toward the clock on the wall. He follows my gaze and cringes to himself.

"Shit. It's already eleven?"

I cover my smile with a sip from my coffee cup and turn back to face the window. I have a feeling the quiet atmosphere outside is compliments of many, many people in a state like my brother Remington.

Compared to the rest of my three brothers, I'm always the early bird who gets the worm, but when it comes to this weekend, it's mostly because I don't drink like a fucking fish. A beer or two is about as far as I get. And without me there to keep them in check last night, I can only imagine how close to dead they all came. This morning, of course—well, it's a whole other story entirely.

Remy sets the Keurig to brew, and a groan escapes his lips as he puts his hand to his head. "I never should've agreed to do tequila shots last night. Ty and Jude are fucking assholes."

Why he'd ever think our youngest brothers would steer him in a good direction when it comes to alcohol is beyond me. Most of the time, he's old and wise enough to hold himself above their standards, but for whatever reason, this weekend, he's been caught in the drunken tide with them.

I quirk an eyebrow in his direction.

"Shut up," Remy snaps, making just the corner of my mouth kick up into a subtle grin.

"I didn't say anything," I counter.

"Trust me, your look implied it all. *Was it the shots—or the bourbon you chose to keep drinking with the shots?*" he mocks in a sarcastic voice that I think is supposed to represent my own. It's even more ironic that, because of my absence, I don't have a fucking clue what he was drinking.

A laugh escapes my throat. Evidently, his subconscious sounds a hell of a lot like me.

"Now's not the time for your fucking logic, man," he grumbles, holding his head with his hand and stumbling back toward the bathroom.

My phone chimes inside the pocket of my jeans, and I pull it out to find a text from our baby sister, Winnie. A successful physician for the New

York Mavericks and married with an eight-year-old daughter, she may be the youngest Winslow sibling, but she definitely isn't a baby anymore. The pigtailed, knobby-kneed version of Winifred that we all grew up with is a distant memory at this stage in our lives.

Winnie: *Anyone in jail?*

A small grin raises one corner of my mouth as I type out a quick response.

Me: *Nope.*

Winnie: *Everyone still alive?*

Me: *Yes. Although, the hangovers Rem, Ty, and Jude are going to be facing today will probably make them wish they were dead.*

It takes a special amount of alcohol to make three grown men not even realize they were missing the fourth member of their group.

Winnie: *Let me guess…Ty started with the damn tequila shots, and Jude succumbed quickly to the peer pressure.*

I might not know the exact details of last night's debauchery, but after forty-one years on this earth studying these morons, I have a pretty good idea.

Me: *Something like that.*

Winnie: *I'm thankful at least one of my brothers is sane. Taciturn, but sane.*

I shrug to myself. What can I say? I am who I am. Still, I wonder what Winnie would think of her one sane brother if she knew all the things about me I don't tell her.

Winnie: *Oh well. I'm just glad it's your job to deal with them on the flight back home and not mine. I've never been good with barf bags. Love you, Flynn!*

I shake my head on a soft smile.

Me: *Love you too, smartass.*

"You texting with that hot blonde from last night?"

I lift my eyes away from the screen of my phone to find Ty looking at me from the large leather sofa in the center of the living room. Jude sits beside him with his head resting back against the big plush pillows and his eyes sealed shut.

With dark circles under both of their eyes and stiff jaws punctuating their faces, it appears my prediction was correct.

Looks like the hangover gang is officially all here.

"What was her name, by the way?" Ty asks.

"Who?"

"The hot blonde who wanted to fuck you," he comments on an annoyed sigh. "You know, the woman in the tight red dress at that karaoke bar off the Strip."

Jude quirks one eye open to look at Ty. "We went to a karaoke bar last night??"

Ty's face morphs from discomfort to hilarity, and a raspy chuckle jumps from his lungs.

Though, it takes Remy to actually answer Jude's question. "Yeah, bro. And it was your stupid fucking request."

Jude glances at all three of us in bewilderment.

"You do one hell of a Journey rendition, my man," Ty chimes in and nudges Jude's shoulder with his fist. "And apparently, Flynn needs to get his eyesight checked because he can't remember when a woman who looks like Farrah Fawcett back in the day is flashing fuck-me eyes at him."

I don't know how to break it to these motherfuckers that I wasn't even there for the red dress-sporting Farrah Fawcett, but I'm thinking the best option is to not. It'll be a hell of a lot more fun this way.

"She wasn't even the hottest woman we saw yesterday," Remy responds, and Ty's face scrunches up in blatant disagreement.

"My ass, she wasn't the hottest woman in Vegas. Who the hell do you think topped her?"

"Didn't you give some woman in the casino a five-hundred-dollar chip, Casanova? Are you telling me you did that shit for nothing?"

Awareness heightened at the mention of Daisy, I instantly shift myself onto the arm of the couch to study their conversation more closely.

"What? I didn't give anyone shit. Did I?" Ty asks, humorously horrified at his own lack of memory.

"I thought you were going to pull a Jude and marry her in Vegas, dude," Remy remarks. My chest involuntarily squeezes at how close to on track he is with the wrong brother. Except for the love thing, of course. Flynn Winslow doesn't fall in love.

"Technically, I didn't find love in Vegas, bro," Jude adds. "I met the love of my life in New York, while she was pretending to be the bride-to-be at a bachelorette party and I was pretending to be an exotic dancer and giving her a sexy lap dance."

Remy just stares at him. "You realize that sounds insane, right?"

Jude just smirks. "Oh, I'm aware."

"Enough about Jude." Ty butts into the conversation. "What's on the agenda today? A little pool time before we have to get on the plane to go back home?"

"Enough about Jude?" Jude retorts. "This is my bachelor party, you fuck."

"Don't know about the pool time. It's already after eleven," Remy answers, ignoring Jude completely.

"What?" Ty shouts, outraged at time's perpetual motion. "The fuck you say it's after eleven."

While my two youngest brothers bicker over their need to be attention whores, I use that perfectly timed distraction to slide my phone into my back pocket, set my empty coffee cup into the sink, and grab my keys and wallet and already packed duffel.

"Hey, where are you going?" Remy calls as I open the door to the suite. "We have to pack all our shit and get ready to go."

I give him a flick of two fingers toward my duffel and a cock of an eyebrow. "Speak for yourselves. I'm packed. I'll see you shitheads downstairs." Remy scowls as I let the door fall closed behind me, but just before it settles into the jamb, I push it open again. "Oh. And don't forget to leave a tip for the housekeeper."

The door slams shut, and I head for the elevators. I've got an hour to get a *real* cup of coffee, find a spot in the hotel to people watch, and hope that maybe, just maybe, I'll get a glance of a wild mane of curls before we need to head to the airport and leave Vegas behind for good.

ELEVEN

Flynn

The sounds of Vegas have managed to follow me into McCarran International Airport. Even while sitting at our gate and waiting for our flight to New York to board, my ears ring with "the slot machine soundtrack" every damn casino in the city plays to lure tourists into thinking they need to get in on the gambling fun.

I know New York isn't the quietest city in the country, but I'll take the sounds of honking taxis and street traffic over the *ching-ching-ching* Vegas song and dance any day of the fucking week.

If I had my say, and if family and business weren't keeping me as a full-time New Yorker, I'd permanently live in my desert house, where silence and the sound of the wind are about the only things that fill my ears. My Vegas residence might be close to the Strip, but I made damn sure when I bought and built that property that it was far enough away from the casino chaos.

Yet you didn't mind all that ching-ching-ching when there was a mane of curls and big green eyes adding to the ambiance...

I'd be a liar if I tried to refute that sentiment. It appears the only thing that made Vegas interesting was Daisy Diaz.

Actually, Daisy Winslow, *the woman—your wife—whom you hoped to spot before you left the Wynn but came up empty-handed.*

"I swear to God, I shit a toddler in there. Little cherub cheeks and big fat arms, I didn't even look back after I flushed the toilet because I don't think there was even a chance my crap was going down," Ty announces on his return from the restroom, climbing over the suitcases and bags under his and Jude's chairs and collapsing into the pleather.

"You're fucking nasty, dude," Remy remarks, pulling his sunglasses down over his eyes and sinking farther into the airport seating.

"What? I haven't been able to pinch one off all week. Traveling and booze make me constipated as a motherfucker."

"Ty, I'm not even remotely drunk enough to be having this conversation right now, and I can smell the booze seeping out of my pores." Rem puts two fingers to the bridge of his nose. "So, can it with the literal shit-talk, for fuck's sake."

"I'm just saying," Ty says on a whisper then, focusing his monologue at Jude, a willing listener. "It was a violent showing by my intestinal system. I didn't know the old girl had it in her, to be honest. I thought I was going to die in the bathroom. See Ty Winslow at his eternal resting place, kind of thing."

I step away from the group on a shake of my head and look for anything I can do that'll be far enough out of earshot that I don't want to puncture my own eardrums anytime soon—or admit that they're a hell of a lot funnier than I want them to be. Just down from our gate, I spot a cluster of slot machines in the center aisle of the airport, mostly abandoned by passengers as they wait to board their impending flights.

Daisy's bouncy curls flash through my mind like a trailer for a movie, and I move on a whim. Toward the slot machines, around the group of them in surveillance, and then finally, to take a seat at the distinctly memorable buffalo game in the middle.

I still fucking hate these things, but a smile almost cracks through the fatigue a weekend in Vegas with my three brothers has created on my face, and I find myself feeding the slot a twenty-dollar bill.

I'm credited immediately, and as any guy with balls would, I hit the max bet button and take my chances with a spin of the reels.

They're off to the races, dinging and calculating and loading into the most random fucking line pattern in the world with buffalo and sunrises and wolves and all kinds of shit that shouldn't have any part in real gambling. There's no science to it. No figuring it out. No skill. It's all blind luck based on the spin of a digital machine.

Nevertheless, something evidently good happens in my favor, the lights and sirens firing wildly into the otherwise silent cacophony of the Las Vegas airport. I can practically feel the sneers from hungover passengers, their bloodshot eyes finding me from behind the solace of their big hats and dark glasses to gift me with a glare.

That part of it, I'll admit, gives me a little bit of joy. So much so, that I find myself nearly grinning when my brothers Ty and Jude gallop over like a couple of lost puppies on an exploratory adventure.

"What the hell? Are you playing the fucking slots?" Jude remarks, his gestures just about as grand as his jubilant words. I roll my eyes at his obvious observation and hit the button to bet again.

"Oh my God, you are," Ty concludes, every bit of the PhD he holds clearly having been earned.

"I never thought I'd see this. This is like a unicorn. A leprechaun at the end of the rainbow. A glitter fairy in a neon forest," Jude rambles, taking out his phone to get a picture of me.

I pay him no mind as I push the button again, the buffalo making a wholly obnoxious running in a stampede kind of sound when I hit the correct combination to win a bonus game.

"I'm putting this in my wedding scrapbook," Jude continues, pulling his phone to his chest and hugging it like an idiot. Ty laughs, which only encourages his behavior. "In fact, I'm going to text it to Sophie now so she can add it to the rehearsal dinner slide show. This is like getting a candid shot of Bigfoot without the photo looking like you snapped it with a potato."

A lesser man might cave to their bullshit—might snap verbally or physically by leaving—but I'm more than used to my brothers by this point in my life. For God's sake, it's always been like this, even when we were kids. They're rowdy and mouthy, and if it weren't for the distinct line of all our jaws, I'd swear I was birthed from a different set of loins. Or, at the very least, the mailman's son.

But we are definitely blood related, that fact known by all four of us and our baby sister and muddied by the reality that our biological father peaced out on his family when we were kids.

I spin again, and another bonus round pops up. Once again, I've managed to double my money. I smile a little, thinking of how excited this would make Daisy and picturing the expression on her face when she realized it was even more thrilling when my tongue was spinning her reels.

Fuck, she makes a good face when she comes. Pretty and memorable but not off-puttingly over the top like some women I've been with. She's uninhibited without dramatizing her reactions like some kind of act. I don't need the moans of a porn star from my partners—just undeniable acknowledgment that I'm making them feel good.

And Daisy knew just how to acknowledge. Instantly, I'm struck with the regret of taking a shower this morning, effectively rinsing off her scent and replacing it with my own.

"Sophie's adding it to the queue now, Flynnbot," Jude announces with a toothy grin. "Not to worry."

I shake my head in amusement.

"See, Flynn, this is why all the ladies flock to us," Ty interjects. "Just like last night, you insist on being, like, the world's greatest mime or something. I don't even think I heard you say one thing last night."

Jude scoffs. "Like you remember anything about last night, bro."

"Hey, man, I was just celebrating you! My baby brother is getting married! That's huge."

"Come on," Remy announces, his face completely pinched in annoyance and all of my brothers' bags hanging from his shoulders. "They're boarding our flight, assholes. Time to get home and not drink for an eternity."

I smile a little at Remy's pain. He's two years older than me, so I know, at his age, he has to be feeling this shit pretty good.

"Bullshit," Jude denies. "You're drinking at my wedding, bro, because that's what you do at *all weddings*. You dance, you celebrate, and you drink like a fish in the name of the happy bride and groom."

Not all weddings end with a happy bride and groom, I think to myself, and when I look over at Rem, I note his face has already shifted. No doubt going to a dark, nearly fucking morbid place as he remembers *his* almost-wedding of nearly a decade and a half ago, and all three of the rest of us see it. It's like a pin in a shrieking balloon—just like that, *pop, all the shit-talk is done.*

Jude and Ty step forward and take their bags, and without a word, Remy stalks in the other direction, headed for our plane.

"*All weddings?* Why'd you have to say it like that?" Ty whispers harshly to Jude as we all hustle along behind Remy toward the gate.

I smack Ty on the back of the head and pass them. "Just drop it."

The last thing we need on this long flight home is to spend all our time reliving the absolute hellfire of witnessing Remy getting ditched at the altar.

That might've been over a decade ago, but the memory still holds some serious power.

All we need right now is to get home, sleep off this wild weekend, and get back to normal.

And that *we*... Well, thanks to a certain woman with emerald eyes and wild curls, it definitely includes me.

TWELVE

Daisy

What a day.

From the instant I took an Uber from Flynn's house and met Damien and my coworkers at brunch, my schedule has been jam-packed with all sorts of work shit. From meetings with potential furniture and fabric distributors for future staging projects to a big conference at the Wynn where Damien and Thomas updated us on the firm's goals and plans for the next two years, I barely managed to get back to my room, pack my stuff, and make my evening flight back to LAX.

You were so busy that you almost forgot about the craziness of last night's wedding bells.

I sigh and look out the window of the plane, watching as the world below passes me by. The sun is setting in the evening sky, and clouds and desert and a weekend of actions I never expected cross my vision.

It feels big and uncontainable, and I feel as small as this view of the world suggests I am. I'm just a tiny speck of life, and all the hugely consequential things I'm hyperventilating over right now are barely even a blip in the universe.

Thankfully, though, for as anxiety-inducing as it all is, the result is an otherwise unattainable level of peace. My life here in the United States will be safe. My job is secure. My dreams have the room to breathe, to fly, to go on.

I must be lost in the tangled web of my thoughts because the gentleman next to me taps my elbow to get my attention and smiles when I turn around. He's a sweet-looking old man, likely in his eighties if the worn skin, knowing eyes, and scraggly gray hair are characteristics to go by, and I look to him expectantly.

He smiles bigger then, pointing above his own head to the looming flight attendant and drink cart that I've completely failed to notice.

"Oh!" I say, a little startled. I have no idea how long they've been trying to get my attention. "I'll just take a water."

The flight attendant smiles, her white teeth shining through a pink-lipped smile, and I don't know what it is about the poised, calm manner of her expression, but it sets me off like a firecracker.

"You know what, make that a vodka with cranberry. And…well, and the water too."

The old man to my right glances toward me briefly before going back to his book. The flight attendant makes my drink after going back and forth to the front for the nip of liquor, and I fidget in my seat so much that the old man leans away from me slightly.

My knee bounces, and my hand thrums out a rhythm on the newly abandoned armrest.

Okay. Okay. Everything is fine. Totally and completely fine, but like, better. Because my problems are solved, I've officially cleaned out the cobwebs from the inside of my vagina, and I'll have a story to tell my future grandkids one day that will officially make me the favorite grandma. All is well.

I try to smile as the flight attendant hands me two plastic cups, one with booze and one with water, but I'm pretty sure it comes off a little psycho for her taste, because she quickly kicks the release at the bottom of the cart and moves on—all the way to the back of the plane after flagging the other attendant behind her to pick up where she left off.

"Great," I murmur to myself before turning to the old man next to me. "I'm running people off now. I bet I'd run you off too if there were any empty seats on this plane."

"What was that, dear?" he asks, placing his bookmark in his paperback and glancing toward me.

I shake my head as the heat of my embarrassment rushes my cheeks. *Jesus, Daisy. What are you doing? Running your mouth to strangers now?*

"Nothing, sir. I'm sorry for bugging you," I apologize. "Just ignore me."

"Oh dear. You were the victim of a mugging?" he asks, horrified understanding seeping into his eyes as he takes a look at my stiff drink with sympathy.

A mugging? *What?*

"No, no," I emphasize with a shake of my head, realizing he must have misheard me. Safe to say, my cheeks have stoked a permanent flame at this point. "Not a mugging. Just…well…just a little issue with work that led to me marrying a stranger."

"A strangler?" he asks, aghast.

"No! No strangler!" I rush to explain. "Lucky I did not come in contact with a strangler. Although, I guess, I probably could have in my mental state last night. But Flynn's not that. He's actually a good guy. At least…I think. I mean, he's pretty dirty in bed, as it turns out, but that's neither here nor there. He was nothing but nice to me from the moment I met him. He's just…a stranger."

Mr. Old Man looks perplexed, and I can only fucking imagine what he's doing with that overshare of information. *Christ, what's wrong with me?* Even with the awareness of that little self-reflection, for some reason, I keep going. I don't know why. Maybe because I don't feel like I can tell anyone I actually know because of all the shame and humiliation and legalities, but venting to this guy feels like a much-needed exercise in emotional expulsion.

"It's a little weird that we got married by a drag queen Marilyn Monroe, but I have the marriage certificate and I'm pretty sure it's legal, so that's all that matters, right?"

"I can't say that I know a whole lot about Justin Trudeau. I've never had a chance to get to Canada."

The irony isn't lost on me. Of all the things for him to mishear in the midst of my immigration mess, it's about my home country of Canada. I laugh. "I'm from there."

"Yes, I have been to Delaware. My wife June and I vacationed there once in 1970. The Bridge Swallow Resort," he remarks, his face transforming at the fond memory. "I've no idea if it's still there or not, but you should go. But not with the strangler, dear, I beg of you. Find a nice boy."

My man, we are having two very different conversations here.

I look back out the window to swallow my laugh and, inevitably, think of Flynn. The idea of him as some sort of psycho serial killer is…well, it's comical. I'm not even sure why, what with the completely limited amount of information I actually have about him, but he just doesn't even remotely strike me as the type.

He's quiet. Calm. Assured. His character actually speaks of the kind of inner peace I've never known. It's settled. It's confident. He doesn't need all the flashy recognition from being a public figure. He doesn't need the spotlight. He's content to just be.

I mean, I've never met a man so willing to let me spew my word vomit all over him for hour after hour without losing his cool or begging off or talking over me so he can take control of the conversation. Flynn listened—and not just in a superficial way in an effort to be polite. He paid attention to every word I said, I could tell.

I turn back to the old man and do my best to enunciate clearly for this part of the story time. Partially because I want to make sure he hears me, but mostly because I want to make sure I hear myself. "Don't worry. My time with him has officially come to an end. Just a crazy story from Vegas that'll live in my history book forever." I nod, resolute. "It was one night, and I'm leaving here in a better position than when I came. Period. That's it. The end."

Technically, I still have paperwork to file with USCIS, but that's just semantics at this point. Pretty sure the hard part—finding a willing man to marry me in the name of saving my ass—has been achieved.

The old man nods sagely, his eyes full of wisdom and agreement and the perfect amount of kindness I need to take a full, uninhibited breath.

"You're exactly right, dear," he says then, making the corners of my mouth turn up with a smile. "Some stories are meant to teach you—the heart is a muscle that doesn't bend."

What? No, that's not what I—

"Don't back down. If you really love him, that man'll be yours in the end."

All I can do is smile through nervous tears as they bust their way out of my eyes of their own accord.

Come on, Daisy. He's just talking nonsense. He's not even having the same conversation as you. You can't seriously be considering anything he says as valid...can you?

I look straight ahead and lift my vodka cranberry up to my lips and take a gulp. Now that my subconscious is asking the tough questions, my plane neighbor isn't the only one hard of hearing.

I hold out my left hand in front of me and inspect the gold band intently. It shines beneath the overhead light above my seat, and I silently wonder why I'm still even wearing it.

I mean, it's not like this is a real marriage.

Eventually, I take the ring off my finger and slip it into my pocket and lean back into my seat.

Home, I tell myself. *Just get back to life as usual. Normal. Day-to-day. And put Flynn Winslow in the only place he belongs—front and center on the immigration paperwork.*

And that, my friends, is that.

THIRTEEN

Tuesday, April 9th, Los Angeles

Daisy

I am back in the land of Hollywood, where the views are beautiful, the smog is never-ending, the sun is always shining, and your odds of spotting a random celebrity at every Starbucks in the city are surprisingly good.

It's been over a year since Damien Ellis offered me a job and I packed up all my belongings and traveled across the border to move in to my new home-away-from-home—*Los Angeles*. Growing up in Canada, Vancouver to be specific, I never thought I'd call a big American city like LA home, but here I am, living and working and thriving.

Well, I *was* thriving, until I managed to put a prominent snag into my American dream dress and sew it up with a *marriage pact* patch, of all things. I mean, what world am I living in, and is it financed by the Hallmark Channel?

Ha. Not likely. The Hallmark Channel doesn't showcase movies revolving around immigration fraud, and they certainly don't include men who dirty-talk like Flynn.

I've been back from Vegas for less than forty-eight hours, and to say I've yet to wrap my mind around what went down in Sin City would be the understatement of the century. I've been like the Energizer Bunny, just pacing back and forth while I beat the same dang drum of truth over and over again.

I'm *married* now. I'm someone's *wife*. Wedded. My knot is tied, my chain has a ball on the end of it, I'm as hitched as one of Gwen's past flavor-of-the-month's fifth-wheel camper.

Married. To someone I hardly know and who just so happened to make a pact with me that ended in us saying "I do" in front of a drag queen Marilyn Monroe.

And all of that doesn't even consider *the fact that we had the hottest sex of my life before parting ways.*

I let out a sigh. *Nope, not going there.* No way in hell am I going to step foot in that minefield of sexual confusion.

Because, *technically*, I'm still illegally living and working in the United States, and correcting the type of problem that involves Uncle Sam definitely takes priority over the Flynn-inspired charley horse in my vagina.

There's no time for excuses or procrastination. I have to do what I need to do to rectify my expired-visa situation, and I have to do it now—even if it has nothing to do with what I should be doing on a Tuesday in the middle of my workday.

Somehow, I'm going to have to pull a rabbit out of my hat and fit in my actual work to-do list, which is a mile long, at the very end of the day. It'll be tough, but I'd look like shit in an orange jumpsuit and I'm certainly not photogenic enough to make a mugshot look good, so there's really no other option.

Goodness, what has your life come to that prison is a potential outcome?

The mere idea of living a real-life *Orange is the New Black* situation urges my lungs to seize and short pants of air to burst out of my throat. Mentally, I feel as if I'm holding myself together by one single, already-shredded thread.

Knowing I need to talk to someone before it severs entirely, anyone who might be able to rationally talk me off this ledge, I grab my cell phone and call the one and only person who could fulfill that role—Gwen.

It rings four times before the line clicks open.

"Daisy!"

Oh, thank goodness. Relief fills my chest, but that's quickly squashed when static hovers over the rest of her words.

"Darling! I'm…you…call…"

I squint and hold the phone as close to my ear as physically possible. "Where are you? I can hardly hear you."

"…here…I…trip…it's…"

"What?"

"I said…"

And then, nothing.

A few seconds later, the line clicks dead. Immediately, I try to call her back, but it goes straight to voice mail.

Well, *shit*. This certainly isn't helping me work through my existential, I-got-married-for-a-green-card crisis. I try to call her back another three times, but eventually, I give up when a text message from an unknown number chimes through on my phone.

Unknown: Daisy, darling, it's Gwen. My phone isn't working on the boat. I think we're too far out to sea for me to get service.

Too far out to sea? What the heck is she talking about?

Me: Huh? Where are you?

Unknown: Me and the girls found a half-off Groupon for an Alaskan cruise.

Me: You're on a flipping discount cruise right now?

Unknown: Don't worry, darling. It's a Norwegian.

Like that's supposed to make me feel better?

Unknown: I'll be back in two weeks.

Oh, for Pete's sake.

Unknown: Is everything okay?

Um, *no*. Everything is not okay, but there's no way I'm going to unload all my drama on her while she's supposed to be enjoying a cruise with her friends. And I'm certainly not going to do it via text message.

Truthfully, this is all so crazy that I don't even know what her reaction will be, but it looks like I'm going to have to wait to find out.

Me: Everything is fine. Have fun and be safe! Love you.

Unknown: Love you too, Daisy.

On a sigh, I set my phone back down on my desk and try to get back to finishing up what I've spent the majority of my workday on—getting a damn green card.

Let me tell you, the application process to obtain a green card through marrying a United States citizen is anything but the simplistic process I imagined it to be. Several forms, over fifty pages of information to read through, and a bunch of other shit that my brain is having a hard time comprehending are what I've been sorting through since I sat down at my desk in my small office inside the EllisGrey downtown LA building.

Just...forget everything else and focus. The sooner this gets done, the sooner your life won't feel like such a clusterfuck.

As I scroll through the mostly filled-out application I downloaded onto my laptop, I try to pinpoint the areas of weakness. Apparently, when you want to obtain a green card, they want to know everything they possibly can about you. It's all understandable, but it's nerve-racking as hell when you're doing it under the pretense otherwise known as my-marriage-is-an-immigration-fraud.

Racing heart. Shaking hands. Erratic breathing. Is this what criminals feel like?

Pretty sure, legally, *once you send in this application, you* are *a criminal...*

Oh, for fuck's sake. This is why criminals have to find a way to remove their conscience. I roll my eyes at myself, ignore all the red flags my yet-to-flee inner voice is throwing my way, and refocus my attention on the application.

Part 1: Information About You

I scan the long section closely and verify that I've dotted all my i's and crossed all my t's. It's pretty standard stuff, and I take heart in the fact that it doesn't require even a single lie.

On to the next.

Part 2: Application Type or Filing Category

Welp. I married a US citizen for a green card.

I cringe over the reality, but I bite my lip and check off the box that applies—*immediate relative of a US Citizen.* You know, because, as of a few days ago, I have a husband. I also remind myself that he offered to marry me. Not the other way around, so if anything, this is all my husband's fault.

A husband who is probably the most reserved man I've ever met and have known for all of twenty-four hours, tops, and who gave me the kind of sex that made my toes curl back so far, I'm surprised they're not permanently stuck to my heels.

Dear God, *the sex*. With Flynn Winslow. *My husband*. Memories of that night roll behind my eyes like the trailer for a movie.

The way his big hands felt on my body.

The multitude of bad and dirty things he said into my ear.

How insanely good his cock felt inside me.

How deep *he was inside me.*

Holy hot-sex-sundae-with-a-cherry-on-top.

When a persistent throb tries to set up shop between my thighs, I shift in my seat and cross my bare legs beneath my black pencil skirt. It doesn't do shit to curb the confusing discomfort, and it definitely doesn't stop the warmth that spreads across my cheeks or the fact that I dig my teeth into my bottom lip so hard, I almost draw blood.

Holy hell, what am I doing?

Oh, you know, just fantasizing about having sex with your husband whom you barely know and married on a whim because you're a desperate illegal alien in the eyes of United States law…

"Ugh. Stop trying to have a mental spiral, Dais. Now is not the time," I quietly coach myself and run a frustrated hand down my face. "Just finish filling out the damn application."

No matter how uncomfortable this whole ordeal is, I *need* to finish this application. My job, *my life*, it all depends on it. Also, you know, it's imperative to avoid deportation.

My brain wants to fixate on that last word, the scary D-word that I'm refusing to give any merit to, but I shake it off and put my eyes back on the screen.

Part 3: Additional Information About You

A little bit of work history. Education history. Current and past addresses. It's all easy-peasy-lemon-squeezy and done a few minutes later.

Part 4: Information About Your Parents

Well, *hell*. If only I knew who my biological parents even were…

Growing up in the Canadian foster system and not finding a permanent living situation and guardian until I was fifteen have made answering these questions impossible. I don't know anything about my parents—who they were, if they're still alive, where they live, *why* they put me up for adoption.

All I know is that I started in the foster system at birth, and while I did stay with a family for the first two years of my life, I mostly jumped around from foster home to foster home until Gwen took me under her wing as a teenager.

And to be honest, I don't have a desire to find my biological parents. I know a lot of people might feel strongly about this, but to me, it's not something I want to do or feel that I *have* to do.

I am the reason I am who I am today, and any information about my absentee biological parents isn't going to change any of that.

"Uh oh, someone has a very serious look on their face."

I pull my eyes away from the screen of my laptop to find Damien standing in front of my desk. He searches my face closely, tilts his head to the side, and opens his mouth again before I can find a reason for my studious expression that doesn't revolve around the sad truth—*letting my work visa lapse and putting my career at risk.*

"What's wrong?" he questions and starts to walk around my desk so he can take a gander at what has me looking so "serious."

Shit. Shit. Shit.

Quickly, I tap my fingers against the track pad to minimize the application that sits front and center. The very last thing I need right now is my boss finding out that not only did I fuck up my visa, but I impulsively married an American in Vegas just so I could un-fuck it up.

"N-nothing," I answer as he comes to stand beside my chair and places a comforting hand on my shoulder. "Everything is just fine and dandy."

Just fine and dandy? *Goodness.*

"What's that?" Damien quirks his brow, and his eyes home in on my computer.

"Uh…" My words fumble over my tongue as he takes a closer look, and a hummingbird's wing is now my heart as I dart my eyes back to my laptop screen.

"Are those the staging plans for the Laurel Canyon bungalow?"

The staging plans for the Laurel Canyon bungalow EllisGrey will be listing soon are, in fact, what is front and center. *Oh, thank hell.*

"Oh…uh, yeah," I respond and swallow past the uncomfortable knot my thumping heart has pushed up into my throat. "I…um…I just finished those up this morning."

Technically, I finished them up *before* I left for Vegas, but he doesn't need to know that. It's better for everyone if he thinks I've spent my workday doing, you know, work.

"Daisy?"

"Hmm?"

"Are you okay? You look like one of those buildings on TV when they televise their demolition. All sad and tired because everyone knows the big bang that's coming." His eyes are back on me now, and I discreetly suck some much-needed oxygen into my lungs.

Damien Ellis is one of the best bosses on the planet. Kind, hilarious, understanding, and sympathetic to his employees' struggles, he's the kind of man you *want* to work for. The kind of man who inspires and motivates you to be the best you can be. The kind of man who encourages you, challenges you, and helps you evolve in your career.

He's…amazing.

But telling him that I put my job at risk—*the job* he *gave me, mind you*—because I didn't keep track of my visa's expiration date? *No.* That's professional negligence that would be impossible for most bosses to understand, no matter how damn awesome they might be.

"Daisy." He says my name again, but this time, it's in a way that makes me realize just how much time has passed since he asked the question.

"Yeah?"

"Doll, I wasn't born yesterday." A laugh jumps from his perfectly hydrated lips. "I know when there's some kind of emotional drama brewing better than anyone. So, honey bunny, it's high time for you to spill the tea on what's got you acting so weird."

"What?" I feign confusion. "I'm not acting weird. No way. Nothing weird is happening, and I'm not acting weird." When I realize just how weird my rambling response was, I add, "Maybe I'm just a little tired?"

"You're jumpy and fidgety, and if I didn't know better, I'd think you were sitting here watching porn on your company-issued computer."

I choke on my tongue. "Uh, *no*. I wasn't watching porn."

"Taking sexy foot pics for your OnlyFans account, then?"

"Damien!" I exclaim on a laugh. "Oh my God, you're deranged. I don't have an OnlyFans account."

"Personally, I am pro-porn *and* pro-Only Fans. I mean, have you seen the money some of the people are raking in?"

"No, I have not."

"It's a lot, doll. A lot. Anyway…back to your weirdness…" He smirks down at me, but he also quirks a knowing brow. An expression that says, "I know you're not telling me something, and I'm not leaving your office until you do."

Boiling hot water in a bubble bath, the pressure is *scalding*. *What do I tell him?*

I search and scramble to find something that makes sense. Something that's simple enough not to trip me up any time it comes up again, and heaven forbid, something that's not even *worse* than the actual problem I've acquired. I wouldn't put it past myself to accidentally blurt that I went on a homicide spree, given the number of true crime shows I frequently put myself to sleep with.

But Damien is calmly persistent. His gaze is still locked on my face, searching, seeking, trying to decode what sits inside my brain, but doing it in a way that doesn't feel like he's suspicious or interrogating me at all. Which only makes me insanely nervous all over again and certain that if the FBI and CIA and local police departments would only hire gay men to get suspects to confess, unsolved crimes would no longer be a thing.

One drop of sweat drips down the center of my back, and my hands start to feel clammy and my heart just keeps pounding, and the pressure is building and building…

"I got married in Vegas." The words shoot out of my mouth before I can stop them. And trust me, I *tried* to stop them, but my hand slapped against my own lips *after* "Vegas" flitted off my tongue.

"What?" Damien's eyes turn as wide as my ever-growing path of lies, and he blinks several times. "I'm sorry, but did you just say you *got married?*"

Oh boy. I cringe. Nod. Shrug. Nervously giggle.

"In Vegas?"

When I don't answer, mostly because the truth is undoubtedly written all over my guilty face, he scrunches up his nose like he just ate a piece of sweet-and-sour candy. "Let me get this straight… Daisy Diaz got married while she was in Vegas for an EllisGrey work trip?"

"I…uh…I made sure I did it outside of work obligations…?" I respond, as if I'm asking him if that was the reality. "And I'm sorry…" I add, even though I don't know why I'd be apologizing to him about getting married. Obviously, I should be apologizing for messing up my visa, but I'd prefer to take that monumental mistake to the grave.

This is not going well…

Damien just stands there, staring at me for about thirty seconds too long. The kind of silent observation that makes you feel incredibly uncomfortable and makes the urge to start rambling some kind of explanation that will most likely lead to the truth grow like a vine of ivy up a tree.

Don't you dare say another word. Do. Not. Do. It.

"Damien, I have something I need to—"

"I swear, if this is Mateo calling me to bitch about the masseuse I hired for him, I will tear my hair out," he grumbles as he snags his phone out of the inside pocket of his sleek gray suit. He stares down at the screen, and my body threatens to burrow inside the fancy hardwood floor of the office when I realize I was mere seconds away from dropping the biggest truth bomb of my life up in this bitch.

"Damn, I forgot about that." Damien sighs, shoves his phone back into his suit pocket, and points a perfectly manicured index finger in my direction. "Doll, you're lucky I have a meeting to get to right now, but I promise you, I'll be back for that tea."

"There's no tea," I answer, and he calls my bluff with a furrowed brow.

"Before we went to Vegas, you were the only straight girl in the office who didn't let her panties fall to the ground for Duncan Jones," he says and shakes his head on a laugh. "And now, you're *married*. Trust me, there's tea…" He pauses, and then his eyes go wide. "Oh hell, don't tell me you married Duncan Jones…"

"Oh my God, no," I answer honestly. "No, no, no."

"Okay, good." He breathes out in relief. "We're chatting later, though. Kisses!"

And then he's off. Through my office door and back into the hallway as if our conversation didn't just make me age ten years.

Fackkkk.

Head straight to my desk, I let my forehead hit the hard surface with a bang.

God, I'm an idiot.

You're also an idiot who doesn't have time to wallow in misery…

On a deep sigh, I find the will to lift my head back up, run a hand down my face, and pull myself together enough to face my application again. Thankfully, it doesn't take long before I have it ready to print out and sign and mail off to the scary immigration overlords at USCIS.

But it doesn't end there. *Oh, no.* There are more steps. Not only did *I* have to fill out an application, but my *American husband* does, too.

Cell phone out, I scroll through my contacts until I come to a stop at the name Flynn Winslow, open a fresh message box, and start to type out a text.

Hey, it's me. Daisy. Daisy Diaz.

Ugh. That sounds so dumb. *Delete.*

Hi, there! I hope you're doing fantastic!

Goodness. No need to shout at the guy. *Delete.*

Stop overcomplicating this and just be yourself. It's not like the man married you because he's in love with you. He married you because he's trying to help you. No need to put up some façade.

Resigned to just handle shit like I normally do, I proceed to type out a few texts I can actually hit send on.

Me: Hey, American hubby. It's me, Daisy, your lovely Canadian wife. I've downloaded all of the pertinent documentation and applications for my visa. We're going to have to send everything in via the good-old-fashioned mail. The first application that needs to be mailed in is mine, which I've filled out and will be sending out soon. The next is your application, along with the pertinent documentation you need to provide to USCIS.

Me: Just FYI: There's A LOT of information to read through. Like, over fifty pages of very boring, mundane things. And I know this is all just a hassle for you, but I want to make sure I say thank you for doing this. That

is, if you're still planning on helping me get a visa, which I hope you are, because hell's bells, I really, really need the help…

Me: So…I guess what I'm trying to say is, if you're still game, either I send you the forms you need to fill out and a copy of the application I'll be mailing in tomorrow morning, OR I can try to fill them out for you and forge your signature. Personally, I think the former is the best option because, while I'm pretty good at forging signatures, I'm not that great at forging official documentation.

Suddenly panicked that the NSA is going to read these messages, I type out all the things I need to say to cover my tracks.

Me: I'm kidding. LOL. I've never forged anything in my life. And obviously, I'm joking about the visa thing too because ha-ha-ha, we're in love. Wild, wonderful love.

Uncomfortable with all the lying, even when I'm smack-dab in the middle of the biggest lie in the universe, I blather on.

Me: Okay, fine. Once, I forged something ONE TIME, and it was no big deal. Just a minor date change on a document for a travel refund when I was eighteen. I deserved the refund, btw. That spring break trip was something nightmares are made of, and the date mistake was a legitimate typo. I was just making it right.

Once I hit send on the final message, I set my phone down on my desk and tap my fingers across the surface as I wait for him to respond. I also silently wonder why I always seem to word vomit all over this guy.

When my phone lights up with two incoming text messages from the man of the immigration application hour, I grab my phone so fast I nearly drop it.

The first text? Only four words—*Mail them to me.*

And the second? A New York address.

Damn, Flynn Winslow is certainly a man of few words, isn't he?

Yeah, Mrs. Winslow. *He sure is.*

So…he lives in New York full time? Not Vegas? Obviously, since I was in his swanky Vegas home, this is new information. *You mean the home that you had the wildest sex of your life in?*

I shake my head, ignore my snarky inner voice, and wait a little longer, thinking that maybe he'll add to the messages. But when nothing comes, I remember that with all the things I *don't* know about my American husband, there's certainly something I *do*—he doesn't converse just for the sake of it. When he speaks, it's because it's necessary or it means something, period. If the world would handle food and recycling like Flynn Winslow handles words, there'd never be any food shortages, and all of the oceans would be devoid of garbage.

As I stare down at his New York address, the seed of curiosity that's planted into my belly starts to grow. Clearly, I've seen his Las Vegas house, but there's something inside me that can't stop myself from Google searching this new nugget of a peek into Flynn's life.

Technology and the internet make it pathetically easy to enable my nosiness, and within a few typed words and clicks on my keyboard, my screen showcases an aerial view of a swanky building located in Midtown. Certified proof that Flynn Winslow has done really fucking well for himself.

Which only makes me more curious about this man and where he lives and what his life is like…

Me: *Okay…so…I have two questions… Is New York where you live full time? And what do you do for a living?*

Flynn: *Yes. Electrical engineer.*

Me: That's cool. Way above my head, I'm sure, but cool. LOL. I'm an interior designer and stager for EllisGrey. That's a big real estate firm based out of LA.

I'm not shocked when he doesn't respond, but I'm also not done asking questions.

Me: Is that the only thing you do to make money?

I'm well aware that electrical engineers—any engineers, really—make a very healthy living. But from what I've seen of Flynn's life so far, it feels like there's more to his financial story.

Flynn: Investments

Short and to the point. Always.

Me: So, not to sound stalkerish, but I Googled your NYC address, and your building is pretty damn swanky. It also makes the designer in me VERY curious what it looks like on the inside… Did you use the same color palette in your New York apartment as in your Vegas home?

Don't get me wrong, his Vegas home is a stunner. But it could certainly use little eye-catching pops of color here and there to break up the constant use of bland neutrals. *Seriously, Flynn, a little color won't kill ya.*

Flynn: Daisy?

Me: Yeah?

Flynn: Stop talking to me about color palettes.

His response makes me grin. And it also gives me a brilliant idea…

FOURTEEN

Friday, April 12th, New York

Flynn

A little after eight in the evening, I step beneath the awning of my building entrance, offer a curt smile to Carl the evening doorman, and head inside the doors. After a quick stop at the small alcove with the mailboxes, I find a stack of mail inside my metal box and a large package sitting right below it on the floor.

The label is written in very pretty, feminine handwriting, and beside the sender's name—**Daisy Winslow**—sits a little smiley face.

I don't know why that makes me smile, but it does. It also makes me shake my head. The woman is a trip.

I tuck the box under my arm, and instead of being lazy and taking the elevator, I jog up the fifteen flights of stairs to my apartment. I might've just finished a grueling workout with my brother Jude, but I'm always game for more cardio. It keeps me young, fit, and focused.

Once I'm inside, I drop my keys and wallet on the kitchen counter, turn on a few lights, and hit play on my Bluetooth speakers so a little music from one of my saved playlists gives some ambiance. The soft, soothing sounds of Claude Debussy fill my apartment, but the lull of relaxation it provides only lasts until my cell vibrating inside the pocket of my sweats grabs my attention.

***Jude**: You guys, I hate to be the bearer of bad news, but I think we need to move forward with an intervention for Flynn.*

The ongoing group chat. With my crazy fucking brothers.

Ty: What the fuck are you talking about?

Jude: Flynn is on steroids.

I roll my eyes at the absurd accusation and keep reading.

Ty: Bullshit.

Remy: Yeah, I call bullshit.

Jude: Well, maybe you assholes should start joining us at the gym. That motherfucker doesn't quit. Like, ever. And the amount of weight he can lift is absurd. There's no other explanation besides steroids.

Ty: So, let me get this straight, bro, you think Flynn is on steroids because he's kicking your ass at the gym? HAHAHAHAHAHAHAHAHAHA

Jude: Wow, Ty. Way to take a very serious concern of mine and turn it into a joke.

Remy: Serious concern? HA. This just keeps getting better.

Jude: Fuck you, Rem.

Remy: Jude, sweetheart, I just want you to know you have no reason to feel insecure. I think you are very, VERY strong, and I'm proud of you. Even if your fiancée can out-lift you.

On a soft chuckle, I set my phone down on the kitchen counter and open the fridge to pull out everything I need for dinner. After this evening's hard workout—*a workout that apparently has Jude whining like a little bitch*—a meal loaded with protein and iron is imperative for muscle healing and growth.

Steak, asparagus, and potatoes are tonight's dinner choice, and it's not long before I have everything on the stove and cooking. While I wait for my steak to grill, I grab the package Daisy sent and open it.

Inside sits the paperwork I was expecting, but also, something else—two pale-yellow throw pillows.

She sent me fucking pillows? And yellow ones, at that?

A note is attached to one of the pillows, and in her now familiar girlie script, it reads, **If your New York place is anything like your Vegas house, then, no offense, but you need some color.**

I laugh and roll my eyes at the same time. Frankly, I have no idea what would make a woman like Daisy think a man like me wants fucking yellow throw pillows on his goddamn couch, but I can't deny I'm inspired by the confidence it took to make that kind of assessment of me.

Intriguing, that Daisy.

I check the stove, flip over my steak and asparagus, and before I can stop myself, I'm heading out of the kitchen with those two ridiculous pillows in hand to test her theory. Once I toss them on my cognac leather couch, I step back, prepared to disprove her theory.

But instead of clashing annoyance, those two pillows have somehow made my living room feel…cozier? Warmer? I don't know what, but it's not bad.

"Damn, she's fucking crazy," I say out loud and run a surprised hand through my hair.

But she's also right, you drab bastard.

Once I grab the hefty stack of papers she sent my way, I finish cooking my dinner and prepare to do a little—more like, *a lot of*—reading while

I eat. If the US Immigration Department is anything like the IRS, it's best to read all the fucking fine print before filling anything out.

And, just for future tax purposes, I'm going to go ahead and add the important disclaimer that I, Flynn Winslow, think the IRS is wonderful and love paying taxes.

FIFTEEN

Los Angeles, California

Daisy

By the time I get home from my final day of staging the Laurel Canyon bungalow, it's a little after five in the evening. Which, to most, wouldn't sound like a big deal at all, but when you take in the fact that I've been up and at it since four thirty this morning, you'd understand that mama needs to take off these heels and sit on the couch.

It might be a Friday night, but I'll be damned if I'm doing anything but keeping my lazy ass on the sofa and binge-watching something on Netflix.

Once I step inside the front door of my downtown LA apartment, I kick off my shoes, change into my favorite pair of sweats, and plop my ass down in front of the TV. I still have no idea what I'm going to eat for dinner, but if I end up consuming the pint of Ben & Jerry's in the fridge and calling it a meal, I'll be perfectly fine with that decision.

Before I locate my next series binge, I scroll through all the missed emails and messages on my phone. Lord knows, I didn't even have time to stop for lunch, much less check my phone.

Most of the emails are work-related and can wait until Monday morning. There's one annoying text from Duncan Jones about the "rain check," which I promptly ignore, archiving the message into the dregs of my inbox.

I also find a few messages from Damien reminding me that, even though he's been too busy to come back and bug me, he *will* be back for the tea—Lipton or Twinings, he doesn't care which. Spring is the busiest season in real estate, and, in this case, I'm thankful it's prevented my boss from haunting me about my problems that I definitely don't want to talk about. But I have to admit, he's pretty dang funny.

But out of all the missed messages and emails, there's one text that stands out more than the rest.

Flynn: I got the package.

Okay…so, he got the package, but…did he open it? Is he going to fill out the immigration forms I need him to? Or has he decided to just toss them in his fireplace and let hot, fiery flames make it all go away?

So many unanswered questions.

Me: I'm hoping I'm supposed to take this message as your confirmation that you're going to fill out the forms and send them in…

His response comes in a few moments later. Although it's not a yes, it's also not a no.

Flynn: Did you read through all fifty-six pages of this packet?

Me: Of course I did.

I mean, I read *most* of it. Okay, fine, I skimmed enough of it to get all the important shit figured out.

Flynn: So, then you're aware of the clause that states we need to show proof of our relationship, proof that we are living together, and in about three months, we'll be asked to come in for an interview together at their New York office since that's where I'm a resident?

This is the longest message, longest string of words that Flynn has ever said to me, and my only reaction is to blink roughly seven hundred times.

Proof of living together? Proof of relationship? An interview?! Gah, I'm terrible at lying in person!

Surely he's mistaken and is just reading something wrong, even though he's definitely not the kind of guy who seems like he reads things wrong.

Panic sets up residence in my chest, getting my heart all riled up and urging me to hop off the couch and grab my laptop from the dining table. Erratic fingers to the keys, I pull up the USCIS official website and read through everything I can find about applying for a visa after marrying a United States citizen.

I scour every single document at my fingertips, and after God knows how much time has passed, I'm aware of two things—Flynn is right, and I'm *way* more screwed than I originally thought.

Oh. My. God.

SIXTEEN

New York

Flynn

Fresh from my after-dinner shower, water dripping down my neck and chest, I step out onto my graphite-colored bath mat to the chorus of my phone chiming with a sound I'm not familiar with. My eyebrows draw together as I snag a towel from the rack at my side and hurriedly wrap it around my waist.

Quick, long strides eat up the distance between the bathroom and my bedroom nightstand, where my phone is dancing across the surface like a performer on *America's Got Talent.* **Incoming FaceTime Call Daisy** flashes obnoxiously on the screen.

Instead of accepting or declining, I stare down at the screen until it disappears. I don't FaceTime. Ever. Not with my brothers or my sister. Not even with my sister Winnie's daughter—and my adorable niece—Lexi.

Daisy: I'm trying to FaceTime you.

Though it's pretty apparent my Canadian wife isn't privy to my FaceTime track record.

Me: I'm aware.

Daisy: What do you mean, you're aware? Why aren't you accepting?

Before I can even answer her text, she's back at it again, attempting another damn FaceTime call.

Shit. Despite all the times before when someone tried to get me to do some stupid fucking video chat and I outright refused, I find myself tapping the screen on the green phone icon and accepting. I know from even my short-lived experience with this woman that she doesn't give up.

In an instant, Daisy is right there, in all her glory. Her cheeks are flushed pink, her lips are full but set in a firm line, and her unforgettable wild curls fall across her shoulders like satin. It's only been a week since we spent a wild night in Vegas together and got hitched, and yet, a sense of shock over her beauty takes up residence in my chest.

Fuck. She really is beautiful in a way that I'd almost convinced myself to forget.

But also, she has seriously crazy eyes right now. The depths of green are like a midnight forest, and her pupils are wide with anxiety.

"What are we going to do, Flynn?!" Daisy exclaims and tosses her hands up in the air. "I mean, how are we supposed to show that we're living together when we're not living together? That doesn't seem like something we can fake, and I'm in LA and you're in New York, and I just don't even know what to do right now!"

She runs an erratic hand through her long curls, tossing strands over her shoulder once her fingers reach the bottom of the tresses, and when she's finished fidgeting with her hair, she stands up—while still holding the phone in front of her face—and starts to pace in what I'm assuming is her living room and kitchen.

"This is completely fucked," she mutters. "And since I've already sent in my application, it's not like I can go back in time and say, '*Oh, I'm just kidding! Ignore that application! It was just a joke!*' I'm pretty sure that would end up with me either in jail or deported or some horrible combination of both."

"You're not going to get deported," I say from a deeply resolute place in my gut.

She meets my eyes, her stare firm. "You don't know that."

Truthfully, I don't know that, but the urge to give her something that might help calm her down was overwhelming. Which, obviously, didn't work at all. Plus, I don't know… For whatever reason, I'm determined to ensure she makes it through this process with her life intact. And when I put my mind to something, I don't fail.

"Okay, fine. I don't know that," I acknowledge. "But I do know that anytime you approach a situation with anxiety and fear, it makes logical thinking difficult."

"So…what you're saying is that I need to calm the fuck down?"

I shrug one shoulder and grin.

"You know, it's pretty hard to calm down when losing my job and deportation are the most likely consequences."

"Understandable." I may not be the kind of guy who wears his emotions on his fucking sleeve, but I'm not incapable of empathy.

"And I feel horrible," she says softly, and her chin starts to quiver. "I feel like I'm making my problems your problems, and it just feels wrong. You didn't ask for any of this. You hardly know me. And you certainly don't owe me anything." A few tears fall down her cheeks, and that doesn't sit well with me. At all.

The last thing I want to do is see this beautiful woman cry. Her vibrancy and enthusiasm are what drew my eyes to her in the first place. It's what captured my attention in the middle of a crowded casino, and it's what led me to doing the craziest fucking thing I've ever done in my life—marry a complete stranger.

"Daisy." I say her name, attempting to grab her attention, but she's looking away from the camera, sucking her bottom lip into her mouth and losing the battle against the tears that keep falling down her now pink and splotchy cheeks. "Daisy," I repeat again, and this time, quite possibly because this is one of the only times I've bothered to repeat something in my life, she meets my eyes. "First of all, I put myself in this situation. I offered. So, you feeling guilty is unwarranted. It's going to be okay."

She huffs out a sigh. "No offense, but now isn't the time to say shit you don't mean."

I give her a knowing look, one she seems to understand immediately. *I never say shit I don't mean.*

"How could you possibly know it's going to be okay? Because from where I'm standing, it feels apocalyptically dismal."

I make a show of looking over my shoulders. "It can't be that bad. I don't see Bruce Willis anywhere yet."

She snorts at that, and my chest lightens. As the flow of her tears starts to slow, I try to infuse the conversation with logic.

"You said you work for a big real estate firm, right?"

She nods.

"Do they just sell in LA or other cities like New York, too?"

"LA, New York, Miami, Vegas are EllisGrey's primary markets, but there're a few other cities on the list."

Bingo. I simply shrug one shoulder, and she searches my face for a long moment before questioning, "Wait…what are you trying to say?"

Although the answer is pretty fucking obvious to me, I can understand that her emotions are running high at the moment.

"If your firm sells in New York, then I'm thinking it's possible that you relocate to New York for a while."

Her eyes turn wide. "Relocate to New York? Why would I do that?"

I almost want to laugh, but I swallow back the urge. "Well, babe, we do have to show proof of living together. And the only way to do that is to actually live together."

"Oh…*Oh my God*," she mutters and slaps a palm to her face. "Of course. Duh. You probably think I'm the biggest idiot right now."

"I don't think you're an idiot."

Worked up and emotional? Yes. But an idiot? Not at all.

"*Move to New York. To live with you*," she says more to herself than to me. Like she's testing it out on her tongue to see how it sounds out loud. "I have no idea how my boss would take something like that." She digs her teeth into her bottom lip. "But it's not like I haven't helped with staging properties on the East Coast before…"

Daisy looks away from the screen of her phone, sighs, and when her eyes meet mine again, the depths of green appear lighter, closer to a jade gemstone than the deep green of the forest.

"Are you sure you're okay with that?" she asks, and my answer is far simpler than I would've ever thought it would be.

"Yes."

Her eyes search mine for a long moment, and then, they flit down to my bare chest. "Holy hell, are you naked? Like, you've been talking to me this whole time while you're naked?"

I almost want to laugh at how quickly her mind changes topics. "I just got out of the shower."

Her jaw drops wide open. "So, you *are* naked?"

"Not entirely," I say and tilt the screen down slightly to show my towel.

"Oh, cool," she mutters, and her eyes flit between my face and chest some more. "Cool. That makes sense!" she exclaims a little too loudly, and her cheeks flush pink. "People take showers all the time, right? I mean, I do. I take showers. Lots of them. And you take showers, and we'll have to take showers in New York because that's what people do, right? Ha. They shower. Which, you know what, that's exactly what I have to do right now. Yep. It's shower time! Okay, I'll talk to you later. Bye."

In an instant, she's gone, but left in her wake is a smile on my face that stretches from ear to ear.

If she gets that adorably worked up over seeing me in a towel through the fucking phone, what's it going to be like when she's actually in my apartment, living with me?

Looks like it's only a matter of time before you find out.

SEVENTEEN

Monday, April 15th, Los Angeles

Daisy

I adjust the nonexistent wrinkles in my silk blouse and check the time on my phone for the fourth time in as many minutes. **8:55 a.m.**

Only five more minutes of anxiety about the sick feeling I'm going to have when I try to explain this mess to Damien. I laugh at myself, briefly, before going back to focusing my breathing so I don't hyperventilate. *I have pre-anxiety to my anxiety. It's the ultimate moment of my millennialism rearing its ugly head.*

With one glance over my shoulder and into the conference room where Damien is spearheading his weekly morning agent meeting, I see that everyone appears to be in the process of standing up and grabbing their belongings.

Immediately, I move my gaze back to his office door and force as much oxygen into my lungs as I can. *Holy shit. It's about to go down.*

After doing a little reconnaissance via Damien's main assistant, Carrie, I know that his schedule is open for the next hour. Which means I have sixty minutes to convince him that me relocating to New York and handling staging the properties on the East Coast for the next three or so months is a really fan-freaking-tastic idea. That it's going to do the work of a spam email Nigerian Prince by enhancing both his *ahem* and his bank account. And I somehow need to do this without spilling the beans on my visa debacle.

No big deal, *right?*

Even though it feels like I'm getting ready to be shipped off to war, that's probably a completely irrational reaction. I hope.

"Well, well, well, if it isn't my favorite little secret-keeper."

The sound of my boss's voice behind me spurs an urge to cringe so strong that I have to dig my teeth into my bottom lip to keep my facial expression halfway normal.

Slowly, I spin on my favorite secondhand black Prada heels and ready myself as Damien strides toward me with a terrifying smirk etched across his handsome face.

"Morning, Dame," I say, trying like hell to keep the nervous titter out of my voice. *Everything* is on the line here.

"Morning, doll." He smiles, slides open his office door, and gestures for me to come inside. "Finally ready to spill the details of your Vegas adventure? Because I'm *dying* for a taste of tea…and a baguette." He chuckles at his penis joke, and all I can do is giggle back, almost painfully avoiding how very aware I am that his point was not at all about a morning beverage and snack. But whatever. Avoidance is all I have to keep myself emotionally afloat right now.

I hold up the to-go Starbucks cup clutched in my left hand and punctuate the gesture with a wiggle of my wrist. "I don't have tea, but how about a morning caramel macchiato?"

An amused laugh jumps from his lungs, and he sidles around his massive all-glass desk to sit down in his black leather desk chair. A desk chair, mind you, that's a ten-thousand-dollar Arne Jacobsen Egg Chair that's exactly sixty years old and has the kind of perfect patina on the leather that would make any interior designer or vintage furniture lover weep tears of joy.

The man has impeccable taste. Expensive-as-hell, but impeccable, nonetheless.

"Party pooper."

I shake the frilly coffee drink again, and he sighs.

He curls his index finger toward me. "Hand over the macchiato, and no one gets hurt."

I set the still-warm drink on his desk and take a seat in one of the chairs across from him. "You're welcome, by the way," I add as I watch him enjoy his first sip.

"Thank you." He winks. "But if you're not here to gossip, what has you bringing me my favorite drink and pacing outside my office for the last thirty minutes on this lovely Monday morning?"

"I wasn't pacing."

"Weren't pacing? Dais, I'll probably have to have someone come out and refinish the Brazilian hardwood in front of my door."

I roll my eyes, and he laughs.

"Fine. Maybe I was pacing…a *little*."

"Come on. It can't be that bad. I mean, what? Are you here to tell me you want to quit?" He laughs at first, the presumed absurdity of his statement laying on his funny nerve. When I don't say anything, though, his mouth drops open.

"Oh my God! Daisy Diaz, you're not trying to quit your job, are you? Because I swear on everything, I will—"

"No, no, no," I quickly respond. "I don't want to leave. I… I just… I…" I pause, trying like hell to figure out a way to verbalize what I actually do need.

"Daisy girl, you're making me nervous here. Stick your finger down your throat if you have to and ralph that shit up!"

"I'm not trying to scare you," I say, but it comes off as more of a whine than anything else. "I just… I need to move to New York." The words come off my tongue way more direct and harsher than I intend, and it doesn't take long before I'm backtracking. "For a little while. Not, like, permanently. Just…three months or so. That's it. That's all I'm wanting to ask you."

"*Excuse me?*" He furrows his brow. "You want to move to New York for three months?"

"Yes?" I respond, and when I realize how uncertain I sound, I swallow and reiterate with a firmer repeat, "Yes. That's what I need."

"And why *exactly* do you need this? Have you taken a position with the New York City Council? Applied to be an extra in the remake of Mary Kate and Ashley's *New York Minute*? What's going on with you?"

"They're remaking *New York Minute*?" I ask, suddenly distracted.

"Daisy!"

I hold up both my hands in defense. *Sorry.* But to be fair, I am a child of the Mary Kate and Ashley generation.

"I have to go to New York because…" *My whole career, my whole life, depends on it.* "Well, you know I got married. And…I…want to…spend more time with my husband. We don't know if we want to live on the East Coast or West Coast, and I figure this is a great way for us to figure that out. And, you know, we're newlyweds, and we should be together and… Yeah, that's pretty much why."

"So, you want to move to New York to spend time with your mystery husband that you married in Vegas, whom I know absolutely nothing about? Am I getting this right?"

"Mm-hmm." I suck my button lip into my mouth and then quickly add, "Obviously, I would be staging properties while I'm there. I want to work for you. That hasn't changed."

"Okayyy…" He pauses and runs confident fingers over his chin. "What's this husband of yours's name?"

"Flynn. Flynn Winslow."

"And how long have you known Flynn?"

Like…a week?

"Uh…not that long."

"He can't move to LA?"

Well, no. He's a resident of New York, and I sent in an application to Immigration stating that very fact. Obviously, though, I can't exactly tell my boss that.

"It's not a good time…" I pause and then quickly add, "For his job. Yes. His job needs him to stay for now. That's why."

"And what does he do exactly?"

Thank God, it's something you actually do know about him!

I almost want to slap myself over how insane my life has become that I'm thrilled I know the answer to a simple question like this. About my freaking husband.

"He's an electrical engineer." *And some kind of investment stuff that you haven't gotten the full story on yet, so technically, you don't even completely know this answer…*

"Interesting." Damien smirks. "And what made you decide to marry this mysterious electrical engineer in the first place?"

Obviously, he's fishing for information. And I'm willing to bet ninety percent of that has nothing to do with work; it's purely because Damien is a nosy little biotch.

Though, I can't really blame him. I'd be asking him the same exact questions if the roles were reversed. I mean, our relationship's foundation might revolve around boss-employee, but ever since he headhunted me to work for his company, we've grown to be fairly close friends.

"I don't know. Because it just felt…right?" *You know, how any good marriage proposal feels when it's done to prevent you from getting deported.*

Damien's mouth straightens into a firm line, and I know I'm going to have to do a hell of a lot better to convince him my marriage to Flynn isn't a total lie done in the name of my visa-expiring ass.

Come on, Daisy. It's time to really amp up the insta-love, love-at-first-sight, he's the most amazing man you've ever met factor. Because right now, it sounds more like you've scheduled a root canal rather than married the love of your life.

"I know it was impulsive to marry someone I just met, but…" I pause, searching for the right words to make Damien believe this marriage is the real deal. "He's the one, Dame." *Who will save my ass from getting deported.* "My…person. I can't really explain how I know this, but I just know. Everything is right when I'm with him. And trust me, I never thought I believed in love at first sight, but…yeah… I married Flynn because he's my soul mate. He's my forever."

"Your soul mate?"

I nod fervently. "It's as if I've known him all my life. As if I'm destined to be with him."

"And this is why you want to go to New York? To be with him?"

"Yes."

Damien thinks it over for a long minute, running his hand across his hair and searching my face closely. "You have to understand this is a shock. I know for a fact you weren't dating, weren't even looking. Hell, to be honest, I often wondered if you were a closeted lesbian or something."

I snort. "I'm not a closeted lesbian. Though, I admit I considered it once when I first started here and met Nikki."

"Girl, I hear that." A burst of laughs leaves his lips. "Someone needs to get her to spill the details on her skincare regimen because, I swear, she looks airbrushed."

Nikki Fellows is a fortysomething goddess who is one of EllisGrey's top-selling agents. She doesn't look a day over twenty-five, and her skin always has that dewy, vibrant glow you only see on high-fashion models in makeup commercials. It's almost disturbing how perfect she is.

I honestly don't know if it's Botox or good genetics or some super-secret fountain of youth she has in her background, but homegirl is one of the most beautiful women I've ever seen in my life. And she's smart and nice too.

"Maybe the next contract re-up, you should consider adding that into Nikki's requirements."

"You're diabolical. I love it." He smirks and takes a sip from his coffee. "Now, if you don't mind, I need to catch up on some emails or else Thomas will turn psychotic."

Thomas is the Grey half of EllisGrey. And while Damien is mostly laid-back, relaxed, and cool, Thomas is a Type-A nightmare. Very nice but *very* demanding. Truthfully, if I were working under him, I'm not sure I would've lasted in my career.

It's not like your career is exactly stable right now as it is…

Damien's eyes are already on the screen of his computer and his fingers move quickly across the keys, but I continue to sit there, still uncertain about the whole reason I came into his office in the first place.

"So…uh…New York?" I question gently, and Damien's gaze lifts to mine.

"Doll, I'm a gay man whose favorite movie is *You've Got Mail*," he answers with a cheeky grin. "Like I'd ever stand in the way of soul mates."

My shoulders sag, and a whole double-lungful of toxic air I didn't know I was holding floods the room in a rush.

"Though, I want you to finish planning out the staging on the Santa Monica, West Hollywood, and Beverly Hills properties. I figure that'll take you at least the week, and then you can go."

That's another two weeks of work, but leaving in one is better. Even that feels like an eternity in "anxiety years." I'm just going to have to fit it all in somehow.

"Of course."

"And most of the listings you'll be working on will be mine. Not Thomas's. So don't let that demanding bastard force too much work on you."

I nod, more than happy to agree to that stipulation.

"Update Carrie on your temporary transition to the East Coast," he adds, and I know that's my cue that this conversation is done.

But as I leave his office, I can't deny that relief isn't the only emotion I'm currently feeling. Even a week is a hell of a lot of time to lose when I'm supposed to be showing that Flynn and I are a married, in-love couple.

Most newly married couples don't live on opposite ends of the country.

They live *together*. In the same state, same city, same *house*. So, how in the hell are we going to show proof of our relationship when we're thousands of miles away from each other?

It's not long before I'm pulling my cell out of my jacket pocket and firing off a text.

Me: We need to talk. Call me as soon as you can, please and thank you.

And then, when I think about the awkward way I ended our last conversation—*when I found out his hot bod was only covered by a damn towel and proceeded to ramble like a moron*—I type out a second text and hit send.

Me: Also, please don't FaceTime me when you're in a towel again because this is a serious, non-towel-wearing conversation.

Once my words fill our text box and I reread what I wrote, insta-mortification sets in.

Oh my God! Why did you send that?! Fix it!

Me: Ha. I'm kidding, obviously! Call me in whatever you like! Fully clothed, balls out, rocking out with your cock out! Doesn't matter!

Ha-ha-ha, I'm an idiot.

Me: Holy hell. Can you just go ahead and ignore all of that?

Me: Oops. Besides the call me part. Still do that. Okay. Bye.

EIGHTEEN

Daisy

After spending ten minutes on self-loathing and theoretical questions about life brought on by my text faux pas with Flynn, I eventually invested myself in finishing my staging plans for one of the properties Damien wants done before I relocate to New York, and my workday just sort of flew by.

I didn't have time to sit and stew, and for that, I'm thankful. Because now that I'm done with my task list for the day, each and every one of my thoughts about those messages has come back with full force.

Hindsight is a bit of a bitch, and I realize now that my messages probably came off as a confusing combination of weird-as-hell and oddly serious. *Not exactly the impression I'm going for*, which, of course, makes me want to fix it. The solution teasingly seems like it rests in more messages. But thankfully—in part because of my age, and in part because I'm a lifetime member of the foot-in-the-mouth club—I know that's not *actually* true. It will, however, probably make me sound like a crazy, nagging shrew to a man who's done nothing but try to help me, and that's the very last thing I want.

On a sigh, I drop my phone back onto my kitchen counter and busy myself with grabbing a yogurt and some granola. It's a little after nine in the evening and this is a terrible dinner, but going to the effort to cook or order takeout at this point feels akin to starting a 5K run knowing my blood sugar is already low.

Regardless, I only get through one bite of my yogurt before my phone starts ringing from its abandoned spot on the counter, and I slip-slide across the kitchen like a newborn colt on a patch of ice trying to get to it in my stocking feet. I fumble and bumble attempting to set the yogurt down with the spoon inside, and I finally pick it up on what I know to be one of the last notes of my ringtone without looking at the screen.

"Hello?"

"Hey, Daisy," the caller says, the rich rumble of his voice immediately recognizable. A whole-body shiver starts at my toes and curls right into my buzzing brain. It's weird, but I think the rarity of my new husband's words ups their potency or something.

"Flynn." I giggle involuntarily. "On the phone. Talking."

"You asked me to call."

"I did. You're right. It's just…you, on the phone, where you literally have no option but to talk in order to communicate. It's almost nonsensical."

It's as if the man has a set quota of words per day, not to be exceeded. In the modern age of social media, where everyone is pretending to be the very best version of themselves by spewing bullshit from their keyboard at every turn, that's refreshing, to say the least.

I wonder what percentage of total words in his lifetime have been used while in the bedroom?

My cheeks flush pink when memories of the one and only night I spent with Flynn Winslow fill up my head like helium in a balloon. Holy moly, he didn't hold back any words that night. If anything, he was completely uninhibited, and his frequent use of words only spurred my pleasure further.

That was a hot night. *One for the damn record books.*

"Daisy?"

"Yeah?"

"You wanted to talk?"

"Oh, *right*," I respond and cringe through an embarrassed smile. Clearing my throat, I yank my mind out of the gutter and focus on the actual priority. "So, I have good news and sort of bad news, I guess. I got the okay from my boss for my move to New York, but since I have a few more staging projects to finish up, I probably won't be able to get out there for another week. Possibly ten days if my plan to work like a dog comes up a couple barks short of a tail wag."

The silence stretches out for what feels like forever.

"Flynn?"

"A couple barks short of a tail wag?"

My cheeks warm as I suck my lips inside my mouth before popping them back out. "Of everything I said, that's the part you heard?"

"I heard the rest. That was just the part that interested me."

"The fact that it's going to be at least a week before I can move out there doesn't concern you?"

"I can assume from your tone that this isn't the answer you're looking for, but no, it doesn't," he answers matter-of-factly. "We've both sent USCIS everything they need for the application. From where I stand, everything that needs to be done is getting done, and I don't see a problem with it taking a week for you to move out here."

"Okayyy…but wouldn't you say it's a bit of a problem for showing proof of our marriage?"

"I think they'll understand there's a transition period, babe. Lives take time to shift."

"And, what? We just don't talk to each other all that time to make the anticipation grow stronger?" I retort. "That's sketchy as hell, Flynn. It's going to toss up all the red flags for the immigration overlords and make them suspicious of us. Of me. We're going to have to think of other things to do to show we're together and *want* to be together."

"I'm a reasonable guy, Daisy, and I made an agreement with you. All you need to do is tell me what you think we should be doing, and I'll do it."

When I picture him standing there, most likely in his apartment in New York, holding a phone to his ear and having a conversation with me I can almost guarantee he'd rather not be having, plus the FaceTime call in his towel and everything else he's done for me up until now, I know that's true. Flynn Winslow has an irrefutable track record of keeping his word to me.

"I think…" I pause and, for some reason, find myself fumbling over my words. It makes zero sense, but I can only chalk it up to already feeling like I'm asking him for far too much. "We…uh…need to show proof of our relationship through other ways. Like…text messages…phone calls…you know, that sort of thing. And also, probably delete any damning evidence of contractual indifference from our previous conversations…"

"Okay."

One word. Just like that, and he's already agreed. Call me a sadist, but this feels too easy.

"Are you…uh…sure?"

"Daisy."

Right. This is good. Great, even.

My need to get the ball rolling as soon as possible is too strong to deny. The call switched over to speaker, I pull up our text chat and type out a message—*How was your day, hubby?*

Once I hit send, I say, "Okay. Check your text messages."

"My day was fine," he responds, and laughter barrels from my belly and straight past my lips.

"Flynn!" I giggle. "You're supposed to text me your answer back. You know… for *evidentiary support.*"

"Right. I just have one question."

"Of course! Go ahead!" I respond, kind of excited to be able to feel useful for once.

"Will Bruiser Woods be partaking in these conversations too, or is Elle the only split personality of yours I need to be on the lookout for?"

"Flynn!" I shriek, both tickled by his highly unexpected knowledge of all things *Legally Blonde* and slightly embarrassed by his teasing.

"Don't you think it's important that we show proof through text messages, too?" I ask him once my laughter subsides. "Phone calls are great—I mean, it will show Immigration that we stay in constant contact, but they won't be able to see what's said in our phone conversations. And in order to really sell it, I think they need to see the text conversations. Don't you?"

"They need to see text conversations or fake text *conversations* showing we're in love and shit?"

"Um, the latter."

"But you want us to be on the phone, too?"

"Yes," I answer.

But Flynn doesn't say anything else. Not in text and not on the phone, and the silence makes my heart quicken its speed, uncertainty driving the pace.

God, he must think I'm a total nutjob, and he's about to lose my number any minute. Or worse, turn me in to Immigration himself.

"Look, I know it's weird and awkward to text each other while we're on the phone, but…I need the buffer, you know?" I try to explain my intentions, even though I don't really understand what I'm trying to achieve here. "This whole thing is making me freak out a bit…" Okay, *a lot*. "And I just don't know what to say or do or how to show that we're in love when we barely even know each other—"

"Check your messages."

"What?" I ask, but a few moments later, a new text fills our chat.

Flynn: My day was pretty good, babe. How was yours?

"Oh." Okay, so maybe he doesn't think I'm a total nutjob. Just, like, a partial nutjob. Not put-her-in-a-padded-room nuts, more like, yes, she's crazy, but it's tolerable.

I don't hesitate to type out a response to his message. Truthfully, I've been thinking about it for about seven out of the last twenty-four hours, so it's pretty curated.

Me: It was good, but I miss you. I hate being this far away from you. I hate waking up and finding out that you're not there. And going to bed without you beside me? Completely miserable. How many days until I'm in New York with you again? Because from where I stand, it feels like a thousand.

Flynn: I miss you too.

A sigh leaves my lips when I read his latest text. "No offense, Flynn, but you're going to have to say more than a few words for this to work. I mean, we are supposed to be two people who are crazy about each other and miss each other and all the things, you know? Our text conversations should show love and excitement, but they should also show passion. We're two people who desperately want to be together but have to be thousands of miles away. It's going to look weird if I'm penning a novel of adoration and you respond with *yeah*."

His hearty chuckles fill my ears, and I furrow my brow.

"Wait...are you laughing at me right now?"

"No offense, but you sound like an acting coach."

It's my turn to laugh, but my nerves turn it to hysteria pretty quickly.

I've never been one to spend time imagining my future husband, but I do know, if I did, it definitely wouldn't have been like this, where my husband wasn't even my husband at all but a man who made a commitment out of pity in order to help keep me from losing my job. It all feels kind of pathetic when I think about it.

"I'm sorry. I know I sound like a rambling psycho and I'm probably making no sense, but the importance of all this, of getting this visa and keeping my job, is making it hard for me to be rational."

I shut my eyes and run a hand through my hair, but when Flynn says, "Check your messages," into my ear once more, my focus is back on the screen of my phone.

Flynn: *Do me a favor and tell me what you're wearing right now, babe. In explicit detail, so I can imagine it perfectly.*

A breath gets caught in my lungs, and I open and close my mouth several times in an attempt to form words. *What the hell? Is he...is he sexting me?*

"I can't be sure...but...are you sexting me?"

"You want it to look real, right?"

Numbly, I nod, the words on the screen still burning into my eyes.

"I'm expecting a response," he adds.

Okay, Daisy, you said you wanted this. Well, the ball is officially in your court...

I've never sexted with anyone in my life. Kind of sad, I'm sure, but true—I am a sexting virgin.

Maybe the only sexting virgin left on the planet at this point in the modern-technology age.

Don't make a big thing out of it, Daisy. Just…sext him back.

I glance down at my clothes, and when I see that I'm still in the skirt and blouse I put on for work this morning, I decide that this isn't nearly sexy enough for this conversation. And before I know it, I'm stripping out of my work clothes until I'm left wearing something that feels appropriate for the sexting cause.

An imaginary notification bings dramatically in my head: *Libido has entered the chat.*

NINETEEN

New York

Flynn

Daisy: Your favorite white lace panties and a tank top.

If this conversation weren't intended for fake purposes, those words would probably make me hard.

Me: Fuck, I want to taste you. I'm about ten seconds away from hopping on a plane to LA…

"Holy moly, that was really good," Daisy whispers, almost like USCIS has our apartments bugged or some shit, and I have to work not to laugh audibly over the open line. "Like, really good. I don't even know what to say to that."

"Simple. Say whatever you think the Daisy who's in love with her husband would say."

"Okay…" she whispers, and when it sounds like her fingers are tapping across the screen of her phone, I wait patiently for her response. I'm just about to pull the phone away from my ear to look when she shouts, "Oh no! Oh my God! I didn't want to send that! Ignore that one! Don't look at that one!"

It's too late, though; the text is already on the screen of my phone before she can stop it.

Daisy: I want to see your big penis.

When I read her response, I have to bite my lip over how fucking adorable and awkward it is. Almost as good as telling me I could call her while I'm *rocking out with my cock out.*

But also, that message, oddly enough, made you hard.

Me: *If I were with you right now, where would you want my big cock? Between your pretty lips or inside your wet cunt?*

Her breath hitches. But to my pleasant surprise, instead of dissolving into another hysterical spiral, she sends another message through.

Daisy: *Both*

Me: *I need you to do something for me right now, babe.*

Daisy: *What?*

Me: *Slide your hand down your belly, beneath your panties, and push one finger inside your cunt so you can tell me how wet you are.*

She moans a little into the phone, and my cock jerks.

Daisy: *Wetter than the first night you fucked me on your kitchen counter.*

Fuck me. The visual is immediate and potent. I couldn't forget that night if I tried. Every moment, every memory, like how tight and perfect Daisy felt wrapped around my cock and how damn mesmerizing she looked when she came, is available for instantaneous recall.

Me: *Pump your finger in and out of your perfect cunt. And each time you slide it out and back in, I want you to pretend it's my cock filling you up.*

Her soft moan bounces from the speaker, and my cock twitches beneath my boxer briefs.

I imagine her hips shifting to accommodate me as she works herself, and a throbbing ache starts to form below my stomach.

Okay, yeah, the soldier is officially at full attention.

And our pretend messages don't feel at all pretend anymore. The drive to make her come is intense and overwhelming, and I know without a shadow of a doubt, I won't be able to sleep without hearing it.

In the interest of keeping both of our hands free, I click my call over to speakerphone and lay the phone on the bed next to me.

"Your pussy is a perfect fit around my cock, Daisy," I say, reaching into my boxer briefs to stroke myself lazily.

Her breath catches on my name, and I swear, all I need is one word to know all the things she's thinking. Pleasure, excitement…panic over the fact that I'm switching up the carefully crafted plan from messaging to outright phone sex.

"Are you wet enough that my cock will melt, baby?" I ask roughly, wishing like fuck that I could feel the juice of her perfect pussy rather than the dryness of my hand.

"Oh yeah," she hums, her words shifting from a moan to a groan. "Mm-hmm."

"Tell me what I feel like, Daisy."

"You feel…good. God, Flynn, I want to come so badly."

"Then come. Don't hold back. Don't stop. Rub your clit while I fill your pussy up with my come."

"Oh God. Oh *yes*! Oh shit, I'm coming so hard, Flynn."

Pearly fluid shoots from my dick onto my hand, and I bite into the flesh of my bottom lip to soften my groan. It's guttural, and if I let it fly at full strength, it's sure to pull her out of the perfect bliss of her postorgasmic haze.

That's the last thing I want to do.

Because my wife is finally calm—free from anxiousness and content enough to rest. And that's exactly where I'd like her to stay.

"Goodnight, Daisy," I say softly into the speaker.

Her giggle is soft and satisfied. "Um… Goodnight, Flynn."

Yeah, it is a fucking good night, indeed.

TWENTY

Wednesday, April 17th, New York

Flynn

"Can I get you boys anything else?" our waitress asks, and Rem flashes a friendly wink at her that makes me roll my eyes. He plays the part of a lothario pretty well, but I know in actuality that my brother Rem is nearly celibate. Okay, maybe not celibate per se, but he's way less active than he likes to portray, and I know it's because his past still cuts deeper than he'd prefer.

Even if he's grown up since Charlotte left him at the altar, even if he knows now that she wasn't the right fit for him, the mark of an event like that changes a man. Changes his perspective on the amount of effort on love that's worth it.

And as far as Remy's concerned, he keeps his levels pretty close to zero. For the last decade or so, it's actually been the thing we have most in common—careful, methodical, transactional-style relationships.

It feels a little weird to be sitting across from him now, given the state of my arrangement with Daisy, almost as though the universe has shifted.

"I think we're all set. Thanks, Carol."

"All right, honey. Just holler if you need anything."

Carol heads back toward the kitchen, and I shake my head on a chuckle. Apparently, my eldest brother has become a regular at Don's Diner since I brought him here a couple of years ago, and I had no idea.

"What?"

"Pretty friendly with the waitstaff, eh?" I retort, and he flashes me a small grin.

"Don's has the best burgers in Brooklyn."

I raise my eyebrows pointedly. That's exactly what I told him on our first visit, and he practically told me to fuck off.

My my, how the tide changes when fuckers learn to not be such snobs.

Brooklyn used to be borough non grata with Remy a couple years ago when he thought it was all hipsters and young twentysomethings, and now it's one of his favorite parts of the city. It also just so happens to be the one area where I hold a lot of rental properties. I dove into this real estate market about fifteen years ago, when everything was just on the cusp of booming but you could still buy properties for relatively low prices. As a result, I got a leg up on a lot of the revitalization crowd, and my properties generate a substantial portion of my income.

"What have you been up to anyway?" he asks. "I feel like I haven't talked to you since Vegas. Hell, I feel like I didn't talk to you all that much *in* Vegas."

Oh, you know, just sending in immigration applications for my wife—that you don't know about—and making arrangements for her to move to New York so we can keep up our relationship façade for the big interview in a few months…

"You were all too drunk in Vegas to talk clearly to anyone." I shrug and make a point to change the topic of conversation to something that doesn't make me have to lie to my brother. "How's the market looking these days?"

"The market?" Rem looks up from the fresh plate of burger and fries the waitress just dropped off at our table, and his face turns amused. "Oh, so this lunch had stipulations."

"Not stipulations," I correct. "Multiple motivations."

Rem laughs. "I should've known when *you* of all people suggested lunch, there was more to the story than shooting the shit."

He's not exactly wrong. Out of all of our siblings, I'm the least likely to make plans for lunch just to catch up. And it's not because I don't like spending time with my brothers and sister—I do. They're my favorite people I know, actually. I just fucking hate small talk.

"I take it you've got some profits you're wanting to dump?" he asks around a bite of French fries.

"Possibly."

"How much are we talking?"

I pull my cell out of my pocket and shoot my accountant a quick message.

Me: *What's our excess for 2nd quarter?*

He gets back to me pretty quickly.

Allen: *$500,000.*

I meet Rem's eyes. "A decent amount."

He sighs. "A decent amount can be anything, you fuck. How many figures we talking? Four, five, *six?*"

"Six."

"Damn, bro. I should've invested in real estate when you told me to."

I grin, and he shakes his head.

"I don't think I'd dump it all in the market right now," he says, switching from teasing brother to sage investor. If anyone knows the stock market, it's Rem. "How much risk do you want to take with it?"

I shrug. "Moderate."

"All right, I'll look at a few things and email you some options I think will give the most return on your money," he updates, but then he pauses, meets my eyes for a long moment, and laughs. "And to think, you went through all that college to become an engineer, and here you are…asking me about fucking stocks."

"I still do engineer shit."

"When exactly?"

"Whenever I go to my office."

He laughs. "So, almost never."

I just shrug and take a bite of my burger. He can think what he wants about my work life. I don't really give a shit.

Truth be told, for the past six years, my passive income from real estate and investments has made it so I don't have to work full time as an engineer, but I spent so much time building the company that it aggravates me too much when I think about walking away from it all. As long as I'm able, I'll keep doing both.

My phone vibrates in my pocket, and I pull it out to find three new messages from Daisy. The first two are pictures of a lamp and a couch, followed by *What about these? Should I bring them?*

We've been playing this game for the past forty-eight hours, and I know it at least started as a way for her to breach the text message barrier formed by where we left off—with me telling her to use her fingers like my cock to stroke herself.

Her sending me pictures of random things in her apartment and me telling her she doesn't need to bring them is a way to keep the lines of communication and *evidentiary support* for USCIS open and flowing without having to address the dripping wet pussy in the room.

Me: No.

Daisy: Are you sure? Because I could easily hire movers to transport from LA to New York…

A weird combination of a sigh and laugh escapes my lips.

"Who is that?" Rem asks, and I look up to find him staring at me curiously, but I just shake my head and type out a response.

Me: My apartment has furniture, babe.

"Dude. Seriously. Who are you texting?" he questions. "I sure as shit know your fucking accountant wouldn't make you smile like that."

"When he's messaging me with high-profit numbers? He sure as fuck does."

"Whatever," Rem retorts. "This is a different kind of smile, and you know it. Who's the girl?"

"My wife," I answer simply with a flicker of eye contact.

"Oh yeah. Sure, Flynn. You're just sitting here, texting your fucking wife," he says, rolls his eyes, and laughs as if I just said the most absurd thing on the planet. And then, he just goes back to eating his burger as if I didn't just tell him I have a wife.

Sure, it's probably because he thinks I was joking, but this is me we're talking about, not fucking Ty or Jude.

I don't bullshit. Ever.

My phone vibrates again, and I check the screen to find another message from Daisy.

Daisy: Besides clothes and shoes, I feel like I'm hardly bringing anything, Flynn. What about dishes? Do you have enough dishes? Or glasses? How about silverware? No one ever has enough silverware.

I know her well enough by now to understand that she's going to send me about six or seven additional rambling text messages before she's finished.

So, I give her time to ask all the questions her little heart desires and go back to eating lunch with my brother. You know, the first person I've actually told that I'm married, and he doesn't believe me.

Pretty sure he's going to believe you soon enough when Daisy is living in your apartment…

The silence is marred only by our chewing as my phone buzzes frantically from its spot on the table, and Remy's eyes narrow slightly as he watches it. When it nearly falls to the floor from shaking itself so much, I pick it back up and scroll through what she's sent me.

Daisy: Okay, so I'm guessing by your lack of enthusiastic agreement, that's a no to cutlery.

Daisy: How about bath towels? I have these really great towels I got from Pottery Barn, and I swear they're the softest towels you'll ever feel against your skin. I know guys act like they don't care about shit like that, but let's be real, no one wants to dry off with sandpaper.

Daisy: Fine. No bath towels. And I guess if you have really crappy ones, I'll buy new and leave them at your place after I leave. Your skin will thank me.

Daisy: Should I bring my own pillows? Comforter? Sheets?

Daisy: Gah. I'm an idiot, and we need to delete all these messages because they are insanely suspect and do the opposite of saying we're in love. They scream "This chick is frauding the system and needs to be deported ASAP."

Daisy: Oh my God. Delete that one too.

Daisy: P.S. Has anyone ever told you that texting with you is impossible? I never know what you've read and haven't read because you're not answering me.

Daisy: Delete that one too.

I'm smiling when I finish reading, and without thinking, I type out the first message that comes to mind.

Me: Love you, Daisy.

The words come so naturally that I don't even catch myself until I put the phone down on the table again and look back up and into the weight of my brother's stare.

I think we're both wondering the same thing. *What, exactly, is really going on here?*

TWENTY-ONE

Monday, April 22nd, New York

Daisy

If you're looking for peace and relaxation, do not go to JFK Airport. Do not marry a man to save your residency in the United States, do not move across the country, and do *not* do it within a week's time.

I juggle my carry-on and big backpack through the narrow hallway that leads to baggage claim, hoping to find some peace away from the bustle of passengers running for their flights and lining up way too early, but it's nothing like I hoped.

It is a madhouse. Every baggage claim is surrounded by impatient passengers who have just arrived, and the people who have managed to get their bags are careening through the crowd with their luggage like it's the Indy 500.

Honestly, I'm surprised to see that it's this busy on a Monday evening, but I'm a naïve Canadian who's been living her life at an energy-depleting level for the last week, and New York eats its young for breakfast. I really hope I survive.

Swallowing thickly, I set my backpack down on the floor and take a minute to blow some of the wild curls of my hair out of my face. There's a river of sweat running down my back from anxiety, and I need to calm the eff down if I have any hope of getting all my shit off the baggage belt and out to a cab.

Okay, Daisy. You can do this. You're an independent woman, for Pete's sake. You've been on your own most of your life, and this isn't any different now.

Gathering myself, I check the board for my carousel number, and with my bags slung over my shoulders again, I head for the crowd standing around it. I have to dodge a group of rowdy twentysomething men with golf bags and nearly get run over by a woman with a screaming toddler sitting on her carry-on suitcase, but I make it to the shiny silver oval just as the red-siren-light thingie on the top starts to buzz.

Preparing, I drop my bags to the tile at my feet, tie my curls back in a loose ponytail, and adjust my favorite cutoff jean shorts. A couple of jigs and hops on my toes, and I'd be a boxer in the corner of the ring readying for her fight.

I take my position to the side of the conveyor belt bringing the luggage to the carousel and wait. In a shocking twist, I'm startled when the white of my bags is the first thing I see cresting the top of the hill and dumping onto the shiny silver metal.

Woo-hoo! This almost never happens!

I jockey through the crowd, using gentle elbows to make my body seem bigger than it is, and lean over the edge as I wait for my luggage to get to me. Having them right in a row is a challenge, but thanks to all my hyping, I'm gamed up and ready.

I step forward and latch on to the first handle and then the second, and I grit my teeth against the weight of them as I pull two of my suitcases with both of my arms and lift.

Unfortunately, between the weight and the instability of the soles of my poorly planned sandals, the bags and the carousel lift *me*, instead of the other way around.

Shit, oh shit! I scream internally as the panic of being dragged along in front of the people waiting for their luggage overwhelms me. *Do something, Daisy!*

Within a second, I'm fully aboard the carousel, the handles of my bags still in my hands as I ride around the oval like an airport cowboy. People start to shout for security—and I'm so tangled in myself and my hysteria that I can't figure out how to get free.

Before I know it, the conveyor looms ahead, the bulky weight of the bags it's spitting out dangerously apparent by the sound they make when they slide to the bottom.

Oh God. Oh God! *I'm going to be crushed!*

I'm a little ashamed to say that the first and only line of defense I can come up with is to close my eyes, but that's probably why it's so shocking when large hands scoop under my knees and around my back and lift me free of the chaos.

A yell of panic swells in my throat, but when I open my eyes to the tall handsomeness of my contractual husband, all my terror recedes like a wave.

Holy shit, Flynn?!

He sets me down on my feet, and I pull my white T-shirt down until only the small sliver of my stomach that's supposed to be exposed is left in the breeze.

My eyes feel so wide they might take over my face, and my chest heaves with the exertion of my debacle.

"That was a bit of a close call, huh?" he asks as if I haven't just single-handedly brought shame to the city of New York.

"W-what are you doing here?"

"I came to pick you up from the airport," he answers simply, only then releasing his hold on my hips he'd been using to steady me.

"You came to pick me up?" I question, dumbfounded. I… Well, I don't know what I thought. But I didn't think this. "We didn't make any arrangements, and I figured I was going to meet you at your apartment."

He frowns. "Daisy, there was no way in hell I was going to make you navigate the New York craziness by yourself after a long flight. That'd be cruel."

I search his vivid blue eyes for a long moment, for something, anything, to calm the racing beat of my heart and the twisted, almost painful warmth in my chest. I don't think I've ever known what it's like to have someone other than myself this invested in my well-being.

"So…uh…since you're here, mind helping me get my bags off the carousel? I'm still fresh off adrenaline from that near-death experience a few minutes ago, and I'm not sure if I'm ready to give it a second go just yet."

He grins. Nods. And steps forward to snag the large white suitcase that started the clusterfuck in the first place. As he pulls it off the carousel, I point to the one next to it. And then another one.

And *another* one.

"That's it," I finally declare once four large—and heavy—suitcases are off the track and sitting beside me. "I took your advice and packed light," I say through the embarrassment.

The sarcasm makes Flynn laugh, and my chest inflates dramatically. *Gah, that might be the best sound ever.*

I have the immediate and almost overpowering desire to make it happen again.

Flynn handles my shitshow of bags with ease, leaving me with only my backpack and carry-on to manage.

He looks strong, confident, calm, and—dare I say it—content.

As we make our way out of the airport and head in the direction of Flynn's car, I can't stop myself from thinking that if I were an innocent bystander watching our interaction, I might actually believe that we are husband and wife. In a serious relationship, at the very least.

Which, I guess, is a good thing, right?

For getting a green card? Yes. For your future sanity? Probably not.

TWENTY-TWO

Flynn

The elevator dings our arrival on my floor, and I jerk my chin for Daisy to go ahead of me and her four suitcases. She's been relatively silent since we left the airport, choosing instead to spend her time surveying the city around her as we drove, saying only a singular "wow" when I drove my Range Rover into the underground garage beneath my apartment building.

I know it's a lot—moving here, across the country, to the apartment of a man she barely knows—so I don't push her. She'll have plenty to say in her own time; I'm pretty much sure of that.

I hand her the keys to open the lock, and after pushing the door open, she heads to the kitchen first, located right off the entryway hallway, to divest herself of her backpack and carry-on—and then performs a slow spin into the living room. The floor-to-ceiling windows at the side make the light so bright that a gentle dust floats in the air, and the leather of my cognac-colored couch almost shimmers.

Her yellow pillows sit in each corner of the couch, and she smiles when she sees them. She circles around to the back of the couch to look out the windows again and perhaps take in the whole room at once, and the motion light in the back hallway clicks on.

"Mm," she hums. "I see this place is just as teched-out as the one in Vegas."

I shrug. It's practical to be able to see where you're going with minimal effort.

"The pillows look great," she continues then. "Really liven up the place."

My shoulders rise and fall again. "I'll take your word for it."

She giggles at that, turning to look again at the room and any of the details she may have missed, when her gaze snags on the fireplace—or more specifically, the painting above it.

It features a laughing woman with curly hair and vibrant eyes, the strokes of the paintbrush soft and wispy in a way that completely belies the masculine overtones found throughout the rest of my place.

Now that I look at it closely, it's remarkably similar in its resemblance to her in both physicality and personality.

"That painting…it…it seems out of character for you."

I nod. "It is. But my great-great-aunt painted it many years ago and promised it to me when she passed. It's been hanging there ever since. I'm pretty fond of it, honestly."

Perhaps that's why I became so enamored of Daisy so quickly. Normally, I don't take a weighted interest in anyone's life but my own.

Daisy nods, her eyes watching me closely for a long moment before moving on almost suddenly.

"What's down this way?" she asks with a small jerk of her head toward the hallway.

I raise my eyebrows, and she laughs, adding, "Right. Only one way to find out with Mr. Mysterious."

She walks to the end of the hallway, peeking in briefly to a linen closet and a half bathroom on the way, and then opens the door—after a nod of permission from me—to my bedroom.

The gray brick on the opposite wall stands out in the light from the windows, and the industrial shelving on one side of it boasts its emptiness.

"There's nothing on those shelves," Daisy points out immediately, making me laugh.

"I know."

She shakes her head and then startles, her head jerking toward me. "Is that it?"

"What do you mean? To the apartment?"

"Yes. To the apartment. That's it?"

I shrug. "Yeah."

"There's…there's only one bedroom in this apartment?"

I raise my eyebrows, and she immediately shakes her head. A long-winded babble is coming, I can feel it.

"How is that possible? H-how? I googled your building, and this building doesn't look like the kind of building that has apartments with only one bedroom in it."

"I didn't know that was discernible from the outside."

"Well, it's not! Obviously! Because here I am in a building that shouldn't have any one-bedroom apartments, in a one-bedroom apartment. Your house in Vegas has multiple bedrooms, Flynn. Why doesn't this have multiple bedrooms?"

"Because this isn't Vegas. This is New York. And I've only ever been able to sleep in one bed at a time."

"You're not funny right now. This isn't funny. Where am I supposed to sleep?"

I glance to the bed and back at her, and her eyes spin like flying UFOs. "In the bed with you? *Every night?*"

"Only the nights you want to be in a bed."

"This isn't funny, Flynn!"

"Listen, Dais, it is what it is. It's not a big deal. It's not like we haven't slept in a bed together before."

"We didn't *sleep* in that bed at all, Flynn."

No, we definitely didn't sleep, and it was fucking glorious.

I grin, and she practically chokes on her own saliva.

"Come on," I tell her, leaving the room. "Let's go. You can worry about the bed later."

"What? Go? Where are we going?"

I don't answer. No. I don't *dare* answer.

TWENTY-THREE

Daisy

Flynn pulls to a stop in front of a gorgeous Uptown brownstone that makes me believe in the movie version of New York. The trees are large and mature, and the street is calm. I can practically picture Tom Hanks asking Meg Ryan what would have happened with them if they hadn't been enemies from the start.

I don't know why we're here, though, and the anticipation has me on edge. *Does Flynn have another house here? Perhaps with more than one bedroom?*

I nearly laugh aloud at myself, but Flynn opening my door and holding out a hand to help me climb out of his Range Rover seems to startle it right out of me.

"Where are we?"

He doesn't answer, instead guiding me across the sidewalk and up the steps to ring the doorbell. You *don't* ring the doorbell at your own house. "Uh…" I look around in confusion. "Are we at someone's house?"

"Yeah," he answers matter-of-factly. "My sister Winnie's."

"What?!" I question, but he's already added knocking to his arrival alert system, apparently unsatisfied with the speed of response from the bell. "Flynn. This is your family's house?"

He nods, completely at ease with the insane situation. "It's family dinner night."

"Are you kidding me?" I retort as quietly as I can, but it's hard to have volume control when your heart is pounding in your damn ears. "You didn't think I needed time to prepare? I barely know you. You barely know me! I mean, what are we even going to tell them? What if they ask—"

"Shoot!" Flynn says suddenly, tapping me on the back and turning around. "I forgot the cookies in the car. Be right back."

I swing my hips hard and lunge for his wrist as he retreats, but it's too late. He's down the steps and passing the couple of spots to the car and walking around to the trunk in no time.

The front door swings open, and my nervous jaw clamps closed like a Venus flytrap.

"Uh, hey," an attractive, dark-haired man I've never seen before says, looking around me curiously. "Can I help you?"

Everything inside me tries to speak, but I'm, for all intents and purposes, mute for the foreseeable future. My throat feels thick and my vocal cords paralyzed. I don't know what to say, so I hope Flynn hurries the fuck up or something.

The door swings open behind the now narrow-eyed man with a little puff of spring wind, revealing another man I actually know, walking down the hallway toward us.

The five-hundred-dollar casino chip gifter. Flynn's brother Ty.

When my eyes lock on him with what must be recognition, the man at the door turns toward him and groans loudly. "Oh. She's with you. I should have fucking known."

Without another word or even a hello, the man retreats back down the hallway, smacking Ty on the shoulder as he goes. Ty approaches the door and me, his eyebrows drawn together curiously.

With a long look up and down my body and face, he finally shrugs. "Well, you certainly *are* my type. Did I ask you to come here tonight?"

"No," I manage to murmur with a shake of my head. *God, apparently, he was so drunk that day, he doesn't even remember me.* "I'm—"

But he already has me by the elbow and pulls me inside. "Come on. Let's head to the kitchen and get a drink. We're about to start dinner soon."

I twist frantically to look over my shoulder, searching for Flynn with wild eyes as the door closes behind me.

Oh my God. How did you manage this one, Daisy? Not only have you entrapped one Winslow into marrying you for a green card, now you've got another brother thinking he's dating you?!

Before I know it, we're standing in the center of a bustling kitchen, and there are people pretty much everywhere. Loud chatter, laughter, and the sounds and smells of dinner being made overwhelm my senses.

"Well, dang!" Another attractive guy with light-brown hair and blazing blue eyes I recognize as another one of Flynn's brothers shouts at the top of his lungs. "I thought that was gonna be Flynn at the door. For once, I can actually attend family dinner because we're not working around Winnie's schedule and doing it on nights I'm at work. I'm ready to enjoy this feast!"

"Stop whining, Jude," a beautiful—almost ethereally, really—trim brunette with smoldering green eyes tells him. "You know Flynn will be here any minute. He's reliable."

Ty laughs beside me, and a whole new wave of panic renews as he wraps an arm around my shoulders. "Unlike the rest of us, right, Sophie?"

She shrugs. "You said it. Not me."

Instantly, it feels as if everyone's head turns in our direction, and I almost choke on the saliva in my throat from the pressure of it all.

What are they going to ask me? Who do I tell them I even am? How in the fuck am I going to explain this little moment when Flynn finally comes inside?

They're going to think I'm a tart, for cripes' sake.

But the stares are temporary, and to my surprise, everyone is back to their own conversations and tasks. No questions. No insults. No recognition, really, whatsoever.

If anything, his family notices my presence, and then…moves right the fuck on.

What the heck?

"Come on, everyone! Food is ready!" an older woman I think might be Flynn's mom calls out. "Time to eat!"

I watch as a few women begin to carry platters of food into the dining room, chatting happily with one another as they go, and I'm torn between asking if they need help or burrowing into the nice hardwood floors of the house.

Overall, the current sentiment makes me feel as if I've either turned invisible and I don't know it, or they couldn't care less who I am.

Ty puts his hand to my lower back, thankfully not in a creepy way, and leads me into the dining room. Flynn is still nowhere to be seen, and I'm starting to get really close to bolting. *I mean, I'm a fake wife. If I leave burning rubber on their floors on my way out the door, it'll only be really weird for another three months or so, right?*

Ty pulls out a chair for me, and without much of a choice other than the Road Runner scenario, I take a seat in it. Flynn's voice finally—thank God—breaks through the chaos, and I bob and weave my head like a fucking emu to get a look at where he is.

Person after person stops him for a greeting on his way down the hall, giving hugs and backslaps and big, huge smiles that they in *no way* gave me. I'm an intruder in their lives, and I feel terrible for showing up unannounced.

When Flynn finally gets to the mouth of the dining room, I lasso his gaze with the frantic panic of my own and wait for him to figure out what to do. He gives me a kind smile as Ty takes the seat next to me, and I want to murder him for it.

This is not funny, Flynn Winslow. I'm on the edge of a cliff here!

Evidently recognizing the severity of my anxiety, Flynn wastes no more time stepping into the dining room, approaching Ty at the table, and tapping him soundly on the shoulder. Ty looks up at him curiously.

"You mind moving so I can sit beside my wife?" Flynn says without preamble, making me nearly choke on my tongue. And I'm not the only one floored by the simple statement—the entire room brimming with people comes to a *screeching* stop.

Did he just… Did he just introduce me as his wife?

I don't miss the way the attention of the room has now come right back to me, and this time, it is *different*. No apathetic glances here. Nope.

Holy shit. Either this is really intense, or my face is on actual fire.

"I'm sorry," a blonde with blue eyes and a friendly face says, the first to speak. "Did you just say *wife?*"

Only moments later, Ty turns to me. "You're here with *Flynn?*"

I nod. "I-I… Well, I tried to…um…say something, but—" My voice shakes, and my bones vibrate all the way inside me. Flynn notices and puts a calming, steady hand to my shoulder, effectively shutting me up.

"Ty, it's your own fault that the whole family, including *you*, automatically assumes any new woman at family dinner is here with you."

"That's because he's a manwhore."

"Jude!" the woman who I'm now positive is Flynn's mom snaps. "Language! There are little ears at the table!"

Those little ears are an adorable blond-haired girl who just shrugs and giggles. "Uncle Jude says stuff like that all the time, Grandma."

"Because I'm a genius, right, Lex? Statistically, only geniuses use swear words." Jude winks at the little girl, completely ignoring his mom's scolding, but an older man on the other side of the huge table and his female companion start to snicker.

"You know you've got problems when you don't even know which woman at the family function is yours. Now, Ty, please remember, this woman right here is your aunt Paula. My wife."

"It's not funny, Uncle Brad." Ty groans, and the whole room erupts in rabid laughter.

"Oh, yes. Yes, it is," the man who opened the door for me earlier says. "And this is my house, so even if it weren't, I can laugh if I want to."

Immediately, the room dissolves into utter chaos. People yelling and shouting and shoving at one another while Flynn's head bounces back and forth at a million questions coming from different directions.

I watch him closely as he shakes his head, puts his fingers into his mouth, and lets loose with a whistle that will probably wake up the dogs in Brooklyn.

"Everyone, shut up so we can get this over with. Yes, I'm married. And this gorgeous woman right here is my wife, Daisy," Flynn says, and my jaw hits the top of my pencil skirt. *Does he…does he actually think that's going to calm them down?*

I blink so many times I almost give myself motion sickness, but I'm immediately startled back into equilibrium when the room erupts into chaos *again,* and the entire room of people starts shouting at the same time.

Flynn throws his hands up in the air and shoves Ty out of the chair next to me to fill it while I try to pick out anything I can through the bedlam.

"Mom, am I having a stroke?"

"Your wife?!"

"You're married?! How? How is that possible?!"

"What the fuck, Flynn?"

Yeah, my thoughts exactly—*What. The. Fuck?*

I search Flynn's eyes for signs of, you know, an aneurysm or something that would explain his complete mental breakdown, but shockingly, I don't find any. He looks normal.

I turn back to the table and swallow hard. There's less shouting, and it seems, the women may have gotten the room organized because it's quieted back to silence. Unfortunately, all eyes, just as before, are on me.

"Winnie," Flynn cautions softly as the friendly looking blonde goes to open her mouth again, and she shakes her head at him and points a finger.

"Be quiet, Flynn."

I swallow hard as her eyes come back to me, assessing me closely. I fidget a little, but by and large, I'm just glad I don't vomit all over the table of food.

Her face melts into a smile, and the breath I didn't know I was holding spreads out all over the room. She sticks out a hand, and I stand up to take it gently.

"I'm Winnie. Flynn's sister," she introduces and begins to point at everyone around the table. "This is my mom Wendy, my uncle Brad and aunt Paula, our eldest brother Remy, Jude and his fiancée Sophie, and my husband Wes and daughter Lexi."

"I don't get an introduction?" Ty grumbles, earning a shush from Winnie. Everyone else waves. I smile awkwardly, waving back.

"It's so nice to meet you. I'm incredibly sorry for our rudeness earlier, but that was Ty's fault," Winnie continues.

"Yeah, yeah, let's shit on Ty all night long."

Remy punches Ty in the shoulder, effectively shutting him up and giving me a chance to respond.

"Thanks. It's really nice to meet all of you, too. And I don't blame you for the confusion…it was confusing."

Ha-ha-ha. God. Someone help me.

"Well," Winnie replies, looking around the room and meeting everyone's eyes in a way I can tell means something. "We'll get the details later. For now, I want to say welcome to the family. And I'm sure," she adds, eyeing everyone closely again, "everyone at this table feels the same way."

"Of course, of course," Uncle Brad says with a nod and a raise of his glass. "Welcome to the family, Daisy!"

The whole room joins in, and their unexpected kindness causes my heart to flip-flop in my chest.

Flynn's hand moves to my thigh underneath the table to give it a squeeze, and when I meet his gaze, he offers a reassuring smile.

What in the world have I gotten myself into?

TWENTY-FOUR

Flynn

Daisy was silent the entire ride home from my sister's house and locked herself in the bathroom as soon as we got back to "get ready for bed." It's pretty obvious that she feels I blindsided her by taking her to my family dinner without warning, but while it might seem a bit cruel to an outsider, I still think I did the right thing.

Daisy has shown time and time again that once she gets locked inside her head, it's nearly impossible to get her out. Her panic takes her in an endless circle of indecision, and I didn't have the time to both tell her the news of tonight's family dinner and fuck the anxiety out of her before we got to my sister's. We were running late as it was.

Still, I'm aware I'm going to have to deal with the repercussions of my decisions, and I'm ready for it.

I open the group text message with my siblings to kill a little time while I wait for Daisy to get ready to face me, and fucking hell, it's busy. If I didn't have it on Do Not Disturb, my phone would be on its way to being diagnosed epileptic.

Remy: We're going to fucking discuss this later, Flynn Winslow. Seems to me now that our lunch conversation should have been expanded a little bit.

Jude: Dude, I cannot believe you're married before me, you fucker. I didn't even know we were racing, or I would have tried harder.

Winnie: How did you meet? What was your first date like? Was it love at first sight?

Ty: Does no one even care that Flynn fucking scooped a woman right out from under my nose?

Remy: She was never really with you. He was married to her before family dinner, you dumbass. Plus, the bastard even told me he was married at lunch last week.

Winnie: WHAT? YOU KNEW?

Remy: Relax. I only sort of knew. I didn't exactly believe him.

Jude: You didn't believe Flynn, dude? He's the only one of us who doesn't lie.

Remy: I remember that now. Obviously.

Ty: She really looks like a woman who'd be my type, though. Like, I feel as if I know her.

Jude: DUDE. Shut up. This really isn't about you.

Winnie: Seriously, Ty. I want answers from Flynn. Not to hear you whine.

Ty: Wow. Brutal, sis. Brutal.

The door to the bathroom finally cracks open, and I immediately click the button to lock my screen and set my phone down on the kitchen counter.

She's walking on eggshells, but not because she's afraid she's going to upset me. No. She's a woman at the very end of her rope, trying not to explode all over everything.

As far as I'm concerned, though, the sooner the big boom happens, the sooner I can start putting the pieces back together.

"Go ahead," I prompt. "Let it rip. I know you want to."

"God, Flynn!" She tosses up her hands and stomps the rest of the way into the kitchen. "This is just a lot, you know? First, I arrive after traveling across the country a week after giving my boss a practical ultimatum, almost die on the luggage carousel, and then, I find out there's only one bedroom! And after that, we go straight to your sister's house without any warning from you, and everyone thinks I'm there with your brother because you left me to fend for myself! And everyone was staring at me and looking for answers that I don't have to give them! Because this marriage is a pact marriage, and I don't actually know all that much about you!"

I nod, and she takes a deep breath, gearing up to go again.

"And your sister! She's so freaking nice and kind, and after she knew that I was with you and not your brother Ty, she was so welcoming and interested in me and jumping to include me. I'm having lunch! With her and Sophie! Next week! Did you know that?"

I shake my head because, no, I didn't know that.

"I am! Because they were so sweet and I couldn't say no, and so now I'm having lunches with your sister like it's a thing! Like we're a real thing! *Oh!* And Sophie! She was so excited that she asked me to be a bridesmaid in her and your brother's wedding! A bridesmaid, Flynn, in your brother's freaking wedding!"

I raise my eyebrows.

"And I wasn't prepared for any of it! Because you didn't think it was important to tell me that we were going to your family dinner tonight! I don't know what to do with that." She inhales a deep breath, and I'm not surprised when she keeps going. "I mean, we probably should've at least worn our damn wedding rings! Your sister kept asking me, and I had to come up with a random excuse about them being fitted at the jeweler! When she asked me which jeweler, I pretended to have a coughing attack and told her I have a history of asthma—which I don't! But I do have a growing web of lies with your family!"

"What would be different if you'd known ahead of time?" I interject, and her chin jerks back.

"What?"

"Would you not be going to lunch with Winnie and Sophie?"

Her eyes narrow.

"Or Sophie and Jude's wedding? Would you have said no to being in it if you'd prepared ahead of time?"

"No, Flynn, that would be *rude*. But that's not the point—"

"It is the point, Dais. None of the results would have changed, but the amount of stress you'd have felt leading up to it would have been exponentially higher. You have a tendency to freak out a little."

"I don't freak out *that* much."

"Daisy."

She huffs. "Okay. So, I freak out. But the decision to freak out or not should be mine and mine alone. I'm Julia Roberts, dammit, and I say who, I say when, I say *how much*!"

I stalk toward her with quick, deliberate strides, and she tilts her chin back dramatically to keep her eyes on me during my approach.

Her breathing quickens as I put my hands to her jaw and tip her head back even more, running the pad of my thumb over her plump pink bottom lip.

"You're right. I'm sorry."

"I am? You are?"

I nod. "Even though I was trying to protect you from feeling anxiety I didn't think you should have to feel, I should've given you a heads-up."

"Okay," she breathes out through a whisper.

"Okay, you accept my apology?"

"Yes, I accept."

"Good." I waggle my eyebrows. "Now it's time to relax."

"Time to relax?"

I nod briefly and then seal my lips to hers. She gasps, and I immediately slip my tongue into her mouth.

She tastes minty and fresh from brushing her teeth, and the smell of her hair when I'm this close envelops me like a cloud of fog. The urge to recreate our first night together and lift her onto the kitchen counter to eat her out is strong, but the need to normalize her first night in our bed is even stronger.

Hands to her ass, I lift her up until her legs wrap around my hips and her arms around my shoulders, and I turn to head down the hallway to the bedroom with her in my arms.

She's light and easy to carry, but the things she's doing with her tongue inside my mouth are a little bit more of a distraction. We bump into the wall once or twice but eventually make it to my room. Her back hits the soft material of my black comforter, and moonlight filters in through the window, illuminating the features of her face and the gloriousness of her curls spread out above her head.

Fuck, she really is beautiful.

One day soon, I need to see those lips around my cock. But not tonight. Tonight, I need to be inside her. She needs to feel me inside her—so goddamn deep she won't even know she's in a bed, let alone my own, when we're done.

I pull her pajama shorts down the length of her legs, taking her pretty pink panties with them, and then scoot her up onto the bed until her shoulders touch the pillows.

"Hold on to the headboard," I instruct, taking her hands in mine and placing them where I want, rather than waiting for her to process the order and carry it out herself. "I'm going to fuck you hard tonight."

She needs it, I know, and if I'm completely honest, so do I. Seeing Ty's hands on her so casually felt…not good. I didn't like it, and as much as I can't exactly explain why that is, I'm ready and willing to do what I need to make myself feel better about it.

And fucking Daisy until neither of us can breathe sure seems like it'll make me feel better.

Stroking two fingers through her center, I find Daisy wet and ready enough for me that neither of us has to wait any longer.

"Keep your legs open," I tell her. "I want you as deep as I can go."

Eyes wide, she nods and complies, spreading her thighs apart to make room for my hips to fall in between. She feels like heaven against me, and my already hard cock jerks in anticipation.

With only a little maneuvering, I slide inside with ease, going slowly to give her time to adapt. I push past the limit, until the hilt of me is beyond the entrance of her, and she kicks her head back in response. Her eyes close, her fingertips curl into the comforter below, and her mouth rounds in pleasure.

That's it. "That's a good girl."

Out and in again, I score a path for my thrusts while upping the tempo with each one. She pants slightly, the jolt combined with the relentless stroke at her most sensitive nerves making it hard to keep enough air in her lungs.

"Oh. My. God," she forces out, her words a staccato to match my hips.

"Yeah," I agree with her, moving my hands to go over the top of hers on the headboard. "Your pussy is gonna remember me tomorrow."

"Uh-huh," she agrees.

"My cock is going to remember you too," I admit then.

Truth is, I'm starting to think certain parts of me might never forget Daisy.

TWENTY-FIVE

Daisy

After I lost my shit on Flynn about blindsiding me with his family dinner, he apologized and proceeded to wring my body dry with crazy, hot sex and an intense orgasm that still has my legs feeling weak.

Personally, I'm more than okay with that sequence of events. Even if half of them threw me for one hell of a loop.

Although, it's a bit of a dangerous game. I mean, if every time I get mad at Flynn he gifts me with an actual apology and an orgasm, I might be tempted to start making up reasons to be mad at him.

Not to mention, I'm finding that during and after sex, Flynn is far more talkative and freer with his words. Which is how I managed to get him engaging in a round of pillow talk with me in the darkness of his bedroom.

"So, that's Ty's thing?" I question with a raise of my eyebrow. "He just brings random women to family events?"

"Pretty much." Flynn smirks. "And it's never the same woman twice."

His brother Ty is quite the character. I mean, he just went along with the possibility that I was there as his date even though he didn't even recognize me.

"What about your dad? Why wasn't he at family dinner?"

"My dad left when we were kids," Flynn whispers in answer to my question about the patriarch's absence from the gathering. He strokes his fingers softly over the small of my back while I lie naked on my belly, my head turned on its side to face him on my pillow.

"I'm sorry," I murmur back.

"I'm not," Flynn declares easily, his position mimicking mine and his voice quiet. "He left five rowdy kids to be raised alone by a sweet woman who didn't deserve abandonment. I don't need a dick for a dad just to say I have one. I have Uncle Brad and Aunt Paula and my mom and my brothers and sister, and that's all I need."

I want desperately to add that he has me too, that I'm in his corner and always will be, but the truth is, I don't really know. We're an arranged marriage, designed and executed for the sole purpose of maintaining my residence in the country. But the night in Vegas and tonight—and the phone sex too—it's all crossed a line into territory that I can't quite explain.

There's passion and intimacy and interest there—I can *feel* it between us—but as far as I can tell, that's as far as any intentions go for Flynn. No matter our easy companionship or the explosive chemistry we have in the bedroom, when the clock strikes midnight on my immigration crisis, Cinderella will go back to LA again and the prince will move on with his life.

"I don't have a dad either. Or a mom, for that matter. I grew up in the foster system in Canada." Flynn's fingers never stop moving on my back, but somehow it seems like the pressure of his touch changes or something. "I do have Gwen—she took me in when I was a teenager, but she's not really a mother figure per se. She's more of a slightly mature girlfriend." I shrug into the soft linens of his—well, *our*—bed. "Nevertheless, I'm thankful for her. I don't know where I'd be if she hadn't made sure I got a chance to start adulthood on my feet."

I chuckle a little as I realize how much Gwen and Flynn have in common. "And thanks to you, I don't have a bashed-up face from my epic adulthood stumble."

Flynn doesn't say anything, as usual—though, he *has* been uncharacteristically open tonight—instead tucking a piece of my loose hair behind my ear.

My eyes feel suddenly heavy, the weight of the move and the dinner and the one-bed situation leaving me in a potent exhale. I blink against the lure of sleep, eager to hear more soft secrets from my fake husband, but the pull is too strong.

I'm no match for the solace of sleep, and the next thing I know, the only thing I see is the black backs of my eyelids.

TWENTY-SIX

Tuesday, April 23rd

Daisy

My toes curl and my calves tighten as I stretch my arms to the ceiling and blink through the soft morning sunlight cutting through the windows and across my comforter-covered body. I roll over immediately to stretch myself in the cat cow position, and it's only when I'm done that I realize where I am—which is *not* in my LA apartment.

My groggy eyes transition quickly to alert, and I sit up in the bed, pulling the comforter up over my bare chest as I go. The room is pretty self-explanatory in its emptiness, but that doesn't stop me from surveying the walls as though Flynn's going to pop out of a secret Batcave behind one of them at any moment.

His empty shelves stick out like an ugly thumb, and I wonder if he's even considered filling them with some very manly décor. Nothing fancy, just, like, a plant or two and some heavy black stoneware and maybe, like, one gold accent.

I rub at my lips with my pointer finger and my thumb as I flip through the rolodex of New York vendors in my head who I know have that kind of stuff on hand. I'm only a shelf and a half into my design plan when I shake myself awake from la-la land with a scrub of my face and a shimmy.

"Stop it, Daisy. The man doesn't need you and your design aesthetic throwing up all over his loft."

With an internal scoff, I push the comforter off with a toss, pausing slightly when the gust of wind from my brusque motion sends a tiny piece of notebook paper flying off the bed and onto the floor.

I hop down and scoop it up quickly, and then I read through the short-stroked, manly scroll.

Daisy-

At work.

-Flynn

Oh. Well. I mean, I guess that makes sense. Of course he has work. His life didn't stop just because I got here.

Even if your own issues mean you're a little disappointed that it didn't…

Moving on from the bed to the closet where one of my suitcases lies open for its unpacking, I dig through recklessly and toss on the first pair of sweatpants and T-shirt I come to. I have a lot of my life to get organized today so that I can be ready to focus on work when I start tomorrow, but I need coffee first.

I pad my way down the hallway on careful feet, just in case Flynn's note about going to work was a recent deposit and he hasn't actually had time to leave, and peek into the main living area of the apartment with a crane of my neck that rivals several safari animals, even with their far more accommodating physiology.

It doesn't take but a moment to ascertain that this space, too, is empty. My lips purse and my shoulders settle as my body takes a beat to adjust. Walking normally then, I make my way behind the sofa and around into the kitchen to the coffeepot in the corner. The coffee itself, sugar, and mugs are all in the cabinet directly above, making my ability to set up the pot and switch it to brew swift and painless. For that, I'm thankful.

The pot spits and gurgles as it works to produce my precious nectar, and I take that time to snoop a little bit more. Dishes are in the cabinet two down from the stove, spices in the one directly to the left. The counters are pretty devoid of things, both in decoration and functionality, and I make a mental note to see if he's got a toaster somewhere.

I'm not high-maintenance, but some peanut butter toast on my way out the door to work in the morning wouldn't go amiss.

During my scan, I notice my purse sitting on the corner of the island counter and walk immediately to it to dig through its contents and sort them. My phone, which I know is still inside, will need to be charged, and the shiny key I'm guessing Flynn left for me sitting next to my bag needs to be secured on my key ring.

My stomach flutters as I slip the gold metal through the split in my silver ring, and I press myself into the counter in an attempt to stop it. *My oh my, how strange this normally huge milestone feels.*

The move in. The next step. The declaration of intentions. Normally, that's what the exchange of keys or codes or any general method for making yourself at home in someone else's residence would mean, but not for us. For us, it's a requirement in our charade with USCIS, and for Flynn, I'm sure a necessity so that he doesn't have to babysit me twenty-four seven.

I've just pushed the key past the final millimeter of the split, securing it in place with the rest of my own when my phone starts to ring wildly on the counter, my volume set quite apparently to the max.

"Jesus," I groan, swiping quickly without looking at the screen to stop the nearly violent playing of Gwen Stefani's "Don't Speak." Evidently, a couple of months ago, I found the idea of making a song with that name my ringtone ironic. Right now, in the midst of my emotional confusion, it's just obnoxious.

"Hello?"

"Daisy, doll! I'm officially back on dry land!" Gwen declares excitedly. "Ready to hear all about my favorite girl and her exciting life in the States!"

Oh shittt. What am I going to tell Gwen about all this?

With her gone on the cruise for the last two weeks, I haven't even thought about how I might explain the fact that I'm married to a man I barely know in order to keep my *exciting life in the States*.

Gwen's an open-minded, fluid person, but I'm pretty sure if her pseudodaughter told her she climbed on the back of the bike of a man she didn't know and expected herself to come out alive, she'd kind of object. If that pseudodaughter then told her she went on to marry him, move all the way across the country, and lie to pretty much everyone she comes in contact with, I'm pretty sure she'd call the police.

Gah.

"Daisy? Are you there? These stupid cell thingies never get good reception."

Speak, for the love of everything. Say something.

"Sorry, Gwen. I'm here. I was just… Yeah, you were breaking up. How was the discount cruise? Was it the dollar store version of Alaska or the real one?"

Gwen laughs. "I guess I don't know for certain, as Kammie didn't want to get off the boat, but the pictures I have *look* real."

I'm not surprised by this info. Kammie is the one broad in their girl group who always manages to put a snag in the plans.

"Okay, but I'll have to see the evidence to believe you."

"Of course, darling, I wouldn't have it any other way."

"Why wouldn't Kammie get off the boat?"

"Something about her facelift scars showing in the reflection of the snow."

"Right. Of course. I mean, what else would it be, right?"

Gwen's laugh rolls like a soft melody, the ease of our normal conversations obviously—thankfully—conveying on her end. For my part, I'm so freaking nervous I could wet myself if I uncrossed my legs.

"What about you, my little flower? How's work? And Damien?"

It might seem a little strange on the surface for Gwen to be asking about Damien, but the truth is, I started blurring the boss, employee, childhood guardian line a while ago. I've included them in the details of each other's lives and forced them together more than a few times. Hell, not even a month ago, I forced Damien to sit on a FaceTime call with Gwen while she taught me—*and* Damien, because I dragged him into it—how to paint lilies like it was some kind of virtual chat with Bob Ross.

"Work is good. Damien is still Damien. A powerhouse in Prada with no time for anyone's shit." I take a deep breath and pause to gather myself for the best truth I can come up with—the half-truth. "I'm actually in New York."

"New York? Oh, that's exciting! For the day or for the week?"

"For three months, actually."

"What? Three *months*?"

"Yep. Dame had some special projects over here he wanted me to be involved in," I lie, closing my eyes against the overwhelming wave of guilt nausea. *Lie, lie, lie.*

"Wow! That's pretty incredible, but three months is a long hotel stay. Even hopeless wanderers like me need little touches of home every now and then. Is he flying you home on any of the weekends?"

I nearly draw blood from my tongue, working to keep myself from freaking out and spilling all the beans all over this phone conversation. "No, no trips home. But I'm… Well, I'm in an apartment not a hotel, so it's not so bad."

"Damien has a company property, I guess? No way you managed a three-month lease somewhere."

"Mm-hmm. Something like that. I'm not really sure of the details."

I roll my eyes into my head and suck my lips into my mouth. *Gah*. I have to get off the phone. I can't take much more of this.

"Well, that's great, love. I hope you have the best time. Oh, and don't forget to give yourself some time away from work. Living somewhere on assignment like that, it's so easy to grind yourself into the ground twenty-four hours a day. Treat yourself sometimes, okay?"

"Okay, Gwen. I'll try."

"Kisses, sweetie. My cab's here to take me to the airport in Seattle. Let's chat again soon."

"Okay. Safe travels."

"Thanks, darling. Bye!"

"Bye," I wheeze, hanging up the phone with absolutely the last vestige of control I have left and dropping it to the counter. I immediately double over and grab my stomach, the cramps of discomfort from deceit wreaking havoc.

That was hard, I reason, *but it was also for the best.* Ultimately, this whole charade with Flynn is short-term. It's going to come to an end, and if I'd told Gwen about it now, I'd have to explain why we were breaking up then. Because it is going to end—*even if it didn't seem so much like it was going to last night*—and this will just be a blip in my history.

Gwen didn't need to know. Now, though…I need a distraction. I glance over to the yellow pillows on Flynn's beautiful leather couch, and an idea strikes me.

I won't do much, I swear. Just enough to calm my nerves.

Yeah, that's the ticket.

My hands shake slightly as I trim the last of the flower stems from the bouquet I got from the street vendor downstairs. They're bright Gerbera daisies, reminiscent of the ones from our wedding with Marilyn, and it's only now, in the light of Flynn's nearly fucking renovated apartment—*good going, Daisy*—that it occurs to me what a poor choice they might be.

Cripes, what in the world is Flynn going to think about all this?

His couch and chairs are rearranged atop a new rug, he's got new, tight black velvet barstools—one of which I'm sitting on—and cream-colored kiln-fired stoneware in the center of his island, and the regular non-Batcave entrance shelves in his bedroom are no longer empty. I also, kind of, maybe, changed out the hardware on both his kitchen and bathroom cabinets to a soft brushed brass that really livens up the masculinity of it all and added a throw blanket to the back of his leather couch so you can sit on it in shorts without getting cold.

I've never seen Flynn flip out, but I'm pretty sure if there were going to be a time, coming home to a completely rearranged apartment by his temporary, not-for-real wife would do it.

What was I thinking?!

The sound of Flynn's keys in the door lock startles me into motion, and I jump up from my spot, scooping up the scrap of newspaper with the flower trimmings into my arms and speed walk it over to the trash. I push the matte black vase with the daisies to the center of the counter and back toward the windows frantically, only stopping when the flesh of my palms touches glass.

This way, if things get really bad, I can just heave myself backward and hope that the force of my body is enough to make the double panes shatter.

Maybe plummeting to my death from the fifteenth floor is a little dramatic, but that's where my mind goes in an emotional emergency of this caliber.

The door finally creaks open what feels like several light-years later, and as expected, Flynn takes one quick gander at the apartment and freezes dead in his tracks.

Oh crap, oh God.

"I can put it all back!" I blurt suddenly, my muscles stretching and tightening into little iron rods.

Flynn glances from me to the apartment again, scanning the space closely, and then…well, he shrugs.

I nearly explode. "A shrug?! A *shrug?* That's all you have to say?!"

He shakes his head at me, sighs, and steps forward to lean his formidable weight into his strong, tanned hands on the island. *It's a motherfucking hot position, I'm not gonna lie.*

"My great-great-aunt's painting is still there." He shrugs *again.* "I don't give a shit about the rest of it."

"Y-you don't?"

He gives me one small shake of his head. "Looks nice. And the leather on the couch is cold. Blanket'll probably be good."

"I filled the shelves in the bedroom too," I admit quickly. "I may have gone a little overboard on the plants."

He lifts a hand and gently flicks the brightest orange daisy in the vase in front of him. "More flowers like the ones from the wedding?"

My breath catches in my throat and makes it hard to swallow. *He remembers.* "No. Just greenery."

He lifts his shoulders a final time and, if I'm not mistaken, even grins a little. My heart flips over inside my chest. "I'm sure it looks good." He turns to the drawer behind him and comes back with a stack of paper menus, tossing them to the counter in front of himself. "How about I order some takeout? Clearly, we've both been busy today."

"Yeah," I agree. "Takeout sounds good."

To be completely honest, life with Flynn altogether is starting to sound a little too appealing.

TWENTY-SEVEN

Tuesday, April 30th

Daisy

"Where are we on the Santa Monica property?" Thomas Grey asks the speaker in the center of the conference table. His demanding voice is a routine staple of our company start-the-week-right phone calls—which, yes, do occasionally occur on Tuesdays if Monday is too busy, and no, the irony isn't lost on me—but I'm usually on the other end of them, making big, dramatic eyes at Damien while he pantomimes his jokes.

I'll admit, sitting next to serious Thomas while my new East Coast coworker Tara Insley shoots eye lasers at me from across the table isn't quite the same good time.

"Daisy, what's your timeline on getting Frederick in there for listing photos?" Thomas asks me since I'm the one who did all the planning for the staging on the property before I left LA.

"About three days," I answer, even though I know Thomas doesn't like to get any answer other than one that would involve a time traveler. "The setup is there, but Frederick doesn't have any availability before that," I clarify with a gulp.

Thomas holds my eyes dangerously, and I hold my breath under his scrutiny. I mean, I know I'll have to take in some fresh air soon if I don't want to pass out, but if it takes him that long to tell me if three days is okay or not, I'd probably rather be unconscious anyway.

Luckily, though, he doesn't question my timeline, instead agreeing with a brusque nod before moving on and passing the pulpit to Damien to do his cross-checks. Tara's foot knocks into mine under the table—accidentally, I'm sure—and she smirks a fake apology.

I hope you nick your ankles to all hell the next time you shave, I hex in my head. It might seem a bit over the top to be mentally passing out hexes toward your coworker, but Tara Insley hasn't been anything but a passive-aggressive, evil shrew to me since I arrived in New York.

"Tom, what is your team's ETA for the Miami and Vegas properties that just came under contract?" Damien asks, switching the focus to the Grey team of EllisGrey. "I'd like to see us capitalize on the spring market and get those listed within the month."

A few agents from Thomas's team speak up, giving the rundown on where they're at in the process, and my brain begins to zone out when the legal side of real estate starts getting discussed.

It's not that I don't want to understand the legal side of things; it's just that I *can't understand* it. At all. You know? Just give me properties to use my interior design skills in, and I'm happy.

This is a perfect example of why, if I ever go out on my own and make Daisy Designs its own brand name, it will revolve solely around the design side of things. No contracts, no listings, just interior design for homeowners and staging work for real estate firms.

Ultimately, that *is* my big dream. To run my own company.

Which explains why my pride is somewhere down around my knees with this whole immigration thing. That big dream is far easier achieved in the United States than Canada. Don't get me wrong, I love Canada. Always have and always will. But the market in the States holds far more opportunity.

I *need* that green card like I need my next meal.

"Daisy," Thomas calls, grabbing my attention again and making me sit up straight.

"Yes?"

"You'll be working with Tara on Damien's new Greenwich Village property. Time is of the essence with getting it out there, so I need the two of you to pool all your connections to make it happen."

Of course. Why wouldn't I be assigned to direct teamwork with Cruella's spawn?

"You got it, Tom."

"Good. Then get out of here. You two don't need to hang out for the rest of the call. Just get started."

Tara and I both nod dutifully, pushing back in our chairs and climbing to our feet in the conference room. Tara rounds the table, and I hold open the glass door like we haven't spent the last week of work together solidifying our opposing positions in a lifelike game of *Mortal Kombat*.

Dirty looks, underhanded trick questions in front of Thomas, giving me wrong times and addresses for properties and vendor appointments, "accidentally" squishing my food in the back of the break room fridge, and telling the entire office she saw me drying my blouse under the hand dryer in the bathroom—thanks to an unfortunate coffee spillage event—because I apparently have some sort of glandular problem, are just the tip of the iceberg of her full-frontal assault, and this is only my fifth official day.

Now that we've been assigned to work together, I might have to invest in a bodyguard. My vote is, of course, for Kevin Costner, but I'm not sure he makes people who try to defraud the government a priority in his schedule.

I step outside the door behind Tara and follow her swaying hips down the hallway to her office. So far, she hasn't even acknowledged my presence.

She steps inside, rounds her desk, and takes a seat in her chair. I lean into the doorway, keeping the jamb in front of me as a shield of defense.

"Uh, hey, Tara?" I question, making her head pop up almost violently.

"What?"

"I thought maybe we should get a plan together—"

"I don't have time right now. I have a lunch engagement." Technically, so do I, with Winnie and Sophie, but I figured, given Thomas's urgency, I'd reschedule. "I'll email you the details I have from my vendors, and we can go from there."

Right. Okay, then. *I guess I'll go to lunch with Winnie and Sophie after all.*

I turn to leave, but Tara calls me back. "Oh, and Daisy?"

"Yes?"

"You have something in your teeth…" She points to her own mouth in example. "Right there."

What a bitch, waiting to tell me until the meeting was over, when we were in the conference room alone for five minutes before it started. I hope she gets on a local train on the way home instead of the express and hits every goddamn stop.

I sure hope lunch is filled with friendlier waters. I'm not sure how much more I can take today without going psycho Daisy Mae on someone's ass.

Bilbow Gardens is an adorably over-the-top restaurant with cascading florals all over the ceiling and walls, neon signs behind every booth, and pink dimpled leather on the seats. According to Winnie, her husband Wes knows the owner. And I'm thinking that's probably how she managed to get us a cozy booth in the back corner of the place, away from the hustle and bustle of the kitchen and lunchtime rush.

"So, Daisy, you have to tell us what Flynn is like as a husband," Sophie says through a big smile on her side of the booth. "I'm dying to know. I've spent a lot of time picturing Jude as a husband—my husband—you know, but it can't be at all what Flynn is like. Is he serious all the time? Does he wear socks to bed? I have to know!"

Winnie nods vigorously. "Oh my God, yes. I need to know too. I don't even know what Flynn is like as a brother, he's so freaking mysterious. Tell me all his secrets, please."

I shift in my seat, trying not to give away just exactly how nervous I am. Any new bride would be feeling the jitters as she sat down with her sister-in-law and another future one and tried to make it into the club, but just like with everything else, my situation is even more complicated. Because I'm not a rosy-eyed newlywed in love, and I don't know all that many secrets about Flynn—almost assuredly not any more than his own sister has learned about him in a lifetime.

Aside from the length and girth of his penis, which I'm guessing Winnie isn't all that interested in knowing, I really don't have a lot of value to add to this conversation.

Still, with a lick of my lips and a deep pull of air into my lungs, I give it my best shot. I agreed to this lunch with them, and they're really fun, nice people. I don't want to disappoint them almost as much as I don't want to disappoint Flynn. Plus, I could use the endorphins from the gossip if I'm going to go back to the land of Tara after this.

"Flynn is…" *Dirty, hot, sexy, good with his tongue…* "Surprisingly easygoing. He's never in a bad mood, and he doesn't get upset if I rearrange his stuff. He's a really laid-back kind of guy and somehow always seems to know how to quiet my tendency for anxiety and freaking out…" *…by fucking me until I can't see straight.*

Winnie's eyes dance, and Sophie leans forward onto her elbows. "And?"

"And…I actually haven't seen him use the bathroom yet. Like, I'm not sure he does," I say with a teasing grin, and Winnie's and Sophie's smiles turn to laughter. "I mean, his diet is, like, pretty clean and healthy. His breakfast usually looks like it's portioned out with the perfect amount of protein and carbs and fats like someone is going to take a picture of his plate and put it in a damn nutritional book. All the while, I'm shoving a bowl full of Lucky Charms down my throat. Honestly, he's the only person I know who actually does the whole "everything in moderation" thing, so maybe his body doesn't even produce any waste or anything. Frankly, I'm considering buying stock in the Febreze company because I use so much air freshener trying to pretend I don't have to go either. Just yesterday, I almost overdosed on the chemicals. Seriously, the cloud of mist in there rivaled the smog in Los Angeles."

Winnie snorts, and my smile grows right along with my confidence to continue my little newlywed stand-up routine.

"As for the socks in bed, I think all of his clothing just evaporates off him, especially at bedtime. One minute, he's dressed, and the next, he's not." I shrug, and Winnie groans her face into her hands.

"Oh God. I'm not sure whether to get excited that I'm related to a superhero or be disturbed by the vision of my brother's clothes evaporating into thin air."

"Be impressed," I say easily. "Your brother is *very* impressive."

Sophie dissolves into hysterics, and Winnie squeals. My cheeks are red and heated with embarrassment, but it's the *good* kind. The kind that makes my chest ache a little because it's not going to last.

"It must be genetic, then," Sophie says with a waggle of her brows and adds to Winnie's suffering so much that she lifts her hands to her ears and pretends to keel over.

"What's wrong, Winnie? Isn't Wes *impressive* too?" Sophie teases relentlessly.

"Oh God, you're terrible. Both of you."

I'm overcome with laughter, but Sophie keeps going for both of us. "Horny, Winnie. I think the word you're looking for is *horny*. Jude's on some ridiculous kick that we can only have sex every other day leading up to the wedding. Some kind of sacrifice to the Fortune-Teller Gods, he says. I'm dying here."

I suck my lips into my mouth and shift in my seat. Flynn and I haven't had sex since the night I got here, and Sophie's right—it's killing me. Hell, I think that's probably seventy-five percent of why I'm letting Tara Fuckface Insley get to me so much. I keep waiting for him to take charge and fuck the anxiety out of me, but no matter how many coy looks I've given, we still just climb into bed and go to sleep.

"Oh, sweet Jesus. The fortune-teller?" Winnie murmurs, putting her hand to her chest.

"What? You know something about it?"

Winnie nods and then shakes her head. "It's been…well…fifteen years or so? Before Remy's wedding, they all went to a fortune-teller, and she had all these things to say about the trajectory of all of their love lives."

"Remy's married?" I ask in confusion.

Winnie shakes her head. "No. It never happened. Charlotte…" She pauses and licks her lips. "It was a long time ago, and it was *bad*. She left him at the altar. I swear that's why all of my brothers have avoided commitment like the plague."

My throat tightens exponentially. "What'd the fortune-teller say about Flynn?"

Winnie waves me off. "Oh, I don't know. They've all been pretty tight-lipped about what she said, honestly, but I know Jude feels like she was right about him and Rem." Winnie glances up at my face, which I'm almost positive is as white as a sheet, and smiles sympathetically. "Oh, honey, don't worry. You and Flynn are together, and you're happy. Whatever that fortune-teller said, you've obviously got your lives figured out."

I force a smile, but inside, I feel sick. Flynn and I…we don't have anything figured out at all. And when Winnie and Sophie find out in two and a half months, they're going to hate my stupid, lying guts.

TWENTY-EIGHT

Flynn

I turn the page in my philosophy book, the sheets and comforter resting comfortably at my hips, and watch Daisy as she dances from one spot in the room to another, propping her toes up a little so she can rub lotion down the length of her pretty legs. She's got on a long black-floral satin robe that dusts the floor with every bend and obstructs most of my view, other than the tanned length of skin that runs from her calves to her toes.

"Lunch with your sister and Sophie was really great. They're both so fun and funny," she says, glancing at me over her shoulder.

"Mm," I hum, looking down at my book, but when she shucks the robe and bends over again, my eyes move right back to her. This time, there's nothing blocking my view of her sheer panties and thin white tank top. My cock twitches under the covers and starts to harden immediately.

She hasn't dressed like this for bed since she got here, and she can't seem to keep herself from adding to a rolling ramble, so it's not a secret that something is different, even if she thinks it is.

"I really needed that after the week I've had at work," she says, and her hands keep spreading that fucking lotion up and down her legs, her fingers lingering every so often, and her eyes keep looking toward me like she's trying to make sure I'm watching the show. "It's…good, you know? But it's a transition. It's not at all like working with my boss, Damien, in LA. He's kooky and spirited, and the people here are pretty serious, I guess."

I hum. "Mm-hm. Sounds like New York."

She laughs then, finally finishing with her lotion and heading toward the bed with slightly wild eyes. "It does, doesn't it? Pretty clichéd if you ask me, but I'll take what I can get. I mean, I'm so appreciative of everything you're doing, and I'd never dream of suggesting that this isn't the nicest opportunity anyone's ever given me. You don't owe me sympathy, you know? You've done a great job of welcoming me. Better than I expected, to be honest, and I just want you to know that—"

"Daisy," I interrupt, forcing her to take a breath. Any more words per second and I'm pretty sure she's going to spin off into the atmosphere like a cartoon rocket.

"Yes?"

"What's really going on here?"

"What do you mean?"

I raise my eyebrows and reach out to run a hand across her sheer panty-covered hip with one hand and tweak the peak of her very obvious nipple through the material of her top with the other. "Is this for me?"

"Is what for—"

"Daisy," I call, stopping her evasion before it starts.

"It's for you. I just…well, we haven't had sex since the night I got here, and I thought maybe—"

"I like it."

"You do?"

"Hard not to like anything that shows this much of your body, babe."

Her cheeks flush under the attention, but her nipples also harden noticeably. She likes when I'm direct, even if it embarrasses her at the same time.

"You want me to fuck you?"

She nods jerkily. "Yes."

"Okay," I agree easily, tossing my book onto my nightstand, grabbing her by the hips, and depositing her in the bed with a roll to put her beneath me. I palm her breast in my hand and suck her nipple into my mouth through the cotton of her tank top, and her head flies back immediately. I stop then, waiting for the haze to clear and her confused eyes to come back to mine. "The clothes are great, Dais, but if you ever want me to fuck you, all you have to do is ask."

"Flynn."

"It's not a chore. And it's not an obligation. Fucking you is fun," I disclose with a smile.

"It is?"

I scoot down suddenly, shoving the hem of her top up to expose the bare skin of her breasts and grin even bigger. "Oh yeah. In fact, I think I'm gonna fuck your tits tonight."

She looks almost disappointed, and I can't help it then. I laugh.

"Don't worry. I'm gonna fuck your perfect little cunt too."

Up and down, her chest heaves with the intensity of her excitement. I climb off her and the bed, shuck my boxer briefs to the floor and climb back astride her, my hard, angry cock bobbing above its waiting home between her breasts.

I thumb both nipples until she moans, and then I slip my dick between her lips to moisten it. She sucks ravenously, eager to get in as many licks as I'll let her before taking it back again.

Damn, she never disappoints.

"I see your mouth knows how to do a lot more than talk."

She hums around my girth and doubles her efforts under the praise. I pull back when a tingle in my spine threatens with my climax and scoot back down her body to position myself, ordering, "Wrap your tits around my cock."

She complies, grabbing a handful of breast in each hand and closing them around the slick length of my dick. The resulting picture is fucking amazing.

"Fuck, every part of you looks good wrapped around me."

Slow and steady, I start up a stroke between the flesh of her breasts while she plays with her nipples, her tongue spiking out to lick at her desperate lips.

"You want my cock back in your mouth, don't you, dirty girl?"

"Yes," she agrees with a cry, her beautiful, heavy tits bouncing with my every thrust.

"You wanna suck the come right out of me, don't you?"

"Yes," she breathes through a nod, frantic.

Fuck yeah, I want that too. I want to coat the back of her throat with my come and watch her swallow it, but I'll be damned if I'm going to spend myself in her throat when she went to this much effort to get me between her legs.

"Next time, baby."

"No, Flynn, now," she complains, and I shake my head.

"No. Right now, I'm going to fuck you with your ass in the air so I can spank the self-doubt right out of you."

"Flynn."

"You want sex, Daisy, you ask me for it, understood?"

"Yes, sir."

The way the word sir rolls off her tongue has the power to push my mind to dirty fucking things—things she's not ready for now but will be one day soon if I have anything to do with it.

"Good," I whisper, leaning forward to take her mouth with mine in a deep kiss. She moans into my mouth, which only enhances her gasp when I grab her by the hips, flip her over, and rip her sweet little sheer panties right off her body. "Now, get your ass up."

She does as she's told, sinking her chest into the mattress and straddling her knees until her ass and pussy are all I can see. She's so fucking perfect, I can't help but run my tongue over everything in sight.

This Daisy—my Daisy—tastes better than any fucking flower smells.

Thank fuck she's ready for me. I position and seat myself to the hilt in one aggressive stroke, making her cry out into the pillow beneath her head. Deeper and deeper, I push myself back into her on every downstroke, almost as though I can permanently attach myself if I try hard enough.

She meets my hips with her own, rearing back into me with fervor and zero inhibition, and I feel a twinge somewhere inside.

No woman has ever given herself over to me like she does—has submitted to the faith that I'm going to take care of her every need like Daisy is willing to do.

It turns me on and sets off all my alarms at the same time. Because the more I have of Daisy, the more I'm starting to wonder how I'm going to fill up all the empty space inside myself without her.

TWENTY-NINE

Monday, May 6th, New York

Daisy

I finish fluffing my curls, give myself one last look in the mirror, and then shut off the bathroom light to head for the kitchen. Flynn is still in there rooting around, getting ready for work. I can hear him, and the thought of seeing him after the things we did last night is both exciting and terrifying.

Ever since my seduction scene last Tuesday, Flynn's been working my body in ways I never knew were possible. Backways, sideways, pretzelways—I've officially been in every position known to man. And every time, just when I think we've done everything there is to do, it just gets hotter.

Last night, he ate me from behind with a vibrating plug in my ass. *My ass!* The door I always thought would swing only one way. The thing is, I don't even know how he convinced me—because he didn't have to. I just wanted it. Everything Flynn does feels good. Everything Flynn does takes me to a place of freedom from thought I didn't know existed. And he does it in a way that I don't even question it.

But the more nights I spend not questioning the things he's doing with my body, the more days I spend very much questioning just what in the hell it is we're doing here.

In a couple months, this whole charade is going to be over, and what? I'm just supposed to be ruined for all other men for the rest of my life?

I don't know. I don't *know* what Flynn's thinking or what his plans are when our time is up, and I don't know what he even does when he goes to work every day, and the absolute fuckton of mysteries are starting to wear on me.

Hell, I'm still wondering about that whole fortune-teller thing Winnie revealed at lunch a few weeks ago. Although I'm pretty sure the only reason I haven't asked him has more to do with fear and that I'll find out he's supposed to marry some six-foot blond, Swedish supermodel named Greta than anything else.

So far, I know he goes to the gym with his brother a few nights a week and that he gets private work calls well outside of his nine-to-five. And according to his sister Winnie, I'm not the only one in the dark. As far as I can tell, everyone in Flynn's life is.

You also know that he's into kinky sex, which has taught you that you're into kinky sex.

It's true that I might be an emotional freak in the streets, but Flynn is a freak between the sheets. I didn't even know that sex could feel *that* good until him. And sure, some of that has to do with that well-endowed penis he's packing, but a lot of it has to do with the way he knows how to take control, the way he knows how to work my body, and the intuitive way he always knows just how far to push my limits without making me feel unsafe.

I grab an apple from the drawer in the fridge and some peanut butter from the cabinet and put it on a plate so I can cut it up, all the while Flynn scrolls through his phone and puts his coffee cup to his lips silently.

I'm not sure what breaks inside me while I watch him, his perfectly chiseled jaw and his dark, damp hair curling around his forehead, but when it does, I can't stop myself.

"Where do you work?" I ask without preamble, dropping my knife on the counter and leaning into it while I wait for him to look up to me.

Bright-blue eyes find mine and search, and then he sets his coffee cup on the counter. "At 1350 Sixth Avenue, Manhattan. On the twelfth floor."

Semishocked that he was so openly specific, I pick up my knife again and nod. "Well, okay then."

Flynn smirks at me; I can feel the weight of it even as I slice manically through my Golden Delicious, and when I'm done, I can't help but meet his eyes again. He raises his eyebrows—just as he always does when there's more to be said and I'm avoiding it.

"I just… I don't know… I thought maybe it'd be a good idea for me to know where you worked. You know, in case of an emergency."

"Right."

I narrow my eyes on his simple answer that lets him off the hook way too easily and up the ante. "Maybe we should have lunch one day. To keep up appearances. I could meet you at your office so I could see a little bit about what you do, and we can go from there."

"Great," Flynn agrees, shocking the hell out of me as he sets his coffee mug in the sink and winks. *Winks.* Flynn Winslow, the most stalwart man on the planet, winking…at *me.* "How about tomorrow? I would today, but I've already got a business lunch with my accountant."

"T-tomorrow's great," I stutter, overwhelmed.

"Good," he praises me then, stepping forward and placing an unexpected kiss on the apple of my cheek that gives me a full-body chill. "I'll see you tonight, then. Maybe we'll get tacos."

"Tacos? On a Monday?"

"Live dangerously with me, Daisy." He laughs and reaches out to tuck a few of my curls behind my ear. My skin doesn't miss the cool sensation of his gold wedding band.

He's wearing his wedding band? When did he start doing that?

I discreetly tap the ring on my left finger with my thumb, even twirling it around a little. *Welp, he probably started wearing it around the same time you started wearing yours…*

I'm sure it doesn't mean anything, though. It's just to keep up appearances.

All I can do is nod as Flynn steps out the door because I'm left wondering just how fucked I'm going to be emotionally if this is the Flynn that lives behind the taciturn curtain. I already knew the quiet Mr. Mysterious was great. But an emotionally available witty wizard who now wears his wedding band out in public? Well, that's a horse of an entirely different color.

God, Daisy. Do not fall in love with your contractually bound, marriage-pact husband. Only a fool would do that.

My phone buzzes on the counter beside me, startling me from my cold, hard stare at the door.

Damien: *How's it going in New York, doll?*

I sigh. *Not great.* Not only has my war with Tara escalated to epic proportions—*think walking into a shocked office of people because she told them she'd heard I died*—but I'm also getting dangerously close to becoming attached to my fake husband. *Oh yeah, I'm having a grand ole time.* Still, Damien gave me this opportunity despite the burden it put on his office, and I don't want to make him feel like I'm not grateful.

Me: Well, it's not exactly as fun as working directly with you every day, but the Greenwich Village penthouse looks incredible.

Tara and me working together is a joke of a concept, and she puts down literally everything I suggest, but thankfully, Thomas Grey showed up while we were there the other day and agreed with my proposed changes, so she's had to go along with it.

Obviously, that did nothing for my working relationship with Tara other than sully it further, but at least Thomas isn't walking around thinking I'm a complete moron.

Damien: Tara's just jealous that Thomas liked your suggestions more than hers. Also, she's territorial as hell, and sometimes I wonder if she and Thomas are having an affair.

My eyes damn near hit the screen of my phone. Not only did Damien suss out the reason for my ho-hum answer immediately, but the gossip around the villain in my story is juicy enough that Paris Hilton of the early 2000s would slap it across the ass of a pair of terry cloth pants if she could.

Me: You think Tara and Thomas are hooking up??? I thought Thomas was married???

Damien: Tara is too, but that doesn't mean she didn't spread her legs in a raunchy little dance at the Christmas party two years ago while eye-fucking my eastern counterpart to high heaven.

Me: Oh, holy hell.

Damien: Which brings me to your next work task. Keep an eye on those two and report anything suspicious to me immediately.

I almost want to laugh.

Me: Keeping you in the gossip loop is not a work task, Dame.

The last thing I am going to do is blow the lid off a secret affair of some sort. *Hell to the no.* That shit is none of my business.

Besides, nearly deported immigrants clinging to their last chance to work in the country shouldn't throw stones from glass houses.

THIRTY

Tuesday, May 7th

Flynn

The intercom buzzer on my desk phone trills as soon as I place the receiver on the hook from my phone call with the CEO of Tuff Co., the leading vinyl flooring producer in the country, and I scribble my note about equipment setup in their new Texas plant on my notepad quickly so I don't lose my train of thought.

Talk to Jim about thermodynamics repercussions for ventilation system

Tuff Co. has, for the last twenty years, operated their vinyl plants out of northern China, but because of some changes in logistics and politics, they've decided to bring everything stateside to the tax-friendly state of Texas. I've been brought on as a consultant to help work through all the kinks involved in an intercontinental move, including climatological considerations on their state-of-the-art machinery.

It's almost painfully boring, if I'm honest, but it also allows me to keep a residence in Texas on their dime. Since that's one of the next markets I'd like to expand into with my real estate investments, I took the job.

"Mr. Winslow, your...wife is here to see you."

I nearly laugh as Valerie stumbles over the word "wife," but I don't think it's in good taste to make fun of an elder, and my assistant was thirty when I was born. Lord only knows why she clings to working for a silent bastard like me when she could retire with her well-off husband and travel the globe, but for whatever reason—perhaps fifteen years of loyalty—she puts up with me every day.

I don't bother telling Valerie to send Daisy in; after this many years together, she knows what to expect.

Several moments later, the door cracks timidly open, and Daisy peeks her head in, her curls leading the way into the room. "Hi! Am I interrupting?"

I shake my head and wave her in with a hand, so she backs her head out, opens the door farther, and steps inside. "Am I too early? Or are you ready to head to lunch?"

"No, I'm good," I reply, standing to shut off the monitor on my computer and hitting the button to forward all my direct calls to Valerie's desk for the time being.

I round the desk and lean in to kiss her on the cheek, and she bounces on her toes awkwardly, accidentally knocking her chin into my teeth.

"Ope! Whoops! Sorry." She's strangely nervous, and my dick reacts like he's one of Pavlov's dogs. It's twisted as fuck, but Daisy's anxiety has become a distinguishable precursor to a very satisfying orgasm.

If Valerie didn't have the hearing of a bald eagle mid-hunt, I'd toss Daisy up on my desk and work whatever's bothering her right out with an orgasm. As it is, the best I can do until tonight is to distract her with food—the second-best calming agent in my Daisy arsenal.

"Come on. Let's go get some food."

She nods at that, her vibrant green eyes dancing in the sunlight of my office. "You have somewhere in mind?"

I nod. "Head out and hit the button for the elevator. It takes forever sometimes. I'll just grab my phone and keys and meet you out there."

"Okay," she agrees amiably, turning for the door and taking a step.

She's almost out of reach when the urge to have just a tiny part of her overwhelms me. With a quick snap of my elbow, I grab her just above the waist and pull her back, her body twisting on the balls of her feet and falling soundly into the bulk of mine.

Wide eyes and lips in a tiny circle of surprise, she looks up into the center of my gaze just as my mouth comes down on hers in a crush. Open and easy, she meets my tongue with her own in the sexiest fucking dance. She tastes like the black cherry gum I've seen her chew, and my dick jerks against the fabric of my dress pants. My hand sinks into the spiraled curls at the back of her head, and I tilt the angle of her mouth to go deeper.

One second leads to two, and before I know it, two seconds lead to thirty. When I finally regain the sense to pull away, her whole face is glazed and relaxed in a way I know would only be better if she'd had my cock in her cunt.

"Ready for lunch now?" I tease, and she giggles softly before nodding her forehead against my chest.

"Uh, yeah. I think I'm ready now."

"Good," I praise with a squeeze of one cheek of her ass. "I'll meet you at the elevator."

She nods again, this time hustling out of the office without my interference. I round my desk back to the side by the windows and open my top right drawer to grab my keys and phone. Right next to those, I see the letter I pulled out of the mailbox at the apartment this morning—from USCIS.

I grab all three and load them into my pockets, and then follow in Daisy's wake to the elevator. She's waiting dutifully, though I can tell that the stress of waiting for an elevator that might arrive before I do is already counteracting the hard work of our kiss.

I pick up my walk to a jog just to make her feel better, and Valerie eyes me suspiciously the whole time. I roll my eyes at her, and she narrows hers.

She's known me a long while and, quite frankly, knows things about me that no one else does—including the reason Daisy and I got married as she's the one who put the damn USCIS packet in the mail for me. But right now, she needs to mind her own damn business.

I put my hand to the small of Daisy's back as the elevator dings its arrival and escort her inside. Valerie meets my eyes one more time as the doors close in front of us, but I ignore her, turning my focus to my wife instead as she starts to ramble.

"This building is really nice, but it's also kind of confusing."

"Yeah?"

"Yeah, when I came in downstairs, I was expecting the lobby to be a straight shot to the elevator, but it's more like a matrix or something. Like, I kind of felt dumb, to be honest. All the hallways lead back to the beginning, but they're like a hexagon and remind me of being in one of those fun house mirror maze things, you know?"

I smile, but I don't say anything because I know by now, I don't need to. Daisy has absolutely no problem carrying on a conversation herself.

"It actually reminds me of the building where they get into the huge firefight at the end of that movie…you know, the one with Gerard Butler… *Angel Has Fallen!*"

Having seen the movie a couple times, I know immediately that she's actually right. It is startlingly similar to that building. I chuckle.

"I finally had to split my hope between finding your office and finding the office where they were hiding President Morgan Freeman, you know?"

The elevator eases to a stop on the ground floor and opens its doors, and I put my hand to her back again to lead her out of the building. There are a few turns, but if you take the most direct route, it's pretty easy. When we make it to the front doors quickly, she scoffs. "Sure. Work your voodoo magic or whatever, just as I've made it all sound dramatic."

I grin. "I've worked in this building for the last fifteen years, so I think I have a little bit of an advantage."

"Fifteen years? Really?" she asks.

I nod.

"That makes sense, I guess. I've just never been anywhere for fifteen years. It seems so…long."

I laugh. "If it makes you feel any better, I move my desk chair around *a lot*."

Daisy's answering smile is so mesmerizing, I don't even look before pushing the front door open onto the sidewalk and almost take out a guy with a giant inflatable lollipop. He stumbles to the side and swings the thing like a sword, and Daisy's eyes sparkle. "New York is wild, man."

I grin. That it is.

Thankfully, the little diner I like to frequent for lunch is only right across the street, and after a quick jaywalk, we're inside again.

I escort Daisy straight to the table in the back where the framed reservation sign with my name on it sits. She reads it aloud as we scoot into our respective sides of the booth. "Reserved for Flynn Winslow." She snorts. "Come here often, do you?"

I shrug. "Just about every day for fifteen years."

"Wow! Holy shit, you're a creature of habit! I can't believe it. The guy nobody knows anything about does the same dang thing every day."

"You make it sound like I'm some sort of phantom," I say with a laugh. "No one has ever asked me where I have lunch, so I haven't offered it up. That's it."

"No one has ever asked you?"

I shake my head, and Barbara, my favorite quiet waitress, sets a couple of plates with burgers in front of us along with two glasses of water, and then heads back for the kitchen. I glance to the food and then at Daisy. "Is this okay? She obviously just assumed you wanted what I get."

Daisy waves off the food faux pas and pops a fry into her mouth before leaning into her elbows on the table and whispering intently, diving right back into the conversation we were having before Barb brought the food. "Your sister talks like you're ex-CIA, and you're telling me it's all because people don't ask you?"

I shrug. I mean, yeah. If they asked, I'd answer. But I'm not going to fucking gab for no reason. I pick up my burger and take a bite.

"Holy shit. That's…groundbreaking, really."

I roll my eyes with a shake of my head and a dry laugh, and Daisy reaches across the table and grabs my hand to stop me.

"What's your favorite color?"

"Black."

"What's your favorite holiday?"

"All of them that bring the family together."

"What do you do with your free time?"

"Work out. Scope out real estate investments. Volunteer at the homeless shelter Uptown."

She stops her continuous giggle then to get serious. "You volunteer at the homeless shelter?"

I shrug. "Once a month or so."

"God, Flynn." She shakes her head as if to clear it. "You're…well, you're kind of a catch of a husband, you know that?"

"Oh," I murmur, her comment reminding me of the envelope in my pocket. "I almost forgot." Pulling it out, I toss it into the center of the table, her eyes following it and scanning until she makes out the address of the sender in the top left corner. I lean over my plate and take more bites.

Daisy stops eating altogether, and as soon she understands what it is, her whole demeanor changes.

"Oh my God, that's from Immigration."

I raise my eyebrows.

"That's from Immigration, Flynn!" she repeats, this time much more manically.

"Yeah, I know. I saw the address," I reply calmly.

"What does it say?"

"I don't know. I didn't open it."

"You didn't open it?" she nearly shrieks, making a couple of the regulars look our direction. But I don't give a shit who's watching us, so I don't pay them any mind.

"Daisy."

"Okay, you said that, but why? Why didn't you open it?"

"Why don't you just open it now?" I suggest instead of answering.

She nods then, grabbing the envelope and ripping into it without much finesse. The envelope is practically shredded, and I lean down to pick up a stray piece of it that's fluttered to the floor.

By the time I straighten back up in my seat, Daisy is fully engrossed in the letter and chanting the phrase, "Oh my God," over and over again under her breath.

I raise my eyebrows in question, and she says it again, extending the last word like some sort of prayer. "Oh my Gooood, Flynn! They want to do the interview in less than a month! Holy shit, they want to do the interview May 31st!"

May 31st. The day of Jude and Sophie's wedding.

Daisy's eyes have turned wild and crazy as she frantically glances between me and the letter in her hands. "Geez Louise, what are we going to do?"

"Go to the interview?"

"*Flynn*, they said three months, and that's only like a month and a half! They must know!"

My eyebrows draw together. "Know what?"

"About us! About the sham! That I'm a big fat phony who needs to get deported!"

"Daisy, relax." I reach out to place my hand over hers. "They don't know anything. You're Canadian. You're, like, the most nonthreatening type of immigrant. They're probably just ready to push your stuff through."

"I just can't believe it's that soon," she says, her voice despondent in a way I'm not entirely sure I understand. This is good news. The sooner they do the interview, the sooner we know there's no chance Daisy's going to get forced to leave.

"When you get home tonight, I promise to fuck all the anxiety about it right out of you," I respond cheekily and squeeze her fingers.

Her smile is genuine but doesn't quite meet her eyes.

"I have to get fitted for a bridesmaid dress tonight with Winnie and Sophie."

"After, then," I promise, wanting desperately to see the excitement her little question-game had brought to her beautiful face before she got freaked out by the USCIS letter.

She nods, and her smile lights up her whole face, including her eyes. "After."

I may be a creature of habit, but a lot sure has changed in the last month. Most of all, I'm beginning to think there isn't any length I wouldn't go to to see Daisy smile.

THIRTY-ONE

Daisy

I shove inside the dress shop from the bustling city, and I immediately take a breath as the noise settles. It's not that LA isn't packed full of people—it is—but I'm used to having the buffer of my car. *Don't want to speak to someone? Roll up your window and gas it.* Here in New York, I feel a little like I'm volunteering as tribute for the Hunger Games every time I step out onto the sidewalk.

I spot Winnie immediately, perusing a rack of dresses in the center of the store, and make my way over to her. Just as I arrive, a young blonde steps out from behind the rack and moves to join us.

"Hi, Daisy!" Winnie greets excitedly, pulling me into a big hug before stepping back.

"Hi, hi!" I greet back with a pathetically awkward wave. I've been a little off-kilter since finding out that my immigration interview is scheduled for the morning of Sophie's wedding, but I need to shake it off, for Pete's sake. Trying on dresses is supposed to be fun, and I refuse to be the cloud of doom.

"You remember my daughter, Lexi?" Winnie asks, holding out a sweeping hand to the absolutely gorgeous girl in question.

"Oh, of course, Lexi. It's so nice to formally meet you. I'm sorry I didn't get a chance to talk with you more at family dinner."

"That's all right. Logistically speaking, it's pretty hard to carry on a conversation when people are shouting at above one hundred decibels anyway."

When Winnie laughs, I figure it's safe to unleash my smile. "There were a lot of people yelling, weren't there?"

"Yeah. They all thought Uncle Flynn would grow old and die alone. So, a wife was a shock."

I laugh then; I can't not. Surprisingly, it seems like the perfect time to let in a little tiny nugget of the truth. "To be honest, it was a jolt to me too."

Winnie and Lexi both laugh at that, and I take the moment to glance around the bridal shop in search of the third member of our party. "Where's Sophie? Is she not here yet?"

Winnie rolls her eyes good-naturedly and laughs. "Oh no, she's here. She's in the back. Every time we come here, no matter the reason, she can't leave without trying on her dress too."

"Oh, great! I'd actually love to see it."

Lexi snorts. "That's exactly what she said you'd say."

"Well, she was right," I confirm. Plus, anything that delays the inevitable of me getting fitted for a dress I'm not even entirely sure I'm going to get the chance to wear is okay in my book.

Does Flynn even realize the interview is the same day as his brother's wedding?

When we found out about the appointment at lunch this afternoon, he was encouraging, his usual calming force to my emotional nerves, but I don't know if he put two and two together. I mean, once the interview is done, he'll be released from his obligation. I'm sure I'll have to do some things with Immigration on and off as I seek citizenship, but once USCIS declares us legitimate, I'm allowed time in the country to sort my status even if Flynn and I break up. I know, because on a painfully pathetic day while having lunch at my desk to avoid Tara and the rest of the people in the office, I looked it up.

Winnie seems oblivious to my mental wandering, thankfully, as she and Lexi chat about different shoe options for the wedding. Lexi insists that flats are the most practical of all the options, but Winnie contests that then her butt won't look as good.

Evidently a fan of practicality over fashion, Lexi rolls her eyes.

"Well?" Sophie announces suddenly, popping out from behind the back wall in a gorgeous top-beaded satin gown that pools around her feet beautifully. Not very many people in this world could pull off that dress, but Sophie does it in spades.

"Wow, Sophie. You look *stunning*."

"Yeah. I'd say Uncle Jude is statistically likely to get an erection when he sees you."

"Lexi!" Winnie snaps while I choke on saliva and Sophie dissolves into a fit of laughter. "Oh my God, what in the world?"

Lexi shrugs. "Men average eleven erections a day. With the sex appeal of Sophie's wedding dress, it's highly likely one of those will happen when he sees her."

Winnie puts two fingers to her forehead and sighs. "Remind me to check your internet protections again when we get home."

"Why? Is an erection not part of a male's biology?"

"Well, yes, but—"

"And sex appeal has a marked cause and effect, proven by the statistics on its frequency in advertisements."

"Yes."

Lexi's eyes widen as if to say, *Well...what, then?* and Sophie steps in to use Winnie's obvious speechlessness to her advantage.

"Great. Now that we know I'm beautiful in a way Jude won't be able to deny," she starts, stepping down off the platform and forward to place her hands on my shoulders and spin me. "Let's go get Daisy in her dress so Liza can make whatever adjustments are necessary."

Winnie nods, and I go with Sophie's guidance without a fight.

When we round the back wall, Sophie moves from her position behind me to wrap one of her arms in mine, locking out elbows together. "I'm so glad you're here, Daisy. It's a little intimidating being an outsider in this group—even though everyone is nice, obviously—and it's good to have some backup."

My throat is thick, and my nose stings with choked-back tears as they threaten immediately. I feel like a coward and a shrew, but knowing how important all of this is to the whole of my life as I know it, I keep my mouth shut once again.

All I can do is nod, and Sophie mistakes my almost-tears for exactly what I wish they were—the thankful recognition that this family and its bond are the very things I've been looking for my entire life. Togetherness, support, and encouragement from a group of people who'd do anything for you and laugh at any joke you tell. *God, I wish with a desperation I can't describe that it was all real.*

"Aw, Dais. Don't cry now. Tears and chiffon don't mix."

She's right. But neither do lies and a group of people so great they give ol' Alexander a run for his money—and I'm so deep in the middle of that mixture that I don't know if I'll ever get out.

THIRTY-TWO

Friday, May 10th

Flynn

As I snag my duffel from my gym locker, Jude lets out a deep sigh behind me. I glance over my shoulder to find him easing himself off the bench that resides in the middle of the locker room, his movements looking more like those of an elderly grandma after a rowdy game of backgammon than a fit, thirty-eight-year-old man who just got done with his daily workout.

"You good?"

"Am I good? Ha!" He grimaces. "No, I'm not good. My legs are Jell-O. I feel like fucking Bambi, dude. Next leg day, I'm not letting you lead the workout."

A laugh jumps from my lips, and I lift my duffel over my shoulder and shut the locker door. "It wasn't that bad."

Jude scoffs. "My body says otherwise."

"You realize I'm not forcing you to work out with me," I comment and lift my brow to punctuate that sentiment. Truth be told, I never asked Jude to work out with me. Several years ago, he just started showing up and hasn't stopped. I will admit, though, the time together is nice. He's always so chatty everywhere else, but at the gym, he's too busy gasping for air.

"And what am I supposed to do?" he retorts. "Meet Ty at fucking Planet Fitness and do yoga?"

You might think he's joking, but Ty actually does attend yoga classes, along with God only knows what else, and it's all in the name of keeping his revolving door of women spinning and thriving.

Over the last decade, I've yet to attend a family function without my second-youngest brother bringing some random woman along. And considering Ty's never brought the same woman to a family function twice *and* the Winslow clan gets together two to three times a month, that's a lot of fucking women.

"And Rem's day-trading schedule makes him work out at two in the morning like some kind of damn vampire. You're my only viable option," he says, snagging his backpack from the bench and scowling as he shifts on his feet to stand upright. "And right now, I hate you."

"You want me to see if they've got a wheelchair you can borrow?"

"Shut up."

"A motorized scooter? Crutches?" I keep going, sarcasm and amusement lifting the corners of my lips, and Jude flips me the middle finger.

"I like you better when you're being all surly and not saying shit."

He doesn't have to tell me twice.

I shrug and spin on my heel, more than ready to leave the locker room before the after-seven crowd takes over. But I only make it a few steps toward the door when Jude calls out, "Wait… Where are you going, man?"

I turn around to meet his eyes. "Home."

"You don't want to grab some dinner with me?" he questions. "I mean, it's the least you can do for putting me through Satan's leg day."

"Can't. I'm making Daisy dinner."

Last night, she saw an Olive Garden commercial and started rambling on and on about fettuccine Alfredo. I told her I could make it for her sometime, and she looked at me as if I'd just said I was an alien from Mars. Though, it didn't take long for her to make me promise to fulfill my homemade pasta offer ASAP, as in tonight after we both get home from work.

"Oh yeah, *Daisy*." A big, shit-eating grin consumes Jude's face. "Your *wife* that none of us knew about until you'd already married her."

Actually, he *did* meet her. In Vegas. But just like Ty and Remy, he was apparently too drunk to remember, and I'm not going to be the one to tell him.

"Of all the people to get married before me, you were the last motherfucker I expected to pull that trick out of his mysterious hat. I mean, you were all 'I don't do the relationship and marriage thing,' but now look at you. You're someone's husband."

"You don't like Daisy?"

"Get real." He rolls his eyes. "She's going to be a bridesmaid in my wedding, bro. Of course, I like Daisy. Sophie *loves* Daisy. I'm just still trying to figure out where in the hell she came from. Seriously, Flynn, how did you go from the guy who barely even dated to fucking married in the blink of an eye?"

"It's a fake marriage," I answer, giving him the full truth, but it feels foreign on my tongue. Like it shouldn't even be there. Like it's not the truth at all.

His response? An outburst of laughter.

"Oh yeah, okay, *a fake marriage*," he repeats, using his fingers to make air quotes around his words. "Sure thing, Flynn." He rolls his eyes again and keeps laughing as if I just told the biggest joke of the century. "How long did you know her before you got married?"

"Not long."

"*Not long.*" Jude sighs. "That really narrows it down." He eyes me suspiciously, his gaze narrowing as if he's attempting to seek out all the answers by telepathy. "Fuck, you're difficult to read. You're my own brother, and you're still a damn mystery to me. I swear, if you ever went missing, your own fucking family wouldn't even know what to tell the cops."

Funnily enough, he's probably not wrong, but that has more to do with my family never actually asking me anything to give them an insight into my life. It's not that they don't want to, I don't think. They're just intimidated or something. *Daisy isn't intimidated to ask. Hell, she knows you more than anyone has ever known you.*

My phone vibrates in my pocket, and since Jude is busy trying to read my mind, I pull it out to check my messages.

Daisy: Running a little later than I expected, but I should be home by 8:30. We still on for you cooking me a glorious feast?

I grin and shoot her a quick *Yes* back.

But when I look up from my phone, I find that Jude is *still* watching me like I'm the most interesting thing in the locker room. Ironically, I've now told him and Remy the truth about Daisy and me, but the fuckers don't believe me—even after what I told Remy turned out to be true.

Whatever. It's his problem, not mine.

I leave the locker room for good this time, but Jude follows right behind on his shaky Bambi legs.

"It's all pretty fucking nuts, bro," he calls toward my back as I walk past the reception area and out of the gym's lobby doors. "I mean, you're married, *before me*, the guy who had to propose four fucking times before Sophie said yes."

Truthfully, I have not a clue what he's trying to get at here, and I don't care to know. He and Sophie are getting married, and Daisy and I already are. End of story—*almost.*

Jude looks out toward the street and then back at me. He searches my eyes with scrutiny again, until eventually, he asks, "Why did you get married, dude? Like, what the hell changed? You're the most rational person I know, and it seems like this marriage was on a damn whim. Like it just dropped out of the sky. I like Daisy, I really do, but this is all so unlike you." His eyes go wide and imploring. "Oh shit, you're not in the middle of a fucking nervous breakdown, are you?"

Pretty sure anyone who is in the middle of a nervous breakdown doesn't realize they're in the middle of one, but in the name of not getting him all worked up, I keep that shit to myself.

"I'm good, man."

"You sure?"

I sigh. Nod. And I almost end the conversation right there, but something inside me makes me want to put Jude at ease. "Daisy is…better than I ever imagined she'd be," I tell him. "She's hilarious. Fucking adorable. Talks enough for the both of us. She makes life fun."

And you actually really fucking like her.

I can't deny that ever since Daisy came blazing into my life, I've been the opposite of bored. This last month is the most I've laughed in a lifetime, I'm certain.

She's also the first woman you want *to spend time with. A lot of fucking time, in fact…*

"Are you in the mafia? Is that what it is?" Jude questions out of fucking nowhere. "Or is it the CIA? Are you an undercover agent living a double life, and you can't tell anyone about it?"

"Who knows," I answer through a shrug and hitch my duffel higher on my shoulder. "Maybe I'm not even your actual brother. Maybe Mom's in on it too."

For an instant, Jude's eyes look so big they might pop out of his skull, but then, he reaches out to punch me in the shoulder. "You're such an asshole."

I shake my head on a chuckle, and it's then that I notice the T-shirt he changed into after our workout that had him whining like a baby. White cotton material with a variety of badges spread all over his chest and stomach and back and arms, and the words "The Secret Club" embroidered across his right pec.

"I'm the asshole?" I retort and nod toward his attire. "Says the man who's standing in front of me in a T-shirt that looks like he joined the Girl Scouts."

Jude glances down at his chest and grins. "Sophie got it for me. Well, actually, I got Sophie the first one, and then she got me one too. It's a *Secret Club* T-shirt."

I still have no idea what that means.

"The badges have to be *earned*." He waggles his brows. "You want to know how I earn my badges?"

I shake my head. "Nope."

"What?" he questions. "Why not?"

"Because it's pretty damn obvious it's related to sexual shit, and I'd prefer to stay oblivious to your sex life."

"Like I'd even fucking tell you. What happens in the Secret Club stays in the Secret Club."

"Fantastic," I respond and decide it's high time I got the hell moving. Not only do I have a dinner to make, but I need to stop at the grocery store to pick up a few things.

Jude calls out toward me, something about being a dick, but I just lift my hand in a wave and head toward the subway. Though, once I find an empty seat toward the back of the train, I can't stop myself from starting some shit on my youngest brother's behalf.

Phone in hand, I fire off a text in the ongoing group chat with my brothers.

Me: Jude's in the Girl Scouts now. And, personally, after seeing his T-shirt with all the badges he's earned, I'm really proud of him.

Knowing my brothers, it's only going to take that one text to get them going.

Ty: Aw, congrats, bro! Let me know when you're selling cookies because I'll buy a shitload from you. Especially Thin Mints. Those fuckers are like candy-coated crack.

Remy: That's awesome, man. What's your troop number?

See what I mean?

Jude: I'm not in the fucking Girl Scouts, you idiots.

Ty: But you earn badges?

Jude: Sophie and I earn badges.

Remy: So, you and Sophie are in the Girl Scouts?

Jude: I'm thirty-eight fucking years old, and I'm a man, bro. I'm not in the Girl Scouts.

Ty: But you earn badges?

Jude: Yes. It's a thing between Sophie and me, and Flynn is just being a lying prick.

Remy: Are you sure you're not in the Girl Scouts?

Ty: Right? It sounds like the Girl Scouts.

Jude: Fuck you guys. It's not the damn Girl Scouts, it involves orgasms, you dicks.

Ty: Dude, does your troop leader know about this? I feel like you guys are going to get kicked out.

Jude: FUCK YOU GUYS.

Ty: Okay, but don't forget to let us know when you're selling cookies.

Jude: I HATE ALL OF YOU. ESPECIALLY YOU, FLYNN. I KNOW YOU'RE READING THESE TEXTS BUT NOT RESPONDING, YOU CRYPTIC BASTARD.

I smirk to myself and slide my phone into my pocket. I know I keep shit close to the vest, but I can't deny this conversation gave me a hell of a lot of enjoyment.

My phone buzzes a few more times in my pocket, most likely Ty and Remy still razzing Jude, but when the subway comes to a halt at my stop, I grab my duffel and head in the direction of the grocery store.

I have a meal to cook and a wife to feed.

THIRTY-THREE

Daisy

"Honey, I'm home!" I exclaim as I walk through the door. Keys on the cute table I set up by the door, I kick off my heels and head straight into the kitchen with two bags of groceries where the delicious aromas of cheese and pasta and garlic fill my nose.

"Oh wow, it smells good in here."

Flynn glances over his shoulder as he drains hot water from the pasta. "Dinner is almost ready."

"After the afternoon I've had dealing with Tara and her dramatics, this is the best news I've heard all day."

"I take it the Wicked Witch of the Real Estate East is still alive and well?"

His commentary makes me giggle, but it's also a pleasant surprise. Over the past few weeks, Flynn has received more than an earful regarding my lovely—more like, *horrible*—coworker, and apparently, he really did listen to everything I told him. "Oh yeah, alive and well and probably out buying a new broomstick as we speak."

I get to work on putting away groceries that consist of some fruit, yogurt, and frozen meals that can be cooked very quickly.

Once everything is put away, I refocus on the man at the stove. In just jeans and a white T-shirt, Flynn looks...well, hot. With his tight ass and muscular back and biceps bulging beneath cotton, I could take a photo of him right now, post it on my Instagram account, and have thousands of men and women go nuts in a matter of minutes.

And thirst traps aren't even my aesthetic, but I know Flynn would spur a reaction.

Probably because he's doing exactly that to you right now...

I make a valiant effort to shift my focus and note the creamy white sauce that bubbles in the skillet. I grin and walk over to the stove to discreetly dip my finger in for a quick taste test, but I'm stopped in my tracks when Flynn's arms wrap around my waist.

"Don't even think about it," he whispers into my ear, and before I know it, my bare feet are no longer touching the floor and I'm being carried over to the kitchen table. My ass is in the chair a few seconds later.

It's then that I realize the table is already set with plates and napkins and cutlery. A vase with a bouquet of flowers and two already-lit candles sit in the center.

Holy moly, this is fancy. Like a romantic dinner date.

Well, even if it's temporary, he is your husband.

An annoying pang sets up residence in my chest, but I don't have time to question its cause because Flynn is leaning down and pressing a soft kiss to my lips.

"You stay right here."

"Right here?" I tease, smiling up at him. "In this chair?"

He smirks. "Yes."

"What if there's a fire?"

"I'll handle it."

"What if I have to go pee?"

"Hold it."

"What if—"

He cuts me off with another kiss and proceeds to whisper firmly against my lips. "Keep that little ass of yours in this chair while I plate our food—or else."

"Or else what?" I waggle my eyebrows. "You gonna spank me?"

"Oh, baby, don't tempt me." A deep, hearty chuckle rumbles his chest, but before I can do exactly that, he's turning on his heel and heading back to the stove to plate our dinner.

Forget the dumb stove and spank me with your penis!

Okay…that was weird.

Mind you, the dinner smells delicious, but all that spanking talk has my appetite focused on something else. A myriad of dirty-as-hell thoughts fill my head, and I shift a little in my seat.

There has to be a way to put a pause on this dinner and revisit it a later time… I mean, that's what microwaves are for, right?

"Stop thinking whatever you're thinking and prepare to enjoy the feast you demanded."

I look up to meet Flynn's amused gaze as he sets two platefuls of fettuccine Alfredo with garlic bread on the table.

"How do you know what I was thinking?"

"Because you've got that look," he answers cryptically and sits down in the chair across from mine.

"What look?"

He just smirks, doesn't answer my question, and grabs his fork to dig in.

"I didn't have a look," I state, but he is completely unfazed. "*I didn't have a look*," I repeat, but Flynn just twirls pasta around his fork to take a big bite.

"Eat your food, babe," he says once he finishes chewing. "After dinner, if you want to try to tempt me into spanking your sassy ass, be my guest."

Damn, can he read me that well?

I put on a show of acting like I'm innocent and narrow my eyes at him. "I wasn't thinking about that."

"Then what were you thinking about?" he challenges, calling my bluff.

"Uh…" I pause. *Shit.* "Um…couch…*es*…I was thinking about couches. For a new listing."

His steady gaze drips with "I call bullshit."

"Shut up," I retort on a snort and proceed to take my first bite of Flynn's fettuccine Alfredo. The instant the creamy pasta hits my taste buds, I practically fall out of my chair over how damn good it is. "Holy hell, you can, like, really cook."

Flynn looks up from his plate, and I don't miss the amusement that flashes across his eyes. "Were you expecting something inedible?"

"No… Well, maybe? I don't know, but this is insanely good," I answer, and an apologetic smile lifts the corners of my mouth. "I wasn't doubting your cooking skills. I just didn't know what to expect."

"You were expecting something revolting, which is why you brought home two bags of groceries," he retorts with a sly grin.

"I wasn't."

He just stares at me.

"Okay, fine. I was. I mean, I hoped you would exceed my expectations, but just in case the meal didn't turn out, I grabbed a few easy-to-make options to have on hand as a backup."

"You brought home microwavable freezer meals, babe. I think it's safe to say you were anticipating a fucking disaster."

"I wasn't!" I exclaim through several giggles. "I mean, I might've had the fire department on standby just in case, but…"

A soft, raspy chuckle jumps from his lungs.

"So…is this meal a one-hit wonder? Or can you cook more things?" I question and take another bite of my pasta. "Because, seriously, Flynn, this is otherworldly."

"I can cook, Dais. Lots of shit," he comments. "And I do recall I've made you a few things before. Steak. Eggs. Grilled chicken."

Okay, he has a point. He *has* cooked for me a time or two, but this is, like, gourmet kind of cooking. The type of cooking that involves spices I've probably never even heard of.

"And how did you learn this awesome skill?"

"I don't know." He shrugs. "My mom, my aunt Paula, a few cooking classes here and there."

"Wait…Flynn Winslow took cooking classes?"

He furrows his brow. "That's strange to you?"

"I don't know…" I look up at the ceiling and then back at him. "Maybe? I mean, you're like the big, bad, sexy leather-jacket dude on a Harley, but you also cook like Julia flipping Child? It's unexpected."

He just smirks and dives back into his food.

And since I'm starving and this is the best damn fettuccine Alfredo I've ever tasted in my life, I do the same. But also, I make a mental note of the newest insight into Mr. Mystery.

He can cook. Like, *really* cook.

He's even taken cooking classes!

I don't know why but the mere thought of Flynn in a cooking class makes me smile.

"Why are you smiling?" he asks, surprising me, and I look up from my plate again to meet the depths of his ocean-blue eyes.

"Because I'm a woman who loves delicious food, and one who just found out she's married to Wolfgang Puck. Wait, no, Emeril Lagasse. No! Curtis Stone. Yeah, he's the cutest of them all." I wink. "Plus, the idea of you in a cooking class with a chef's hat on is an amazing visual."

He shakes his head on a laugh. "I've never worn a chef's hat in my life."

"Oh, don't even try to ruin this visual, Flynn. In my fantasy, you're definitely wearing a chef's hat."

"In your *fantasy?*" he questions with a raise of one curious brow. "If you want me to fuck you with a chef's hat on, all you have to do is say so."

"You wouldn't, you liar."

He just stares back at me, and I know instantly, he actually *would* do that. Flynn Winslow is a man of his word. And he's also a man I'm always desperate to find out more things about. Things that no one else knows. Only me.

Yeah, yeah, yeah, but what about the chef's hat fucking, Daisy? Or the spanking? Those sound promising...

"Flynn!" I call toward the living room where I know post-dinner Flynn is currently relaxing on the couch, watching whatever boring sports game is on ESPN. "Your presence is requested in the kitchen!"

A minute later, he's standing in the doorway, and his eyes survey my setup on the counters.

"What is all this?"

"Cake baking time," I answer and hold out the paper chef's hat I made just for him. "Here. Put this on."

When he doesn't take it, I stand up on my tippy-toes and shove it on his head. After one pat to his broad, firm chest, I grin up at him. "There. Perfect."

"What's the plan, Daisy?"

I wink and hold up a box of Betty Crocker cake mix. "The plan is to let me see Chef Flynn in action."

Pretty sure the real plan is to entice Chef Flynn to bang you...

"Anyone can make cake from a box, babe."

"Yeah, well, it's what you had in the cabinets," I answer on a shrug. Plus, I, personally, don't have a clue how to bake a cake from scratch. That would've required far too much Googling for what I'm actually trying to achieve here.

Cake is great. Fantastic, even. But getting Flynn to do dirty, sexy things with me? Well, that beats cake every day of the week. And, trust me, I'm a cake-lover from way back. I could write a twenty-paragraph essay, APA formatted, *with* the bibliography, on my love for it, but nothing beats a naked Flynn getting me to do bad-girl kinds of things.

"And don't worry, I made us both chef's hats for the baking cause," I add and snag my white paper hat from the counter and pointedly put it on my head.

A smile whispers across his mouth, almost lifting his lips up at the corners.

"So…Chef Winslow, are you ready to get started?"

"Do I have a choice?"

I shake my head, and his smile is visible now.

"Let's bake some shit!" I exclaim, fist-pump the air, and grab him by the hand to drag him the rest of the way to the counter where I have his KitchenAid mixer set up. "First of all, I've always wanted one of these mixers, and I'm almost positive I've never dated a man who owns one."

"Married," he corrects me with a playful tap to my butt, and I giggle.

To my surprise, Flynn actually gets to work, grabbing the box of cake mix. But he doesn't do what I expect him to do. Instead of checking the instructions on the back and opening the package, he returns it to the cabinet and proceeds to get out containers of flour and sugar.

"What are you doing?"

"If we're baking a cake, we're doing it right."

"Wait...you know how to make a cake? Like, without Betty Crocker's assistance?"

He doesn't respond. Instead, he grabs milk and butter and eggs from the fridge and proceeds to start adding shit to the bowl locked inside the mixer.

With a flick of his wrist, the mixer is on and spinning around the wet ingredients.

"Oh my God, this is better than I even imagined," I mutter more to myself than him and snag my phone off the counter. "I have to get photo proof of this or else your sister won't believe me."

Flynn chuckles at that and tries to grab my phone with a playful hand, but I dodge his movements with a few bobs and weaves. "Traitor."

I grin and snap a quick action shot.

And just for good measure, I take three more photos of big, bad Flynn standing in front of the KitchenAid mixer with a paper chef's hat on his head.

To be honest, the whole scene is far hotter than I ever thought it could be. Like my own personal food porn, but minus the food.

Hello, ovaries. Please don't explode.

But before I can even fire off a message to Winnie, my phone vibrates in my hands with a text.

Duncan Jones: *Daisy, baby, how have you been? Damien told me you're in New York for the next couple of months, and since I'm going to be in the Big Apple next weekend, I was wondering if you wanted to schedule that rain check. Pretty sure you owe me a date. ;)*

"God, no! No, no, no, no!" The Michael Scott GIF of him reacting to Toby's unexpected presence in the office flashes in my mind. And then another stupid text chimes through.

Duncan Jones: *I won't take no for an answer, and I promise you'll have the time of your life.*

"Uh…*excuse me?*" I question out loud, staring down at the screen of my phone in irritation. "That's not how it works, bucko."

"Everything okay?"

I glance up to find Flynn looking at me with concern, and the sounds of the mixer have been silenced by the off switch.

"Yeah," I answer through a sigh. "Just some unwanted attention from a guy I worked with at the LA office."

"Unwanted attention?" he asks, and I hold my phone out toward him so he can read the text messages.

"Well, he sounds like a real fucking prick," Flynn comments, and I shrug.

"He's…a little overzealous."

"He won't take no for an answer," Flynn repeats Duncan's words. "That's not overzealous, babe. That's harassment."

"I don't think he realizes that."

"Who is this fuck?"

"Just some agent at the fir—" I pause for a moment when all the pieces of the puzzle fall into place. "Actually, you've seen him. You know who Duncan is."

Flynn quirks a brow.

"He's the guy you thought I was running away from at the Wynn. Right before I made you take me for a ride on your bike and wed me into holy matrimony."

A smile lifts the corners of his mouth, and moments later, his fingers tap across the screen.

"What are you doing?"

With one more tap to the keys, he hands my phone back, and I look down at the screen.

Me: This is Flynn Winslow, Daisy's husband. It's time you lose her number. That is, unless you'd like for both of us to join you on the forced "rain check." If that's the case, then name the time and place, and we'll be there.

Oh, holy macaroni. *Pretty sure he just threw down the gauntlet.*

I don't know whether to be grateful or freaked out. I glance from my phone to Flynn's face to my phone again. I can imagine Duncan's head is spinning over the news that I'm married, but I'm not exactly mad about that.

I'm just… I don't know? Shocked? Confused? But also, oddly happy.

The Flynn I met in Vegas was quiet, a bit surly even, but the Flynn who's standing in front of me now, the one who just played texting-knight-in-shining-armor feels different. He's still Flynn, but he's more fun-loving, more open, freer with his words. He's just…*more.*

And all that more is really starting to get to your heart…

"Dais, what good is having a husband if you can't use him to run off douchebags?" His question is rhetorical and highlighted by an amused rasp in his voice.

I look back up to meet his steady gaze and open my mouth to respond, but I quickly shut it when I realize I don't know what to respond.

His point is undeniable. The odds of Duncan texting me again are probably below zero now, and I'm not upset about that reality. The first time I met him, I thought he was just the office flirt, but the more I've gotten to know him, the more red flags have popped up. Truth be told, any man who feels a woman *owes* him something deserves a swift kick in the dick.

"Promise me this," Flynn adds. "If you end up back in LA, don't let that fuck make you feel like you have to oblige him with your time."

His words sent a shock wave into my chest, and all I can do is nod.

If I end up back in LA? Not when I end up back in LA? As in, maybe, I could end up in New York? With him?

Don't get your hopes up, Daisy. That's not at all what he meant. He meant you'll be free to be wherever you want to be in the country because you won't have to answer to the government. Or him. Or anyone. You'll be alone. Again.

"How about that delicious cake!" I blurt, probably a little too loudly for our close proximity but the exact right volume to drown out my crazy thoughts.

Flynn smirks, and with a flick of his wrist, he turns the mixer back on. It doesn't take long before all the ingredients have been added and the batter is the kind of smooth, silky consistency that contestants on *The Great British Bake Off* would go gaga over.

"Do we get to taste it?" I question, nodding down toward the bowl. "Pretty sure all good bakers test the batter before they commit to putting their cake in the oven."

"Oh yeah," he answers.

Dipping one long index finger into the bowl, Flynn lifts his batter-covered digit toward me and gently swipes it against my neck. The coolness of the batter makes me squeal out in surprise, but he's undeterred. Lips to my skin, he sucks and licks at my neck until the batter is gone, and tingles proceed to shoot down my spine and straight between my thighs.

"Mmm, it's good," he whispers against my neck. "But I need to check one more thing."

His big hands around my hips, he lifts me up and onto the kitchen counter and spreads my legs so wide that my skirt bunches up my thighs. One more finger into the batter, he swipes it across the skin of my inner thigh, just inches away from where the hem of my black panties begins.

"Yep," he says quietly and glances up at me with mischievousness lifting one side of his mouth. "I definitely need one more taste. Just to be sure."

"O-of course," I mutter. "It's always good to be sure about something like cake or cupcakes or brownies or anything with batter, really…"

What are you even talking about right now?

"Glad you agree," Flynn says, and his warm breath brushes against my inner thigh. It's a confusing sensation, the cold of the batter and the warmth of his mouth, but oh my stars, does it feel good.

And it turns downright euphoric when he actually puts his lips to my skin and sucks at the sensitive flesh. His mouth lingers there, sucking and kissing, even occasionally drifting up and brushing against the hem of my panties.

It's heaven and hell. Delicious and painful. And the throb that's taken up residence between my thighs grows so intense I shift my hips a little to try to ease the pressure.

But it's useless. I'm fucking turned on. Insanely turned on, actually. I want Flynn to keep kissing me, touching me, licking me, but I want him to do it everywhere. All at the same time.

"It's good," he says and lifts his mouth off my skin. "But I know it's no match for your sweet-as-fuck pussy."

Oh boy.

His hands slide up my thighs, over the material of my bunched-up skirt and the fabric of my silk blouse. His fingers linger over my nipples, and I have to swallow the urge to moan.

Eventually, both of his hands are gently holding my face, and our gazes are locked as we search each other's eyes.

"What are you going to do to me, Flynn?" I ask, hopeful that all this cake-batter tasting is actually foreplay that leads to something a little more hands-on…*me.*

"First, I'm going to kiss you," he says, and then, after a few soft brushes of his mouth against mine, he does.

His kiss is sweet like cake yet spicy like sex. It's gentle but demanding, and I want it to go on forever. But it doesn't. The instant he pulls away, my lips turn down at the corners. Flynn notices, but the heat in his eyes tells me that he has plans.

"And then, Daisy, I'm going to take you to bed," he tells me and runs his hands through my hair. "I'm going to remove your clothes, and I'm going to kiss every fucking inch of you. Especially that birthmark that sits on your lower back, just above the curve of your ass."

The fact that he knows about that birthmark hits me square in the chest.

"I'm going to kiss your breasts and lick your nipples," he continues. "And I'll probably stay there for a while. An hour, maybe two, because I'm obsessed with memorizing how every part of you works."

His hands move from my hair and slide down my arms until his hand gently grazes the apex of my thighs. "Once I'm done with your breasts, I'm going to do the same thing to your pussy. Lick it, taste it, eat it. And I'm not going to stop until you're begging for my cock.

"And by the time I spread your legs and slide inside you, I'm camping out there for the rest of the night. Until I can't hold back from filling you with my come. Can I do that, Daisy?" he asks and brushes his lips across mine. "Can I take you to bed?"

I don't have to think about my answer.

"*Yes.*" I wrap my legs around his waist and my arms around his neck. "*Please.*"

With his lips to mine again, he kisses me slowly, lazily even, and the unbaked cake batter is a forgotten memory as Flynn carries me out of the kitchen and into the bedroom. And once my back hits the mattress, he removes my clothing.

Each piece that leaves my skin is a teasing reminder of his words that are now replaying in my mind on a loop. And every cell in my body is anticipating what's to come.

I am at his mercy, completely naked and undeniably wanton for everything he has to give. His blue eyes blaze as he stares down at me, and I watch in rapt fascination as he removes his clothes. My eyes don't miss the way his muscles flex with each precise movement or the fact that his cock is already hard, already ready to be inside me.

"You're so beautiful, Daisy," Flynn whispers as he climbs on the bed until his body hovers over mine.

So are you.

And then, always a man of his word, Flynn does all the things he said he'd do.

First, my mouth. My neck and shoulders. The curve of my back.

Then *every* inch of my skin.

And by the time he slides inside me, I am so overwhelmed with need I can't see straight. All I can do is show him with desperate, greedy hands against his skin that I want more. That I want everything he has to give.

It's sweet and slow but passionate and deep. It's everything I want and everything I didn't know I needed.

And it's dangerously addictive.

So addictive that you don't want this to end.

THIRTY-FOUR

Saturday, May 11th

Daisy

I wake up to Flynn's side of the bed empty, the sounds of the shower running in the bathroom, and every muscle in my body reminding me of the dirty, wicked, ah-may-zing things Flynn did to me mere hours ago.

I swear, I'm never going to hear the song "All Night Long" the same again.

Thoughts of last night flood my mind.

Flynn kissing my neck and shoulders and my breasts. His tongue lapping and sucking at my nipples. His face between my legs. His big, strong body hovering over mine as he slid inside me. All the things he whispered into my ear.

The way his blue eyes caught fire every time moans would spill from my lips.

The way he was gentle but deliciously rough at the same time.

Damn, the man is a stallion with a wicked mouth and a big penis. Are you sure you don't want him to be your real husband?

I roll my eyes at myself and shift my focus to waking up.

Hands over my head and toes pointed away from my body, I stretch out my arms and legs beneath the comforter. My muscles are sore and a bit achy, but it's the good kind of discomfort. The one that serves as a delicious reminder of last night.

Once I'm out of bed, I grab my favorite fluffy robe from the closet and stop dead in my tracks when I catch my reflection in the mirror.

Are those hickeys on my boobs? And my freaking thighs?

Fingers to my skin, I tap at the bruised flesh and deduce that they are, in fact, *hickeys*. But why I smile over that truth is something I don't understand. Normally, I'd be a bit ticked off if a man marked me like this, but being marked by Flynn with a bunch of hickeys? I don't know what I am, but it's not mad.

Because you l-o-v-e love it, you little floozy.

Okay, fine. So what if I like the idea of Flynn marking me? Pretty sure any woman would love a man like him giving their body that much attention.

A little niggle of discomfort sets up residence in my chest, and I write it off as another sign of my sex hangover. I'm probably a little dehydrated. Maybe even low on blood sugar, too.

Uh-huh. Sure, that's all it is...

Instead of marinating in my brain's early morning absurdity, I tie my robe around my naked body and pad into the kitchen. Once I start a pot of coffee—*caffeine first, then water and food*—I locate my phone where I left it on the counter, moments before Flynn's and my cake baking turned to insanely hot sex.

Though, before I start to check for missed notifications, I don't miss the fact that Flynn has already managed to clean up our mess from last night. Come to find out, the more time I spend living with him, the more I realize that Flynn Winslow is a man who cleans up after himself.

He's like a unicorn of men. But minus the horn and sparkles.

Oh, but he has a horn. And it's hella big and sits smack-dab between his legs.

I don't know what it is about Flynn, but I swear on everything, my mind has never been this much of a horny harlot until he showed up.

Phone in my hand, I swipe my finger across the screen and start rolling through any texts, calls, or emails I've missed.

An email from Damien that is actually work-related and can be dealt with on Monday.

A passive-aggressive email from Tara regarding the property in SoHo that I staged two days ago. She rambles on for about five paragraphs, but the gist of her words revolves around second-guessing everything I did with the place.

Unfortunately for her, I already sent Damien and Thomas a few preview photos, and they both approved of my design aesthetic.

Suck on that, Tara.

Once I send Tara a friendly but equally passive-aggressive response updating her on the cold, hard facts, I check my text messages and find one from Gwen that came in a few hours ago. *Dang. She must be up early.*

Gwen: Darling, I miss you. How is New York treating you?

Me: I miss you too. And New York is good. Just staying very busy with work.

And, you know, living with my husband that you don't know about.

Ugh. I cringe and run a hand down my face. Gwen is the one person I don't lie to. Ever. And yet, here I am, lying to her.

Gwen: Well, I hope you're not working so much that you aren't enjoying this glorious Saturday. What's that famous saying? All work and no play makes you a dull girl?

A laugh bubbles up from my lungs as I type out a response.

Me: It's actually "All work and no play makes Jack a dull boy." And that quote is from The Shining. It's the part where Jack Nicholson officially goes off the deep end. Right before he tries to kill his family.

Gwen: So, not a good quote for a happy Saturday?

Me: Nope. LOL.

Gwen: Bad quotes aside, do you have big weekend plans? Something fun, hopefully?

Before I can even respond, **Incoming FaceTime Call Gwen** pops up on the screen of my phone.

Oh boy. Nerves tickle my throat, and my finger hovers over the accept button, unsure of what to do. It's one thing to lie to her through text message, but it's a whole other ball game trying to do it while we're face-to-face.

Eventually, though, guilt wins out, and I hit accept by the third ring.

"Darling! It's so good to see you!" she exclaims, and a big grin consumes her face. Her excitement is infectious, and for a moment, I forget about everything but just being happy to see her. Sometimes I forget how lonely my life was before Gwen.

"I missed you. How are Vancouver and the girls and David?"

"Vancouver is the same. The girls are great. And David is starting to get on my nerves, so…" She shrugs but doesn't say anything else.

"So…?"

"It means I don't know how much longer I'm going to keep him around. You know I don't like to strain my attention span."

I snort. "Poor David."

"No," she disagrees with a little smile and a shake of her finger, always a proponent for women having the right to put themselves first like men usually do. "Not poor David. He's become a stage five clinger—to the point that I had to tell him he could not, in fact, attend ladies' night with me last night even though the rule is already right there in the name—so you should actually be saying *Poor Gwen*."

How she even knows the term *stage five clinger* is beyond me, but it's one of the many reasons why I love her.

"Anyway," she hums, but her eyes squint a little when she notes the ambiance—Flynn's apartment—behind me. "Where are you?"

"Uh…at my apartment in New York."

"Oh, so this is the New York place." Her eyes brighten with intrigue as she tries to see through the camera. "Very nice."

"Uh…thanks. I—" I start to answer just as Flynn walks into the kitchen, fresh out of the shower, with a towel wrapped around his waist, and heads toward the coffeepot. I know this because I can see him on the screen of my phone.

Oh *shit*. Quickly, I spin in the opposite direction, so my camera faces the kitchen cabinets instead of the hot man in the towel.

"You hungry, babe?" Flynn asks as he pours himself a cup of coffee, completely oblivious that his towel-covered ass just made an appearance in my FaceTime. "Probably going to run up the street and get some bagels." Frankly, I'm pretty sure he's clueless to the fact that I'm on the phone altogether. *I'll take things that happen when you're known for rambling to yourself all the time for a hundred, Alex.*

He glances over his shoulder to meet my eyes just as Gwen's brow furrows. I wave my hand behind the camera like I'm guiding in the next fighter jet to land on a naval carrier, but it's too late. The towel-covered penis and rich, unmistakably manly voice of my fake New York husband have already made their debut. "Daisy?" Gwen questions, and her voice drops to a conspiratorial whisper. "Is there a man in your apartment?"

Flynn's eyes are wider than I've ever seen them, the curiosity of exactly what kind of bungle I've gotten us into now evidently overwhelming enough that he can't suppress the emotion, and I suck my bottom lip into my mouth, completely unsure of what to say or how to handle this situation. I mean, Gwen knows about my recent move, but she knows absolutely nothing about Flynn or the fact that I'm a married woman.

Shit. Shit. *Shit.*

"Daisy?" Gwen urges, and when I see the concerned look in her eyes, something inside me just snaps. I know I could play it off as a one-night stand or a short affair with a random New York man and Gwen would understand, but it just doesn't feel…right.

It's time for the truth—or, at least, the closest version of it I'm willing to tell before my citizenship is settled.

"Technically, I'm at his place. Our place. Well, our place temporarily."

Gwen just stares back at me through the camera. Clearly, I've confused her so much, she doesn't even know what questions to ask.

"I guess now it's time to tell you that I have some news," I state, and nervous laughter bubbles up from my lungs.

"I'll say."

"So… uh…as you know…I'm…uh…living in New York now."

"Yes. We've established that." Her brow furrows in a way I know is more accusatory than confused. "You told me about the move when I got back from the cruise—I remember the conversation specifically. What I don't remember is any mention of a man, any man, and certainly not one that you're *living with* in New York."

"Well, it's a crazy story…" I pause, trying to explain without Gwen focusing on the fact that I'm a big fat liar.

"I'm waiting on pins and needles here, darling."

"So…that was Flynn…and Flynn is…" I pause again and swallow against the Sahara Desert that has migrated into my throat. "Flynn is…my husband."

Outright shock makes her jaw drop like one of those clowns at a mini golf course. "I'm sorry…did you just say husband? As in, till death do us part, grow old and die, one man for the rest of your life husband?"

"She definitely said husband."

Those words aren't mine, and they definitely aren't Gwen's. Eyes wide, I look up from the screen of my phone to find Flynn looking at me with a laid-back smile, as if it's no big deal that we've just dropped a nuclear bomb of truth in the kitchen.

"My Daisy…my strong, big-hearted, independent, doesn't need a man Daisy is *married*?"

I look between Gwen and Flynn, and all I can do is nod.

"Daisy! What?! How? I need to know all the details, and I need to know them now. Seventy years of men flowing in and out of my life, and I can't imagine committing to one of them. And, what? You found someone to do it with in the Yellow Pages? Fill me in here."

Between one breath and the next, my phone is out of my hands and Flynn's face is filling Gwen's end of the camera line.

"Hi, Gwen," he greets her, still flipping shirtless and only wearing a towel. "I've heard a lot about you. I'm sure you know our Daisy is a bit of a talker."

Our Daisy?

"That she is." Gwen smiles through a startled laugh. "Though, she doesn't seem to be doing a whole lot of it right now." My cheeks flame, and I move farther out of the camera frame of the call. *Oh God.* "Maybe you can explain to me how you fit in here—a whole *husband* I didn't even know about."

"I'm Flynn Winslow," he says without a hint of nervousness in his voice. "It's a pleasure to meet you, Gwen. I know this must be confusing and concerning for you, but I think you'll understand best if I explain it this way—I've never in my life met a woman like Daisy, and I doubt I ever will again. She's the kind of person you don't forget, and given the opportunity, she's the kind of person you don't let go. Understand?"

"Well, this is quite the surprise," Gwen comments, in a way that, to me, is completely nonsensical, a tiny shimmer of tears in her eyes, and Flynn smiles.

"It was for my family too."

"I can't decide if I'm mad at Daisy for not telling me anything or happy for her. Or maybe both."

What the hell? I mean, that's it? She's just done with the questions?

"I think you're probably just happy for me!" I blurt out loud enough for her to hear, too relieved to give my inner skeptic any credence.

"I think I am too, but I also think you have a lot to tell me," Gwen responds, but I take heart in the fact that I can sense a smile in her voice.

"Before I make you give the phone back to Daisy, I have a few questions for you, Flynn."

He nods.

"Are you taking good care of my girl?"

"Always."

"Are you financially stable?"

He smiles. "Yes."

"Any criminal background?"

He shakes his head. "No, ma'am."

"What if I told you I was going to hire a private investigator to do a secret background check on you?"

"I'd tell you to give him my number and address, and I'd be more than happy to give him all the information he needs."

"I think I like you, Flynn Winslow," Gwen eventually responds. "I'm not too happy that you and my Daisy got married without telling me, but I might be able to let that slide."

Flynn smiles. "I hope you will, Gwen."

"Daisy?" Gwen's voice fills my ears, and I know it's time for me to put on my big-girl panties and stop hiding in the corner.

"Yeah?" I respond and take my phone from Flynn's outstretched hand.

He pats a gentle hand to my shoulder and mouths, *You okay?*

I nod.

He leans forward to press a kiss to my forehead before heading out of the kitchen and back into the bedroom.

"So, I guess congratulations are in order, huh?" Gwen questions, and I look at the screen to find her raising a pointed brow in my direction.

"Don't be mad." I cringe. "I'm sorry. I wanted to tell you, but it's all been a bit of a whirlwind and it never felt like the right time and, yeah, I'm mostly just sorry you're finding out like this."

"I didn't even know you were dating."

That's probably because I wasn't.

"Shoot." She shakes her head on a sigh, a horn honking in the background. "You're lucky I have to head out for an art class, but just know, I have a lot more questions for you, missy."

"Understandable."

"Before I go, I have one question for you."

"Ask me anything." *Well, besides why I got married. Don't ask me that.*

"Are you happy?" Her question is so simple, and my answer isn't as complicated as I would've thought it would be.

"Yes," I answer, and it doesn't feel like a lie at all. It just feels…I don't know…right?

"Good. That's good, darling. If you're happy, then I'm happy." Gwen smiles. "Okay, well, I'll definitely be talking to you soon."

"Definitely."

"And one more thing…" She pauses and drops her voice to a whisper. "Is Flynn nearby?"

I shake my head. "In the bedroom. Getting dressed."

She waggles her brows. "After seeing that man in a towel, I can't blame you for marrying him. I would've done the same."

"Gwen!"

She winks. "Kisses, darling!"

And then she's gone, off the screen and leaving me standing in the kitchen, trying to wrap my head around what just happened.

You managed to tell Gwen you're married…but you didn't tell her why you got married. So basically, you're still lying to her…

I lean my head back and blow out a breath.

"You okay, babe?" Flynn's voice snags my attention, and I find him standing in the kitchen again, but fully dressed for the day.

"I will be once you take me for a big fat pancake breakfast with all the fixins."

He quirks a brow. "Why do these pancakes seem like penance?"

"Because they are. First, for being an accomplice in my big marriage reveal to Gwen. And second," I say and pointedly tug the collar of my robe down to show him all the glorious marks he left on me last night. "These."

He smirks when he sees the tops of my breasts and then shakes his head. "You were going to have to tell Gwen at some point, and you can't even pretend to not like those hickeys. Astronauts are taking photos of your smile right now from space."

"Okay, so I might like the hickeys."

"Then why are you trying to start an argument?"

"Look, Flynn, sorry to break it to you, but you married an occasionally crazy person who sometimes is irrational, and since you were the one who helped me break the news to Gwen and blessed me with all these hickeys and orgasms last night, I'm making you take me to breakfast."

"Okay," he says and shrugs. "Pancakes it is."

No questions. No rebuttals. Not even an annoyed sigh.

Just…okay.

Sometimes, Daisy, this man is so perfect for you, it's as if you made him up in your head.

We've been walking for a few blocks, in the direction of a restaurant Flynn said will cure my pancake breakfast cravings, and I've yet to feel anything but content. There're plenty of people milling about the sidewalks, going into shops or grabbing a coffee or whatever it is they plan to fill their weekend with, and I find myself second-guessing my original conclusion that Los Angeles is where it's at.

After being in New York for a while now, I'm starting to wonder what my life would be like had I started my American dream venture here. Would I be happier? Feel more at home?

You already know the answer to that question, sis.

I can't refute the appeal of a Saturday morning in New York. Even dreaded Mondays feel different here. This city has a vibrancy, an undeniable pull that makes you want to be a part of it. It's why people from all over the world travel here to experience it for themselves. There's just something about this town that makes you feel alive, as if anything is possible.

A cool spring breeze brushes against my face and urges a shiver to roll up my spine. I wrap my arms around my chest a little tighter, tucking my sweater closer to my body.

"Here," Flynn says, and I look over to find him taking off his black leather jacket and wrapping it around my shoulders.

"Nope. No way," I refute and try to give his jacket back to him, but he wraps one strong arm around my shoulders and makes it impossible. "I can't wear your 'I'm a hot, bad boy jacket.'"

"What?" He looks down at me with an amused smirk.

"It's, like, a staple of your wardrobe, Flynn. It feels sacrilegious for it to be anywhere but on your body."

"Stake your claim, babe. Make sure no other women pick up on all these hot, bad-boy vibes I'm apparently giving off."

"Now, don't get all cocky about it." I snort, and he just smirks.

I roll my eyes, but I also keep his jacket on. I mean, he might not get the appeal, but I sure as hell do. The instant I saw him all mysterious on his bike with this sexy jacket on, I threw caution to the wind and hopped on the back. Sure, I was in the middle of a pseudobreakdown, but that didn't take away from the irresistible appeal.

Suddenly, I find myself watching all the female pedestrians on the sidewalk closely, gauging their reactions to Flynn when he strolls by them.

Lady in a sweatsuit and with a baby in a stroller? *Double take.*

A fortysomething woman in heels? *Licks her flipping lips.*

A white-haired granny with a black poodle? *Pretty much drools.*

Goodness, if he were my real husband, I'd probably have to consider a tracking device or something.

If he were your real husband, you know you wouldn't have to worry about any of that because Flynn Winslow isn't the kind of man who fucks around on his significant other.

My gaze moves to Flynn, and I can't stop myself from taking inventory of how he reacts to other people…particularly, other women.

Eyes forward, he doesn't really do anything but…guide us through the morning foot traffic. His eyes flit to the same people my eyes flit to—a very attractive brunette in heels, an enthusiastic man singing "YMCA" at the top of his lungs while jogging, a group of teenagers chatting and laughing and bumping into one another—but he never does anything that would raise a red flag if he were my actual spouse.

Don't get me wrong, I don't think a healthy relationship means you shouldn't be able to look. We're all human, and when faced with someone who is aesthetically attractive, it would go against our nature not to look. It's natural. Normal, even.

But you should never feel like your spouse is looking with some kind of intention. You should never feel like your significant other is keeping their options open or that their eyes are showing more interest in someone other than you.

And even in a fake marriage, Flynn isn't that kind of man.

Flynn is loyal to his core and has the kind of integrity that most men wish they had. If he weren't so anti-relationship, anti-real marriage, there is no doubt in my mind that some lucky woman would've probably already locked his ass down.

Thank fuck that's not the case. Though, pretty soon, once all your immigration shit is done, Flynn will be a free man again, and maybe he'll want to give relationships and dating a shot…

I swallow hard against a knot in my throat and refocus on following Flynn's lead as we cross the street and begin to walk past one of the Central Park entrances.

Spring is certainly showing herself inside the gates. Flowers are blooming and greenery is thriving and the action taking place within the park's entrance is irrefutable. What looks to be white-and-red tented booths for a small carnival fill my vision and become a draw I can't resist.

Fingers gripping Flynn's shirt, I tug on the material and pull us both to a stop.

He looks down at me in curiosity, and I nod toward the inside of the park. His gaze follows my line of vision until he spots the tents and the small crowd of people, and then he meets my eyes again.

"Can we go?"

"To a carnival?"

I nod. "I have to at least get one of those funnel cakes."

"What's a funnel cake?"

I blink three times. "I'm sorry, did you just ask me what a funnel cake is? As in, you've never had one?"

"Yes."

"You've never had a funnel cake?" I question again, and he shakes his head on a soft chuckle.

His eyes narrow, and I know him well enough now to know they're saying, *"How many times do I need to answer this question?"*

"Holy shit, Flynn!" I exclaim. "We have to fix this ASAP!"

"But what about the pancakes you were going on about?"

I shrug. "We can grab some after."

His health-conscious mind is shocked. I can see the question written all over him. *"Pancakes after funnel cake?"*

"It's Saturday, Flynn. And we can do and eat whatever the hell we want on Saturdays because calories don't count on the weekends."

He laughs at that, and I take it upon myself to grab his hand and pull him toward a tent that has the words **Funnel Cakes** written across the front of it.

We only have to stand in line for a few minutes before we pay the kind man with the rotund belly ten bucks for two funnel cakes. And once the paper plates filled with the greasy dough and covered in powdered sugar are in our hands, Flynn looks at me like I've lost my ever-loving mind.

"You are going to eat that cake, and you are going to love it," I state with an index finger toward him. "I don't care that you're Mr. I Like To Eat Healthy. Today, you're going to cheat it the hell up and savor the greasy deliciousness of a funnel cake with me."

I've watched the routine way in which Flynn almost never misses a workout at the gym and selectively chooses his meals and snacks. Basically, most of what he puts into his body is devoid of processing and is packed with the kinds of nutrients that would make my family physician back in Vancouver sob out of happiness.

And if he does go the processed food route? Well, you best believe the next few meals will be clean with a capital C.

Flynn just shakes his head, but I don't miss the whisper of a smile on his lips.

Yeah, he's going to eat this cake and like it. I don't care if I have to pry his mouth open and shove in each bite. There is no human being alive who should snub their nose at a funnel cake.

"You know, babe," he says and takes my free hand to guide us over to an empty bench. "When it comes to food, you're kind of bossy."

"Because food is important, Flynn," I state and sit down in the empty spot beside him. "Everyone needs to eat. It is the foundation on which our bodies grow."

He eyes me with a knowing look. "This funnel cake is the foundation of a heart attack."

"*If* you eat too many. Everything in moderation."

He laughs and surprises a squeal out of me by pulling me into his lap. His lips are near my ear, and he whispers, "You like having the last word. Love it, even."

"What?" I press my nose against his and stare into his eyes. "No, I don't."

He smirks and steals a kiss. "It's okay. I don't mind."

"Of course you don't mind. You barely talk."

He winks. "And you talk enough for the both of us."

"Just shut up and try the funnel cake." And with that, I tear off a piece of his funnel cake and all but shove it into his mouth. His surprised laughter blows powdered sugar into my face, which creates a domino effect of giggles.

"You like it?" I ask once I catch my breath, but more laughs leave my lips when I realize just how much powdered sugar has managed to get all over Flynn's face.

"I love it. Greasy, sugary, full of fat. A true foundation of nutrients, like you said," he responds cheekily and tears a piece of funnel cake from his plate. But he doesn't put it to his lips. *Nope*. He takes a page from my book and rubs the cake across my cheek before pressing it against my lips.

"Here, babe. Have a bite."

I snort. "What the hell?"

"Oh, that's not how you eat funnel cakes? You don't shove them in each other's faces? I was just following your lead."

"You're such a smartass," I retort, but yeah, I also take that bite because funnel cake. Everyone and their mother loves funnel cake.

And you really love funnel cake when you're eating it with Flynn. Come to think of it, there're starting to be a lot of things you really love with him…

THIRTY-FIVE

Sunday, May 12th

Flynn

Daisy is a bed hog. Covers, sheets, comforter, pillows, she will steal it all. I know this because ever since she moved in with me, I wake up with my head flat on the mattress and my body completely bare of anything.

With a fresh cup of coffee in my hand, I step into the bedroom and note the ridiculous way that my wife is wrapped up in the comforter like a human burrito and how her tiny body manages to take up most of the king-sized mattress.

I smile at the scene as I step closer to the bed and take her in. Her wild curls fan out over the three pillows beneath her head, and her eyelashes flutter ever so slightly, as if she's still sleeping but also still close to waking up.

This woman. She's absurdly adorable.

The soft sounds of music from one of my favorite operas play through the Bluetooth speakers of my apartment, and I carefully sit on the bed beside Daisy. Coffee lifted closer to her face, I wait for her brain to make sense of the familiar scent.

It doesn't take long. Daisy loves coffee. It's her morning go-to.

Her green eyes open slowly and meet mine. They look almost emerald in the light of the day, shimmering like gemstones beneath the rays of the sun that have filtered in through the window.

"Morning, babe."

"Morning," she rasps through a still-sleepy voice and clears her throat. A hint of a smile lifts her mouth when she glances down at the cup in my hand. "Is that coffee?"

"Yes."

"For me?"

"Nope."

"What?" she questions and sits up in bed. The comforter falls down her body, revealing miles upon miles of gloriously naked skin.

"I'm kidding," I say with a small grin and carefully hand the fresh cup of joe to her.

She grabs it greedily with two hands and takes a sip. "Oh, that's good. That's real good. And made to perfection. Thank you."

I know it's made to perfection. Two sugars with a little creamer, that's Daisy's preferred coffee style. After living together for a while now, I know more about Daisy than I've ever known about anyone. Her little quirks, her favorite foods, the fact that when she says she'll be ready in ten minutes, it really means thirty.

"What are you listening to?"

"'Un bel dì, vedremo.'"

She tilts her head to the side, and a wry grin covers her mouth. "I'm sorry… what?"

"It's from the opera *Madama Butterfly*."

"You like opera?"

"Yes. You don't?"

"I don't know." She shrugs. "I've never really listened to it."

"Have you ever been to an opera?"

She shakes her head.

"That's…sad, Daisy. Everyone should experience going to the opera at least once in their life."

"Flynn Winslow likes opera. Wow. That is…quite the revelation."

"That surprises you?"

"Uh…yeah," she answers through a giggle. "But then again, I'm finding you're full of surprises. I mean, I never would've pegged you as a guy who went to culinary school."

Her exaggeration makes me chuckle. "A few cooking classes, babe. Not culinary school."

She just grins. "A motorcycle-riding, leather-jacket–wearing chef who loves opera music. You are an enigma."

"As are you, Daisy," I answer and reach out to tuck a few of her curls behind her ears.

"Oh, I'm not that interesting."

I strongly disagree. She's the most interesting woman I've ever met.

My hand trails down her bare arm, across her bare belly, and I don't miss the way goose bumps cover her arms when the music playing in the background reaches a climax that almost always gives everyone the same reaction.

"This song is…powerful," she says, her voice quiet as she listens intently.

"That's opera."

She looks at me quizzically, and when my eyes flit down to her bare breasts and belly, I get an idea. A brilliant fucking idea that is one-hundred-percent selfish on my part.

"Would you like to play a game, Daisy?"

"What kind of game?"

"A game that will show you just how powerful opera music can be."

She quirks a brow but then shrugs. "Okay, sure."

Fuck yes.

Carefully, I take the cup of coffee out of her hands and set it on the nightstand. She pouts, of course, but I just shake my head and gently ease her back down onto the bed. "This won't take long. And stay right here. I'll be back."

Out of the bedroom and into the living room, I grab a pair of noise-canceling headphones and the remote for my speakers.

Once I'm back in the bedroom, I climb onto the bed and position myself right between, thanks to my devious hands, her now-spread thighs.

Her mouth forms a little "O" of surprise when she realizes the intimacy of our position. "Is this game a sexy kind of game?"

I nod. Her eyes light up.

"I'm going to show you that opera music is so powerful, you are going to have the most intense orgasm of your life. And it's only going to take about three minutes."

She laughs. Outright. "Three minutes?"

I nod again. "Yeah, babe. Three minutes and you're going to be seeing fucking stars."

I don't wait for her response. Instead, I gently place the headphones over her ears and help her relax back into the mattress.

She keeps looking at me skeptically, but it only makes me smile. Because I know in just a few minutes, she's going to feel the kind of pleasure that'll make her think she's having an out-of-body experience.

From my phone, I choose the one song that will seal her pleasurable fate— "*Nessun Dorma.*"

Sung by Luciano Pavarotti, the one and only man who could sing it to perfection.

I know this piece like the back of my hand, and once I hit play and the music is flooding into Daisy's ears, I engage in my selfish desires of putting my mouth on her.

Without preamble or hesitation, I bury my face between her thighs and lap and lick my tongue against her. She's sweet like honey, and every time her hips jolt forward from the sensation of my mouth, it makes my cock grow harder by an inch.

Fuck, this is heaven.

I wish I could stay here all fucking day, licking and sucking and feasting on her. But I'm on a time limit, and I know, very soon, the orchestra and Pavarotti are going to start hitting the notes that will spur the most powerful orgasm Daisy has ever experienced and wring her fucking dry.

My mouth wrapped around her clit, I suck, flick my tongue, and suck and suck *and suck* until her body starts to vibrate beneath me. Her moans grow louder by the second, and when her hands go to my hair, gripping the strands so tight it makes my damn skull hurt, I know she's there.

Fuck yes.

Incomprehensible shouts escape her parted lips as her climax consumes her.

Tears stream down her cheeks, and her body shakes and trembles beneath me, and I never stop eating and sucking at her. I ride out her orgasm right along with her, and I don't stop working my mouth against her until I feel her body go lax.

My chin resting on her belly now, I stare up at her as her breasts heave up and down with panting breaths.

"Holy shit," she mutters. "Holy fucking shit."

With shaky hands, she takes off her headphones and looks down at me in shock. "What was that? What just happened to me?"

"That's opera, baby."

She snorts. Giggles. Shakes her head. "That was insane. I felt…like I was in my body but not in my body. Hell, I don't think I'll be able to walk anytime soon."

I grin.

"But you know what I can do?"

"What?"

She doesn't respond, but a mischievous smile kisses her mouth as she sits up and crawls down toward me. Her fingers are on my boxers, pulling them down before I know it, and my cock pops free of the cotton constraints, still hard from watching Daisy come.

"What are you doing, babe?"

"I need to make you feel good, Flynn."

She needs. She fucking *needs*.

Daisy leans forward and puts her mouth on me. Slow and teasing at first, she wraps her lips around my cock and begins to gently suck at my length.

Well, *fuck*. It feels good. *Too good*. And watching the way she greedily takes me into her mouth makes it even better.

I watch the way her eyes fall closed, as if it's giving her actual pleasure to do this to me. I feel her warm breath against me as small moans escape her throat. And I don't miss the covetous way her hands grab at my thighs and abdomen and chest.

Daisy is a fucking goddess. A woman who surprises me at every turn. A woman who gives me the kind of pleasure I've never experienced before.

You could spend forever having weekends like this with her, and it still wouldn't feel like enough.

THIRTY-SIX

Friday, May 17th

Daisy

"Good morning, Daisy," a smiling, happy woman in a pair of medical scrubs with cute kittens all over the material greets me as I step into an exam room. "I'm Susan. I'll be the nurse who'll be helping Dr. Fields do your physical today."

She glances at her clipboard. "I have a note here that this physical is for immigration requirements, correct?"

I nod. "Yes."

"Okay, great. I'll make sure Dr. Fields has the forms she needs to file with USCIS." She gestures with one arm toward the lone, white-paper–covered exam table in the room. "You can go ahead and take a seat."

I follow her instructions, and the paper beneath my skirt-covered butt rustles and crinkles as I adjust my hips and cross my legs.

I don't know what it is about doctors' offices and hospitals, but they always have the same smell. A weird, everything-is-sterile odor that shouldn't remind you of being sick, but for some reason, it does. It's a conundrum, I tell you.

"I'm going to ask you some questions, get your vital signs, and then Dr. Fields will be in to do her examination."

"Sounds like a plan, Stan," I blurt but then cringe. "I mean, that sounds great."

Besides the strange odors, places where medical shit occurs always make me uncomfortable. There's just something about a random stranger in a white coat asking invasive questions about your life and daily habits that never sits well with me. I mean, can you take me dinner before you start asking me about how many sexual partners I've had? Sheesh. I don't want to start an intimate relationship with you; I just want you to tell me if this mole on my back is normal.

Truthfully, I have the same issue with the dentist.

Luckily, Susan doesn't appear to notice the giant pink weirdo in the room and gets on with the show.

"Have you experienced any illness in the past two weeks? Cough, runny nose, fever, body aches?"

"Nope."

"Since we don't have your immunization records, we'll have to do a full blood work-up to check your titers for all of the diseases USCIS requires. Is that okay?"

Ugh. Blood work. Another reason why I hate going to the doctor. But it's not as if I have a choice in the matter. If I want a green card, I best be showing my veins.

Internally, I cringe and grit my teeth, but externally, I nod. "Okay."

"Any pertinent past medical history we should know about?"

"Not that I can think of. I don't take any daily medications or anything. And my only surgery was a tonsillectomy when I was eight."

"What about a history of drug use, excessive alcohol use, or smoking?"

I shake my head. "Nope."

Although, all this immigration stuff might lead me to drink…

"Have you ever been pregnant before? Have any children?"

"No."

"Is there any chance you might be pregnant?"

I start to open my mouth to say no, but then, I'm hit with the truth of Flynn's and my relationship. We've had sex. A lot of sex. And we've never once used a condom.

Way to be responsible, Daisy.

Susan stares at me, and I laugh nervously.

"I…uh…don't think I'm pregnant. I mean, I've obviously been having sex with my husband because that's what married people do, you know." *Good God, Daisy, just get to the point.* I clear my throat. "But I'm on the Depo shot. Have been for five or so years now."

"Okay." Susan just nods and jots something down on her clipboard. "Per the guidelines we have to follow for USCIS, we have to do a pregnancy test. But since we're already drawing your blood, I'll add an HCG level check to your labs."

"What's an HCG level?"

"Pregnancy hormone check," Susan updates and sets her clipboard down to grab a blood pressure cuff. "If you were to be pregnant, your HCG levels would be elevated."

If you were to be pregnant.

If I were to be pregnant?!

I don't know why those words hit me straight in the gut, but they do. If I were to be pregnant, that would certainly cause quite the conundrum in an already complicated situation. Frankly, I don't even know what I would do with that kind of information.

What you *would do? What would* Flynn *do?*

"We get everything back pretty quickly," Susan adds. "Usually within twenty-four hours."

"And I take it you call me with the results?"

She grins and wraps the cuff around my arm. "Yes. If anything comes up in your blood work related to your titer levels or HCG levels or any kind of out-of-the-norm results, we'll call you."

"So, like a no news is good news kind of situation?"

A soft laugh leaves Susan's throat. "Yes."

I blow out a breath as Susan puts her stethoscope to my arm and checks my blood pressure, but my mind is pretty much a million miles away while she finishes whatever else she needs to do.

Including drawing my freaking blood.

Normally, I'm a lunatic with needles, but the realization of Flynn's and my carelessness related to sex has provided quite the mental distraction. It's like my brain is busy doing fucking parkour up there, trying to figure out what the consequences of an unplanned pregnancy with my contractual husband would be.

How would Flynn even react to that kind of news?

I honestly don't know the answer to that, but it doesn't matter because I'm on birth control. Obviously. So, all these mental gymnastics are a pointless endeavor.

But it's certainly interesting that you weren't exactly terrified over the idea of being pregnant. If anything, you were busy with what Flynn would do...

I shake my head to try to dislodge my obviously crazy thoughts. Now is not the time to have a psychotic breakdown. Surely USCIS will frown upon reading that Dr. Fields has deemed me to be medically insane.

The big immigration interview might be just around the corner, but I'd bet money they'd cancel that shit real quick if a physician sent in paperwork that said I'm a nutcase.

Which is why you need to chill out, you psycho. Just take a breath. And wait to lose your shit for after you leave this office.

Sweet mother of mercy.

―――

As I walk out of Dr. Fields's office, fresh from an exam and a blood draw and whatever else they had to do to me to make USCIS happy, I head for the subway.

I don't know why the whole pregnancy question threw me for a loop, but it did.

Both Dr. Fields and Susan assured me that if anything came back outside of the norm—titer levels showing I need a vaccine, or you know, the big P-word—they'd call me. Otherwise, they'd just send everything over to USCIS, and I'd get a copy at my interview.

But there's no way I'm pregnant…right?

Even when you're on birth control, there's a way. And yours just happened to involve a sexy-as-hell man with a big cock.

Goodness. My mind has to stop fixating on pointless things.

I roll my eyes so hard I almost bump into the man in a khaki trench coat walking in front of me on Fifth Avenue. Yes, Flynn and I haven't exactly been using condoms, but I'm on freaking *birth control*, have been for years now, and I don't feel pregnant.

Not a single symptom, to be honest. No nausea or sore boobs or whatever else women have to deal with when they're with child.

As I pass a Walgreens on the corner, I almost consider going inside and grabbing a take-home pregnancy test, but before I can step through the automatic doors, logical thought wins out. Just because a nurse had to ask me if I was pregnant doesn't mean that I'm pregnant. Geez.

Maybe you secretly want to be pregnant? Maybe, deep down, you wish you could have Flynn's baby?

"Oh, for the love of everything. I have got to stop," I mutter to myself and hitch my purse up higher on my shoulder. I don't miss the strange look I get from a woman eating her sandwich on a bench, but I put my head down and focus on getting my ass to the subway so I'm not late for work.

I have an apartment in Nolita to stage, and I'll be damned if I give Tara even an extra five minutes of time to start making changes on my design plans. The woman is a little too into farmhouse chic, and the three-bedroom, three-million-dollar loft EllisGrey has under contract is the opposite of shiplap and barn doors.

Not that there's anything wrong with a little Chip and JoJo influences. I've seen *Fixer Upper*, and I adore everything the Magnolia brand stands for, but this loft is not the place for it. It needs a minimalist design with sleek, sophisticated touches.

Once I make it onto the subway, I find an open seat across from a college-aged guy with headphones on and a book in his lap, and I proceed to take my cell phone out of my purse and see what I've missed.

A few work emails.

And a boatload of texts inside my group chat with Winnie and Sophie.

Sophie: I am freaking out. FREAKING OUT. How is my wedding less than two weeks away?! I haven't even decided how I'm going to wear my hair or what shoes I'm going to wear with my dress or whether or not the caterers should serve shrimp cocktail at cocktail hour or…basically a million other things I've yet to figure out.

Winnie: But you have your dress. Which is downright gorgeous. And you have everything else figured out with the caterer. It's all good in the wedding hood, my soon-to-be sister-in-law. You have no reason to worry.

Sophie: You swear it's going to be fine?

Winnie: Promise.

Sophie: Can you also promise that my soon-to-be-husband isn't going to do anything crazy like plan a flash mob in the middle of our reception or give me a lap dance while he's taking off my garter?

Winnie: Uh…

Sophie: Winnie!

A laugh jumps from my lungs as I read their exchange. Pretty sure Sophie is asking Winnie for a promise that she cannot guarantee.

Winnie: What? You know I have no control over what my crazy brother does. Jude is nuts. I'm just thankful it's him and not Ty that's getting married. Truthfully, the only wedding I looked forward to was Flynn's because he's so damn laid-back, but he just up and married Daisy without inviting any of us.

Winnie: P.S. I love you, Daisy! And while I was mad at you both when I first found out, I'm only thankful that I have you as my sister-in-law now.

Instantly, I go from laughing to staring down at the phone with a knot in my chest. I'm starting to feel like such a fraud for lying to Winnie, for lying to everyone about the truth of Flynn's and my marriage.

A marriage that will come to an end soon.

My interview is the morning of Jude and Sophie's wedding. Which means, if all goes well, not too long before their actual wedding, Flynn and I will no longer need to keep up the fake-marriage pretenses.

And even though his family has accepted me with open arms and started to feel like my own family—feel like the family I've always wished I'd had—I'll have to move back to LA and go back to my life there, and Flynn will go back to living his life here.

A life that doesn't include me.

THIRTY-SEVEN

Flynn

I flip two steaks on the skillet and turn to grab some seasoning, but when I spot movement out of the corner of my eye, I turn to find Daisy setting her purse and keys on the counter. Normally, she announces her arrival in some adorable way like "Honey, I'm home!" or "Flynn, I'm starving! Feed me!"

But tonight, she came in like a fucking ninja.

"Hey, babe," I greet, but it's like she doesn't even hear me.

Daisy's face is devoid of her normally bubbly expression, and her eyes are distant, as if she's too busy inside her own head to even notice her surroundings.

"Babe," I repeat, and she looks up to meet my eyes.

"Hi," she responds, but her voice is quiet, timid even.

"You okay?"

She nods, but that's all she gives me. No rambling explanation or adorable hand movements punctuating her words. Just…a nod.

"How did your appointment go?" I ask, and when she furrows her brow in confusion, I expand. "Your physical…?"

"Oh," she acknowledges, and her mouth forms a little "O." "It was fine."

I might not be the type of man who has a track record of long-term relationships with women, but I have a sister and a mother and an aunt who have shown me that "It's fine" never means that.

Fine means the opposite.

"Are you sure you're okay?"

"Yep." She nods again. "Just tired, I guess. It's been a long day."

"Would a steak help make the day not feel so long?" I grin and nod toward the skillet.

"I'd love to say yes to that, but…" She pauses, cringes, and explains, "I'm not hungry, and I still need to finish up some staging plans for a property by tomorrow."

Daisy not hungry? Not talkative? And choosing work over her favorite Friday night Netflix binges that she always forces me to join in on?

I can't shake the sense that she's shutting me out. Like, she has shit on her mind that she doesn't want to talk to me about. It's the opposite of what I'm used to with her. Sure, sometimes it takes her a bit to open up to me, a sort of rambling in circles before she reaches her end destination, but she always gets there in the end.

Though, tonight, she appears steadfast in not saying much. Not saying anything, really.

And that's not sitting well with you.

But before I can decide if I should ask more questions and try to figure out what has her in such an off mood, Daisy is out of the kitchen.

Damn, it appears she just wants some space. From you.

I turn back to the skillet and flip over the steaks, but the idea of eating right now isn't holding the appeal it did ten minutes ago.

Stove off—and steaks most likely ruined—I set down my spatula and head into the living room where Daisy is sitting on the sofa with her laptop in her lap. Her fingers move across the keys in quick succession, and I decide right then and there she needs something to help take the edge off.

Whatever is causing that edge, I don't know, and I'm hopeful she'll eventually get around to telling me, but if there's one thing I know how to do, it's to help my woman relax.

To make her feel *good*.

I grab the edge of the coffee table and slide it away from the couch. Daisy's feet fall to the floor, and she looks up from her laptop screen in confusion.

"Don't mind me, babe. Just keep doing what you're doing."

She scrunches up her nose, but her eyes widen as she watches me get to my knees in front of her.

"Flynn...?"

"Like I said, don't mind me. You keep working," I tell her and place both of my hands on her thighs and spread them farther apart. I'm thrilled that she's wearing a skirt and all it takes is my fingers sliding her panties to the side to reveal her gorgeous pussy. "In fact, ignore me completely."

I dive right in, face between her legs, I latch my lips around her clit and gently suck.

Daisy's hips jolt forward. "Flynn!" she exclaims, but for the first time since she got home, she also giggles. "You're insane!"

After one long stroke of my tongue against her, I smack my lips in approval. "Yes, baby, I am insane for this sweet-as-fuck pussy of yours."

And then, I get back to work. Sucking and licking and eating at her. Sliding my tongue inside her and feeling the way her walls clench around me.

I give her no mercy. I don't hold back. And I enjoy every fucking second of her on my tongue.

She moans, and her laptop falls to the cushion beside her. And eventually, her fingers find their way into my hair, urging me to keep going.

"Good girl," I whisper against her. "I want you to feel good. I want you to come hard on my tongue. Will you do that for me, Daisy? Will you let me make you come?"

"Y-yes. God, yes."

Once her breaths become tiny pants of air and her legs begin to shake, I know that, in a matter of seconds, Daisy will fall off the cliff and straight into the pleasure abyss where all she can do is feel good. Where whatever had her so quiet and reserved when she got home this evening will no longer be weighing her down.

She doesn't disappoint. She *never* disappoints.

Her moans turn raspy, sexy-as-hell, and just as she hits her peak, I look up to watch the way her full lips part, her cheeks flush, and her breasts heave up and down.

Fuck yes. That's my wife.

THIRTY-EIGHT

Saturday, May 18th

Daisy

Eyes bleary and brain begging for coffee, I shuffle out of the bedroom and down the hallway.

After I came home last night, all stressed out and anxious and locked inside my own head, I was prepared to burrow myself into work that could've waited until Monday and just…I don't know…ignore—*more like, avoid*—everything.

But the night took an unexpected turn.

A "Flynn's head between my legs" kind of turn, and next thing I knew, we were naked, in bed, and I was giving my best impression of a rodeo queen while he was gripping my ass and whispering dirty things into my ear.

Sometimes, it feels like Flynn just intuitively knows when I need a distraction.

Because he does. Which begs the question, what are you going to do without him?

As I step into the kitchen, the soft sounds of classical music playing from the Bluetooth speakers fill my ears, and I find Flynn sitting at the table with a newspaper in his hands. And not the digital newspaper most people read from their phones, but the *actual* newspaper with real paper and ink.

I don't know why, but there's something so sexy about a man reading the newspaper. Especially when it's Flynn and he's wearing only a pair of boxer briefs.

Boxer briefs that give quite the show of the kind of heat he's packing...

"You doing okay over there, babe?"

I blink past the fantasy fog and realize I'm just standing in the middle of the kitchen, staring at him quite…crudely. Well, *hell*. Apparently, I'm a pervert.

Flynn quirks a questioning brow, and I bumble my way through an awkward nod, mumbling, "Mm-hmm," as I head over to the coffeemaker.

"Coffee, huh? Seemed like you were headed in my direction."

I glance over my shoulder and find him smiling at me in a way that makes me wonder if he has any clue how attractive he is.

Seriously. Why's he gotta be so damn good-looking?

Hand to my hip, I turn around and face him with a cheeky grin. "Maybe I was. But now I'm thinking you should come over here."

Flynn doesn't hesitate to set down his newspaper, get out of his chair, and stride straight toward me. I'm in his arms between one beat of my heart and the next, and his lips move against mine, slowly provoking an ache to stir between my thighs.

He deepens the kiss and slides his hands into my hair, and I'm *allll* about the direction this is heading, but Flynn slows the movements of his lips until he ends our embrace with a soft press of his mouth to mine. "Morning, babe."

A few seconds later, he's back at the table with his newspaper in his hands and his eyes scanning the pages.

Um…excuse me? Hello? Please, sir, I'd like some more.

I stare at him, as if my eyes alone have the power to get his attention, but he doesn't look up from his paper. Mind you, a paper that isn't feeling as sexy as it did before. If anything, it's now the world's greatest literary cock-block, and it's ruining my selfish need for more attention from Flynn.

Slightly annoyed and now far hornier than one woman should be upon just waking up and without her proper caffeine fix, I pour myself a cup of coffee and mentally prepare myself to lure the oblivious man at the kitchen table through other means.

Okay…think, Daisy. What's sexy? What's something that no man can resist?

Knowing full well that I'm currently wearing only a simple silk nightgown with nothing underneath, when I go to get my favorite French vanilla creamer from the fridge, I take my sweet, sweet time and make a show of bending over to reach the container from the middle shelf.

I'm talking, someone call the Academy and let them know there's a new actress in town, any second Meryl Streep will be calling me for tips, kind of show.

When I feel the sensation of my nightgown sliding up my thighs, I know, *I fucking know*, that my milkshake that brings all the boys to the yard is on full display for Flynn.

Are you sure that's what milkshake means in that song?

Frankly, no, I don't know that, but whatever. Just work with me here.

I pretend to rummage around in the fridge—*my ass and hoo-hah still hanging out in the wind*—and then I steal a quick glance over my shoulder to check my target.

Is Flynn's gaze resting joyously upon my ass? Nope. *That would be a negative, ghost rider.*

Not even kidding, the sexy bastard is *still* looking at his paper. I'm flashing goodies like it's Mardi Gras and he's got the beads, but he's just reading the newspaper like it's any ol' Saturday morning that doesn't include his wife practically spread-eagled in front of the fridge.

What is in that paper? The key to eternal life?

I'm starting to feel like a bit of a brat for being so annoyed that Flynn isn't giving me attention, but damn it, that's what I want. Throw a red dress on me and call me Veruca Salt because I want Flynn's eyes on me and his hands on me and his big, perfect, beautiful cock inside me, and I want it all right now.

On a quiet sigh, I shut the fridge door and actually use the creamer for something other than an excuse for me to bend over and entice Flynn to show me his penis. But once I get my coffee all made and take a few sips, I decide to give it another shot.

Ain't no rest for the wicked-ly horny, amirite?

Up on the counter with a little hop, I sit in the type of—*hopefully*—seductive position that has my body facing Flynn.

"Reading anything interesting over there?" I question as I make a point to spread my thighs as far as they can go.

"Just the usual shit."

Four words. No eye contact. That's it.

Okay, yeah, I've had about enough of this nonsense…

I hop off the counter and stride right over to the man who is apparently oblivious to all the "I'm horny for you" signs I'm sending his way. And it doesn't take long for me to edge myself onto his lap, making damn sure I'm between him and that dumb newspaper that's stealing all my thunder.

Flynn doesn't react, though. Instead, he flips to the next page, something involving the business section, and even adjusts his hands so we can both read the paper together.

"Anything in particular you want to read, babe?"

Your penis. I'd like to read your penis.

"Nope." I purse my lips.

"Here, can you hold this for a sec?" he asks and puts the newspaper into my hands.

"Sure." I discreetly roll my eyes. "Love to."

"Fantastic."

I almost roll my eyes again, but when his big hands grip my ass and lift me off his lap for a brief second, I'm surprised to feel the warmth and hardness of his cock slowly sliding between my legs.

Oh myyyyyyy.

My nipples tighten. My pussy clenches. And over what feels like the longest seconds of my life, Flynn eases himself inside me until his cock is completely filling me up.

I'm talking, inch by motherfucking inch, he pushes his cock inside me. It all feels so good, so intense, that tears fill my eyes and I have to bite down on my bottom lip to stop myself from shouting out over the soft music that's still playing from the speakers.

But Flynn doesn't say anything. He just fills me up and then gently takes the newspaper back out of my hands and goes back to reading. Hell, he even flips through three pages with me just sitting there, on his lap, with his cock inside me.

What is happening right now?

Whatever it is, it just might be the hottest, most confusing thing you've ever experienced.

I shift my hips, and the sensation that builds inside me causes a little moan to escape from my throat. This is…intense. And insane. And feels So. Damn. Good.

"You wanted my attention, that much was clear," he whispers into my ear, and the warmth of his breath urges a shiver to roll up my spine. "So I'm going to tell you again—because it seems like you didn't really hear me the first time…if you want sex, Daisy, *all* you have to do is ask."

Oh, holy hell.

"What kind of attention does my girl need right now?" he asks and brushes his lips up the side of my neck. "Did she just want to feel my cock inside her? Or does she want more than that?"

"More," I whisper back. "Lots more."

He sets down the newspaper and places his big hands on my legs. With a squeeze, he spreads them until they're as wide as they can go, completely astride his lap, and grazes his fingers from my knees to my inner thighs.

"You want me to fuck you?"

I swallow. "Yes, please."

In an instant, the newspaper flies into the air and Flynn's coffee cup hits the hardwood floor in a crash. My back is on the kitchen table, and my nightgown is up and over my breasts, leaving my body bared for his covetous gaze.

He stares down at me, his blue eyes heated, and his big hands adjust my thighs until they're perfectly wrapped around his waist.

"Anytime you want my cock, Daisy," he repeats as he slides himself back inside me, "all you have to do is tell me."

I moan. Flynn doesn't repeat himself, ever. The fact that he's doing it now is such a turn-on, I can hardly keep my eyes from rolling back in my head.

"You don't need to work to get my attention," he whispers and grabs both of my breasts in his hands. "Because, baby, you always have my attention."

His words make me clench around him, but they also spur a pounding rhythm to vibrate my chest and hiccup the breaths falling from my lips.

This man, I swear, he's too perfect for my own good. He's *everything*. And I'm having a hard time seeing a future where I won't want his attention.

But the immigration interview is scheduled, planned, and set in stone, and I know in the cold, dark, scary part of my heart what comes when it's finished.

No Flynn. No sex. No forever. None of the attention I can't see myself walking away from. *Which means you've got thirteen days to figure out how to rewrite your vision of the future.*

THIRTY-NINE

Friday, May 24th

Daisy

I finish stacking the vintage books I purchased at a secondhand shop in Greenwich Village and step back to check my work.

Yeah, that's perfect, I think to myself as I note the way the worn-in spines and hues of dark blues and greens and maroons really bring out the dark wood of the shelves inside the bonus room that is being staged as an in-home office and library.

In a week's time, this expensive SoHo loft will hit the market, and I'm confident EllisGrey's client will receive multiple bids on this beauty.

Empty cardboard boxes stacked, I head back into the open and airy living area to find Tara scuttering around on her heels like a woman on the warpath.

I roll my eyes to myself. I swear, staging days with her are something straight out of a horror movie. She snaps at everyone and everything, and the joy that usually comes from bringing a design vision to life is severely compromised by her overall sour attitude.

I mean, does she even like this job? Sometimes I really wonder.

My phone vibrates in the back pocket of my black dress pants, and I pull it out to find a text.

Flynn: *I just received a delivery. At my office. Any idea what that's about?*

I smile. *Why, yes, I definitely do.*

Me: If it contains two very beautiful but still STRONG and MANLY vases that provide a little color for the shelves behind your desk and an abstract painting to hang on the wall by the door, then yes, I might know something about that delivery…

Honestly, after seeing Flynn's office for the first time a few weeks ago, I couldn't stop myself from adding a little design aesthetic to it. I'm hoping my emphasis on the men-friendly buzzwords helps it go over a little more easily.

Flynn: You know what would be a better pop of color in my office?

Me: A gorgeous throw rug for underneath your desk?

Flynn: Your bare pussy. On my desk.

Me: Flynn Winslow. Are you sexting me???? In the middle of a workday????

Scandalized or not, when it comes to sex with Flynn, an opportunist I am. I quickly throw another message into the mix. Also, Yoda I'm not, but there are only so many days left to feel Flynn inside me, even if it's just a visual via phone sex.

Me: If you ARE sexting me, then put your money where your mouth is and send me a dick pic.

I mean, there's nothing wrong with trying, right? What's the worst he could say? No?

And having a picture of Flynn's gorgeous penis on my phone for the rest of time isn't exactly a negative.

Ha. You'd save it to a damn USB stick just to have a backup.

Flynn: I'll do you one better.

Me: *Oh, really? I'm all ears.*

Flynn: *I'm leaving my office right now. A good girl who wants to get fucked can meet me at home in about 20 minutes.*

I look at his text and across the room to where Tara is now bitching at one of the burly movers tasked with delivering and setting up the staging furniture for this loft.

I shouldn't…*should I?*

Back to Tara, I note the way her face scrunches up with disdain when the man doesn't give her an answer she likes.

Only seven more days, my mind whispers. *Seven more days until the interview and your current cozy bubble of blissful sex and happy days with Flynn will come to an end.*

And just like that, I'm decided.

"Tara, I have to run to the office really quick," I announce in a rush, already starting the process of heading toward the door to grab my purse.

"What?" she questions back and looks at me like I just told her I'm going to set this loft on fire for the fun of it. "*Why?*"

Because I need to go have sex with my husband before he's not my husband anymore.

"Uh…" I pause and search for a reason, any-fucking-reason. "Uh…Damien just texted, and he needs me to send him a few files from an LA property I helped stage. It's urgent."

Her narrowed eyes call my bluff, but I ignore her.

Instead, I offer a wave over my shoulder and head out the door before she can ask me anything else.

Of course, the instant the loft door shuts behind me and I step on to the elevator, I pull my phone out of my purse and fire off a text.

Me: If anyone asks, you needed me to send you very important papers about an LA property today.

Damien: And why would I need that?

Me: Because I wanted to play hooky, and I needed an excuse that didn't end in Tara gouging my eyes out with her nails.

Damien: I hope this hooky at least involves something awesome and not going to the fucking dentist.

Me: That was one time! And there's nothing wrong with liking clean teeth.

Damien: Daisy.

Me: Relax. This hooky involves…sexy kind of things.

Damien: You mean, you're sneaking out of work to go home and fuck your hot husband?

Me: Something like that.

Damien: Since I'm technically your boss, I think I'm supposed to tell you I'll let it slide this time, but don't make a habit of it.

Damien: But as your friend, I'm saying… I got your back, doll.

Don't make a habit of it? Not to worry, Dame. *This habit of mine has a seven-day expiration.*

FORTY

Tuesday, May 28th

Daisy

At half past five, I step out of the entrance doors of EllisGrey's New York office in Manhattan and stop just before I get past the outside awning. Rain falls from the sky in harsh, unrelenting waves, and I glance down at my favorite white silk blouse and sigh.

This is the opposite of what I want to be wearing right now.

It's times like these that I wish I were the type of person who planned ahead. The kind of organized person who checks the weather and brings umbrellas and raincoats and slicker boots when there's a prediction for rain.

But I've never been that person. Hell, I don't even own an umbrella.

I check the time on my phone and realize I have exactly thirty minutes to get across town to the bridal shop where my bridesmaid dress for Sophie's wedding is waiting for pickup.

Also not ideal for this kind of torrential rain situation.

I start to weigh out the taxi versus subway pros and cons, both of which seem to end in me giving my best impression of a spring break wet T-shirt contest, but the sound of my phone ringing from my purse stops me before I can decide which is the lesser of two evils.

Incoming Call Flynn flashes on the screen, and I answer it by the second ring.

"Hey, you."

"Where are you?" he asks, and I look up at the protective canvas barrier above me.

"Welp. I'm standing underneath the awning outside my building and trying to decide how to avoid the rain while I run across town to get my bridesmaid dress. You don't happen to have access to a teleportation device, do you?"

He chuckles. "What about an umbrella?"

"Well, that would certainly help, but how are you going to get it to me?"

"By car."

"So…you're going to send a car to drop an umbrella off to me?" I question on a snort. "That sounds like a waste of resources."

"Not if I'm driving the car."

I tilt my head to the side. "Huh?"

"I'm half a block away," he expands.

"For real?" I question. "So, you can drive me to the shop to get my dress?"

"There's no need. I already picked it up for you after I got my suit."

The surprising, downright fan-fucking-tastic news makes me fist-pump the air. "Oh my goodness, Flynn! You're my hero!" I exclaim so loud it startles the man working security at the entrance doors.

"Stay put. I'll be there in a minute," he says just as I look toward the street to see him pulling his Range Rover to a stop in front of the building. There's a smile in his voice—an easiness he's acquired when it comes to dealing with me that steals my breath unexpectedly.

He's parked illegally and New York traffic is showing its disdain through obnoxious honks and middle fingers, but Flynn is undeterred. Out of the driver's side door, he heads my way with an actual umbrella in his hand. Rain soaks his dark hair and his white T-shirt as he jogs toward me.

Holy hell. An actual hero. My heart feels as if it wants to burst out of my rib cage, and the burning, stinging pain in my jaw gets more and more intense. Tears, it seems, are trying their damnedest to make a showing right now, but there's *no way* I'm letting some sappy emotion about all of this coming to an end ruin the moment for me.

"Hey, babe," he says with what just might be my favorite Flynn smile. It's a signature smile of his where just one corner of his lips quirks up, but it always reaches his eyes in a way that makes the blue look bright like a clear, summer sky.

"Hi, handsome." I smile up at him. "Was this a coincidental pickup or intentional?"

"I didn't want you to have to deal with the rain." He leans forward to press a soft kiss to my lips, and then he pops open the umbrella and leads me to the Range Rover with it safely hovering over me.

My heart lurches. Talk about some kind of romantic.

Almost like what a real-life, married husband would do for his wife.

Once I'm buckled inside the car and Flynn is pulling away from the building, I glance over my shoulder and spot his suit and my bridesmaid dress for Jude and Sophie's wedding hanging off one of the hooks by the back passenger doors.

Only three more days until their big day. *And three more days until pickups from my knight in shining armor go up in a fantastic ball of immigration interview smoke.*

Where in the hell did the time go?

FORTY-ONE

Thursday, May 30th

Daisy

I adjust the nonexistent wrinkles on my dress and follow Flynn's lead across the sidewalk and toward the entrance doors of The Penrose.

"You ready to deal with my rowdy family?" Flynn asks with a little grin. "Because, you know, if you want to skip the madness and head back to our apartment for a quiet night in with my cock inside you, I doubt anyone will notice."

I snort. "We're both in the wedding, Flynn. I'm pretty sure they'll notice if they're short a groomsman and bridesmaid at the rehearsal dinner."

He just shrugs. "Hey, later tonight, when my uncle Brad is trying to get you to dance with him, just remember this conversation."

I playfully slap a hand to his chest, and he opens the door to usher us inside.

I don't know how it happened, but one minute, I felt like I was arriving in New York, and now, I'm stepping inside the Upper East Side gastropub that is hosting Jude and Sophie's rehearsal dinner.

And tomorrow, you'll be interviewed by USCIS.

I swallow hard against the anxiety that wants to move into my throat. *Now is not the time to focus on that.* Instantly, I force myself to think about the happy couple we're celebrating tonight and plaster a smile on my face as I follow Flynn's lead through the venue.

The Penrose is packed to the brim with everyone who loves and adores Jude and Sophie. The aesthetic touches my designer heart, fitting perfectly in the middle of vintage and contemporary. It's cozy, with wood and brick elements throughout, but the light fixtures add this cool, modern vibe.

If anything, this place is authentic and fun and just suits them perfectly.

Flynn takes my hand and guides me toward our assigned table, but on the way, we're stopped by several familiar faces for hugs and greetings. His mom, Aunt Paula and Uncle Brad, Ty and some woman with big boobs and even bigger jade-colored eyes named Mindy, every step we take, it feels as if another person pops up to say hello.

And the instant Lexi sees us, she sprints across the hardwood floor and wraps both of her little arms around us. "Hi, Uncle Flynn and Aunt Daisy!"

Aunt Daisy. Gah. That pulls right at the heartstrings.

"Hey, Lexi Lou." Flynn smiles and releases my hand to lift Lexi up and into his arms. "Whoa, did you grow?"

She rolls her eyes and giggles. "Of course, I grew, Uncle Flynn. That's part of childhood development."

Her reaction makes me smile, but it also spurs an ache to form inside my chest. I rub at the annoying discomfort and try to focus on the big night—Jude and Sophie's rehearsal dinner. Tomorrow, the happy bride and groom will be happy wife and husband.

And tomorrow, you could find out that you and Flynn no longer need to keep up the marriage façade.

"Aunt Daisy?"

I blink out of my thoughts and find Lexi back on her feet, staring up at me. "Yeah, sweetheart?"

"My Mathletes competition final is in two weeks."

"It is?" I ask, trying like hell to act as excited as I should be. "That sounds like a really big deal, Lexi."

"It's the state championship. Do you want to come?"

I nod and try to ignore the ball of emotion that has found its way into my throat. "Of course I want to come. I wouldn't want to miss that for anything."

Yeah, but you can't actually say you'll be there. Because you'll probably be back in LA by then.

Flynn smiles over at me and wraps his arm around my shoulders. He reaches out and rubs the top of Lex's hair affectionately. "Consider us both there, Lexi Lou."

"I'll let my mom know to save two more seats," she says. "So, fifteen seats total so far. And if Uncle Ty brings one of his girls, that'll be sixteen seats."

One of his girls? I'd probably laugh if I didn't feel like the room was closing in on me.

"Daisy!" Winnie calls from the other side of the room. "Get over here, sis! We're having a bridesmaids' powwow in the other room." When Ty starts to head that way, she quickly points an index finger in his direction. "No boys allowed!"

He puts a hand to his chest and feigns discomfort. "You wound me, sis."

"I swear to everything, Ty, if you try to mess with any of the bridesmaids tonight or tomorrow, I'll wound you for real."

He just grins like the devil. "And what if the single bridesmaids can't resist me?"

"Oh, they will," Winnie adds. "Because I've already told them you have an incurable venereal disease."

"Jesus, Win."

She cackles and then meets my eyes again. "C'mon, Dais!"

"Looks like you're being summoned. Have fun, babe," Flynn whispers into my ear and presses a gentle kiss to my forehead. "See you in a bit."

The kiss is simple, chaste even, but it does nothing to help my emotions. Every cell inside my body loves feeling a sweet gesture like that from Flynn, but it's all just part of the game we've been playing…*right?*

A game that will soon be over.

The pact we made will be complete.

And like Flynn said from the beginning, no strings will be attached.

The lie we've been living will no longer be needed. Soon, everyone will know the truth. Winnie and Sophie and Flynn's mom and brothers, Uncle Brad and Aunt Paula, adorable Lexi, everyone will know I'm a fraud.

Everyone who's become the family you always wished you'd had.

Tears threaten to fill my eyes, but I blink them away. I refuse to do anything that will ruin Jude and Sophie's big night.

You can't change the reality of the situation. All you can do is put on a happy face and get through the night without falling to pieces.

Yeah. I can't change any of it. All I can do is make the best of it.

And you definitely can't change the fact that you've fallen in love with your fake husband.

Frank Sinatra serenades the room, and Flynn pulls me tight against his chest. We float across the dance floor in between the other couples in attendance at Jude and Sophie's rehearsal dinner.

"This is just a taste of what's to come tomorrow night!" Uncle Brad announces and proceeds to dip Paula and plant a smacking kiss to her lips.

Paula giggles. Ty cheers them on. And Flynn just shakes his head on a low chuckle that makes his chest vibrate against mine.

All in all, it's been a pretty good night.

Dinner was delicious. Jude and Sophie appear so damn happy it makes my heart twist against my ribs. And I managed to pull myself together enough to help celebrate the soon-to-be husband and wife.

Flynn presses a soft kiss to my forehead, and I have to shut my eyes for a brief moment to not let it affect me. But hell, it's affecting me.

Every innocent touch, kiss, caress from him feels so right that it's wrong.

Wrong because he's not my real husband. He's not the type of guy who does relationships. He made that fact clear from the get-go. Flynn is just a kind, genuine man who helped me in my time of need. And it's highly likely that, as of tomorrow, my time of need will be a thing of the past.

"You know what I think?" Winnie's voice grabs my attention, and I glance to my right to find her and her husband Wes slow dancing together. "I think the two of you should plan a wedding."

Flynn smirks. "Sorry to break it to you again, Win, but we already did that."

"Yeah, I'm aware. But I'd like you to plan a wedding that I can actually attend."

Wes smirks. "Like you should talk, baby. We got married on a beach in the Bahamas. And only you, me, and Lexi were in attendance."

"Shut up, Wes!" Winnie squeals and smacks a hand over his mouth. He just laughs and playfully bites at her fingers in a way that makes her giggle and yank her hand away from his face.

Flynn is amused by the whole scene. I know this because a genuine smile kisses his perfect mouth. But me, on the other hand? Well, I'm overwhelmed. Confused. And my heart is starting to take up a breath-stealing rhythm inside my chest.

I'm a fraud. A liar. A phony. A fake.

And even though I never anticipated the aftermath of Flynn's and my marriage, I'm starting to comprehend just how many people our web of lies has ensnared.

Not to mention, your heart.

Guilt pitches a tent inside my stomach, and I have to remove myself from the dance floor, away from Flynn and his family, and just…away from everyone I feel like I'm going to disappoint far too soon.

I step back and out of Flynn's arms, and he looks down at me with a quirk of his brow.

"I…uh… I think I need to…uh…" I pause, searching for a reasonable reason to leave. Sure, most of the guests have already left, but I doubt me springing out of the restaurant like my ass is on fire is going to occur unnoticed.

"I'm tired," I explain lamely. "I think I'm ready to call it a night."

"Okay, babe." Flynn doesn't ask any questions. He just…places a gentle hand to my back and guides us off the dance floor and toward our table where I left my purse.

But this isn't what I want him to do at all. The more time I spend with him, the harder this whole thing is getting. The more he treats me like a fucking princess, the more I realize I'm far past the point of having just *some* feelings for him.

I have *all* the feelings for him.

I just need space. Away from him. Away from his family. Away from my lies.

Far away from tomorrow's fate…*and the inevitability of a broken heart.*

FORTY-TWO

Flynn

"You guys heading out?" Rem asks, giving me a slap on the shoulder and a shake of my hand.

"Yeah, man." I look right beside me to where Daisy should be, anticipating her smile and ramble, but she's nowhere to be found. I grace Rem with a return slap on the shoulder and glance around the room for my favorite bouncy head of curls. It's only when I look all the way across the restaurant, at the double doors that lead out the front, that I spot that very hair making an abrupt departure.

"Everything okay?" Rem asks, observing me so closely that I can feel it without even having to look.

Honestly, I don't know. One minute, Daisy was with me, and in the span of two minutes when I was grabbing money out of my wallet to tip the waitstaff, she was gone.

Maybe she's sick?

That possibility doesn't sit well with me, and I don't offer Rem any explanation. Instead, I excuse myself with an "I'll see you tomorrow" and head for the exit. I don't even bother saying goodbye to Jude or Sophie when I pass them at the bar, despite their being the guests of honor, and I don't seek out anyone else from my family to let them know we're leaving.

I'll see them at the wedding tomorrow anyway, and after forty-one years of silent goodbyes, there's no need to start announcing my departure now.

The instant I step outside, I'm hit with a cool night breeze and the vision of Daisy hauling ass in the opposite direction of our apartment.

What the hell is going on?

I break into a jog as I trail behind her quick feet, and thanks to long legs and good genetics, it only takes half a block for me to catch up with her.

"Dais," I say in a quiet voice so as not to startle her from behind. "What's wrong? Where are you going?"

She doesn't respond, stalwart silence in the face of a tense moment a first for her, I'm sure. I quicken my steps and fall in step beside her, reaching out to grab at the soft part of her arm just above her elbow. She keeps walking, even with my hold, but the streaks of wetness down her cheeks that shimmer beneath the soft glow of the streetlamps are unmistakable.

Clearly, she's not okay, and as much as she might need this game of cat and mouse, I can tell by the ache in my chest that I need to know what's wrong even more. "Daisy, hold up a minute," I state and wrap my arm around her shoulders to pull us both to a stop. "What's going on? Are you sick?"

She averts her eyes. "I just needed to get out of there."

"I get that, trust me. I know the whole scene with my family can be overwhelming, but you're going in the opposite direction of our place. Let's go home."

She shakes her head and digs her teeth into her quivering bottom lip, her voice a scratchy version of itself. "Your place."

"What?"

"It's your place. Not mine. Not ours. It's *yours*."

I reach out to place both hands on her cheeks, but when she steps back to avoid my touch, it feels as if someone just put a line of barbed wire in my chest. This isn't the anxious, chatty Daisy I know. This woman is cold. Detached. *Determined*.

"What am I missing here, Daisy?"

"I can't do this anymore."

"Do what exactly?"

"This!" she blurts out and finally meets my eyes. Tears are now streaming down her cheeks, and she gestures between us with an erratic back-and-forth of her hand. "*Us*. Me and you and all the lies. I can't do this anymore, Flynn. I can't do it to you or your family. I *won't*."

"What are you talking about? You're not doing anything to me or my family."

"They think our marriage is for real, Flynn! They think I'm going to be around! Winnie treats me like a sister, and your mom treats me like a second daughter. Everyone has welcomed me with open arms and kind hearts, and I'm about to shit all over them!"

"Daisy—" I start to say, but she's quick to cut me off.

"No, Flynn!" she shouts so loud I'm certain that everyone within a one-mile radius can hear her. "There's nothing you can say that will make this okay. I'm sorry I ever brought you into this mess. I'm sorry for the aftermath that you're going to have to shoulder when I'm gone. I'm just sorry about all of it."

Aftermath when she's gone?

Tomorrow is her interview. The day she'll find out if her application was approved and if USCIS will give her a green card. If it all pans out the way it should, our marriage will no longer be needed, and she can move back to LA.

She can go back to her life that doesn't include you.

We could get a divorce and it wouldn't affect Daisy's immigration status. I know this because I already did my research. She'll be free to continue on with the process and eventually get citizenship in a few years if she wants.

She won't need you anymore.

I place a hand to my chest when a sharp pang shoots beneath my ribs. Everything inside me feels as if it's ripping apart at the seams.

"Just let me go, Flynn," she says, and her voice shakes when the words leave her lips.

No. I'm not ready to let her go.

"Your interview is tomorrow. We can talk again after," I force myself to concede through a throat so tight it's hard to breathe. I grab her hand and turn to walk to the apartment, but she yanks out of my hold and effectively spins me back around to face her. Her eyes are pained and her body is crippled under the weight of her yell as she leans forward and roars.

"I don't give a shit about the interview!"

"You've got to be shitting me right now, Daisy. All of this…everything we've been through… It's for nothing?"

Her whole jaw shakes as she buckles on a sob, and it's all I can do not to reach out and gather her in my arms. It'd be a wasted effort, I know, because with the way she's lashing out right now, I know there's no way she'd let me.

"So, that's it? You're just done. After everything you've been through, we've been through, you're just going to, what? Walk away? Go back to Canada? Give up everything?"

"I'm sorry," she says, swiping angrily at her tear-soaked cheeks. I step forward, desperate enough to provide her comfort that I have to try, but she's having none of it.

Two more steps back and she's put even more distance between us.

"I'll stay in a hotel until I make arrangements to go back to Canada. And I'll send someone to get all my stuff from your apartment. I promise, this will be the last time you have to deal with me and my problems."

"What the fuck?" I question, and the calm of my voice is long gone. "I have no idea what brought this on, but it's fucking irrational, and you know it. You're not thinking clearly about this."

"Not thinking clearly?" she retorts with wide, blazing eyes. "I've caused a fucking disaster with your family. Your mom, Sophie, *Winnie*, they're going to be devasted when they find out that we've been lying to them the whole time. Trust me, I'm thinking clearly."

"So, that's it, then? Your mind is made up, and you're just going to walk away from everything?" *Walk away from me?*

"I hope one day you'll be able to forgive me for dragging you into this. I hope one day your family will understand that I really do care about them and I never intended to hurt them."

I can't fucking believe it. She's *actually* saying goodbye right now.

And I fucking hate it.

"Dais—"

"I'm so sorry, Flynn," she whispers, and without another word, she turns around and walks away. Down the street, and across at the light, I watch her retreating back until my chest feels like it's going to explode.

Every cell inside my body wants me to follow her. To chase her down. But for some reason, I just stand there, frozen to my spot, and watch her walk away until she's just a blip in the darkness.

Until she's completely gone and all I can do is head home. *Alone.*

FORTY-THREE

Daisy

I can't stop crying.

Not when I told Flynn goodbye. Not when I walked around New York like a vagabond in the night, unsure of where to go or what to do. And definitely not when I finally gave up and checked in to the first hotel I spotted.

Luckily, the receptionist at the Holiday Inn Express paid my emotions no attention and let me book a room.

I hold the keycard in front of the door handle, and once the light beeps green, I push inside, only to snag my heel on the threshold and force my body to catapult forward. With a panicked hand to the wall, I just barely prevent myself from eating carpet.

Fantastic. Someone just snap my picture and plaster my face right above Webster's definition of *disaster*.

I throw myself onto the hotel bed, shove my face into one of the pillows, and groan. I can't be sure, but I think I fucked up. Big-time.

Oh, you definitely fucked up. You're an idiot for walking away from him like that.

I feel like a big fat coward. Like someone who ran away from her problems and left Flynn to deal with the aftermath by himself.

Hmmm…ran away from her problems? This sounds oddly familiar…

I turn onto my back and stare up at the ceiling. I shouldn't have done that.

I shouldn't have just left him like that. I should've stayed and been there when his family finds out the truth.

It's not too late for that…

I swipe the never-ending tears from my face and hop off the bed to where I left my purse on the floor by the door. Phone in my hand, I spot a missed call from an unfamiliar number and a voice mail.

My heart beats wildly in my chest as I tap play on the message, but when "Hi, Daisy, this is Dr. Fields" fills my ears, all my hopes pop like a balloon with a needle in it.

I don't know what I expected. Flynn calling me from a random number? It makes no sense, but I'm not exactly the most sane person at the moment.

"I have an urgent update that I need to relay to you, so please call me back as soon as you can. This is my cell number, and I'll be available any time, day or night."

Urgent update? What in the hell does that mean?

I tap on the number beside her voice mail and hit the phone icon to call.

The line rings four times, and I almost hang up, but by the fifth ring, she answers.

"This is Dr. Fields."

"Hi, it's Daisy. You just left me a message."

"Daisy Winslow, right?"

I swallow and shut my eyes. "Yes."

"Well, Daisy, I want to first apologize because the lab we sent your blood to made a very big error."

"Okay…?"

"When they entered everything into the system, they somehow mixed up your results with another patient's results, and while all of your lab work was still normal, your HCG levels came back high."

"What does that mean?"

"Your blood work showed that you're pregnant."

Time halts. Brakes squeal. The world stops spinning.

"I'm sorry…*what?*"

"You're pregnant, Daisy. And estimating by your HCG levels, I'd say you were about five to six weeks when you were in my office, so you're probably seven to eight weeks along now."

I shake my head. "T-that can't be."

"I can understand this comes a shock, especially since you're finding out two weeks later than you should have. Again, I really apologize for that."

"But I'm on birth control. The Depo shot. I have been for years now."

"Birth control isn't one-hundred-percent effective, Daisy. Do you remember the last time you had your shot? Or the last time you had a period?"

My last period? Fuck, I don't know. I'm not the organized type that keeps it all marked on a calendar. I'm more of the type that finds out she's on her period when she's in a bathroom stall at a restaurant and Aunt Flo decides to ruin her underwear.

And my shot? I mean, I've been getting it regularly, every three months, even since I moved to LA.

Yeah, well, you're the woman who forgot to renew her work visa, so it's highly possible you've messed something up here…

When I think back to the last time I had my Depo shot, I know that it was Christmastime because Dr. Lowe's waiting area was decked out with garland and stockings and a giant tree in the corner.

Which means it was December. And it's May, almost fucking June.

"I'm pregnant," I whisper and lift a hand to my mouth. "Holy shit, I'm pregnant! How did I not notice that I'm pregnant? Isn't that something that a woman should know?!" *Oh my God. I'm one of those women who end up having her baby in the toilet because she's clueless!*

"Every woman's body reacts differently to pregnancy, and while some experience a lot of symptoms in the first trimester, some women don't. Maybe you're one of the lucky few who doesn't have to deal with morning sickness and constipation." She laughs, but I sure as shit don't feel like laughing.

I am in the midst of existential absurdity, and it feels like I'm the butt of the universe's biggest cosmic joke. I mean, who finds out they're pregnant with their fake husband's baby on the same night they walk away from their fake husband, even though they don't want to walk away from their fake husband at all because, in all actuality, they love their fake husband so much they wish he was their real husband?

Apparently, you *are this woman.*

My life is an absolute dumpster fire, and this news just added gasoline to the already blazing flames. If I'm seven or eight weeks pregnant, that would mean…*that you and Flynn literally consummated your marriage in Vegas.*

"Daisy, are you there?"

"How do you know for sure?" I blurt out and begin to pace the small space in front of my hotel bed. "I mean, if the lab results got all screwed up, how do you know that I'm really pregnant? Maybe it's another one of your patient's labs. Maybe I got a pregnant woman's HCG result mixed with my labs! Maybe you've called the wrong woman!"

Or maybe, you're the pregnant woman, you no-period-having, missed-birth-control-shot lunatic.

"I can assure you, it's your results," Dr. Fields responds, and her voice is surprisingly calm for handling a raging psycho. "And while HCG levels are a definitive test, Daisy," she continues, but I'm already done with the conversation, "I want you to follow up with an OB-GYN in the city. Her name is Dr. Marissa Summers. She's really—"

"I have to go!" I cut her off and don't wait for her response.

Instead, I shut my phone off and throw it onto the bed, grab my purse, and head right back out my hotel room door in search of the nearest Walgreens or CVS or whatever the hell place is open this late and has pregnancy tests.

No way I'm pregnant. Obviously, they've made a mistake…*right?*

FORTY-FOUR

Flynn

The peace and quiet that usually come with stepping into my apartment don't give me the relief they normally do.

Instead of feeling relaxed, I feel as if I'm about to crawl out of my fucking skin.

I can't deny that I was hopeful Daisy would've somehow ended up back here. That she would've changed her mind and I would've found her sitting on the couch.

But she's not. Daisy is… gone.

And you didn't do a damn thing to stop her, you dense motherfucker.

In the kitchen, I tug the fridge door open with a harsh pull of my wrist and grab a beer. But I barely have the top popped off and the bottle to my lips when several pounding knocks echo into the otherwise silence of my apartment.

My heart races with anticipation, and I don't waste any time striding into the entryway and yanking the door open.

But the one person I want to be on the other side isn't there.

"That was quite the show back there," Rem says by way of greeting, and I furrow my brow in question. "You know, in the street, with you and Daisy."

I stare at him, and he takes it upon himself to step inside my apartment and shut the door with a kick of his boot.

"You motherfucker, you lied to me. You lied to *everyone*."

Normally, I might feel angered by his aggressive approach, but I'm all tapped out. After I watch Daisy walk away, my entire body feels numb, and my mind is thriving off the kind of emotion a man like me purposefully avoids.

"You know, I knew it was all so ridiculous. I fucking *knew* something was off with the whole situation." He walks into my kitchen and grabs himself a beer. "I expected something like this from Ty, but not from you."

I have nothing to say to that. Don't care to say anything to it, actually.

Because your concern right now isn't about Rem or your family. It's about her.

"How in the fuck did you end up marrying a random stranger to help her get a green card?"

Damn, he really did hear the whole blowout in the street.

"I know your usual MO isn't to say shit, but you're going to have to ante up an explanation, my man. And I promise, I'm not leaving until you do."

"You know her." Those are the first words that have come out of my mouth since he barged in here on a rampage and started making himself at home.

"What?"

"You met Daisy. In Vegas."

He stares at me like I have two heads, and I use that time to take several needed gulps from the beer that's still in my hand.

"What do you mean, I know—" He pauses midsentence, and I can see the wheels turning inside his mind. "Wait…she's not the chick Ty gave money to at the slot, is she?"

I nod. *Bingo, brother.*

"What the hell?" he questions, but it's more to himself than to me. "Damn, I knew she looked familiar."

Yeah, well, now you know why.

"For fuck's sake, Flynn," he mutters and runs a hand through his hair. "How did you get dragged into a fake marriage?"

The fact that he'd even insinuate a woman like Daisy would drag me into anything makes my spine prickle with irritation. A woman like her doesn't drag a man into any-fucking-thing. A woman like her makes it impossible not to come willingly.

"I didn't get dragged into it," I answer firmly. "I offered."

"You're fucking with me."

I shake my head.

"You offered to be get married to a complete fucking stranger?" A sharp laugh escapes his throat. "This just keeps getting better and better, doesn't it?"

The truth is, I think I fell in love with Daisy the first moment I saw her. Some part of me offered to save her because, deep down, I knew she'd save me.

The realization is so acute, so visceral, that I lose my grip on the beer in my hand, and it crashes to the floor in a bubbling mess of broken glass and booze. But all I can do is stand there and watch the beer make a river on my hardwood floors.

Rem looks from the floor to me and back to the floor until, eventually, his gaze locks on my face.

"Oh no," he says. "I'm…such a fucking idiot," he says quietly and sets his beer down on my coffee table. "I know that look. I've felt that look. You love her. You're in love with her."

I don't deny it. I don't even stay silent or just offer a nod. I face the truth head on.

"Yeah, Rem. I love her."

"Shit, I'm sorry." He shakes his head and runs a hand through his hair. "I just came blazing in here, all fixated on the fact that you were lying to me, but I didn't stop to think about what was actually going on with you. I'm a real fucking bastard."

I nod. He chuckles, but it's devoid of amusement.

"I didn't plan on it," I admit. "When Daisy and I made the pact, I didn't plan on it ending like this."

"Yeah, well, that's usually how it goes. I mean, when I asked Charlotte to marry me, I didn't plan on it ending with her leaving me at the altar. But love is a real motherfucker."

And that right there, seeing what Rem went through, still goes through because of it, is exactly why you've stupidly tried to avoid it this whole time.

My mind drifts to the distant past, and I think about the night of Rem's bachelor party when all four of us Winslow brothers were young and had our whole lives ahead of us.

I think about how excited Remy was and how ridiculous Jude and Ty were.

I even think about the stupid fortune-teller that Jude made us all go to after a stripper had all but torn Rem's boxer briefs to shreds with her stiletto.

You mean the fortune-teller who correctly predicted Rem getting left at the altar? And the same one who also correctly predicted Jude would make a bet that would change his life?

Instantly, the words crazy Cleo said to me ring loud and clear in my mind.

"There will be a night, though. One wild, unexpected night in a seemingly predictable life where you, my sweet boy, will make a pact with a stranger from which there will be great consequence."

Holy fuck.

One wild night. A pact with a stranger.

How in the hell did I miss this?

Probably because you wrote Miss Cleo off as a nutjob.

"What are you going to do?" Rem asks, pulling me from my racing thoughts, and I look at him long enough to come to a final conclusion.

"Make sure that fucking fortune-teller is wrong about the consequences."

"Huh?"

"I gotta go, Rem," I say and snag my keys, phone, and wallet from where I left them on the kitchen counter. My mind is made up, and there isn't a damn thing anyone can do to stop me.

"Go? What the fuck are you talking about?"

"Lock up when you leave."

And that's the last thing I say to my eldest brother before the door of my apartment slams shut behind me.

FORTY-FIVE

Daisy

I'm alone in the bathtub in my hotel room, and about twenty pregnancy tests are scattered along the edge of the tub and the floor and the sink like some kind of pregnancy-obsessed hoarder lives here.

And every single one of them tells me the same thing—**Pregnant**.

Holy fucking shit.

I'm pregnant, my immigration interview is tomorrow, and mere hours ago, I lost my ever-loving shit and told my fake-husband/real-baby-daddy that I'm done and moving back to Canada.

If this weren't my actual life, I'd probably think it was a joke and have a good laugh about it.

But all I can do is sob.

Big fat tears stream down my cheeks, and I just stare at the grout work of the tiles and wonder how in the hell I managed to get here.

Eventually, I find the will to get out of the tub and tip-toe past the pregnant evidence. Once I pace a little in front of the flat-screen TV, I grab my phone out of my purse and tap the screen to check for notifications. But when I realize I must have turned it off after I panicked over Dr. Fields's big news, I turn on the damn thing and decide that I need to call the two people who might be able to help me sort all of this out.

The screen comes to life quickly, but I'm immediately hit with a low battery notification. I rummage in my purse for my charger, but I quickly realize it's not with me; it's at Flynn's apartment.

Son of a bitch! Can't anything go right tonight?

Hopeful that I have enough juice to at least make this call, I get Gwen on the line first, then Damien, until we're all sitting on a three-way FaceTime.

It's late—very late, actually, even for West Coast time—but there's no complaint about it because the second they both spot my splotchy, tear-stained face, their reactions are basically the same.

"Daisy? What's wrong?"

"Oh my God, doll. Are you okay?"

"I have something I need to tell you," I say, biting the bullet of truth through a shaky voice. "I've lied to you both."

"What are you talking about?" Damien questions, and Gwen tilts her head to the side.

"Lied about what, darling?"

I stare at them, the words not coming as easily as I'd like.

"Daisy?" Gwen questions gently. "You know you can tell me anything and I won't be mad."

Her kind words are my undoing.

"I didn't marry Flynn because we were in love!" I burst out in a rush. "I married him because my US work visa expired, and he offered to help me get a green card! And now everything is fucked, and I left him because the lies became too much and I was feeling too much and I shouldn't have been feeling too much because it's all fake, and now I'm going to have to move back to Canada without a job and I don't know what I'm doing with my life anymore! It's like I'm purposely trying to destroy it!"

Gwen's eyes nearly bug out of her head.

"You did what?" Damien's chiseled jaw turns to jelly. "You married Flynn for a green card?"

I nod and swipe my hand across my face to clear my blurred vision. "It's why I'm in New York. We had to show proof of living together for Immigration."

"Well, this is certainly some news," Gwen mutters.

"You should've told me, Daisy," Damien states, and his lips turn down at the corners. "I could've helped you. I mean, I'm sure there was another work-around for an expired visa that didn't include marrying a stranger."

I grimace through more tears.

But even if you could go back in time, you still wouldn't change any of it.

The realization hits me straight in the chest, and I have to swallow back another onslaught of tears. Though, it only half works. I'm still crying, just not sobbing like my hiccuping lungs and shaky throat would prefer.

"Damn, doll, when you go, you go all the way, don't you?" Damien questions rhetorically. "So…you married Flynn, but now, you're not with Flynn? Did I get that right?"

I nod and rub an irritated hand down my face. "Tonight, at Flynn's brother Jude's rehearsal dinner, I lost it. I stormed out and we had a big fight in the street, and I told him I couldn't do it anymore."

And then you booked a hotel room, found out you're pregnant, and took twenty tests just to verify.

Internally, I cringe. And I decide right then and there that even though

I'm done with the lies, I can't tell them the full truth. I can't tell them I'm pregnant before Flynn knows I'm pregnant.

That would feel completely wrong.

"Why did you do that?" Gwen asks in her always-comforting tone.

I shrug. Sniffle. "I don't know what came over me. But I guess the guilt of what we were doing, and the lies we've been telling everyone, reached a breaking point I couldn't handle. I just couldn't keep living the lie. I couldn't keep acting like we were this happy couple in front of his family when, deep down, I knew it would all come to a crashing end soon."

Are you sure that's the only reason?

I'm sure.

"I'm sure that's why I left," I say out loud, but it doesn't make me believe it more. If anything, saying the words only makes it painfully clear that there are two sides to this story of mine.

And it doesn't do anything to convince Damien and Gwen.

"Doll, no offense, but even though I'm still trying to catch up with the fact that you went through with a shotgun wedding because your work visa expired instead of just telling me, you don't seem all that sure right now. You seem like a fucking mess, and I have a feeling that's why you called Gwen and me. Because you're the opposite of sure."

He's right. I know he's right. The guilt and shame in our lies only make up half of the truth. Probably way less than half, if I'm being honest with myself.

"I love him," I blurt out, and finally, the words match what's inside my heart. "I'm in love with Flynn. We may've gotten married on a green-card whim, but I've fallen in love with him and I…wish our marriage was real.

I wish it wasn't going to come to an end. And his family? Well, I love them too. They're the family I always wished I'd had when I was a little girl in foster care. I feel like I belong with them. Like I can be myself with them."

Gwen's eyes turn soft, and she lifts one hand to wipe below her eyes. "Aw, darling. I'm so sorry."

"Damn, doll." Damien sniffles. "Why in the hell did you walk away from him, then?"

"I don't know," I cry and swipe at my face. "Because Flynn isn't a relationship or marriage kind of guy. Because we made it clear from the beginning that this was a no-strings-attached kind of thing."

"But he married you."

"Yeah, but it was a fake marriage."

"A fake marriage that involved you moving in with him, spending time with his family, and being all up in his personal space."

I stare at him through my tears.

"Doll, are you sure he doesn't feel the same way? I mean, fake marriage or not, he sure seems like he was committed to you."

"He's just a loyal kind of guy, Dame. I promise you, this isn't a romance movie where the girl and guy end up together in the end."

Gwen lets out a soft sigh. "Darling, you can't be sure about that until you actually tell him how you feel. Which, it sounds like, is the one thing you haven't done. The man I talked to on the phone talked about you like he *saw* you, Daisy. The real you. Why do you think I got over the whole thing so quickly?" She snorts. "It wasn't because of his six-pack abs and handsome smile, I can tell you that."

It…it wasn't? I just assumed Gwen understood because she has a thing for man candy herself. I never considered that she saw something more.

"I think you need to tell him, Daisy," Damien agrees.

All I can do is nod. But it's not because I agree. It's because they both seem so hopeful that I can't find the courage to tell them that my immigration interview is tomorrow, and thanks to me, Flynn won't be there.

Yeah, but are you going to be there?

I look down at my stomach, where, I now know, sits a tiny baby that's growing inside me. A baby who deserves a mom and a dad and a happy, healthy home.

"I've fucked this up for more than just myself," I mutter, and both Gwen and Damien look at me in confusion.

But neither has time to say anything, because the battery on my phone chooses that exact moment to give up the good fight. The screen goes black, and I'm on my own again.

And all I can do is stare down at the wedding band that sits on my left hand. The ring I don't seem to ever take off.

Now what are you going to do?

FORTY-SIX

Friday, May 31st

Daisy

I stand outside the massive federal building and check the time on my phone again.

8:00 a.m. glares back at me.

Time is almost up, Daisy.

I don't know how long I've been standing outside the USCIS building, but considering I checked out of my room at six this morning, I know it's been a while.

So long, in fact, the security guard at the door is probably starting to wonder if you're casing the place…

"Hi," I greet him from across the sidewalk, the courage to speak just barely popping out of its hole like a little prairie dog. "I have an interview. At nine."

He doesn't respond or alter the deadpan stare from his face. He's all business, and I'm the furthest thing from it. Truth be told, I'm one small skip away from emotionally exploding all over this city sidewalk.

"I guess you could say I'm a little nervous."

When I realize I'm not going to get anything out of Stone Cold Steve Austin at the door, I take a few steps away and force myself to sit on a bench that's positioned off to the side of the building. Far away from Officer Serious but still close enough to actually walk into the building.

That is, if I decide to follow through with the interview.

I lean my head back and look up at the early morning sky. The clouds are shades of pinks and blues and silently make me wonder which color will soon become a staple in my life.

Pink or blue? A daughter or a son?

Hand to my stomach, I feel around my belly for any sign of pregnancy. I'd like to think I can feel a slight fullness in my lower abdomen, but truthfully, besides my out-of-whack emotions, the only reason I know I'm pregnant is because of Dr. Fields and the twenty or so sticks I peed on last night.

I'm pregnant. With Flynn's baby. And I don't know what to do.

You do know. You need to woman the hell up and go to that interview and make damn sure you can stay in this country long enough to tell Flynn you love him and you're having his child.

But how do I explain the obvious reality that my husband isn't at my interview?

The question urges me to stand back to my feet and play the all-too-familiar role of crazy-lady-pacing-outside-the-building.

My husband really wanted to be here, but see, there was an emergency. He fell off—

That is not going to work.

Flynn is very ill. We had Taco Bell last night, and I'm sure you can understand how that can end badly. You definitely wouldn't want him here, stinking up your bathroom. Ha-ha…I'm an idiot.

My husband is—

Out of nowhere, two arms wrap around my shoulders and pull me back into a hard, firm chest. I shriek out in surprise and start to fling my arms at my attacker, but that's quickly stopped when "Daisy, calm down. It's me." fills my ears.

I spin on my heels and come face-to-face with the one person, *the only person*, I want to see right now—*Flynn*.

"W-what are you doing here?"

"We don't have much time, babe," he says, and in a matter of seconds, my feet are off the ground and I'm in his arms, cradled close to his chest. Across the street and into an empty alleyway, Flynn doesn't set me on my feet until we're completely alone.

"I'm calling in my IOU."

My head jerks back. "What?"

"The night we got married, you said you owed me, and whenever I wanted to call it in, I just needed to tell you. Well, I'm calling it in now."

Normally, I'm not the quiet one in our conversations, but right now, that's exactly what I am.

"I don't want you to leave, Daisy. I want you to stay and make a real go of this with me. And quite frankly, I think you owe me the chance to try."

He wants me to stay?

"You want to try to make a real go of it with me?" I repeat back, my whole body shaking with the overwhelmingly relieving feeling of my adrenaline crashing. *I'm not going to have to fight at life alone anymore?*

"More than anything I've ever wanted," he says and takes both of my hands into his. "You make me better, Daisy."

But will he still want that when he finds out the truth? That our lives are going to be a lot more complicated than a couple of raging horndog fake spouses?

"I don't want to go back to my quiet life without you. I don't want to do anything without you. I—"

The urge to tell him everything, to lay it all out on the table, is too strong, and without thinking, I blurt out the words right in the middle of him talking.

"I'm pregnant!" I exclaim just as Flynn finishes with, "love you."

Holy hell, he loves me? *He loves me?!*

"I love you too!" I shout at the same time he asks, "You're pregnant?"

Tears threaten and a giggle bursts uninvited from deep, deep in my chest. For once in my life, I'm going to shut up and let someone else do the talking. Flynn deserves that. *Flynn deserves everything.*

"You're pregnant?" Flynn repeats again, this time on an awed whisper.

I nod, and emotion floods my eyes for what feels like a million reasons. Worry, happiness, elation, concern, *fear*, it's a kaleidoscope of feelings rushing through my veins.

"You're pregnant," he states this time, as if he needs to hear the words out loud for himself.

"Yes," I answer, and the need to give him an explanation—to assure him I haven't been hiding this—is too strong to deny. I can't be quiet anymore. "But I didn't know until last night. After I left The Penrose. The doctor who did my physical called me, and yeah, even though I didn't really believe her, it only took a two-hundred-dollar trip to Walgreens and a gallon of Sunny Delight for me to comprehend that I am, in fact, pregnant. Apparently, seven to eight weeks along."

"My baby is inside you," he says and reaches out to gently place his left hand—the one that *still* showcases his gold wedding band—onto my stomach. "Right there. That's our baby."

I nod, and the tenderness of his touch allows the relief of tears to spill down my cheeks. "Yes. That's our baby."

"A life-long contract we can't deny," he says and lifts me into his arms. "You're staying. With me. Forever. I'm going to love you both with everything I have." He presses his lips to mine, and all the fear and anxiety that are spilling out from my eyes and down my cheeks turn to pure happiness.

"You're my wife, Daisy. The one and only woman I want to spend the rest of forever with," he whispers against my mouth. "Hell, you've been my wife all along, even when I was too dense to realize it."

"Even when I was telling myself that this was all just a fake marriage," I say quietly and lean back to search the depths of my husband's eyes. "Deep down, I knew it was real, Flynn. I don't want anyone else. Just you."

He kisses me again, but this time, it's fiercer, more passionate, and it's not long before my legs are wrapping around his waist and my fingers find their way into the thick tresses of his dark hair.

"God, I've missed this. I've missed you," he says between kisses. "I know it's only been ten-fucking-hours, but I can tell you it's been the longest ten hours of my life. I spent last night walking all over this fucking city, checking far too many hotels trying to find you."

I lean back and meet his eyes again. "Why didn't you call me?"

"I did, on and off the whole damn night," he answers and presses a trail of kisses down my cheek and against my neck. "But it just kept going to voice mail."

"Shit." I cringe. "I sort of, kind of, maybe turned it off for a bit, and then the battery died." But I also moan. Because Flynn's mouth is on me. I can't not moan when his mouth is on me.

"Next time you get upset about something, upset with me, promise me you won't do that. Promise me you won't run away from me without giving me any idea of where you're going. I was really fucking worried about you."

"I swear." I gently bite down on his bottom lip and tug. "Cross my heart."

"Fuck," he mutters and slides his fingers into my hair to deepen our kiss again. "I know we need to go into that interview soon, but I need you, babe. I can't think straight. I have to be inside you."

"What?" I question with wide eyes, but also, a desperate, throbbing ache makes itself known between my thighs.

"I have to be inside you, Daisy. Right now."

Oh, holy moly. This man. He's *my* guy.

Master of my universe.

Father of my child.

And crazily enough, my fake husband who, without a doubt, is my *real* husband.

He's also the only man who spurs the kind of sexual desire and intensity that have me sliding my panties to the side and going right along with his quick-fuck-in-the-alley plan.

"That's my girl." He smirks, and my nipples tighten beneath my dress—the same rehearsal dinner dress I've been wearing since last night thanks to my emotional-breakdown-freakout-and-bolt moment.

Flynn doesn't waste any time, though. In a matter of seconds, his pants are unzipped, and his cock is filling me up in the way that only he can.

"Daisy. My Daisy," he mutters and greedily presses his mouth to mine. "I needed this. I needed you."

I've spent most of my life, even as a kid, thinking I didn't need anyone. But I was wrong.

I needed him too.

FORTY-SEVEN

Flynn

"Daisy, how long have you and Flynn been living together?" Fran, the all-business USCIS agent, asks, her eyes filled with a healthy dose of suspicion.

Though, after forty minutes of sitting across from this woman, I'm not entirely sure a suspicious demeanor isn't just a staple for her. Fran is the kind of woman who takes her job seriously. She lives and breathes her position within the immigration department, and she even takes pride in her own American citizenship.

I know this because every photo on her desk includes her in various patriotic gear. American flag T-shirts and hats, shooting off Fourth of July fireworks, Fran's pictures show she's an all-American kind of gal, and I can appreciate the display. Any old girl—even a country—has her problems, but I can't deny she's been pretty great to me. Hell, without "her," and her roots in tradition, I'd have never gotten here with Daisy.

"Uh… Well…I moved to New York April 22nd," Daisy answers, and her knee bounces in erratic movements beneath the table. "Basically, as soon as my boss would let me shift my work duties from the West Coast to the East Coast, I made the big move."

Fran nods, jots something down on her notepad, and Daisy glances at me out of the corner of her eye.

She is completely freaked out by this interview, but truthfully, I'm enjoying it. This is Daisy at her most beautiful, her mouth moving a mile a minute and her curls bouncing with every move. Watching her work through her emotions in the middle of the room for the world to see makes me fall in love with her all over again. As such, I couldn't feel any more at ease. There's nothing in this world realer than Flynn and Daisy Winslow.

She's my wife, the mother of my child, and the only person on the planet from whom I'd answer an uninvited FaceTime call. She might've burst into my world like a spiraling tornado of long-winded words and crazy eyes, but fuck, I'll forever be grateful she did.

There's no way in hell I'm going to let Fran do anything but approve her green card. My wife is going to stay right here, with me, and that's the only future I'll accept from here on out.

I reach out to place a reassuring hand on Daisy's still-bouncing knee, and her movements slow to a stop. Her body even tilts toward mine ever so slightly, and my whole chest swells with my smile. I fucking love it.

I love her. *Everything* about her.

I love the way she gets insanely excited over things like funnel cakes in Central Park and rambles when she's nervous. I love that she lets me do crazy shit like fuck her in an alleyway because I can't stand to not be inside her, even if that means she's sitting in this interview with still-flushed cheeks, wet panties, and snags from the alleyway brick on the back of her dress.

I love that when I wake up in the morning, I know there's going to a head full of unruly curls on the pillow beside mine and that all the blankets will be wrapped around Daisy like she's a Chipotle burrito.

I even love the way her messy ass leaves dirty dishes in the sink for me to clean, and I love that when I'm not in the mood to talk, she won't mind—she's got enough to say for the both of us. At the end of the day, there's no one I'd rather have on my team.

"Do you plan to stay in New York?" Fran asks, and Daisy is quick to respond.

"Yes." Her answer is straight and to the point, and while we haven't broached the whole "Where are we going to live?" question, I know my wife well enough to understand that she means it.

Looks like we're staying in NYC.

Though, if LA were where Daisy wanted to be, I'd pack up my shit, sell my apartment, and move without hesitation. I don't give a shit where we live, as long as we do it together.

"Flynn's family—our family—they're here. I've never had the kind of support network I have here, and…" Daisy's voice catches a little with the admission, and I squeeze her thigh to bring her comfort. "I can't imagine my life without them in it."

Even robotic Fran cracks a little at that, licking her lips and looking down at her notepad in a way that makes me think she might be fighting tears. When she looks back up after a nod, however, her professional armor is back in place.

"Great. Okay. Well, it looks like we just have one more question to finish up. Is there anything that you didn't note on your application that you feel compelled to tell USCIS today?" Fran's attention is fully focused on my wife—I suppose since she's the technical immigrant here—and Daisy's reaction isn't one of calm and cool.

Her eyes grow big, and she looks over at me like she's a woman with something to hide.

Shit, babe, relax. It's fine. I squeeze her thigh again, but her eyes only get more expansive.

I try to hold her manic gaze, but her eyes move from me to Fran and then back to me, and she repeats that circuit another ten times. All the while, the silence is growing to the kind of intensity that Fran just might be wondering if Daisy is some kind of undercover Canadian terrorist who actually did commit a murder.

Which, truthfully, would be quite the turn of events, considering Canadians are about the nicest fucking people in the world, but anyone who is staring into the depths of my wife's currently crazy-fucking-eyes probably wouldn't feel at ease.

Do something, man!

"I think what Daisy is trying to—" I start, but I'm quickly cut off by the beautiful maniac sitting beside me.

"I have a child!" Daisy yells out so loudly, it startles Fran's pen out of her hands.

"You have a child you didn't mention on your application?"

"Yes!" Daisy exclaims but then shakes her head. "Wait… No. I mean, I haven't had a child yet. I have one in my stomach. Growing inside me," she rambles, even pointing to her belly as evidence. "I'm pregnant. Knocked up. Bun in the oven…" She pauses and then points two finger guns in my direction. "By this guy, obviously! My husband. Flynn Winslow. He's the guy who did it. Got me pregnant, I mean."

Well, fuck, Dais. You could've, maybe, kept the finger guns holstered.

I shut my eyes for a brief moment, but then, I smile like a fucking fool. Though, I guess that's what happens when you're in love; you become a goddamn buffoon for the woman who owns your heart.

Fran looks at me and then at Daisy and then back at me.

"We just found out today," I explain with a knowing smile and wrap my arm around Daisy's shoulders, pulling her closer to me. "And, well, I'm sure you can understand why my wife is a little on the excited…" I lower my voice to a conspiratorial whisper. "Antsy…side. We're both over the moon with the news."

"Yeah… Flynn's right… I'm…uh…kind of an easily excitable person if you haven't noticed," Daisy chimes in. "So, I apologize for all the shouting."

"I see." Fran just nods and jots more shit down on her notepad.

No congratulations or soft smile. Just…a fucking nod. Obviously, that reaction does nothing for Daisy's current worked-up state.

I squeeze her thigh again for reassurance, but before I can get her to relax back against my arm, Fran is back with the same unnerving question.

"Is there anything *else* you feel compelled to tell USCIS today that you didn't note on your application?"

Daisy's knee is off to the races again, bouncing up and down in quick succession. "Anything else besides that I'm pregnant?"

"Yes," Fran responds, and her lips stay in the same firm line they've been in since we sat down across from her.

Oh fuck. Here we go.

"Uh…" Daisy pauses, and her eyes are so big I can actually see my reflection in her pupils. "I don't think so… I mean…"

"We haven't had a change of address," I calmly respond. "Daisy is still working with EllisGrey. They have offices in Manhattan."

"Yep. Yep. Yep." Daisy nods so many times I fear her head might roll off her neck. "Same address. Same job. Same Daisy and same Flynn. Same awesome marriage. Just a baby in the belly!" she exclaims again, and the finger guns are back out and blazing.

Goddamn, she's cute. A fucking mess, but cute.

Discreetly, I reach out with one hand and ease the guns back into Daisy's lap. "I will say that with a baby on the way now, we'll definitely be looking at other apartments in the city because our current place is only one bedroom. I'm assuming we'll need to update USCIS with any change in address?"

"Yes," Fran answers firmly. "Within thirty days of your move, you need to update us by mail or through the online form."

I nod, look over at Daisy, and realize her mouth has morphed into the biggest smile I've ever fucking seen. I'm talking, the Joker's smile pales in comparison to this all-teeth, megawatt force.

While Fran makes more notes on her notepad, I subtly tilt my head to Daisy, but it only makes her smile grow bigger. *Shit.* Pretty sure all the emotions of the last several hours and her pregnancy hormones and this fucking woman with the face made out of stone are about to make my wife break.

Dude, you're going to have to get her out of here.

Yeah, I have to get this interview show on the road. The sooner I can get Daisy out of this room, the sooner I can take her home and fuck the anxiety away until she can relax.

"Well, Fran, this has been a real pleasure," I say and reach out to pat Daisy's knee. "And I really appreciate the professional manner in which you conduct these interviews."

Fran looks at me through narrowed eyes.

You're going to have to do better than that, my guy. Really hit her with the charm.

Fuck me. I inhale a discreet breath and prepare myself to be the kind of man I most certainly am not—*a small-talk schmoozer like my baby brother Jude.*

"Fran, I'm sure you don't get to hear this as much as you should, but the United States of America is lucky to have you at the helm of the immigration process."

Her eyes become *less* narrowed.

"So, thank you for your service," I say with a proud nod. "I know this isn't an easy job."

She purses her lips. "No, it's not."

Daisy adjusts in her seat a little, almost as if she's going to chime in with something, but I know that is the opposite of what we need right now. No offense to my gorgeous, beautiful, amazing, intelligent wife, but in the name of her and my sanity, I need her to sit tight while I extract us from this situation.

"Just out of curiosity, how long does it take for applicants to find out if they've received a green card?"

"It depends," Fran responds. "Some applicants find out during the interview. Some have to go through a longer process."

I feel Daisy tense up beside me, but I keep my cool.

"Sounds like very stringent protocols you follow."

"Oh, they are," Fran comments, and I almost sense a smile on her firm lips. "*Very* stringent."

"That's great to hear." I smile at her. "A relief, to be honest. I appreciate your dedication to the monumental responsibility you're tasked with."

"Wow. Well, thank you, Mr. Winslow."

"Are you going to need us to come back for another interview?" I question nonchalantly and use all my strength to keep up the loathsome small talk while ignoring the tension that's vibrating off Daisy's body.

Fran looks down at her notepad. Then at Daisy. Then at me. Her eyes waver a few times, but eventually, she says, "No, sir. You will not need to come back for another interview. I feel I have obtained all the information I needed for your wife's case, and I am happy to report that I will be recommending her for a green card."

Thank fuck.

"Really?" Daisy questions and hops up from her chair. "I get to stay in the country? I get to live here? With my husband?"

Fran nods. "Yes, Mrs. Winslow."

"Oh my God, Fran!" Daisy shouts and jumps around on her feet. "I could kiss you right now!"

"Please don't do that, ma'am."

"So, we're all set?" I quickly ask, and Fran nods.

"Yes. Good luck and congratulations."

"Thank you!" Daisy squeals and jumps into my arms. "Thank you, Fran! I love you, Fran!" she continues to shout, and I don't hesitate to carry her right out of ol' Fran's office.

Once I get us safely on the elevator and behind closed doors, I set Daisy to her feet and kiss the hell out of her.

"Babe, I love you," I whisper between kisses. "But, fuck, I was scared shitless you were going to break in the middle of that interview."

"Oh my God," she says through a giggle, her lips still permanently attached to mine. "Is that why you started talking so much? I had a moment where I thought you'd been abducted by pod people."

"Says the woman who kept shooting fucking finger guns at the immigration agent."

"I didn't know what to do with my hands!" She giggles some more, and it's the best sound I've ever heard in my life.

"Fuck, baby, once you started smiling like you were trying to get your mouth to reach your damn hairline, I knew I had to do whatever I could to get you out of there."

"And boy oh boy, am I glad you did." Daisy snorts and hops up to wrap her legs around my waist. She places erratic kisses all over my face, and I don't hesitate to squeeze her luscious ass with my big hands.

"Now that you saved me from being deported by Fantastic Fran, what's next, husband?" she whispers against my mouth.

"First, home, so I can fuck you senseless. Then, we get ready for Jude and Sophie's wedding."

Daisy giggles, but then, she leans back and stares deep into my eyes. "And then what do we do?"

"We spend the rest of our lives together."

Her responding smile lights up my whole fucking world.

"There will be a night, though. One wild, unexpected night in a seemingly predictable life where you, my sweet boy, will make a pact with a stranger from which there will be great consequence."

There's only one thing Cleo failed to mention that night in her dark, velvet-draped room—*that Daisy would be the kind of consequence I would pray will never change.*

EPILOGUE

Ten hours later...

Daisy

I take a bite of delicious wedding cake and look across the room, where I spot Flynn standing in a corner off to the side of the dance floor, chatting with his brother Remy.

I don't yet know all the details of what happened between them last night after the rehearsal dinner, but from what I understand from Flynn's limited explanation, Remy broke open our huge Pandora's box of lies and dragged Flynn through a tense questioning.

My shoulders sag. And to think, while he was going through all that, I was finding out about the little bambino in my belly. To say the past twenty-four hours have been a bit of a roller-coaster ride would be quite the understatement. But I can't deny I'd ride that crazy roller coaster a million times over if it meant I'd end up in the same place—married to Flynn, with a precious baby on the way.

As I place another bite of cake into my mouth, an approving moan falls from my lips, but that's quickly overcome by what sounds like a text message notification.

Quickly, I locate my purse beneath my chair at the head table and realize both Damien and Gwen have been trying to reach me since my dead battery abruptly ended our FaceTime chat.

The whole screen looks a little like a psycho-killer movie massacre, but the last two texts in the group chat are...downright dire.

Damien: Okay, that's it. I'm getting on the phone right now and calling everyone I know until it leads me to Liam Neeson's number, and when I get him on the phone, I'm going to pay him as much money as it takes to fly to New York, feel if the wind is blowing from the east, and find your cute little stranger-marrying ass.

Gwen: Michael, my boyfriend from ten years ago, has "connections." I'm waiting for a text back, but we did enough freaky stuff that I KNOW I can blackmail him into using them if I have to. Maybe he, and this Liam, can team up.

Holy hell. I'm an asshole.

Me: You guys, I am so, so, so sorry. My phone died last night, and it's a very long, crazy story, but all you need to know is that I'm good. Fantastic, even. I love you both so much, and I swear, I'm doing really, really good.

I hit send and add one more message to the chat.

Me: Oh and, Damien, I need to permanently stay on the East Coast.

Damien: You're good? YOU'RE GOOD?!! Listen, missy, I'm going to spank you so hard the next time I see you, and I've already visualized the whole scene happening on the West Coast. So, you'd better give me a damned good reason if I'm going to mentally rearrange my vision to accommodate smelly New York.

Me: I'm in love with my husband and he's in love with me, and yeah, I'd kind of like to keep living with him.

Damien: Well...hot damn! I guess you're off the hook, then. Because that's a pretty good reason.

Damien: Happy for you, Daisy. Even if you're a little biotch and made me cry!

Gwen: *Time to settle in, darling.*

Me: *Settle in? For what?*

Gwen: *Happiness.*

"Come dance with me." Warm hands wrap around my waist, and I glance back to see Flynn standing behind me, resting his chin on my shoulder.

"Everything go okay with Remy?"

"Yeah." He nods. "We're good."

"Is he…mad at us? At me? For…lying to everyone?" I ask just as I lock the screen of my phone and set it on the table.

"No, babe." Flynn shakes his head. "He gets it. But even if he were pissed, it wouldn't fucking matter. You and I are a package deal."

"A package deal. I like that." I smile and reach out to adjust his tie. "Did you…tell him…about…?" I question, and Flynn places a gentle hand to my belly.

"No, but that's only because it's Jude and Sophie's night," he answers and holds out a hand toward me. "We'll tell them soon. But for now, how about that dance?"

I don't hesitate to place my hand in his and let him lead me out onto the crowded dance floor. In a matter of minutes, I'm tucked safely into his arms and we're swaying around the room to the music.

I look around the venue, taking in all the familiar faces that have become some of the most special people in my life. Uncle Brad and Aunt Paula giggle like teenagers as they dance across the room.

Lexi cackles as both Wes and Winnie dance with her.

Ty steals an amused Aunt Paula from Uncle Brad's arms.

And Jude stares down at Sophie like she's the only woman in the whole wide world.

Damn, they look so happy.

"Do you want a wedding like this?" Flynn whispers quietly into my ear, and I look away from the happy bride and groom dancing in the center of the ballroom to meet his eyes.

"Like a wedding do-over?"

He nods.

"And replace our glorious memories with Marilyn Monroe?" I smile and shake my head just as I stand up on my tippy-toes to press a kiss to his lips. "Never."

Flynn places his hands on my hips and searches my eyes, but I already know what he's silently asking.

"I love our wedding day memories just as they are. I don't want to change them."

"I feel the same. But…I do have something serious to tell you."

Panic seizes my breath. "What?"

"I never took back the rental dress and tux. So, I'm pretty sure we can expect a charge on our next credit card bill."

I stop in the middle of the dance floor. "Are you serious?"

He nods. Smiles. And leans forward to press a soft kiss to my lips. "At the time, I didn't understand why I wasn't ready to return them. Now—now, I do."

Be still my beating heart.

"Well, holy hell, I don't think I can be upset about the bill now!" I yell with a playful slap of his chest. "Flynn Winslow is a secret, sentimental softy."

"Only for you, babe." He winks and places a gentle hand to my stomach.

"Our baby is in there," I whisper, and emotion builds in my throat, urging tears to prick my eyes.

Never in a million years would I have guessed Flynn would be the father of my child, but now that our tiny baby is growing inside my belly, I've never felt more blessed in my whole life.

Flynn bends over to place his lips to my belly, a soft, discreet press of his lips over my bridesmaid dress, before standing back up to pull me into a tight hug.

"When do you think we should tell everyone?" I ask when I see that his mom and Winnie and his brothers and Uncle Brad and Aunt Paula have now made a circle around Jude and Sophie on the dance floor.

"Let's handle it like our wedding."

I tilt my head to the side. "What do you mean?"

"My family is fucking crazy. We'll tell them after the baby is born."

Laughter bursts from my lungs. "Pretty sure they're going to know before the baby is born, you know, with the whole, this belly of mine is going to get much bigger thing. Probably, like, scary bigger."

"I can't fucking wait." He rubs my belly again, and we both look toward the center of the dance floor to find a giggling Sophie sitting in a chair and Jude striding up toward her with a big, sexy smile on his face.

Sophie's sisters and a few of the other bridesmaids start to throw one-dollar bills toward the happy bride and groom, and Flynn smirks down at me.

"Just think, babe, all these crazy motherfuckers are *your* family now."

I smile up at him. "They sure are."

Talk about a dream come true.

Two months later…

Flynn

"I feel nervous." Daisy flashes a shaky smile in my direction, and I reach out to take her in hand in mine.

"There's nothing to be nervous about, babe."

"I know." Her free hand fidgets with the paper on the exam table. "It's just that…I don't know…I hope everything is okay with the baby."

"It will be, Dais."

She starts to open her mouth again, but when the door to the exam room opens, she quickly snaps it shut and watches as a woman in a white doctor's coat walks inside.

"Good morning, Daisy. I'm Dr. Summers. How are you feeling today?"

"Do you want the real answer or the fake answer?"

The doctor grins. "The real answer, always."

"Well, I've been better." Daisy shrugs. "Morning sickness has been kicking my ass the past few weeks."

She's not joking. Every morning, like clockwork, I wake up to Daisy in the bathroom with her face in the toilet.

"I can imagine, Daisy, but I will tell you that, generally, once you're well into the second trimester, those symptoms will start to dissipate."

"I have everything crossed that's the case," Daisy answers and looks over at me. "I'm sure my husband feels the same. My morning puking now serves as his alarm clock."

Dr. Summers laughs and meets my eyes. "And I take it you're that husband?"

I nod and smile. I'm proud as hell to be Daisy's husband, but that doesn't mean I'm ready to get chatty with everyone now.

"Well, are you two ready to see your baby today?" the doctor asks as she puts two latex gloves over her hands.

"I think so." Daisy flashes a nervous smile in my direction.

"Of course, we're ready," I reassure, but I glance over my shoulder to the door. "But we should have two more people who want to be here for the ultrasound. They should be arriving any minute."

Daisy looks at me quizzically, but I don't offer any explanation.

"I always say, the more, the merrier," Dr. Summers comments and begins to set up her ultrasound equipment. "A baby is something to celebrate."

"Flynn, who else—" Daisy starts to ask, but three knocks ringing against the door interrupt her midsentence.

Slowly, two heads peek inside.

"Did we make it in time, darling?"

Daisy's jaw nearly hits her chest. "Gwen?"

"And Damien!" a jovial male voice exclaims as he steps into the room.

"*What?*" My wife's smile is infectious, and she glances between Gwen, Damien, and me. "Did you do this?"

I shrug. "I might've had a part in it."

"Had a part in it?" Gwen teases. "He was the mastermind behind it all."

"Plus, there was no way Gwen and I were going to miss this for anything," Damien chimes in. "It's not every day that your best girl gets knocked up."

Daisy snorts, but when more knocks sound against the door, she's looking back at me.

"Flynn! How many people did you invite?"

"Technically, he didn't invite us," my sister Winnie answers as she steps inside the exam room. "But there was no way in hell we weren't going to be here."

And right behind her, Lexi, Wes, my mom, Aunt Paula, Uncle Brad, Jude, Sophie, and Remy file inside. To say it's getting tight in the room is an understatement.

Oh, you've got to be fucking kidding me.

Remy notices my scowl, though, and steps up to whisper in my ear. "It's the first baby in the family since Lexi, dude. We couldn't fucking help it."

When he pulls back, a shiny pool of a tear glistens in the corner of his eye. Just like that, any remark I might have made is silenced immediately.

"Well, this is quite the crowd we have here," Dr. Summers comments with surprised eyes. "I guess…well…everyone just try to find a spot?"

"Oh, don't worry, we'll manage because there is no way in hell we're missing this," Sophie responds with a smile. "Love you, Daisy!"

"Okay, well, I guess we'll get started," the doctor says as she squirts gel on Daisy's belly.

"Wait! Don't start without me!" An all-too-familiar voice fills my ears, and I look back toward the door to see my brother Ty sliding inside the exam room.

Daisy looks at me with shocked eyes, and I raise both hands in the air. "I only invited Gwen and Damien. I don't know how everyone else managed to get here."

"You should've invited us, you bastard," Ty comments, and Remy reaches out to slap a hand to the back of his head.

"What? He should have. That's our niece or nephew in there."

"Um…can someone…turn the lights down?" Dr. Summers questions, and Uncle Brad starts to hit every damn switch he can find, causing all the lights in the room to go on and off erratically.

"Wait! Not that one!"

"This one?"

"No, the one by the door, sir," she directs, and after we've all experienced the kind of light show that would be labeled as an epilepsy risk, Uncle Brad finds the one damn switch the doctor meant.

"Okay, that's great. Thank you."

"Not a problem, Doc!"

"Don't be so proud of yourself, Bradley. You nearly gave us all a seizure," my mom chastises, but thankfully, Dr. Summers ignores the peanut gallery and focuses on the ultrasound.

"Okay, Daisy, let's see your baby."

"Yes! Let's do it!" Jude cheers. "I got fifty bucks that it's a girl!"

"I'll take that bet, brother. I say it's a boy!" Ty joins in, and Jude scoffs.

"No way God will let another Winslow brother enter this world!"

"Boys, I brought you into this world, and I will take you right out of it if you don't shut up."

"Sorry, Ma," Ty says, but the bastard is grinning like a kid.

"Okay, then," Dr. Summers announces. "*Now*, are you ready to see your baby, Daisy?"

Daisy nods, inhales a deep breath, and her eyes become riveted to the screen.

For once in her life, my wife is speechless, and I can't stop myself from stepping closer to her side and taking her fingers in mine. I lift her hand to my mouth and press a soft kiss to the back of it.

I can still hear my fucking brothers whispering about their goddamn bets behind me, but when the vision of a tiny, fluttering heart is on the big ultrasound screen, I can't focus on anything else.

"Well…Daisy…this is Baby A," Dr. Summers announces, and Ty is the first one to start asking stupid questions.

"Baby A? You guys already named your kid?"

"And this, right here, is Baby B."

"What's A-B stand for, Flynn? That some kind of acronym?" Uncle Brad questions, but I'm too busy blinking my eyes one thousand fucking times.

"Uh…um…" Daisy mutters and looks up at me. "W-what did…?" Her eyes shoot back to the doctor. "I'm sorry, but did you just say Baby A and B? As in, t-two babies?"

"I did." Dr. Summers smiles. "You're having twins."

Instantly, the room erupts into fucking chaos.

"*Whaaaaaaat?*"

"*Twins! I'm going to have two more grandbabies!*"

"*Dude, this is nuts!*"

And all I can do is stand there, holding my wife's hand against my chest, and look at the two profiles of Daisy's and my babies.

Twins. My wife is having twins.

"Flynn…I don't even know what to say," Daisy whispers, and I lean down to press a kiss to her lips.

"Me either." A shocked laugh escapes my lips. But when I stare into her eyes, a thin sheen of emotion blurs my vision. "I love you."

Her lip quivers. "I love you too."

"We usually have to wait until your twenty-week ultrasound to find out what you're having, but Daisy, I know the sex of your babies. Would you like me to tell you?" Dr. Summers asks, and Daisy nods.

"You're having two boys, and since they share a placenta, I'm pretty sure they're identical."

And just like that, the room is back to chaos.

"Two more Winslow boys! Holy shit! Watch out, world!"

"I can't believe this!"

"You owe me fifty bucks, bro!"

But when I look down at my wife with tears welling up her eyes and a smile cresting her lips, I swear, she's never looked more beautiful or happy than she does right now.

Damn, this woman, she's made my life.

"Well, I guess this all only really leaves me with one option," Ty says cryptically, stealing the thunder in a room full of showboats.

"And what's that?" Winnie asks smartly, a sarcastic grin lighting up her space.

Ty scoffs. "To fall in love, obviously," he says with a *duh*-like shake of his head. "And to do it bigger and better than the rest of you."

Famous last words, bro. Joking or not, those are some *very* famous last words.

THE END

Love Flynn, Daisy, and the rest of the Winslow crew and want to read MORE Winslow Brothers?

Well, we have *great* news!

You can cure your Winslow Brothers' cravings right now and find out what really happened during Remy's bachelor party in this FREE novella!

GOTTA HAVE FATE!

https://dl.bookfunnel.com/1dvqktv6el

It's completely **FREE** and not-to-be missed!

AND

You can preorder the next book in the *Winslow Brothers Collection* today!

The wild and crazy Ty Winslow is next.

The Secret is coming soon!

Completely new to the Winslow Brothers?

Grab *The Bet* to read all about how Jude and Sophie fell madly in love. Trust us, you won't regret it.

BEEN THERE, DONE THAT TO ALL OF THE ABOVE?

Never fear, we have a list of nearly FORTY other titles to keep you busy for as long as your little reading heart desires! Check them out at our *website: www.authormaxmonroe.com*

COMPLETELY NEW TO MAX MONROE AND DON'T KNOW WHERE TO START?

Check out our Suggested Reading Order on our website!

www.authormaxmonroe.com/max-monroe-suggested-reading-order

WHAT'S NEXT FROM MAX MONROE?

Stay up-to-date with our characters and our upcoming releases by signing up for our newsletter on our website: *www.authormaxmonroe.com/newsletter!*

You may live to regret much, but we promise it won't be subscribing to our newsletter.

Seriously, we make it fun! Character conversations about royal babies, parenting woes, embarrassing moments, and shitty horoscopes are just the beginning! If you're already signed up, consider sending us a message to tell us how much you love us. We really like that. ;)

Follow us online:

Facebook: www.facebook.com/authormaxmonroe
Reader Group: https://www.facebook.comgroups/1561640154166388/
Twitter: www.twitter.com/authormaxmonroe
Instagram: www.instagram.com/authormaxmonroe
TikTok: vm.tiktok.com/ZMe1jv5kQ
Goodreads: https://goo.gl/8VUIz2

ACKNOWLEDGMENTS

First of all, THANK YOU for reading. That goes for anyone who has bought a copy, read an ARC, helped us beta, edited, or found time in their busy schedule just to make sure we stayed on track. Thank you for supporting us, for talking about our books, and for just being so unbelievably loving and supportive of our characters. You've made this our MOST favorite adventure thus far.

THANK YOU to each other. Max is thanking Monroe. Monroe is thanking Max. We know, *we know*! We do this every book. Every. Single. Book. But guess what? We're going to keep doing it because that's how we roll. If you don't believe us, we challenge you to go read all of them and see for yourself. HA-HA!

THANK YOU, Lisa, for continuing to kick ebb with our flow. We could NOT do this without your goddess-like ways. WINE! WINE! You get wine!

THANK YOU, Stacey, for making the insides of our book look so damn pretty and rolling with the crazy schedule punches we throw your way. You are the absolute best!

THANK YOU, Peter (aka Banana), for rocking our covers and making Flynn Winslow look like the sexy, charming, perfect good-time guy that he is.

THANK YOU, John, for joining the team like a Bond movie character who has to parkour his way onto a moving train! To the future!

THANK YOU to every blogger who has read, reviewed, posted, shared, and supported us. Your enthusiasm, support, and hard work do not go unnoticed. We love youuuuuuuuuuuu!

THANK YOU to the people who love us—our family. You are our biggest supporters and motivators. We couldn't do this without you. Although, it should be noted, sometimes you guys are hella distracting. But the ones who are the most distracting are under the age of eleven, so we're not going to hold that against you. HA-HA.

THANK YOU to our Camp members! You guys are the best! THE BEST, we tell you! You've made Camp the coolest place to be and one of our favorite places to go to procrastinate. We can't wait for all the fun we've got planned for this year!

As always, all our love.

XOXO,

Max & Monroe

Made in the USA
Monee, IL
21 January 2022